Mel Stein is best known as the personal business manager of Paul Gascoigne and Chris Waddle. Brought up in North London, Mel Stein was taken to his first football match at the age of three by his family, who were fanatical Arsenal fans. To the horror of his relatives, in 1951 Mel defected to Newcastle United when they won the FA cup. He has remained a loyal supporter ever since and is confident that at last, in 1996, they will have some silverware to silence opposition fans.

Stein qualified as a solicitor in 1969 and became involved in football and sports law in the mid eighties. He has been responsible for conceiving and launching the first Sports Law Post-Graduate University course in the United Kingdom, jointly between his law practice, Finers, and King's College, London, from where he graduated. He was involved in Waddle's transfers from Newcastle to Spurs, Spurs to Olympique de Marseilles, then back to Sheffield Wednesday, as well as Gazza's moves from Newcastle to Rangers in Scotland via Spurs and Lazio. Over the past dozen years he has also represented many other leading players. He is the author of five non-fiction books on football, including the authorised biographies of Paul Gascoigne and Chris Waddle. Mel Stein is married and lives in North London with two football-crazy sons and a long-suffering wife.

Marked Man

Mel Stein

HEADLINE

First published in Great Britain in 1995
by HEADLINE BOOK PUBLISHING

First published in paperback in 1996
by HEADLINE BOOK PUBLISHING

10 9 8 7 6 5 4 3 2 1

ISBN 0 7472 4906 7

Typeset by Keyboard Services, Luton, Beds

Printed and bound in Great Britain by
Cox & Wyman Ltd, Reading, Berks

HEADLINE BOOK PUBLISHING
A division of Hodder Headline PLC
338 Euston Road
London NW1 3BH

For WJ who stopped me being a marked man, and for Len who helped him along with DS, JHC and TC, all at ABG, SF, HF, GC, JS, JZ and AZ (who deserves more than being the friend who went to the ballet) all my other loyal friends in Southgate, PL and AL, JHB, CW, PG, DB, JR, JC (who's already had one dedication), their respective wives and especially RW and the late lamented Misty who always kept me company. And for the Marilyn B. and Clemy who somehow or other got left out last time around.

CHAPTER 1

The man stood in the watery Spring sunshine without a coat, in defiance of the chilly wind that blew across the empty stadium. Hertsmere United did not possess the luxury of their own training ground, they trained where they played, right here in Park Crescent. Despite the meteoric rise of the club from the Southern League to the old Conference, then into the Football League when poor old Wychavon went into liquidation, the stadium had remained the same. With its walls pushed out and the police satisfied as to safety, it held twelve thousand people. The big clubs could bring that number of travelling fans with them and, whilst the close-packed hostility of the Crescent was at times worth a goal, twelve thousand paying customers could not generate enough income to meet the sort of wage bill the players' talents – and their agents – demanded.

David Sinclair looked across the pitch at the players who were dribbling balls through a maze of cones under the direction of the coach, Ray Fowler. Fowler's barrack-room voice carried clearly across the field.

'Come on you load of lazy bleeders. You may have been satisfied with a point at Newcastle, but I fucking wasn't.'

Of the manager, Phil Reynolds, there was no sign. He'd taken him on board as a track-suit man but nowadays you were more likely to find him wearing Armani. Still, Fowler was a good coach, the players respected him, and there was no doubting that Reynolds' hand was still on the rudder when it came to team selection and tactics. They made a good partnership, Reynolds and Fowler, and with the experienced Stuart Macdonald leading the side on the pitch, Hertsmere were having the most successful season in their history. In the top half of the League, into the semi-final of the FA Cup and knocked out unluckily in the semis of the Coca Cola.

As chairman, Sinclair knew he ought to be a happy man. Watching the team he'd helped to build he tried to erase every other thought from his mind. They were shooting in at Greg Sergovich, the huge Slav goalkeeper. Macdonald hammered one to his left and the keeper, with a sudden show of grace that belied his size, swooped across, caught the ball and neatly threw it out again, all in one motion. Sinclair took in a deep breath. He loved this game, loved its beauty and its passion, loved its balletic grace even on a morning such as this.

Instinctively he looked for Mickey Wayne in his number eleven shirt. Merely in training Wayne gave him a thrill, a frisson of excitement every time he got the ball. But of Wayne there was no sight and he felt somehow let down, as if this was to be symbolic of the shape his day was to take. Sinclair's uncle had actually played for Hertsmere in their non-league days and his father had proudly taken him as a six-year-old to a match. 'That's my brother, number eleven,' his dad had said, and from that day onwards the green and white striped number eleven shirt had always held a mixture of romance and fascination for him. Not that there'd been much romance about his Uncle Tim galloping down the left wing, but since then he'd seen so many better players wearing that shirt for Hertsmere that time had softened the harsh picture he'd had of his uncle's sparse talents.

But of all the players he'd seen Mickey Wayne was the best. He'd been the best since he'd been a kid and he knew it. He'd played as a schoolboy that first season in the league. A couple of tough old pros had tried to soften him up with some crunching attempts at tackles, but they'd never got near enough to connect. Since then many wiser and better players had been left looking at thin air as Wayne ghosted away.

They'd been lucky to keep hold of him as they'd moved upwards through the leagues, cutting through opposition like a knife through butter. It had all seemed so easy, not just for Wayne, but for Hertsmere too. Laughing in the faces of the so-called professional pundits who predicted their imminent doom with all the confidence of soothsayers announcing a warning against the Ides of March, season after season they'd gained promotion until they'd finally found themselves in the Premiership, the poor relation none of the richer clubs liked to visit.

Sinclair ran his hand over his slightly greying hair. At forty with all the pressures he had to bear it was hardly surprising that the grey was showing through, the only surprise was that he had any hair left at all. He shrugged himself into the contours of his hand-made Savile Row suit, straightened his silk tie and reluctantly dragged himself back to the problems of the day.

He shielded his eyes against the sun and turned to walk through the tunnel. A tall figure, rugged rather than handsome, David Sinclair was nevertheless the object of the fantasies of most of the female catering staff. But only one woman could intrude into his affair with football. He'd been married once, when very young, and all he had to show for it were huge alimony payments and Holly, his eighteen-year-old daughter.

Holly never missed a match and ever since her mother had walked out when she was only five she had sat next to her father every Saturday, home or away. It never occurred to Sinclair to regret he'd not had a son. In Holly, with her mother's fair hair and perfect skin and his own determination and passion for football, he had the best of both worlds. Strangers mistook them for lovers, and as far as Sinclair was concerned if any man tried to win his daughter's heart he would have to win over her father's mind as well. Yet, there was something cold and aloof about her that put off potential boyfriends, and few got close enough to discover that was just a cover for shyness.

She had just finished her 'A' levels and although she had a place at Bristol to read politics she had decided to take a year off.

'A year off from what?' her father had asked her that morning. 'You've done nothing worth taking a week off for, let alone a year.'

'Dad, these exams have really taken it out of me. I can't face another load of studying just yet. I thought maybe I'd go to Europe for a while, watch a bit of football, see the sights...'

'And who's going to maintain you in the manner to which you've become accustomed?' he'd smiled.

'You're becoming Victorian.' But she was only teasing and, as she smiled back at him, he knew he was lost.

He felt as if he was losing on all fronts. The day had not started particularly well. He'd already had a two-hour meeting with the club's bank manager and now he had an appointment with Lennie Simons, Mickey Wayne's agent, to be followed by a board meeting. It was not the sort of day to find him bouncing out of bed all ready to meet it. He'd not bounced out of bed for a while now, although if he'd been asked thirty years ago what he wanted to achieve, his reply would have been the ownership of Hertsmere United Football Club. Whilst his classmates supported the likes of Arsenal, Spurs, Manchester United, Liverpool or perhaps more eccentrically Palace or Millwall, for Sinclair the real heartbeat of the game was outside the league. They might only get two hundred people and a few legendary dogs to watch them but he still seized upon Hertsmere with proprietorial enthusiasm. He could not wait to get home from school, to get out into the road wearing his precious green and white Hertsmere shirt – the real thing, not a replica, a gift from his uncle. In his childish games anything was possible, Hertsmere at Wembley, Hertsmere at Anfield, at Old Trafford, St James's Park, even in the European Cup Final. Now in his lifetime he's seen it all, except Europe.

But the ten-year-old standing on the weed-strewn terraces, whilst his team of part-timers toiled away, hadn't known about the dark underside that came with success.

Sinclair had made his money in property, starting with conversions of houses into two or three flats, then moving on to building individual houses and from those to developments of his own, both residential and, more often now, commercial. The market was no longer that attractive, but any business problems he might have took a back seat whilst he concentrated on the football club. It was a drug and he was hooked. Success, and the price the club had to pay, that was what his three meetings today were all about, and if the second was to be no better than the first then he might as well go home and get his old Subbuteo set out of the loft.

'If you're not out playing football, then you're in playing Subbuteo,' he could hear his mother's voice screaming at him. 'If one more of those little men gets into my Hoover I'll throw the whole lot away, so help me, You'll never get a living out of football. Why don't you open a book once in a while?'

Yet, maybe this season's team would change everything and they'd qualify for Europe either through the League, or more dramatically and indeed realistically through the Cup. He'd cried when they'd lost in the final of the old Littlewoods Cup to a harsh penalty decision in the last minute, but then, perhaps, they'd not been ready. The great God of football rolled the dice and that had just not been Hertsmere's day for sixes. The bank manager with whom he'd had his early morning meeting had talked of rolling the dice as well. Almost everything he'd said had been in metaphors, as if he was programmed for nothing else. Frank Marsden was new to the job and he brought with him little sympathy and even less personality. It had been a sad day when Billy Thornton had been pensioned off. Bill was Hertsmere through and through and, for no greater reward than a guaranteed match-day ticket in the directors' box, had time and again put his neck on the block for Sinclair and the club. And Sinclair had never let him down even when it had meant ploughing more of his own money into the kitty or tying up personal assets with guarantees. All of that counted for nothing with Marsden, who appeared to know nothing about football and to want to learn even less. He was young, no more than thirty-five, but he had the pomposity of a man twice that age, wearing a three-piece suit, his hair cut strictly short back and sides, his spectacles, Sinclair speculated, most likely National Health.

'I want to see weekly management figures, Mr Sinclair. I need cashflow for the year, you have to get some sort of system in place to support the level of overdraft my predecessor gave you. Quite how he got it passed by Head Office I have no idea. Anyway it's shoulders-to-the-wheel time. We have to fall in step with the march of progress if we're to see the light on the road to Damascus.'

'It's not that sort of business. If we get a Cup run like we've had this year it makes an enormous difference to our figures. If we're riding high in the League we'll get more TV coverage and that means more money as well and, of course, if we get into Europe, well then that's jackpot time.'

The bank manager was unimpressed.

'I'm afraid we have to leave jackpots in their proper place in Las Vegas. You can't rely on a random roll of the dice. It's all ifs and buts. Every business may have an upturn if it gets more customers. Yours is no different. What's good for the goose is good for the gander. I, too, am accountable to my masters.'

Sinclair had not given up.

'Look, I've brought with me the plans for a new stadium. You'll see it'll be just off the motorway rather than in the town centre. It includes its own American-style shopping mall, parking, leisure facilities. I think we can pre-let the supermarket and tie a new sponsorship deal on to the back of the project. I've brought all the figures. There'd be an all-seater stadium with a thirty-five thousand capacity...'

'And how do you know you'll get that number of people to fill it? What's the phrase? Fair-weather supporters. What happens if you're demoted?'

'Relegated,' Sinclair corrected him.

'Whatever. What happens if the weather's bad?'

'It's all under cover.'

'The roads are unpassable, the surface unplayable, a week without income will be a week without bread.'

Sinclair sighed. The man just did not want to understand. If Hertsmere were riding high, thirty-five thousand people would dig their way through a blizzard to watch them play.

'No,' the bank manager continued, 'rather than extending facilities I think we have to consider seriously reducing them. There must be some assets of which you can dispose. Cash, I think, is the answer to your problems. Birds in the hand rather than in the bush.'

'Assets?' Sinclair asked, as if he'd never heard the word before.

'Yes, players. They appear to be your only assets. At present you appear to be fiddling while Rome burns.'

Sinclair felt like screaming. He'd burn his boats by leaping across the desk and hitting Marsden. He even had him thinking in metaphors. Somehow or other he managed to control himself and replied quietly.

'We're not looking to sell, we're looking to build.'

'The new stadium?'

'Not just the stadium, the club as a whole. We've got where we are by some good housekeeping...'

'And the goodwill of my bank.'

'Yes, that too...'

'...Well, I don't know if you can continue to rely upon that. Nothing lasts for ever, you know. I'm prepared to mark your facility forward by, say, twenty-eight days. After that I must see some reduction, either from a sale or some other source. Your little club has only just learned to walk. Running is a bit ambitious.'

It was then that Sinclair had finally lost his self control.

'What other source?' he had screamed at the banker. 'What do you think we're going to do? Win the Pools? Rob your bloody bank?'

But it had all been to no avail. He had been spitting into the wind, and all the way back to the ground in his car Marsden's words had echoed in his mind.

'Sell your assets.'

He loved them all. It was Sophie's choice and he could not choose.

CHAPTER 2

Ninety, ninety-one, ninety-two. Mark Rossetti licked the last second-class stamp and stuck it on the last anonymous white envelope. He paused to divide them into two neat piles, secured each with an elastic band, and then went out for the two-hundred-yard walk to the Post Office. As he closed the door behind him it began to rain. He was not surprised. It had rained on him for the last ten years almost without any relief. It had rained on him ever since the day that Hertsmere had lost to Tynecastle in a Fourth Round FA Cup tie. Only right now he no longer had the money to buy an umbrella. He had spent it all on ninety-two second-class stamps.

As he stood outside the Post Office, the pain in his knee almost immediately brought on by the damp weather, he thought of shoving the letters through the slot marked 'First Class and Overseas'. It was about time he travelled first class again, even if he could not afford the fare. He resisted the temptation. With his luck he'd either get them returned or else none of the recipients would pay the excess postage. And these letters had to reach their destinations.

The old newspaper vendor, whose name he'd never

known, waved to him from the shelter of Southgate Station entrance.

'Hello Marky. Applying to make a comeback are you?'

'Sort of.' He patted his pockets. 'Look, I've come out without any money,' Mark said, not adding that he had no money at home anyway. 'Is my credit good for a paper?'

The old man laughed.

'That goal you scored against Fulham, when was it – eighty-two? That'll buy you a paper from me any time.'

'Nice to know somebody remembers,' Mark replied, putting the newspaper inside his jacket for protection. Thirty-one years old, and all he had were memories. Images of a young man with long, flowing hair, drifting down the wing, suddenly accelerating like a finely tuned sports car, leaving defenders trailing in his slipstream, the ball an unstoppable missile bulging the top left-hand corner of the net, then running towards the fans, drawn by their adulation like a moth to the flame, waiting to be burned alive.

And he had indeed died a decade before. Standing in his smart suit, dark tie, white shirt, his hair neatly trimmed, all on his solicitor's advice, awaiting his sentence. The Chairman of the FA Tribunal, peering over half-moon glasses, looking at him as if he were the lowest form of animal life, when just a few months before he'd tried to buy him for his own club for a million pounds.

'Rossetti.' No Mark, no Mister, this was master and servant time revisited.

'Rossetti, we have heard the allegations against you and listened carefully to what you and your representatives have had to say. However, we find the allegations against you proven. These are serious offences. You are a young man with considerable talents, admired by friend and foe alike. You had a glorious future ahead of you, on the verge of an international career, whether it might have been for this country or Italy, your father's native land. All that is lost to you now. We are in no doubt that on February seventh you offered the sum of twenty thousand pounds to Stephen Cairnes of Tynecastle United as an inducement to assist you in your plan deliberately to lose the match between the two clubs. We are satisfied that you, and you alone from your club, were involved and we shall be dealing with Cairnes at a separate hearing. Our decision is that you be fined twenty thousand pounds and that you be banned from any involvement in the game of football at any level whatsoever for a period of ten years.'

At any level whatsoever ... He remembered helping out at a local school, the pleasure he'd got from seeing the kids actually learn to trap the ball, to keep control, to shoot accurately, and then the look on the headmaster's face, the mixture of embarrassment and hostility.

'You should have told us just who you were ...'

It had been a difficult ten years, a prison without bars. Suddenly to find your sole source of income, the only thing you'd ever really been good at, removed at a stroke, without warning; that was never likely to be easy. His paltry savings had been swallowed in one gulp by the fine. Somehow, he'd pieced together the rest of the money, a few favours called in, a few medals sold, the inevitable Sunday tabloid story. And then there was nothing. Twenty-one years old, and nothing.

His father had died a year later, struck down by a heart

13

attack as he tried to save his cafe from destruction by fire. His mother, born and bred in the Elephant and Castle, had tried to comfort Mark, but it had been to no avail. He had convinced himself that his disgrace rather than the fire had caused the heart attack, had been what really killed his father. His mother carried on the little cafe once the insurers had finally and reluctantly coughed up the money for it to be rebuilt. It had been his papa's pride and joy, and for a while things were so hard for Mark that he was grateful to be allowed to work there, glad of the few tips he received, relieved that no criminal proceedings had ever been brought against him. No money had actually passed hands, what he had allegedly attempted had no real impact on the result of the match, and so with magnanimity the matter had been allowed to rest there. The only bump under the carpet was the corpse of Mark Rossetti's career.

Sally had never stopped reminding him how lucky he had been to avoid a jail sentence. She told him every time they argued, which eventually was all the time. They'd been married just a year when the scandal broke and she was already six months pregnant with Emma. They'd disagreed about the name as well, but inevitably Sally had won, just as she'd won most of their battles; but then she had all the weapons. It was when it came to a forced sale of their house that she left. Emma was two by then and she took the child with her as if to say, 'if you can't keep a roof over our heads what right have you to keep your family?'

Later, much later, he discovered Sally had been having an affair for over a year. It was, of course, with another footballer. She always liked footballers. She liked everything that came with them, their firm, athletic bodies, the pleasure of fame, the sexual energy that came with a victory, the money, the champagne, everything except failure.

Had it been his fault? He knew he'd not been easy to live with when the ban began to bite. He'd had too much time on his hands. Time was the enemy of the footballer at the best of times, too much time to drink, to gamble, too many hours passed in smoky snooker halls or watching endless videos. But as a player he still had the training and the games to break the boredom and, unable to fill the black holes, he gradually found himself sucked into them.

He'd not been stupid at school and he had seven 'O' levels to prove it. His headmaster had wanted him to go on to 'A' levels and university even after he'd been offered his apprenticeship. Mark had thought he'd known better as he stood in the man's study, watching the sunlight create myriad patterns in the desk-top dust, listening to one word in three of the man's advice.

'Career . . . risk . . . solid basis . . . unsuccessful . . . short life . . .'

Now, of course, he could fill in the gaps, complete the sensible phrases. But it was too late.

He missed Sally at first, even missed the sleepless nights when he'd walked up and down the bedroom with the baby in his arms. Yet gradually that pain, too, eased as the numbness took effect, the numbness that he could always find at the bottom of a bottle of Scotch. Eventually Sally remarried. It was then he discovered just how blind he had been to what was going on around him. He knew the new husband, Stuart Macdonald, and it hurt him to discover that he was also the old lover.

There was nothing wrong with Macdonald's career. He'd been a good club player with a couple of England caps to his name, and he doubtless deserved the testimonial year he was now enjoying. The couple had a nice house, a nice car, enough money paid into Macdonald's pension fund to ensure there would be life after football. And Mark hated them. He knew how much better a player he'd been than Macdonald and if he had achieved all that from mediocrity what could Mark have not achieved with flair bordering on genius?

He ran the last few yards to his front door. Peeling paint that might once have been yellow opened on to a rickety staircase which, in turn, led to the first-floor room that passed for an office. Anybody who dared would then have had to climb a flight that was even more of a challenge before reaching the couple of rooms in which he spent what was left of his life. Very few visitors ever saw the small sitting-room filled with furniture he'd salvaged from his marriage and which had fared no better than himself over the years. Southgate in North London was, for the most part, an upper-middle-class area, but nobody would have thought it to look at Mark's property. Chase Side, the main shopping street, had been hit more badly than most by the recession and was filled by a mixture of charity shops, estate agents, building societies and shopfronts plastered with illicit posters for concerts that had long since taken place. It was an area on the slide and it had suited Mark Rossetti's ambitions for a long time.

He collapsed, breathlessly, on to the blue divan which extended into a bed if anybody wanted to stay; but nobody had wanted to stay for a long time. In the past there'd been a few drinking companions who'd crashed out there. Mark would wake in the morning, or, perhaps more often, in the afternoon, to clean their vomit off the bed or the carpet. When he'd finally given up drinking, some three years ago, he'd treated himself to a new carpet, but all that had done was to highlight the shabbiness of the rest of the place.

He rose and looked at himself in the spotted mirror above the old-fashioned fireplace. His black hair was still thick, but no longer worn shoulder-length. Now, soaked with rain, it fell sleekly on to his high forehead until he pushed it back with an irritated gesture of his fingers. His violet eyes hid cautiously amongst the dark circles that testified to his sleepless nights, nights no longer dimmed by alcohol, but disturbed by regret and anger. He'd reached rock-bottom the day he'd been taken into the clinic by the police. They'd found him on the pavement begging passers-by for spare change and only the fact that one of them recognized him saved him the ignominy of the cells. Later, the doctor told him he'd been yelling his head off, screaming at an imaginary referee, calling him every name under the sun; but he could remember none of that any more than he could remember his fingers clutching the bottle of watered-down whisky so hard that it had taken three male nurses to prise it loose. He'd been there for ten weeks. The first month was agony, the drying out, the withdrawal, the fear of recognition, the inability to read the newspapers lest he saw his own name. They'd handed him paper and pen when his hands stopped shaking and told him to list every drink he'd ever taken and what it had cost him. Other patients might put down the price in pounds and pence, but he had to log it in loss of pace, loss of skill, loss of respect. He went to the Alcoholics Anonymous meetings, ate with the other alkies, Pat, Tony, Rob, knew them only by their first names for none of them asked questions of each other.

But he'd come out of the clinic feeling good, the healthiest he'd been since he'd last kicked a ball. His olive complexion had taken well to the daily walks around the park, the long hours spent chatting in the sunshine of the clinic's spacious grounds. He felt ready to face life again and had found himself these rooms, taken the furniture out of storage, borrowed the money to pay the bill and made some important decisions.

Sally had been unimpressed when he'd asked if he could have Emma to stay, despite him having made sure he had a second room just for her.

'And what happens if she's ill in the night and you're too drunk to get up to see to her?'

'I'm finished with all that.'

'You're an alcoholic, Mark. Once a drunk always a drunk. The answer's no. If you don't like it then you'll have to take me to court.'

He'd not had the money for that and he'd probably have lost if he'd tried. Sally had the Hertsmere club lawyer working for her and he was tough and aggressive. There'd been a time when Mark would have answered fire with fire, but now he retreated from the slightest blast of heat.

He went into the bathroom and rubbed himself dry with a thin towel. He couldn't afford to replace it, he couldn't even afford this tiny haven. The landlord, Leopold Schneider, an elderly Austrian refugee who came round every Thursday to collect the rents, had been good to him. When there were weeks that Mark could not pay he came round anyway for a chat and a cup of tea, almost apologetically producing some cake he'd bought from a bakery near his North London home. It was he who had encouraged Mark to start a business.

'You're young. You've time to get back. Look at me. Four years in Auschwitz.' He'd rolled up his sleeve. 'I've a number to prove it. There's no tattoos on your arm. The only numbers you had were on your shirts. Clothes you can always get rid off. I came out. Flesh and bones, and not too much flesh either. I came to this country looking for relations I never found. I survived. I worked hard, bought a property, then another. I started all over again. I tried to forget the camps. The number won't let me. You, Mark, you can forget. You tell me that you've sold all your medals, so what is there to remind you?'

When the first-floor offices had become vacant Schneider invited Mark to use them. They had belonged to an inquiry agent who'd upset one husband too many and had found himself in intensive care for an indefinite period of time.

'It's an ill wind,' Schneider had said. 'He won't be back. Take over the business. Take over the phone number – I've paid the bill. You look the sort of man people might trust.' Schneider had no right to give away something that he did not possess, but it was not the time to take the high moral ground.

He'd known nothing about the business, but, buoyed by his landlord's generosity, he learned quickly. After that it got easier. His first commission had been to locate an experienced debtor to serve him with a writ. He'd ploughed through the electoral roll, knocked door-to-door and had finally struck lucky. The last process server had ended up in hospital with a broken leg after a nasty trip down the stairs but Mark had gotten away with it. A missing child – give encouragement; an unfaithful wife – give discretion; a dishonest partner – give results. He was never going to get rich this way, but enough came in to put food on his table and to pay the rent. Lately, though, business had been terrible. Divorce was so much easier that few people needed an agent to track down an illicit relationship, whilst the recession solved financial problems in a far more brutal manner than any inquiry agent's report.

Once again he had time on his hands, only now he used it constructively. He ran, he worked out at the local gym, he swam every morning with all the retired men and women in the local swimming pool. His ten-year sentence would soon be ended. He felt he could still play at a reasonable level, he just wanted a chance. And then, as Chris Rea put it, God tossed his banana skin down and Mark Rossetti slipped on it. One morning as he ran he felt his left knee go one way as he went the other. He hobbled back in agony, pulling himself up the stairs on all fours. The doctor's diagnosis, when Mark finally made it to the hospital in an ambulance, was short and sour.

'It's your cruceate. Unusual for it to go whilst you're just running, but I suspect you've been pushing yourself after a long lay off. Can't rush fitness. Half the patients I see have wanted to run before they could walk.'

He laughed wheezily at his own joke, then seeing the absence of humour in Mark's face moved hurriedly on.

'We'll have you in and operate, but I think you can forget

about any sporting career. Still, I suppose you were a bit old for that anyway, weren't you?'

For anybody other than a sportsman the operation was a success. He could walk, swim, even jog, but more than that was impossible. Another dream had eluded him. Yet the world of football still lured him back.

Then he'd had his great idea, the final gamble. He'd been off work for nearly three months by the time he hobbled home. The small amount he'd saved was long gone. He was down to the wire, in fact so close to the wire that he could feel it cutting into his flesh.

The joint commission set up by the Football League, the Football Association, the Premier League and the Inland Revenue had just published its report. The Chairman of the Commission, Sir Robert Newman, brought more doom and gloom to the game than even the Taylor Report had done a few years before. Illegal payments, tax evasion, unlawful contracts, dishonest managers, agents, even chairmen. Football had become a monster eating itself, then spitting out its own remnants in disgust at the taste. Money, greed, power, all corrupted and all had eaten away at the beautiful game until the sickly sweet smell of corruption and decay had made the decent spectator, player and official recoil with horror. The message was clear.

'Cleanse yourselves, lest ye be cleansed.'

Mark had read the report on the day it was published, then read it again and again, until he understood every line, every word, every nuance. Then he was ready. It was time to see if football could forgive and forget, if it would draw its own lost sheep back into the fold. He spent hours drafting his letter, discussing it with Leopold Schneider when he called, for there was nobody else to whom he could talk. Then it was finally done. He'd checked the names of each and every club chairman, had the letter prepared so that it looked individually and personally addressed.

Dear —
I have no doubt that you will have read the Newman Report with both interest and foreboding. The message is absolutely clear, namely that if clubs will not clean up their own houses then the Commission will seek powers to do it for them. Just as time was given to you by the Taylor Report to make your stadiums all-seater, so you have time to demonstrate that your own club operates smoothly, efficiently and honestly within the rules. . . .

He had wrestled with the next part long and hard before grasping the nettle.

As you will no doubt recall, I was personally suspended from involvement in football some ten years ago. That suspension has now run its course and I have for the last few years been operating a successful inquiry agency. With my experience of both football and investigations I am writing to you to offer my services upon retainer to prepare an internal confidential, but objective, report on your club. This will enable you to implement any necessary suggestions I may have before matters are imposed upon you by the Newman report.

Then a touch of pathos to pluck the heartstrings.

It had always been my hope to return to football as a
player, but a serious injury has made that impossible
for me at the age of thirty-one. I am therefore seeking
to find my way back into the game I love by utilizing
my own expertise and the experience I have gained
during the past decade. I hope you will at least give me
the opportunity of meeting you face to face to discuss
my proposals and the methods I would use to implement them. In any event I hope you and your club will
continue to have a successful season . . .

It wasn't a great letter, but it was his best shot. He'd
thought of enclosing a stamped, addressed envelope, but
that would have been another seventeen pounds odd, and
he just didn't have it. If there was any justice in the world
he'd get one response and that was all he needed, one
chance. Then he could hold his head up again in the world,
clear the shame of his reputation and live on his goals rather
than his crimes. He shook his head at the word 'crimes'. He
was even starting to feel guilty, having lived with guilt for so
long, and that was the most painful thing of all. He hadn't
tried to bribe anybody. He was innocent.

CHAPTER 3

David Sinclair's secretary brought him in a cup of coffee without being asked. Denise Langley had worked for him for over ten years now. She'd been his secretary at his development company and when he'd told her he'd be spending more time at the club than at the office, she'd not hesitated when he'd offered her the chance of coming with him. She was a thin, shapeless girl of indeterminate age, who had been in love with her boss from the first moment she set eyes upon him and whose love had now developed into a fierce and passionate protectiveness that people challenged at their peril.

'Mr Simons is here to see you,' she said in a tone clearly stating that she approved neither of Mr Simons nor his visit. As if in sympathy with her disapproval Sinclair groaned. Simons was an agent, not just any agent, but the agent for Mickey Wayne. Wayne was not just any player, he was a legend at Hertsmere, if one could be a legend at twenty-five years of age. He was, in the eyes of the bank manager, an 'asset', perhaps not just an asset but *the* asset.

Sinclair hated agents as a breed. There had been a time when he'd banned them from the club. That was just after he'd sacked John Kelly as manager. The fans hadn't appreciated that action, but then they often didn't understand what went on behind the scenes. All they saw was Kelly's smiling face, all they heard was the lilting Irish humour of the man who'd captained Hertsmere to the Fourth and Third Division Championships and whose shrewd management had led them all the way to the top of the Second Division.

What they didn't see was the arrangement he had with one particular agent, Sam Lambert, an arrangement where Lambert paid him cash for every player pushed in his direction, an arrangement where Lambert paid him half the fees he earned from the players. Kelly and Lambert had a good thing going until they got greedy and Kelly tried to get the club to pay Lambert for some services he'd never provided. It worked once and that made them complacent. The next time Sinclair was waiting for them, a threat of police action and the whole history of the relationship came spilling out. Kelly's resignation was on the desk in ten minutes and every other agent was tarred with Lambert's brush. If a player wanted to join Hertsmere he came alone, with a representative of the PFA, or not at all.

There was a public outcry at Kelly's departure, but Sinclair gave no explanation. He went out into the market place and brought Phil Reynolds to the club, Reynolds with all his England caps but no managerial experience, Reynolds who seemed to have settled for a media future rather than one in football; but everything Reynolds said made sense. He was blunt, he appeared to be honest and when he brought those virtues to management he was just as successful as he'd been as a TV pundit. There was life after

Kelly at Hertsmere and it was Reynolds who finally steered them into the top division.

Yet playing football at the highest level it was difficult to dispense with agents entirely. Reynolds wanted to bring big names to Hertsmere and the big names had a greater negotiating power than the names they'd been used to dealing with in the lower regions of the League. It was when Reynolds had missed out on three consecutive signings and offered his own resignation that Sinclair had to surrender. He felt Reynolds was straight and he was confident there would be no repetition of the Kelly–Lambert scenario. And so the agents came back to Park Crescent. Sinclair didn't have to like them, but he did have to deal with them and for the most part he dealt with them himself. They had made themselves a necessary evil.

Denise showed Lennie Simons in and, without being offered a seat, he immediately chose the most comfortable chair in the room, collapsing into it as if he was in his own home. He was in his early forties, yet caught in a curious time-warp of the seventies, hair permed, long sideburns, his eyes hidden behind tinted glasses which overshadowed a Zapata moustache. He liked to think of himself as a character, but to Sinclair he looked like an extra for a cheap porn film on a foreign satellite channel. What really annoyed the chairman was that Simons had little or no interest in football as a sport, and merely saw it as a means of making money. There were some agents that even Sinclair had come to tolerate. They were fans, almost groupies, to whom the money was not the only considera-tion. He didn't have them on his Christmas list but they were saints compared to Simons. For Simons it could have been writers, singers, tennis players or golfers, but it happened to be footballers he was representing and to Lennie Simons they were mobile dollar signs. If a player wasn't moving or negotiating a new contract then Simons wasn't earning and Simons liked to earn. He liked to earn more than anything else in life. He was just single minded which was why he was successful.

'Aren't you going to offer me a coffee, David? Your secretary forgot to ask what I wanted.'

'No. And it's Mr Sinclair.'

'Well that's progress. Last time it was Mr Chairman. Maybe you're warming to me.'

'No again. Look Simons, I'm busy. I've a board meeting in twenty minutes. Can you just tell me what this is about?'

'A board meeting, eh? That's convenient. I think you'll need to discuss what I have to say at a board meeting.'

The agent accentuated the last two words as if they were something slightly unsavoury.

Sinclair tapped his desk impatiently with a heavy letter opener, wondering just how long he might get for planting it between Simons' eyebrows. He controlled himself by noticing that the eyebrows met in the middle, affording him no real target. Simons ignored the menacing noise and look. He'd been dealing with people who disliked him throughout his career and had long ago decided you didn't necessarily get on in life by being lovable.

'I'm here today on behalf of my client, Mickey Wayne...'

'Why wasn't your client at training today?' Sinclair interrupted, then, noticing the small cloud that passed across Simons' face, realized that the agent did not know the answer.

'You'll have to ask my client that question. I don't interfere with anything to do with football. That's between him and the club.'

'So why can't Mickey talk to me directly about his contract. I would have thought that was between him and the club as well.'

'Let's just say that he's shy.'

Sinclair almost smiled. He could think of nobody less shy than Mickey Wayne. He'd talked, rather than played, his way into the England Youth side when Hertsmere were still in the Fourth Division. Now he was a regular in the full England squad if not always included in the team. Yet the occasional differences between him and the England manager, Alex Sharpe, did nothing to affect the multitude of commercial activities which flowed from his looks and personality. For the last two years every tabloid in the land had filled in the close season with rumours of his impending move to virtually every club in Britain and beyond. Sinclair, for his part, had given the lad a new five-year contract just three years before, virtually breaking the bank in the process. It had been one of Phil Reynolds' first acts on assuming the reins of managership and, in securing the future of Mickey Wayne with the club, he had convinced the cynics amongst the supporters who still mourned the departure of the popular John Kelly. Wayne's uncle had acted for him that time around and Wayne's uncle was a fan. Simons was not likely to prove so easy.

'The League regulations say I only have to talk to the player.'

'Yeah, yeah,' Simons said dismissively. 'Look *Mr* Sinclair, I've heard it all before. I've sat in car parks and used players as messenger boys, but we're past all that now, aren't we? I've dealt with the toughest and the best. You don't have to like me. You just have to talk to me.'

'You talk, I'll listen,' the chairman said, angry with himself for being so easily defeated.

'Mickey's not happy, not happy at all. He mixes with the England team. They all talk to each other and he's embarrassed to say what he's earning. He's the poor relation.'

'I'm sure you more than make up for it off the pitch on his behalf. He's the only one of our players who turns up to training in a Porsche – that is when he actually bothers to turn up.'

'I'd do just as well for him off the pitch even if you paid him a proper salary.'

'He's got two years of his contract left. He's on top wages. We can't afford to pay him any more than he's getting.'

Simons lit a cigarette without asking, looked around for an ashtray, but finding none puffed on undeterred, catching the droppings of ash in his hand.

'There are others who will,' he said in a tone markedly different from the rest of the conversation.

'Are you threatening me?' Sinclair had to force himself to stay in his seat.

'Would I do that? Could I do that?' The flippancy was back in Simons' voice. 'I'm merely stating facts. The lad's happy here. He's Hertsmere through and through. You know how many bums he puts on benches.'

'Yes, I know. And as you know he's already got a crowd bonus clause in his contract.'

'Twelve thousand maximum. It's peanuts.'

'It won't be peanuts when we move to the new stadium.'

Simons leaned back in his chair and seemed to find something of all-consuming interest on the ceiling.

'What new stadium, Mr Sinclair? You can't afford it, and you know it. Now if you were to sell Mickey, that would provide a lot of bricks and mortar...'

This time Sinclair was up on his feet. The bank manager had been one thing, but this man was another. Two people in the space of one morning telling him to sell the player who was the present and the future of Hertsmere.

'I think I've heard enough. He's not for sale. I will have another look at his contract. If there's any way we can afford to improve it then we will, although for his part he'll have to agree to an extension...'

'*He'll* have to agree. No, Mr Sinclair. You don't understand the situation any more. It's whether I'll agree.'

He took a good long look around the room making Sinclair aware of how shabby it looked compared to the footballing giants. Simons rose, sniffed as if testing the quality of the air and then made for the door.

'Yes, it's whether or not I agree and, quite frankly, I'm not sure that's going to be possible.' And then the door closed behind him leaving only a bad taste in David Sinclair's mouth and the smell of tobacco smoke in the air.

CHAPTER 4

Mark Rossetti made Leopold Schneider his third cup of tea of the morning. The old man heaped in four spoonfuls of sugar and stirred with scientific precision. It seemed incredible that he put on no weight with his love of sweet things, but with his scrawny frame and black hair, that Mark was convinced he dyed, he looked like a raven hopping from property to property.

'I don't know how you can drink it like that,' Mark said without any malice.

'I was in the camps for six years. We didn't have any sugar. There was nothing that was in any way sweet. You can never get enough of something you've missed.'

He looked straight at Mark as he spoke.

'Are you trying to tell me something, Leo?'

'Well, there's no point in my asking you for something. I already tried for the rent and you tell me that you haven't got it.'

Rossetti took a biscuit from the bag that his landlord had brought with him.

'You'll get fat,' the old man said.

'So what. I've nothing to keep in shape for.'

'You know, when I first came to this country in 1946 I

couldn't speak a word of English. German, Yiddish, yes. English, no. But I have lessons. I learn to speak good. And the teacher tells me never end a sentence with the word "for". It don't sound good. So I don't, but you, who've lived here all your life, maybe you never learned grammar at school. I learned it good. I think I was a little bit in love with the teacher. I see the cross around her neck and I say to myself, Laban, that's my Hebrew name, Laban, she's not for you. Some things you don't have to be taught.'

Mark took another biscuit. He knew Schneider well enough to let him get to his point in his own time by his own route.

'So I'm thinking maybe being a private detective isn't for you, Mark. Working in a restaurant wasn't for you either. You're missing the football just like I missed the sugar. Maybe you're missing your wife and kid as well. I'm not getting any younger. None of my properties have got lifts, to be honest some of them haven't got proper stairs. And the tenants ain't too good either. With my kind of properties I can't be too choosy, so who knows when I'm going to get hit over the head. So I think a bit more and I'm wondering if you could help me collect the rents, look after me a bit, maybe go out on your own. Let an old man have a bit more time to drink tea with his friends. And that way we forget about the rent for a while and also you get to speak to my solicitor about how you get to see the girl. Not that my solicitor is the greatest legal brain since Perry Mason, but with your problems and mine I think he can cope.'

Mark bit his lip. It had been a long time since anyone had been kind to him and he'd forgotten how to react. When he'd been young and famous there'd been no time for kindness. When you gave an interview to the papers, they weren't paying for kindness – they wanted you to get the boot in. It had to hurt whoever was their target that day. And then he'd become the target himself and suddenly he knew what real pain was. Not the passing pain that came from a defender's kick on the shin but pain that was at first there for all to see, before fading into a private ache that was there for ten years, an ache that, perhaps, would never go away.

'I don't know, Leo, I honestly don't know. I'm not saying I'm not grateful for the offer, but I honestly want to see if I can make it on my own. You're dead right about wanting something you've missed. Some Saturdays I watch the football preview on the box and I can actually smell the dressing room through the set. Most weeks I just don't watch at all and then it comes to the results and I've got to switch on. It's like a drug, only there's nobody out there pushing what I need now. I hope you understand.'

The little old man pulled himself out of the armchair with a grunt and a groan.

'You know, Mark, you ought to complain to your landlord about the furniture in this place. I can feel the springs coming through into my *toochas*.'

'I'll tell him next time I see him. You'll be around next week?'

'Who knows? Maybe the Almighty will have come for me by then. Maybe I'll have been mugged by an angry West Indian when I take away his comfortable armchair for my favourite tenant.'

Almost reluctantly, Mark helped the old man on with a thick coat that was several sizes too large for his bird-like frame.

'Did this ever fit you?' Mark asked.

'It's a good coat. Cashmere. I got it from the refugees' association thirty years ago. Maybe they thought I'd grow into it. If you change your mind about the offer let me know next week ... If I'm still alive that is.'

He waved away Rossetti's helping hand and made his own way down the stairs. Mark heard the front door close on his visitor, then, watching from the window, saw him swallowed up in the busy high street. He felt a terrible wave of loneliness sweep over him. Maybe he should have jumped at the old man's offer. He'd meant well by it and he just hoped he hadn't been offended by his refusal. As he'd said, he could always change his mind. Yet by next week who knew whether or not he'd have had a response to his circular letter.

He took up the paper, the newsvendor's face a disturbing image in his mind. He remembered when he'd been a player how one of the old Hertsmere players had ended up selling papers on the street corner. He even recalled what he'd said. 'He's been a mug and he's paying for it. That won't happen to me .' No, not yet, but there was still time for that. And then he'd been asked to turn out in a charity match for the player and he'd said yes and forgotten because he was just too tied up with Sally. He felt the anger rising up inside him, the same anger he'd fuelled with alcohol for so many years. He took a deep breath and muttered to himself the words the clinic had taught him so well. 'When you feel you need a drink count to ten. If you still want it after that then count again. Do the same if you're about to get into a fight even if it's only with yourself. You'll find you can't even remember why you were thirsty or angry.'

He had to do something for himself. At this time of the day Sally would probably be at home on her own. He couldn't bring himself to think of Stuart Macdonald, her new husband. Macdonald who still went training every day, whose legs still smelled of linament, whose photo still appeared in the papers, who still signed autographs for the eager kids. There ought to be a way to have a second chance for those who'd messed it up first time around. There were times when he almost felt guilty himself, when he was sure that if he'd not fallen into the maudlin quagmire of drink and self-pity that he could not only have cleared his name but got his wife and child back as well.

He lifted the phone and dialled Sally's number, surprised that he knew it off by heart. It rang out for some fifteen seconds and he actually felt relieved that he was going to avoid the confrontation, but then as he was going to hang up she answered. The voice still sent a shiver down his spine, for not knowing it was him on the line, it contained the polite warmth she reserved for strangers.

'Sally, it's me.'

Before she even spoke again he sensed her tone change.

'What is it, Mark? Are you drunk again? I thought I told you to contact me through my solicitor if you wanted anything.'

He was determined to keep it polite, knowing from past experience that if he raised his voice the receiver would just be slammed down.

'Look Sally, about Emma. I really think I should see her.'

'Oh, and why is that, Mark?'

'Because I'm her father.'

'It's taken you a while to wake up to that idea. Why don't you phone the newspapers. I'm sure they'll want to plaster that all over the front page.'

'I've had an offer of a job ... and some money to go to court. But I don't want to do that. Surely we can work something out before she forgets all about me.'

'Mark, she never had anything to forget. She calls Stuart "daddy" now. I'll tell you what I'll do, I'll send you a photo. I have to go and pick her up for the dentist. Please don't call again. You know who my solicitor is. Just write to him. It'll cause us both a lot less grief.'

And then she was gone. And once again he was alone in the room where the phone never rang, waiting for letters that might not come, and a photograph of his daughter with which to torture himself.

CHAPTER 5

David Sinclair looked around at the rest of the Hertsmere United board and felt even more depressed. There was Jonathan Black who had flatly refused to sell his twenty-two per cent stake in the club when Sinclair had taken over. Black was a bluff man in his late sixties, red-faced, red-veined, even the hair that grew sparsely on his head was red. He was an architect by profession, with a successful practice made even more successful by some lucrative local authority contracts. He had not needed the money Sinclair had offered him for his shares, even when the figure on the table was far in excess of their real value. The price he had demanded and received for not opposing Sinclair's bid for the club was a continuing and guaranteed place on the board. An uneasy truce had been declared between the two men whilst there was success on the field, but Sinclair knew that as soon as he made his first mistake Black would be waiting to pounce.

Then there was Richard Lee, forty years old, with the cool distant confident look that had made him such an asset in negotiations. Sinclair had thought it a good move to appoint a lawyer to the board when he'd first taken over, and who better than Richard who'd helped him mastermind the

whole scheme. Not only was Richard his own solicitor,
but he was a fan as well, a man who rarely missed a match;
but Richard had changed in the last few years. He'd grown
to like the idea of being a personality, of giving interviews,
of making statements and pontifications that sometimes
were neither the whole truth nor represented the views
of the rest of the board. He dressed as if another interview
was just around the corner, smart double-breasted suits,
immaculate white shirts, topped with a brightly coloured
range of bow-ties that he had deliberately made his
trademark. Sinclair had always considered Lee to be his
man, but now he was not so sure. He was ambitious, and he
had the lean and hungry look of a Cassius about him. It
occurred to Sinclair from time to time that the lawyer might
well have him cast as Caesar in his own little script.

The old man opposite him, his eyes drowsily closed, was
Ben Porter. Ben was 'Mr Hertsmere'. He'd played for the
club as a teenage amateur back in 1925, and now in his late
eighties he was Life President, popular amongst fans,
players and media alike. He had a shock of white hair,
bushy white eyebrows and a thick bull-like neck which gave
him now the look of a fierce animal put out to grass. As far
as the board was concerned he had his annoying habits and
sleeping through meetings was one of them. It was when he
awoke, oblivious to what had been discussed, and began his
rambling stories of the past that he was at his most
disruptive. He had nearly been trampled to death by the
policeman on the white horse in the Cup Final of 1923
between West Ham and Bolton, he'd almost signed for
Arsenal, and he'd not missed a home match since a bout of
pneumonia in 1964. The rest of the board had heard it all

time and time again. Yet, he was harmless and, when he was awake and his mind was clear, there was no doubting he had the good of the club at heart.

The finance director marched to a different beat altogether. Tom Kerr was a sharp young Scot in his early thirties with an acerbic tongue and a grasp of figures that left his fellow directors trailing in his mathematical wake. He'd been foisted on them by the bank some six months ago when the old branch manager, Bill Thornton, knew he was on his way out.

'I'm sorry, David. It's a Head Office decision. A company with an overdraft the size of yours needs hands-on monitoring.'

Kerr was definitely a hands-on man and, as Marsden had said that morning, things had definitely improved since he'd been around. He had trained with one of the big six international firms of accountants and now he was on what seemed to be permanent secondment to the bank. He'd said little when he'd first arrived, but within a month he'd prepared a twenty point report of what he required implementing within the club, some half a dozen to be accomplished within a week.

'At the moment, Mr Sinclair, the financial structure of your club is a thieves' charter. From the turnstiles, to the programme vendors, right down to the ordering of boot-laces, there are opportunities for dishonesty.'

'Are you saying any of our staff are stealing from us?'

'I'm not saying that they are. All I'm saying is that as things stand they have the opportunity. I've seen it all before, a dead turnstile, inflated pricing on equipment, backhander deals with suppliers. I was brought up in the Church of Scotland. I learned from an early age not only "Do not steal," but also "Keep us from all temptation".'

He had a sharp face with a permanent look of disapproval etched around his mouth, spectacles that he disconcertingly put on and off while he spoke, and dark hair parted on the left with computerized precision. He looked as if he were in permanent audition for *Chariots of Fire*. Sinclair wondered how much the uncomfortable meeting he had endured with the bank manager that morning was down to Kerr.

His closest friend and appointee, Freddie Scott, was not there. Whether he'd ever be there again was doubtful. He'd fought a long, hard battle against cancer, which just now seemed to be a losing one. Sinclair had seen Freddie in hospital this week, pathetically thin, yet still up and dressed. His face was clean shaven, but the folds of flesh that hung loosely on the yellowing skin showed nicks and grazes from his determined efforts. Freddie, some twenty-five years older than Sinclair, had been one of the main reasons why he had been able to acquire the club in the first place. It had been Freddie Scott who'd seen something in the young man and persuaded the other directors to co-opt him on to the board and that had been the launching pad for his successful bid for the whole club but, sadly, time had not dealt kindly either with his health or his own printing business. The chaiman had Freddie's letter of resignation in his pocket, but he also had his proxy which he'd used ever since he fell ill. Whether or not he put the former on the table depended on his need for the latter.

The only other person at the meeting was Helen Archer, the company secretary and general manager. Everybody had made a huge fuss about his appointment of a woman when he'd first taken control, but Helen was no ordinary woman, and she was certainly no ordinary secretary. She was first and foremost a football fanatic who knew as much about the game as anybody on the coaching staff. She lived and breathed football and had got her foot into Hertsmere's door by way of a letter asking for work during her school holidays. She'd gone to university at Hull, seen more of the local team than the lecture halls, and then upon graduation had promptly sought a full-time job back at Hertsmere. She'd begun as a general dogsbody, then assumed responsibility for the advertising in the programme, revolutionized the whole publication until it was voted Programme of the Year, before slipping into the post of assistant secretary to Tony Malcom. On his retirement she'd moved into his office and his job and was now one of the youngest and most dynamic administrators in the country. She was a large, jolly girl in her late twenties who would not have been out of place on the touchline of a polo field wearing green wellies. Yet her lack of sexual appeal was an enormous advantage in a world of men. One of the players had once asked her out for a bet and had returned to training the next day sadly shaking his head.

'Did you get her into bed?' he'd been asked.

'I never got her out of Rothmans,' he'd replied, referring to the annual book of records, the footballing equivalent of Wisden. 'She didn't stop talking the whole bloody evening.'

Today, Helen had been her usual efficient self. Everybody

had before them a clean white pad, sharpened pencil, agenda, monthly management figures, the previous meeting's minutes and a cut glass containing the individual's preferred drink.

Sinclair looked at his watch. It was noon. High Noon, perhaps, for him as he thought ruefully.

'I propose we take the minutes as read,' he said.

'Seconded.' This was from Richard Lee, whose boredom threshold was never particularly high.

'Right, may we have the financial report.'

He turned to Tom Kerr. The accountant shuffled his papers, removed his glasses and placed them by his side on the table.

'As you'll see from the figures the position is serious. We have a wages bill that can be met each month provided we average gates of ten thousand. Looking ahead to our fixture list we have some decidedly unattractive visitors to the club, which upon comparison with other seasons might attract crowds of half that figure. We do, of course, have our Cup semi-final, and what I'm suggesting is that we increase our admission prices for the next couple of games by fifty per cent, but give a voucher that guarantees admission to the semi-final and also a ticket for Wembley should we get there.'

'We'll have a riot on our hands with the fans if we stick up prices before the end of the season,' Sinclair said.

'Rather a riot with the fans than an invasion by the creditors,' Jonathan Black interjected.

'I don't like the idea at all,' Sinclair continued, 'we're talking about families who've supported us through thick and thin.'

Richard Lee put up his hand. He always did that before he spoke, as if due deference to formality somehow gave weight to his words. It drove Sinclair crazy.

'Yes, Richard,' he said, hoping the lawyer was going to support him.

'I hear what you say,' Lee began. Sinclair hated that phrase when it came from a lawyer, as it did so often. He'd have to be bloody well deaf not to have heard him considering they were sitting around the same table. And he knew it preceeded him saying something in direct opposition to what he had actually heard.

'I think we have to make the most out of this Cup run while it lasts,' Lee continued. 'We're certainly not setting the League alight and if we lose in the semis then that's our season as good as ended. Once the supporters have paid their money and are in the ground they'll forget what it cost them; particularly if we win.'

'And if we lose?' Sinclair queried, trying to keep his temper.

Kerr shrugged and put his glasses back on, peered at his notes, then removed them again.

'If we lose it doesn't bear thinking about. I believe you saw the bank today, David.' The informality came uneasily to him. 'What did they have to say?'

'I'd have thought you'd have known that already, Tom.'

Sinclair looked around at the rest of the board.

'He says we have to get some capital into the club. Either by the sale of a player or some other means.'

Ben Parker suddenly jerked into life, like a puppet whose strings had been violently tugged.

'Can't sell players now. We did that back in 1932.

Weren't supposed to sell, we were strictly amateur in those days. Got rid of Reggie Thwaite to Dulwich Hamlet. Big mistake. We'd have won the old Amateur Cup if we'd kept hold of Reggie. Killed in the war, he was. Dunkirk. Good player. Strong as an ox. Big centre forward, none of your strikers then. Strikers were folks who refused to work. Took a lot to stop Reggie. I saw four defenders try and fail once. Kraut mine succeeded though. Would have stopped most people, I suppose...'

'So what did you say to the Bank?' Kerr asked, ignoring the old man who'd subsided into a violent fit of coughing.

'I showed them the plans for the new stadium. Explained that we could get the gates to fill it if we just had the backing to build it. He still said we had to get more money.'

'Just to stay where we are?' Helen asked.

'Just to stay where we are,' Sinclair sadly confirmed.

Kerr cleared his throat to get attention.

'Even on my figures we can't gamble on further progress in the Cup...'

'But if we were to get to the final we'd be safe.'

'Perhaps,' Kerr replied cautiously. 'We'd need to win, to get into Europe, but even then success would bring its own problems. Bonuses, requests for higher wages, transfer demands if we didn't pay and then all the bad publicity that sort of thing attracts. I believe you've just had a meeting with Mickey Wayne's representative in that respect.'

'How did you know that?' Sinclair asked.

'I make it my business to know what goes on in this club. It's a shame others don't follow my example. What precisely did he want?'

'More money for his player.'

'And you said?'

'I said he was in the middle of a generous contract, but I'd look at it again.'

Kerr shook his head as if the greed of the world was just too much for him to take.

'That's the sort of problem we'll continue to face. I think we must consider either the sale of players, or the injection of fresh outside capital into the club. I believe Chris Handsel is still anxious to come on to the board.'

'Over my dead body,' Sinclair shouted, unable to control himself further. 'Handsel's a crook.'

'Take it easy, David,' Lee said. 'I'm not sure this meeting's privileged.'

Sinclair sought eye contact with the rest of his board.

'Is anybody here going to tell Handsel what I said?'

He felt sick at the mention of his name. Handsel was mafia, dockland mafia, but mafia for all that. He'd played for, and captained Hertsmere some ten years ago, as a tough, even brutal, defender. On his retirement, attackers up and down the country breathed a sigh of relief, but Handsel himself had entered his family scrap-metal business and quickly earned a personal fortune. Neither Sinclair nor a lot of other people thought it began and ended with scrap, but as Handsel got richer and richer the chances of proving that became ever more remote. Handsel had tried to buy Hertsmere before and failed. Sinclair had no intention of giving him a second chance.

'So, you don't want to sell players and you don't want to deal with Handsel. What do you want to do, David, other than agree to pay players money we don't have?' Kerr continued calmly.

And as Sinclair sought for an answer, he thought this was not the moment to tell the rest of the board that locked in his filing cabinet he had a fax from Roma Cinquante, one of the most ambitious clubs in Italy, offering seven million pounds for Mickey Wayne. The only question was how long he could keep that a secret.

CHAPTER 6

Mickey Wayne rolled over in the bed to look at the clock.

'Fucking hell, is that the time?'

He put his own wristwatch to his ear and realized it had stopped. The woman by his side put a bare arm around his shoulders and tried to pull him back to the pillow where she still lay.

'You see, Mickey, how time flies when you're enjoying yourself.'

'It's gone twelve. I was supposed to be at training two and a half hours ago. The boss will go spare.'

'What time does training finish?' the woman asked innocently.

'About one.'

'Hardly worth bothering. Just lay back, relax. We were having such a nice time. How about a hattrick?'

Wayne didn't move. He stayed bolt upright, wondering not for the first time why she didn't keep her mouth shut and her legs open. The relationship was on his part purely physical and he had no wish to make small talk, or indeed any talk at all.

'You've got a dirty little mind. Have I ever told you that?'

49

'I haven't heard you complaining before. Why don't I show you what's going on in my dirty little mind?'

She moved forward, her head bobbing down towards his lap. Before she could take him in her mouth he grabbed her hair, pulling it back sharply.

'Leave me alone. I've got to be somewhere at two.'

Even as he spoke he rose from the bed, pulling on his tracksuit bottoms.

The woman raised herself on one elbow.

'I love the idea of you not wearing pants. It makes for instant accessibility.'

'I don't wear socks either, it doesn't mean I want to screw you with my feet.'

She pouted, his anger finally hurting her.

'Look, nobody made you stay. You turned up here for a quickie and it's just taken you a bit longer than you thought. As for your feet, I don't mind sucking your toes if it turns you on. It was good enough for that MP bloke, the one who reckons he knows a bit about football.'

'He's a Chelsea supporter. That tells me he knows fuck all about the game.'

He looked around the room in irritation.

'Don't you ever tidy up in here? Where the hell's my T-shirt?'

The woman reached under the sheets, pulled the blue cotton garment out and held it over her breasts in a gesture of mock modesty.

'You couldn't wait to get it off when you got here.'

'And now I can't wait to get it on. Give it here, I've not got time for games.'

'Don't you want to have a shower with me?' she

persisted. She liked the feel of the hot water needles, covering her body, while Wayne pressed himself against her from behind. She liked the sight of his body with its fair down of golden hair, liked the way the water streamed off his finely chiselled face, the way his blue eyes shone through the steam, like the sky breaking through the clouds.

'I'll wash at home.'

'Does your wife shower with you? Do you make love to her in the shower?'

'No, I don't make love to her. I don't make love to anybody. I fuck her, just like I fuck you. I'll give you a ring.'

'Where are you going, Mickey? It's not another woman is it?' This time her voice had lost its teasing note.

Mickey didn't care, he raced down the stairs, the smile almost back on his face. He caught a glimpse of himself in the hall mirror, and instinctively ran his fingers through his long blonde hair. He wondered if he had time to get home, shower and shampoo before his meeting. It was another woman, but not in the way the one he'd left behind would understand. It was amazing the way he could talk to her and still have her pleading for him to return and give her more of the same. Sexual equality, sexual liberation, they'd both passed Mickey Wayne by. As far as he was concerned every woman was there for the taking and should be willing to show her gratitude that he was prepared to give.

He walked around the corner to where he'd parked his black Porsche with the number plate MW 11. There was no point in attracting attention by parking it outside the girl's house. Too many people knew it was his, too many people in the area knew his wife, Laura, for him to take any chances. Laura didn't express surprise or ask questions nowadays when he went out at odd times. He'd surrendered his freedom for the first couple of years of their marriage and now he had recaptured it. He had no conscience about his infidelity. He was a good provider to her and the boy. Whatever she wanted or needed she had, and if all of his plans worked out then she'd have a lot more.

He coughed and spat into the road as he turned off the alarm on the car. The cough was annoying and he'd actually been to see his own private doctor about it. He reckoned the club doctor was useless and as far as Mickey Wayne was concerned the only things in life that were any good came expensive; but all the Harley Street man had done was give him some antibiotics and do some tests. Doctors, what did they know? He'd once played half a season with a broken toe because he'd been passed fit. He could do without spending hours in the surgery. He had no time for it. Maybe, if he felt like it, after his appointment he'd drop by his man's consulting rooms and see if he was any the wiser.

He had little time for anything at present. If he wasn't training or screwing, then Lennie Simons kept him busy, too busy. The problem with Simons was that he couldn't say no. If there was ten per cent in it for him, then he'd commit Wayne to do it. He'd tried to explain to the agent that he wanted more time to himself, but the man seemed unable to hear him, let alone understand.

'Mickey, Mickey, you're a long time dead in this business. You break a leg tomorrow, who's going to want to know you? You have to make hay while the sun shines. Believe me, I know. Now, on Tuesday evening I've got you opening a wine bar ...'

Wayne had taken to avoiding his calls, dodging him like a naughty schoolboy, even if it meant not turning up where he was supposed to be.

Simons had protested.

'How can I explain it away when you don't turn up?'

'You'll think of something, Lennie, you always do. Just for a grand it's not worth it.'

'There was a time when you'd have thought a grand a lot of money. Take your playing contract for example. A real mess your uncle made of that.'

'Just sort it out, Lennie, and tell me when you've done it.'

As Wayne drove he switched on his car phone for messages.

First of all Simons: 'I'm seeing Sinclair, your chairman, this morning, about the contract. I'll let you know what happens.'

Then Phil Reynolds, the manager: 'Where the hell are you, Mickey? Your wife says you left home before seven this morning. The traffic's not that bad. I want to see you this afternoon. Be here.'

Wayne swore under his breath. If Reynolds had phoned his home, then his wife knew he'd not gone training. He was getting reckless about these things. Maybe deep inside he wanted to bring it all to a head, to push her into divorcing him and this was his way of doing it.

There were another couple of messages. Simons again: 'I've seen Sinclair. Why weren't you at training? It doesn't help with the negotiations. Let's get you some more money before you piss them around.'

'Get me the money,' Wayne muttered to himself. Just

how much money did Hertsmere have? Doubtless there'd be a fine for not turning up at training, and probably another if he didn't attend this afternoon. Reynolds had fined him last week just for being late, so he could expect a real hammering for today's little effort – skipping training altogether – particularly as he'd not even bothered to phone.

It was time to move on, to look for the big money, the one jackpot that would give him security for all time. Then he wouldn't have to worry if he broke a leg, wouldn't have to drag out in the evenings to some crummy bar and look cheerful just so that Lennie Simons could push nine hundred worth of used notes into his hand. He didn't like the way the man always took his commission up front, and, truth to tell, he didn't really like the man.

When he'd first started making a name for himself in the game, Simons had driven him crazy. He'd phone him at home, be waiting in the car park after training, wangle his way into the players' lounge after matches. He seemed to be everywhere. His persistence had eventually paid off when Wayne had been persuaded to make a couple of appearances that Simons had arranged, do a couple of interviews that paid more than he'd ever received before. It seemed the easy thing to do to sign an exclusive contract with him after that. He'd thought it would not only stop Simons pestering him, but also be an escape route from all the other agents who pursued him in their efforts to peddle their wares. They all had their own methods of approach, through other players they represented all trying to tell him 'their man' was best, through journalists, even through his own family. But Simons was no worse than the rest of his breed and, with his lack of interest in the sport, at least he didn't bother him for tickets. At the end of the day they were all a bunch of sharks, flocking towards the easy pickings. And now the novelty had worn off. He had too much ready cash, and something was beginning to tell him that Simons' obsession with demanding cash rather than a cheque was going to land them both in trouble.

'I'm not exactly low profile, you know, Lennie. Surely the Revenue will be expecting me to earn big bucks off the field.'

Simons had been cavalier in his reply.

'Of course they will; but we'll show them just enough to satisfy them. Why make the taxman rich? After all, his main aim in life is to make you poor.'

There was a fourth message: 'Mr Wayne, just to confirm our two o'clock appointment. I look forward to meeting you.' The English was perfect, the voice female, the accent unmistakably continental.

Wayne glanced at the dashboard clock. If he went home now his wife would be out collecting their toddler, Darren, from the nursery. He'd liked the sound of the woman's voice, as if she was definitely worth the effort of showering and washing his hair. He put his foot down on the accelerator.

'And I look forward to meeting you too, darling,' he said aloud as he jumped a red light. What were danger signals for, if not to ignore?

CHAPTER 7

Mark Rossetti picked up the three letters from his doormat. It had been a week since his letter had gone out and all he'd had were three replies, each telling him in various degrees of politeness that they had no need for his services. There was no good news today. One letter returned from Chesterfield because he'd incorrectly addressed it, the second a red demand for his telephone bill and the third from his wife's solicitors telling him that if he contacted her directly again they would reluctantly have to apply to the court for an injunction. As if any solicitor ever did anything reluctantly, he thought.

Quite simply he didn't know what to do next. Schneider's offer was still on the table and the old man would be round today in his hopeless quest for the rent. Yet, it didn't appeal to him to become a cross between a rent collector and a minder. He tried to convince himself he wasn't that desperate, but one look in the fridge and his larder told him differently. He went to the fruit bowl and took the last browning banana to eat with his black sugarless coffee for breakfast. At least there was no chance of putting on weight.

He picked up the morning paper which had come with a

note from the newsagent telling him that unless the bill was paid by the end of the week he'd reluctantly have to stop delivery. Everybody was reluctant this morning. He sat himself down and automatically turned to the sports pages. The headlines caught his attention immediately. HANDSEL TARGETS HIS OLD CLUB.

Chris Handsel, not a man that Mark was likely to forget easily, not a man that anybody who met him was likely to forget. He'd captained Hertsmere during Mark's last season, had driven them on with a feverish drive that made every game an assault course. He should have fought in the First World War, trench warfare would have suited him down to the ground. If it was a question of going over the top, then Handsel would have been the first to go every time.

Mark had respected him, even though they could not have been more different players. Mark had the skill, Handsel had the muscle, but as the then manager put it, somebody had to win the ball and Handsel had a better chance than most. With Hertsmere in the Third Division in those days there was never a chance of getting rich with them, but Handsel never seemed to be short of money. Some days his dad would drop him off at the ground in his Bentley. Once another player, who was new to the club, tried to take the rise out of him. Handsel laid him out with one punch that broke the man's nose, but the victim never made a formal complaint. People tended to learn the lesson fast that you didn't argue with the Handsels whether it was on or off the pitch.

Yet, when it had come to his hearing, Handsel, like everybody else, had stood aside. Nobody wanted to give a character reference, nobody wanted to be involved. Mark Rossetti had suddenly become bad news. Handsel had hardly changed over the years. He'd put on a little weight, there was the hint of a double chin, but he still sported the crew-cut that had been his trademark, even if the hair was a little greyer. There could be no disguising the boxer's nose, damaged in a hundred fights on the streets and on the pitch, or the steely grey eyes that threw out a challenge every Saturday afternoon. He'd been a controversial choice as captain with his disciplinary record, but the elevation had been the making of him and, even without Rossetti, he'd led Hertsmere to promotion.

His retirement had come as a shock to management, players and fans alike. For a while he'd vanished from the public eye, preferring to concentrate on the family scrap-metal business, a legitimate concern that jealous competitors claimed covered a multitude of illegitimate ventures. There had been at least one attempt on the life of his father, Ronnie, who'd survived a car bomb with nothing worse than a badly damaged left leg and an aching desire for vengeance. There'd been a rash of mysterious deaths after that. Charlie Woods had been burned alive in a car that went out of control, Tommy Ross seemed to have thrown himself under a train and Joe Benskin had just disappeared into thin air, never to return, all of them Ronnie Handsel's rivals. Peace gradually descended with the Handsels buying out the Woods, Ross and Benskin businesses. The police had shown more than a passing interest but, without any firm proof to link Ronnie or his son to their deaths, eventually moved on.

The article itself was all rumour and innuendo. Mark

knew enough about the press to recognize a planted article. This was Handsel's way of telling the public that if Sinclair could not run the club profitably then he most certainly could. The fans had never really taken to Sinclair. Under his stewardship there had been too many sales of popular players, and now this article was suggesting that whatever the outcome of the season, Sinclair would have to sell Mickey Wayne, probably to a foreign club.

'If I were in control of Hertsmere, there's no way I'd sell Wayne. I'd find out the best price we could get for him and whatever that was I'd put in an equivalent amount of my own money.'

It was big talk and Mark had little doubt that if, and when, Handsel ever took over he'd sell Wayne if the money was good enough and then blame it on the greedy player and his advisers. All these fine words would be long forgotten. Sitting back these last ten years as an observer, Mark had learned far more about the politics of the game than he had ever learned as a player, and clearly Handsel was firing the first warning shots in his campaign. Of all the clubs that Mark had circulated, Hertsmere was the one he wanted most to reply, yet whose reply also terrified him. There were too many people there from his days as a player and he would have to look them all in the eye. However, his anxieties were almost certainly hypothetical. Why should Hertsmere, of all clubs, bring back in a man who had caused them so many problems, brought them so much bad publicity?

He heard the front door open and knew it must be Schneider letting himself in with his key. He had his eccentricities as a landlord and one of them was treating all of his properties as if they were his own home notwithstanding who might be living there.

'Mark, how goes it?' the old man asked as he wheezed into the room and chose the least uncomfortable chair into which to collapse.

'It goes. But not well.'

'No replies, eh? Never mind. Have a biscuit. A cup of tea to wash it down would be nice.'

Mark boiled up the kettle, then handed the cup to Schneider.

'No milk, no sugar. And I suppose no rent.'

Mark shrugged apologetically and the landlord did not press the point. They spoke for some half an hour like old friends, without really saying anything. Finally Schneider rose to leave and, as he was draping the inevitable coat around him, he asked, 'Things must be pretty bad. What about my offer?'

'Give it another week, can we?'

'Of course.' The old man fumbled in the recesses of his pockets, then triumphantly brought out two ten-pound notes and proffered them to Mark.

'No, I couldn't. You've been far too generous already.'

'Go on. Humour me. Treat it as an advance against wages.'

'And if I don't take the job?'

'Then you'll have some income from elsewhere, in which case you can pay me back.'

He pressed the money into Rossetti's hand, and before he could say another word, he was descending the stairs at a dangerous speed.

The flat seemed even more empty after he had left. Mark

read the rest of the sports pages, then, without bothering to glance at the front page and the rest of the news, he crumpled the paper into a ball and kicked it straight into the wastebasket. At least he'd lost none of his old accuracy. He stared at the phone trying to will it into ringing, then lifted the receiver to hear the dialling tone and satisfy himself he had not yet been cut off. It was, in its way, a symbolic life-line to the rest of the world.

He suddenly felt a terrible thirst such as he'd not experienced since they'd taken him into the clinic. Twenty pounds in his hand. He could buy milk and sugar, he could pay off a chunk of his paper bill and he'd still have enough left for a bottle. That was all he needed, just one bottle, and then he could make it last. A nip every time he felt down, enough to remind him of what he had left behind, but never enough to cause any real damage. He had no strength left to argue with himself, and the small voice telling him not to do it receded with every step towards the off-licence, became ever fainter with his request for a bottle of scotch and, by the time he fell asleep in the armchair with the empty bottle in his hand, had vanished altogether.

CHAPTER 8

As Mickey Wayne entered the Covent Garden wine bar he realized he had no idea of what the woman he was meeting looked like. He was half an hour late and he just hoped she would have waited. The traffic had been bad, the parking impossible and he had to leave the car in a position so outrageous that nobody could believe he did not have the right to park there. The lunch-time crowd was just beginning to thin out as he arrived, a mixed bag of lawyers, admen and women, designers and writers all staggering back to doze in their offices, regretting that one glass too many.

He paused to stare through the smoke and she recognized him at once, but even if she had not waved he would have known who she was. She sat at the end of the bar on a high stool, wearing a red silk blouse and a tight black skirt, cut to reveal just enough thigh to be decent. She could only have been in her mid-thirties, but she gave off a professional aura that made it clear she was there for a purpose, not for a casual pick-up. The only jewellery was a subtle gold necklace, which made just sufficient a statement to tell it was really valuable. Her hair was dark and permed, yet worn long in a slightly old-fashioned Hollywood style. It was the face though that gripped him, made him want to race across the room so that people should see that she had been waiting for him, that he had the power to keep such a beautiful woman on the hook. Her eyes were dark, her complexion with just a soft hint of olive, and the high cheekbones only added to the impression of a perfect heart shape, the sort of face that would sell cosmetics by the gross if used in an advertisement.

'Mr Wayne, I hope I can call you Michael. I'm Carla Dandone.' She extended a slim, elegant hand and, as Wayne took it, he automatically looked for rings. There was only one, a gold signet that might have been more in keeping on a man's finger. He wondered who had placed it there, father, husband, boyfriend, fiancé? He was determined by the end of the meeting to have discovered the answer.

'Mickey,' he said, 'everybody calls me Mickey. I'm sorry I'm late.'

'It's no problem. In Italy everybody is always late. Today though I am early. I have nothing else to do in London. You are my reason for being here. And I shall still call you Michael.'

'I'm flattered. What are you drinking?'

'*Aqua con gas.*' She laughed, realizing she had slipped into Italian. 'There, I am already giving you your first language lesson. Water, with bubbles.'

'No champagne?' Wayne was enraptured by the accent, by the woman. She was a different class to his wife, to the other women who came and went, even to the girl whose bed he had just left.

'I think it is a little early for champagne,' Carla said.

Wayne looked at his watch.

'It's gone half past two, I reckon that's late enough.'

The woman laughed.

'I think you are having a joke with me. I mean it is too soon to be celebrating something which has not yet happened, but will happen.'

Wayne felt bold enough to test the water.

'I know what I'd like to happen.'

If she understood him she gave no hint, other than immediately becoming business-like. The preliminaries were over. She waited impatiently while the player ordered himself a glass of white wine and her another water, then they moved to a table in a dark corner where they could not be overheard.

'I am grateful to you for agreeing to meet me when I was so mysterious on the telephone. There are times when the phone is not safe.'

'I couldn't resist a voice like yours,' Wayne replied, moving his hand towards hers. Without the movement seeming deliberate she took her hand off the table and ran it through her hair.

'You know my name. Now let me tell you a little more about myself. I am a lawyer by profession, from Rome. Yet I do not operate simply as a lawyer.'

She paused to search for the right word, her brow furrowing as if the fact that some tiny piece of knowledge was eluding her was too much to bear.

'I do not practise simply as a lawyer. I am also a *procuratore*, an agent for sportsmen ... and women. I represent some of Europe's best athletes, footballers, tennis players, even a boxer and a jockey.'

'Look, I hope I haven't brought you here under false pretences, but I've got an agent already.'

She waved her hands in a gesture of dismissal.

'I know all about Signor Simons. He is about to be a little out of his league.'

'I'm not sure I understand.'

She searched his face for a moment then, seemingly satisfied that he was telling her the truth, she continued.

'I see they have not told you.'

'Told me what?' Wayne asked impatiently, his glass already emptied.

'I shall take it from the beginning. Because of the sort of people I represent there is little that escapes my notice. Throughout this season your progress has been closely watched by several European clubs, Barcelona, Bayern Munich, Monaco, but at the end of the day only one has tabled a bid.'

'A bid? For me? Who is it?'

'It comes from my own front door, from Roma Cinquante. I think they have already sent your club an offer by fax. Sooner or later, probably sooner, for there is no such thing as a secret in Italy, it will be made public. Then I think you will need me and so I come to offer my services.'

'I'd accept your services any time,' Wayne said, giving her what he'd always felt was his sexiest stare.

Again she did not react. It was as if every time he said something she did not want to hear that she was able to block her ears to it.

'I will act as your exclusive representative in your negotiations with Cinquante and also your exit from Hertsmere. I will charge you a professional fee which shall not be more than ten per cent of any monies I obtain for you from Hertsmere and five per cent of the total value of your contract with your new club. If I can obtain any payment from either club directly to me then I will give you credit for that amount. It is as simple as that. If I am able to conclude the deal then you will appoint me to represent you exclusively for the first two years of your stay in Italy. What do you say?'

She turned the full power of her gaze on him and if, at that moment, she had asked him to kill for her he would not have hesitated.

'What do I do about Lennie Simons? I've got a contract with him.'

She smiled, and this time he felt a sense of relief that she was on his side. There was a steeliness that he guessed would make her a dangerous enemy.

'I have made it my business to obtain a copy of the standard form that Signor Simons uses. I take it that is the document you signed. I have already analysed it myself and then, as a safeguard, have shown it to the law firm who are my correspondents in England. I am told that not only is it not worth the paper upon which it is printed, but, how did they put it? It has more holes than the *Titanic*. Your Signor Simons, is, I believe, sunk. That is an English joke, I think.'

'I'm not sure if Lennie would find it so amusing.'

'Perhaps he does not have the same sense of humour as you and I?'

'I need another glass of wine, are you sure you won't join me?'

'Have you joined me, Michael?'

There was hardly any hesitation.

'Yes, I'm on board. I never fancied myself as a passenger on the *Titanic*.'

She extended her hand again, and this time when he took it her grip was firm and determined.

'Good. Now for that drink. Now we have something to celebrate. I think you mentioned champagne.'

CHAPTER 9

The last thing that David Sinclair needed on a match day was a business meeting, and the last person he wanted to meet with was Chris Handsel. Not that the match was too important in League terms, but with the semi-final in two weeks' time it was inevitable that Hertsmere would attract media interest.

They'd already made the headlines over the last couple of days for all the wrong reasons. 'Greedy Bastards', as one tabloid put it, was almost the kindest description of the decision to increase admission prices. When it had come to a vote at the board meeting Sinclair had found himself out-flanked. Lee, Black and Kerr were for it and, to his astonishment, old Ben Porter abstained, muttering that he didn't know anything about money matters, leaving him to use Freddie Scott's proxy and lose by 3–2. Helen Archer had taken him aside afterwards.

'I'm only sorry I don't have a vote. It's fine for Kerr to talk about balance sheets and cashflow, but he's not going to be at the sharp end when our fans find out what we've done.'

The sharp end had been painful. The chairman of the Supporters Club had threatened a boycott of the semi-final, the local paper, one of their best sponsors over the years, had organized a petition, whilst the switchboard had initially been jammed with complaints, then finally given up altogether under the strain. Today was a test of how far they were going to get away with it. Kempton Rovers were not usually great crowd-pullers and they didn't have the biggest of travelling support. Last season the gate had been just under 5,000 and with the prices at their normal level they could have expected double that, particularly as they were putting the first batch of semi-final tickets on sale after the match.

It was Helen Archer who had to organize and administrate the voucher system that the board had conceived and that in itself was a nightmare. There were three matches before the semis. The Kempton match this Saturday, then away to Carswell United on Tuesday, then a visit from Stockton Athletic. There was to be a one-ticket allocation to season-ticket holders, then another ticket upon production of the Kempton voucher, another upon production of a Stockton voucher and, if any had not been taken up by then, production of the Kempton and Stockton vouchers gave entitlement to a bonus ticket. That meant that each voucher had to have two coupons so that they could be re-produced in due course. If any supporter actually battled through that maze to take up his full allocation it would be a miracle.

Helen and Sinclair watched anxiously as the computer, so recently installed by Kerr, began to count up the turnstile admissions.

'How's it going?' Kerr asked, poking his head around the office door.

'It's slow,' Helen replied. 'The visitors' end is quite

busy, although we've had a complaint from their secretary that we're unfairly penalizing their fans with the price increase.'

'What did you say?' Sinclair asked.

'I said we were unfairly penalizing their fans with the price increase. He's not stupid. What else could I have said? That we were going to guarantee them value for money? Lots of goals, sendings off, penalties.'

Denise Langley interrupted them before Helen and Kerr could really get an argument going.

'Where do you want to see Mr Handsel, Mr Sinclair?'

'I don't want to see him at all . . .' But before he could add the directive to take the visitor through to his office, Handsel was already in the room, following closely on the heels of Sinclair's secretary.

'That's not very hospitable, Dave. I remember when I was a player at the club, you were just another fan begging for my autograph – for your daughter, wasn't it? Now I want your signature on a contract, you don't seem to want to oblige. Now that doesn't strike me as being very fair.'

Sinclair hated any diminutive of his name, but felt he'd be falling into a trap if he tried to correct Handsel. If there was anything this man could do to unsettle him, then he was likely to try it.

'Come on through to my office. As you can imagine it's a bit hectic today so I can't spare too long.'

'I wouldn't have pushed for the appointment if I didn't think it was important. And what I've got to say won't take long. I want to watch the match as much as you do. Thanks for leaving me a ticket for the directors' box.'

Sinclair turned to Helen in dismay.

'I didn't...' she began, but was interrupted by Tom Kerr.

'No, I did. And you're welcome. I don't think we've ever met, just spoken on the phone.' He stuck out a hand and introduced himself to Handsel who gripped his hand tightly whilst looking searchingly into his face.

'I'm sure we'll be seeing more of each other, Tommy boy. Come on Dave, let's get on with it. You keep on watching the numbers darling, although by the looks of things so far I can't see your bingo card coming up.'

'I'm sorry?' Helen said.

'Bingo, full house, get it,' and roaring at his own joke Handsel almost guided Sinclair to his own office as if he already owned the stadium. Sinclair found it impossible to sit down as Handsel slumped his large frame into the same armchair that Lennie Simons had occupied just a few days before.

'No, it's all right, I won't bother with a drink, thanks all the same.'

'I can't remember offering you one,' Sinclair said, his lips tightly clenched in anger.

'I find a lot of people I deal with are quite forgetful at some stage in our relationship. I won't beat around the bush. I know the trouble you're in down here. A right pig's ear you've made of running this club...'

'We've played it by the book. If you call being honest being in trouble, then you're right.'

Handsel laughed again. He was wearing a dark double-breasted suit. More in keeping with a funeral than a football match thought Sinclair ominously.

'Honesty? I don't call it exactly honest to blackmail your loyal supporters into parting with their hard-earned cash just so you can make a quick buck from a Cup run. All you're doing is putting off the evil day.'

'And I suppose you're going to make sure the fans know your views, just as you made sure they knew you were in the market for my shares?'

'Going to make sure? I've already said just that in an interview which I reckon they're just about to play on Radio 5. Should make good listening for everybody on their way to the game. Wouldn't surprise me if I didn't get a bigger cheer than the team this afternoon when the crowd sees me in the box. Crown Prince and all that sort of thing. The king is dead, long live the king. That kind of philosophy has always appealed to me.'

'That's strange, Handsel, I never took you for a philosopher.'

'Well, Davey, my son, there's a lot about me you don't know, whilst as far as you and this club are concerned there's not much that doesn't come to my attention. Like the fact you had to fine Mickey Wayne for missing training this week, like his agent's demand for more money, like the offer you've had for him from Italy.'

Sinclair was rattled. He knew all about Handsel's reputation, but that had all been from a distance and now it was first-hand he could see just how he had won that reputation.

'Have you disclosed that in your interview as well?'

Handsel visibly relaxed. Now he was all smiles, all charm, the player that Hertsmere fans had turned into a legend, that they had loved as much as he had been hated and feared by the opposition.

'Come on, Dave. There have to be some confidences between men like us. I don't want to fight with you. I'm happy for you to stay on the board, and I'll leave you enough shares to save your face. I think we'd make a good team, you and me. You the velvet glove, me the iron fist.'

Sinclair shook his head.

'You'd punch your way through me, Handsel. I used to admire you on the field, but now when I watch the old footage from all those years ago I can see you for what you were. You were a bully on the field and you're a bully now. If you'll excuse me I have to go and have a word with the Kempton chairman, that is if he's still talking to me after your broadcast.'

Handsel rose slowly to his feet, the gradual unravelling of his bulk and his height a threat in itself.

'I'll see you in the box then, Dave.'

As he left Sinclair realized that he might not have just meant the directors' box.

CHAPTER 10

Rome is a city of heat and rumours, of life and death, a city full of ancient beauty, but the Cavallieri Hilton Hotel, with its swimming pool, tennis courts and smart modern restaurants could be anywhere at all in Europe, and just happens to be in Rome. The steep road up to the hotel from the city had been awash with cars for the past hour or so as the Roman media roared towards the hotel in a mixture of sports cars and motor-bikes.

April was a little early for the main invasion of tourists, but the lobby of the hotel was jam-packed with journalists and cameramen, the latter photographing anything that moved, and quite a lot that didn't, just in case it might prove of interest at a later date. There was a buzz of noise and excitement, the high-pitched sound of locusts who had just discovered a fresh field of corn. If Claudio Barlucci had called a press conference then there was obviously going to be a big story, because over the years the president of Cinquante Roma had never wasted the time of the Italian media. He had used it, manipulated it. But wasted it? Never.

Barlucci was one of the few powerful men in Rome who had remained untouched by the great scandals of corruption that had swept Italy in the nineties. Not a speck of dust had been allowed to soil or even touch his two thousand pound silk suit. Nobody was prepared to hazard a guess as to whether that was because he was as innocent as the driven snow, or whether his power superseded even that of the twentieth-century Inquisition. He did not hesitate to join in the chest-beating and the shirt-tearing, but he drew the line at donning any sackcloth or ashes. He survived with his reputation and empire intact, his charisma as all-triumphant as ever.

He had fingers in so many pies that he could summon up virtually any menu at will; the media, communications, movies, transport, computer technology, publishing, vineyards, hotels, all had at one time or another captured the roving eye and the grasshopper mind of Claudio Barlucci. Now, at sixty, he seemed less driven in commerce, as if the race had been won; but there was no hint of relaxation in what had begun as his hobby and ended in a consuming passion. Roma Cinquante, Rome's 'other' football team as they had been known. Now they were referred to as just 'Cinquante' or '*Gli Bambini di Barlucci*' and if Sir Matt Busby had bred his famous Mancunian babes in the late fifties, then Barlucci had bought his forty years later.

When he had taken control of Cinquante in 1988, they had been down and virtually out. Relegated to Serie 'B' in 1983, they had struggled even to remain in Italy's equivalent of the Second Division. Roma and Lazio had ruled the roost in Rome for many years, Ulisse had come from nowhere to challenge them and provide a mighty trio of teams in the Italian capital city, but Cinquante had come late to the party to form a quartet of sides with real potential for the title.

For Barlucci, Ulisse were the real rivals. Lazio and Roma were the old enemy, old money, whilst Ulisse were owned by Paolo Versace. Barlucci and Versace went back a long way, the path they had trod hardly strewn with roses. Versace's family had been bankers in Venice when Shylock had plied his money-lending trade. Now, he regarded himself as a merchant prince rather than a merchant banker, and Barlucci had never forgiven him for one insult. In a televised interview he had called the Cinquante owner, 'a common little tradesman who had assembled a team of artisans'.

Well, Barlucci thought, the 'tradesman' was going to have the last laugh. He would build not only the best team in Rome, but also the best team in Europe no matter what the price. Versace might have history and breeding on his side, but Barlucci had made his way in the world with his own hard-earned cash, rather than other people's money.

This season Cinquante had surprised many experts already. It had taken Barlucci four long years to get the team back to Serie 'A', but this season they were neatly tucked into third place, too far behind the two Milanese giants to have a realistic chance of the championship, but far enough ahead of the city's other three clubs to ensure them not only the unofficial Roman crown, but also a place in next season's UEFA Cup.

And it was to next season that Barlucci was already looking. He knew full well that whoever he bought now in the Spring could not be registered to play until the following campaign, but there was no reason why he should not be the first to throw his gauntlet into the ring. He was determined to set the pace, to set the standards that others would have to follow. Already any player fortunate enough to be approached by Cinquante knew that he would have a contract far more valuable than he could obtain anywhere else.

He had acquired Lenoir from France in the November window when Italian clubs could add to their squad for the current season. The exciting Bolivian, Roderigo, had committed himself to sign in July and that was two foreigners out of the three he could field in each League match. Barlucci had no intention of following the precedent set by the likes of AC Milan who would have five or even six foreigners on their books, knowing that by the end of a season some or all of them would be discontented. For the sort of money Barlucci was prepared to pay his foreigners they would play in every match, play until they dropped, and even then be ready to come back for more.

Gradually the reporters drifted away from the bar and the pianist playing automatically on his white piano. They left behind a nuclear cloud of cigarette smoke and an exhausted barman, still stunned by the rush for the free drinks that Cinquante had so generously provided. If Barlucci was going to meet the press, he had no intention of dealing with them on equal terms. The Cinquante president had found that these sort of conferences were more impressive if accompanied by a sense of theatre. The head table was covered by a battery of microphones, even though any normal voice would have easily carried to the back of the room. Draped behind was the flag of Cinquante, the striking purple and crimson cross on white, and the national flag of Italy, both providing a backdrop to action photographs of the season's most exciting Cinquante matches. One large picture was covered by an enormous curtain with draw-strings, also in Cinquante's colours, and as they saw it the journalists could be left in no doubt that they had been invited for an unveiling.

Security staff escorted the writers to their seats, ensuring that the front row was given over to the photographers, who held their cameras ready for action like awkward soldiers awaiting the order to go over the top for the first time. Suddenly the lights dimmed and a fanfare of trumpets greeted the arrival of Claudio Barlucci flanked on one side by the team coach Carlo Rendina, the former international striker, and on the other by his Swiss finance director, Kurt Mansbach. Barlucci towered over them both, his bull-like head topped by a mass of dark curls, his rather bulbous nose and bushy eyebrows making him a cartoonist's dream. The cameras flashed, the noise as sudden and startling as a round of machine-gun fire. With a papal motion of his hands Barlucci signalled for quiet, then looked round the room as if to assure himself that everybody he had personally invited had accepted. He nodded to himself in satisfaction, they were all there.

'Ladies and gentlemen.' The tone still had rough edges, a distant memory of the working-class back streets of Rome where he had been born.

'I am delighted to see you all here today and I trust you found the watering hole that I provided agreeable. I am sure I speak for every true Roman when I say how delighted we have been with the rise of Roma Cinquante, and in particular their many triumphs this season. It is hard to pick out individual highlights, but the 2–1 victory in the San Siro when we were a goal down with ten minutes left cannot escape a mention. Yet, football is not a series of snapshots, it is a continuously moving newsreel and we cannot rest on our laurels. Yesterday's triumphs, even such as that over Milan, are already history and we must be prepared to move forward. I have already delivered to you some of the finest footballers, not just from Italy, but from the world at large. Now I am delighted and proud to tell you that our team for next season will be completed by the most exciting player in English football.'

There was an involuntary mass indraw of breath by the audience. Barlucci still possessed the talent to surprise and, whatever rumours they had floated or chased in their multitude of column inches, a signing from England had not been amongst them. Their respect for Barlucci rose even higher. He was that rare creature, an Italian who could keep a secret.

At a discreet signal, Rendina moved to one side of the concealed picture, whilst Barlucci took the other sash in his hand. The two men pulled in perfect unison, and there for all the Italian Press to see was an almost life-size photograph of Mickey Wayne.

CHAPTER 11

It had not been a good day for David Sinclair. He was not superstitious, but he had felt in his bones that the meeting with Chris Handsel on a match day did not bode well. Even before the kick-off there had been an incident at one of the turnstiles. It had not really been the fault of the employee; he had only believed he was doing his job. But the refusal of admission to Mark Rossetti had been a mistake and an embarrassment that he felt sure was going to feature in the Sunday tabloids. During the period of the ban, as far as Sinclair knew, Rossetti had never tried to get into the ground to see a match. In accordance with league regulations his picture had been posted inside all the turnstile boxes alongside those of the known hooligans who were also banned from the stadium. Yet he'd kept no note of the period of the ex-player's ban, had received no circular from the league to confirm it had expired, and the letter he'd received from Rossetti effectively asking for work had rung no bells either. Consequently, no directive had been given to the men on the gates and when Rossetti had tried to pay his entrance money at Gate 15 he had been told he was simply persona non grata or however that may have been expressed by a sixty-year-old who had received no classical education. It had just been unfortunate that Gate 15 adjoined the press entrance. When the incident had been reported to Sinclair he had groaned.

'Can't somebody go and get him back, apologize and give him a free ticket?'

He'd been told that this was hardly possible given that Rossetti had left in a flood of tears hotly pursued by a *News of the World* photographer and at least three reporters who thought he might provide a better story than the game itself.

They had not been bad judges. A 0–2 home defeat was not exactly the perfect build-up to the forthcoming semi-final. The crowd had not been slow to tell them so either. Just as he'd anticipated, Handsel in the directors' box was a target for their cheers just as Sinclair was subjected to a barrage of abuse from the terraces.

'Chris, Chris, give us a wave.'

And Handsel responded, milked the audience, all the while smiling.

A minute before Holly Sinclair had clutched her father's hand tightly at yet another insult, trying to make him feel her loyalty, to somehow keep the venom at bay. But to Sinclair her support made things worse. If he'd been on his own he could have taken anything they had to throw at him, but it wasn't fair that his daughter had to hear the abuse as well. She may have been mature for her eighteen years, and very much her own woman, yet he still felt he had to protect her. He'd spoiled her and indulged her, but he had never needed to buy her love. Although he'd bought her a little place of her own, she still seemed to spend more time with him, not merely in defiance of her mother's wishes, but because she wanted to. They got on as friends and he hesitated before ever playing the parent. There were times when he worried about her. She had the looks and she had the brains. It was just a sense of direction and purpose that were lacking. Today, though he wished her far away, a million miles away from the chorus of, 'Sinclair's a greedy shit-head.' There was nothing original or literate about the Hertsmere fans, but they managed to get their message across just the same.

It could have been worse. Their opponents, Kempton Town, had missed a penalty, whilst Mickey Wayne had been lucky not to be sent off when he had elbowed the Kempton centre back in the face with the ball out of play.

Wayne's whole performance had been disturbing, a mixture of the indifferent and the malevolent. There had been moments when he had looked at his team-mates as if they were already strangers, and at other times he had been more intent on kicking anything that moved other than the ball. If this was his way of saying he wanted to get away then it was unlikely to have impressed any watching Italians.

If Handsel, Rossetti, Kempton, Wayne and the crowd had not been enough there were the Italians for dessert. Almost before he'd left the box he was besieged by journalists, waving notebooks and microphones in their anxiety to get near him. Barlucci's press conference in Rome had sparked off its own disorganized replica in England.

Andy Sharpe of the BBC was the first to ask a recognizable question out of the babble of voices.

'Mr Sinclair. Roma Cinquante have just announced in

Italy that they've agreed terms to sign Mickey Wayne. Is that true?'

Sinclair looked at the man and then at the TV camera in disbelief.

'No, that's not true.' It was a weak response. He realized that as soon as the words were out. Handsel would have handled it differently, he would have dismissed it with an epithet that was just the right side of acceptable on air, followed by a witty one-liner and a casual dismissal. Sinclair's answer somehow only raised more questions.

'It's not true that he's signed, or it's not true that Cinquante have made any approach?'

How much did they know? How far could he lie his way out of the throng and into the relative sanctuary of the board room?

'This is all news to me. We've heard nothing from any Italian club about Mickey Wayne or any of our players.'

The *Sun* journalist was on him like a panther.

'That's very strange, Mr Sinclair. Barlucci, the Cinquante president, produced a copy of a fax he says he sent you over a week ago, offering £7 million for Mickey, and claimed that things had moved ahead very fast from there. He told the whole Italian press that he'd already had several meetings with the player's representative, and he planned to be in England on Monday to finalize the deal. Now somebody's lying here, Mr Sinclair, and I think the public have the right to know who it is. This goes beyond Hertsmere. Mickey Wayne is very important to the future of English football. I don't think you're going to be a very popular man if you take the money and run.'

Sinclair cursed under his breath. He'd played it all

wrong. He should have known better than to mix it with the press before he knew anything about the true situation.

'We hear you've pushed the price up to £10 million and that Wayne's own deal is worth over a million a year? Is that right?' This from the *Sunday Despatch*.

He knew they'd make up the figures even if he said nothing. They all wrote what their readers wanted to hear and the more pound signs the better would be the response of the man in his pyjamas reading the headlines over his Sunday breakfast.

'I've nothing more to say until I've fully investigated these unfounded rumours.' He made to move away, but found his path blocked by the pack of journalists moving in for the kill.

'They don't sound like unfounded rumours to me,' the *Sun* man persisted. 'Does the player know what's going on? If you've been concealing this from him I don't think he's going to be happy.'

Sinclair was not very happy himself. He could hear the headlines behind the questions being fired at him. He began to push his way towards the solid oak door of the directors' room, but he was swimming against the tide and, short of landing a punch in the full glare of the cameras, it seemed increasingly further away.

It was the woman who came to his rescue. She appeared magically by his side, and just as supernaturally carved a path through the crowd, like a female Moses parting the Red Sea. It was only when the door of the directors' lounge closed behind him that Sinclair realized that not only did he not know who the hell she was, but that she had also tricked her way into the exclusively male domain of the club.

'Patti Delaney,' she said by way of introduction. The voice was deep and mellow, but definitely feminine. The rest of her was feminine too. She wore an obviously expensive leather jacket on top of a designer T-shirt and jeans that looked as if they'd been made specially for her. She was tall, about his own height, her dark hair cut boyishly at the front, but curling down to the collar at the back. Her eyes had that distant look of somebody who wears contact lenses, whilst her skin had a healthy tan that had clearly not been achieved on a sunbed, but had been worked on for all that. Sinclair's eyes, though, focused on her generous breasts, which were clearly unencumbered by any artificial supports as they moved beneath the thin cotton of the shirt even as she spoke.

She gave Sinclair no chance to respond to her introduction, but moved immediately to cash in on the favour merited by her rescue operation.

'Look, please don't think I'm a part of that lot out there. They've all got their own particular axe to grind depending on who they work for. I work for myself so I can afford to tell it like it is. I could see you didn't know what on earth was going on out there. If I may say so, lesson number one in situations like that is simply to say "no comment".' She paused, suddenly sensing the hostile stares of the rest of the board and their male guests.

'Is there anywhere that we can talk privately and where a lady can get a drink?'

Still shaken by his confrontation in the corridor and mesmerized by the defiance of gravity of her figure, Sinclair led her through the rear entrance to the lounge and into his own office. He offered her a chair but she preferred to sit on an arm of it, perhaps sensing the unpleasant smell left by its previous occupants.

'Whisky?' Sinclair asked.

'Fine.'

'Soda? Ice?'

'As it comes.'

He poured a measure, glanced at her and, receiving no request to stop, poured again.

'Thanks,' she said. 'Shall I tell you what your little reception committee was all about? And perhaps in return you might answer a few of my questions.'

'And if I simply say "no comment"?' Sinclair replied, not unkindly.

'Then you'll have learned very quickly.'

CHAPTER 12

It had been a long time since he had cried like a child. Straight from the hearing that had suspended him ten years ago, he had gone home and thrown himself on the bed waiting for Sally to comfort him, but she had not come. He had heard her through the mist that enclosed his head speaking in muffled tones on the telephone and now, with hindsight, he realized that she must have called Stuart Macdonald. To say what? That she had the perfect excuse for leaving?

Today, in its way, had been worse. He did not know what had possessed him to want to go and see a match in the first place. Yet, it was like drink, once an alkie, always an alkie. Only this time football had been the drug and even though he had not had a taste for ten years it had never left his bloodstream. He had not given the slightest thought to the possibility that Hertsmere might still be enforcing the ban. It was history, he was history, at least in the world of football. Although right now he felt inclined to make himself history in the world, full-stop.

He'd toyed with the idea of phoning and asking for a ticket but, frightened of being rebuffed, he had joined a turnstile queue like any other fan. Nobody recognized him, nobody even spoke to him as the line shuffled forward in the odd silence that precedes the roar of noise within the ground. Then, as he passed a ten-pound note under the grill, the old man taking the money hesitated and seemed to check with a list on his counter. Mark had groaned inwardly, thinking that with his luck the note was forged, but the money was genuine; it was only his dawn that had proved to be false.

At first the recognition had been flattering. Ten years away and an old man on the gate still remembered. Then after the brief moment of pride came the crashing fall.

'Sorry, but I'm afraid I can't let you in.'

He'd started to argue, but the crowd behind him were becoming impatient, pushing forward more in their anxiety to get into the ground than any curiosity as to what was going on. Mark had turned away, but it was not going to be that easy. He recognized a couple of sports reporters at the adjoining press-ticket window. When he'd last seen them they'd been youngsters starting out on their careers, but now they'd acquired the scavenging, cynical look that came with the job together with the nicotine-stained fingers and the beer gut. And now they'd seen him, and they seemed to be surrounding him, asking questions, the camera flashing until he felt blinded. Blinded by the cameras, suffocated by the questions, he struck out blindly, knocking a photographer to the ground, providing another photograph for his comrades.

'Come on, Mark, we're on your side,' one of the journalists said, 'just tell us what it feels like to be turned away from your old club. Do you feel bitter about it?'

'Are you still drinking, Mark?'

'Do you think Hertsmere would be better served by Chris Handsel?'

'How does today's team compare to yours?'

The barrage of words bounced around his mind, merging into a cacophony of sound that had him holding his hands to his ears to blot out the noise. They'd followed him up the road, then reluctantly turned back towards the mundanity of the match, all save one, who had fallen into step with him, without speaking. He just stared straight ahead, oblivious to the latecomers hurrying towards the ground, who, in turn, passed him by unknowing and uncaring.

It was his companion who broke the ice and in his surprise at hearing a female voice he turned towards her.

'Pretty hairy back there, wasn't it? Sometimes I'm almost embarrassed by the fact that my passport says I'm a journalist.'

Mark still said nothing, his body tight with tension, his hands visibly shaking.

'My name's Patti. Patti Delaney. I won't pretend that I knew who you were, but one of my colleagues filled me in. I'm afraid you were a bit before my time.'

'If you're going to come out to play with the boys then perhaps you should learn a bit more about the game.'

She put her hand on his shoulder and he immediately pulled away as if from a leper.

'Hey, that's not bad considering what you've been through.'

He stopped on the kerb and faced her full on, his eyes burning with a rage that he knew was unfairly aimed at her.

'Look, I just want to be left alone. You don't know me, I don't know you, and that suits me fine. I had it all from your lot ten years ago and it's time you forgot about me and turned your attention to someone new. There's a lot more dirt in the game than you'll find on my hands so why don't you be a good little girl and run along to see the match. If you get there late there won't be time for someone to explain the rules to you.'

Patti smiled, giving Rossetti the full works she usually saved for commissioning editors who weren't going to pay her enough unless she really tried.

'You know how to flatter a girl don't you? Ten years ago I was doing my "O" levels and fantasizing about another Mark with the surname of Knopfler. As far as football was concerned if a boy I fancied played then I might go to watch him as long as it wasn't raining and there was somewhere I could sit to do my homework. I think it was Gary Lineker's legs that changed all that in the '86 World Cup. Well either that or Chris Waddle's hair. Anyway it certainly wasn't Peter Beardsley's smile. And after that I was hooked, but I missed out on you. You were just a name everybody whispered with reverence. You could have been the best they said. Is that true?'

He wanted to walk on, to leave her behind, but something in her eyes told him she was genuinely interested. In the distance he heard the roar of the crowd signal the kick-off.

'You're missing the match. Your editor won't like that.'

'I wasn't covering the match. I was just going because I like Mickey Wayne.' She hesitated as if the idea had just occurred to her. 'Mark, don't judge all journalists by the worst of our breed. We're not all like that. Give me the chance to interview you properly. When I've finished the article I'll show it to you. If there's anything you don't like I'll take it out and if you still don't like it then I'll scrap the whole thing.'

'I don't know,' he replied, knowing he should just say no.

'You've had a bad day, think about it. Let me have your number and I'll give you a ring.'

'I'm in the book.' If she wanted to talk to him badly enough then she could look up the number. Then he went his way and she went hers.

At 7.00 p.m., desperately needing a drink, he turned on his radio instead, realizing he did not even know the score of the match. His timing was perfect as he heard the announcer say,

'There were sensations aplenty at Hertsmere's Park Crescent ground today. The cup semi-finalists went down 2–0 to Kempton Town, missing a penalty on the way; but the drama was all off the pitch. Cinquante of Rome confirmed that they had made an offer of £7 million for star player Mickey Wayne and the latest news we have is that they are close to agreeing terms with the player's agent. Chairman David Sinclair was booed as heavily as Chris Handsel, the former player and white knight waiting in the wings, was cheered. Not the ideal preparation for the clash with Thamesmead on Saturday week.'

He turned down the sound as the telephone rang, reassuring him that by some miracle it hadn't yet been cut off.

'Hi! Patti Delaney here. I said I'd phone. I hope you're feeling better.' She gave him no time to reply. 'About that interview, I wonder if Wednesday morning would be OK?'

He looked around the room as if seeking some escape

from the voice on the phone, idly flipped his diary to yet another blank page, then despite his better judgement told her to come round at ten o'clock. If he was going to make the papers tomorrow then he might as well go for broke.

CHAPTER 13

Lennie Simons had been looking for his client for nearly forty-eight hours without success and at 4.00 p.m. on Monday afternoon he was fast coming to the conclusion that Mickey Wayne was avoiding him. Simons always prided himself on being one step ahead, but the news that Cinquante were after Wayne had come as a total surprise. He was clearly not merely one step behind in the game, but as yet not even a player.

He couldn't believe his ears when he'd tuned in on his car radio on Saturday afternoon. If none of his contacts in the media had tipped him off, then it could not possibly be true. Yet, there on the TV sports news was Claudio Barlucci in the flesh, and unless the subtitles were wrong, he thought he all but had Mickey Wayne in the bag. He couldn't have signed Mickey, Simons reasoned with himself, not if he hadn't even spoken to his agent. Simons smelled money, but he also smelled trouble. Over the years he'd made sure that everybody knew that he, and only he, represented the player. If the media wanted an interview with Wayne then they came to Simons, if the sports companies wanted Wayne for endorsements then they lined up outside Simons' door. It had only been last week that on Wayne's instructions he'd gone to see Sinclair to try and renegotiate his contract. So why no call from Barlucci in Rome? He tried to convince himself this all had to be a gigantic confidence trick on the part of the Italians. The English club had rejected the Italian's offer and this was their way of making sure that Wayne knew of it; but he did not convince himself and he still had a sinking feeling that somebody had got at the young Hertsmere player. Well, if that was the case they hadn't reckoned with Lennie Simons. He simply had to find out who it was and then get to Wayne. Once he'd spoken to his player there was no way anybody else would be able to muscle in.

He rang around the press boys who, for once, were as much in the dark as he was. He hesitated before he called the other agents. If this was a transfer abroad there were only three or four serious contenders, men who knew the minefields of the continent like the backs of their hands. It would do nothing for his pride or reputation to do the rounds of his competitors. He'd rubbed their noses in the dirt whenever he'd had the chance and he had no favours to call in. Any one of them would have jumped at the chance of putting one across Lennie Simons. They'd all come to him at one time or another with deals for his clients where they were looking to share the commission, but he'd dealt with them brutally. They'd ask for a fifty-fifty split and he'd offer them ten per cent.

'It's better than nothing,' he'd say, 'we don't need the deal, and let's face it, you can't take it anywhere else.' They'd go away, tails between legs, clutching their ten per cent in their hands, muttering grim threats of revenge.

Then Simons held all the cards, but now he was playing a bluff hand, and the recipients of his calls would know it.

He began and ended with Steve Menzies. At fifty, Menzies was the Mr Fix-It of the British football scene. As soon as he heard a whisper of another club's interest he was on the phone to the player, with total and arrogant disregard for any agreement he might have with another agent. That would be fine for the nuts and bolts of the lower leagues, he'd say, but surely it was never intended to cover the intricacies of a major move abroad. He'd convince the player that nobody else could make it happen, nobody else had his experience. With the fish in his net he'd be on a plane or train to meet with the club who it was rumoured wanted to buy him, telling them that nobody else represented the player. Sometimes he'd get appointed by the club as well – negotiate the player out and negotiate him in, he'd be told. Only Menzies would know the depth of the buyer's pocket. Whatever he nominally saved from the budget he was given would be creamed off by him at some convenient stage in the transaction. The players were happy with what they got, but what they got was not necessarily what the club intended them to have. Menzies' philosophy was simple. If they'd be content with £200,000 why give them the £250,000 that was on the table when the £50,000 difference would make him content as well? In the business he was known as 'Measles' Menzies by agents, players and managers alike. He was an infection, an itch which longed to be scratched. Yet, despite his reputation, he nearly always delivered. Simons gritted his teeth as he dialled the number.

'Hello.' Menzies never identified himself until he knew who was calling.

'Steve, it's Lennie Simons.'

'Lennie!' The voice was full of false bonhomie, with a hint of pleasure in anticipation of what was to come. 'How are you, Leonard? Still ruling the world with your boys?'

'Yeah, yeah, Steve. Couldn't be better. Never been busier. And you?' He added the inquiry without any great interest and to his disappointment Menzies decided to answer him.

'Mustn't grumble. It's not what it was. Too many amateurs in the game. Everybody thinks they're an agent nowadays. Player goes into a fish shop and before the lad behind the counter has finished sprinkling vinegar on his chips he's got him signed up. Half of them don't know what they're doing. Give them a player with a bit of talent, a bit of charm, and it's like giving a choirboy a machine-gun. It just reflects badly on us professionals. Anyway, time's money and nice as it is to have a chat, what can I do for you?' He could have added 'as if I didn't know', but that would have been gilding the lily.

'I suppose you saw that Cinquante press conference in Rome...'

'Yeah, they really don't mess about those Italians, do they? I thought you would have been there as Wayne's one of yours.'

'Nothing's settled yet, early days.'

'Sure, sure.'

'I heard somebody else was trying to cut themselves into the deal, maybe working for the wops. I just wondered if you knew who it might be.'

'Lennie, Lennie, you disappoint me. You really want to know if it's me.'

'No, no, Steve. We've had our differences, but I wouldn't expect you to pull any strokes.'

'You mean that you don't think I'd be able to pull a stroke with Mickey Wayne. You're probably right. Well, I hear on the grapevine he's fallen for someone with a bit more charm than me, a pretty little thing called Carla Dandone. She's become a serious challenger in the game over there. Looks and brains. That's a dangerous combination.'

Simons had heard all he wanted to hear. There was no point in further pleasantries.

'We'll see about Signorina Dandone,' he said with venom, and without even bothering to say goodbye to Menzies he cut off the line.

Signorina Dandone was just as frustrated as Simons, and had he known that he might have felt a little better. She'd anticipated the whole world would want to speak to Wayne once the news broke and had arranged a telephone code with him. Five rings first, then cut off, four next, then cut off, wait for the three and answer on the third. As a fall-back she'd given him her direct number and had told him to call her at noon on Monday precisely if they'd not spoken before; but noon had come and gone, still without Wayne picking up his phone either to respond to the code or to call her. Barlucci had been calling her every hour on the hour to inquire as to progress and now his calls were coming in every thirty minutes. It was as if he was trying out a new code of his own.

'We involved you because of your reputation, Carla,' he'd said in the last conversation, 'but your reputation is diminishing with every second that passes.'

And in between the calls out and the calls in she had received a visit from no less a person than Paolo Versace himself. She had the feeling that the president of Ulisse, Roma Cinquante's arch-rivals, did not usually make house-calls and she should feel extremely flattered. By the end of the meeting, however, she felt extremely frightened, and fear was not an emotion that normally troubled her. He had arrived at her office unannounced, although the thought crossed her mind that somebody must have told him she was there. She somehow did not feel that any visit he would make would be a wasted one.

Versace had come into her brightly lit high-tech office as if he were entering a repossessed basement slum. He ran his finger disdainfully along the chair before he seated himself, assured that there were no specks of dust that could soil his light blue jacket and pale blue trousers. He looked as if he would be more at home on a yacht in the South of France than here, although Carla doubted if he was the sort of man who would ever remove his clothes in public. Not that he didn't have a good figure for his age, no hint of fat on the waistline, well-groomed skin that seemed to have been shaved within the last five minutes, and above all the eyes, grey and alive, missing nothing as he took in the room and its occupant at a glance.

'*Avvocata* Dandone, I have heard so much about you, and all of it good.'

Carla did not think it appropriate to reply that everything

she had heard about Versace had been bad. He was one of the most powerful financiers in Europe, his banking network in a dozen countries. Now in his sixties, he still looked very much the ladies' man who had supplied the gossip columnists with so much material, so many photographs with beautiful women. If she had her arithmetic right he was not only on his seventh marriage, but indeed on his way out of it.

'This is indeed an honour, Signor Versace,' she replied, hoping he was not attuned to sarcasm. If he was he gave no hint, but merely bowed his head at the overt compliment, giving her a perfect view of his immaculately coiffeured grey hair.

'Would you like some coffee?' she asked. He raised an eyebrow. Italian lawyers, unlike their other European counterparts, rarely offered refreshments.

'If it is not too much trouble.'

'It's no trouble. As you can see I have it ready.'

She poured him a cup from the percolator that bubbled at her side and which she drank and replenished three times a day. She knew it didn't do her any good, but she was still battling the withdrawal symptoms from giving up her thirty cigarettes a day.

'I understand you are representing the Englishman, Michael Wayne.'

He pronounced the name as if the player had been born and bred in Italy.

'Yes, that's so.'

'And I believe you are some way advanced in your negotiations with my friend Signor Barlucci.'

He was fishing and she knew it.

'I'm sorry, I cannot disclose anything about my client's affairs.'

Versace smiled and nodded.

'Ah, of course. You are an *avvocata*, a lawyer, not a *procuratore*, an agent. I was forgetting.' He paused. 'But perhaps you would tell me what is the difference. I have never understood it.'

'The difference, Signor, is that I am honest.'

'An old-fashioned virtue, and so remarkable in a woman. Tell me, Carla, I may call you Carla, may I not? Tell me, does this honesty and high principle extend to doing the best for your client?'

'Of course.'

'Good, good,' he said in a tone that indicated he had seen the traffic lights change to green as he approached at high speed. He took a sip of his coffee and nodded as if surprised it should be palatable.

'Forgive me, Signor Versace, but I do have a busy schedule today, so perhaps you can tell me what it is that brings you to...' She looked around her own room, seeking a suitable description, and then added, 'My humble abode.'

'You wish me to come to the point. That is good. Perhaps when we have concluded our business you would like to do some work for my companies. We use several lawyers and I am sure you will be a wonderful addition to our little team.'

Carla tried very hard to control her temper. As a little girl she had been a volcano, explosive and volatile, treated with caution by every member of her family, including her politician father. 'I pity the man who falls in love with you,' he had said, but there was no need for pity as yet, because she had no time for love, even if she had believed in it. And her father was dead without pity to bestow.

'Signor Versace. You are not coming to the point. You did not come here to offer me a job, and, as for my joining your little team, I am neither collectable nor a team player.'

'Player, yes. You see we have both finally come to the point.' His tone suddenly changed and, despite her exterior confidence, Carla felt a shiver run down her spine.

'It would make me very unhappy if Wayne were to join Cinquante. We, too, have watched his talents flourish. If he can play like that in English football, how would he play on our Italian stage? He will have time, space. I think he could be as great as Maradona.'

'I'm pleased you're such a fan of my client.'

'That is well put. I am a fan. I am not like that fool Barlucci. I do not make rash promises in public, promises he may not be able to keep. He has dug a hole for himself and when Wayne joins Ulisse then the Cinquante fans will bury him in it, like the jackals they are.'

Carla rose from her seat behind the desk. She was only five feet six, but as far as she was able she towered over the seated Versace.

'You just don't understand, do you? If Cinquante can finalize their deal with Hertsmere, and I can finalize Wayne's deal with Cinquante, then he joins them. I don't deal with two purchasers at once and I can't be bribed. If things fall through with Barlucci, then it is a different story. But, believe me, if there is anybody else who comes in for the player they will jump the queue ahead of you. Now, if you'll pardon me, I have some work to do for real clients who pay me for my services.'

For a moment Versace sat dazed by the onslaught. People did not speak to him like this, at least not twice. Then he eased himself out of the chair, his body uncoiling like a snake being raised by a charmer's pipe. It was Carla's turn to step back as his anger seemed to fill the room.

'You are young, Signorina, and you have much to learn. Your father was like you and look what happened to him. Blown up by the mafia because he dared to face up to them. The mafia are not dead, my dear young lady, but only sleeping. Wayne will not join Cinquante whatever you and Barlucci may think or do. Save your time and your energy for the real clients. If you meddle in things that are beyond you I will make sure that in order to earn a living you will need clients to pay for your body, not for your mind. *Buon giorno*, Signorina.'

He closed the door quietly behind him, as if he had no further need to demonstrate his power by slamming it.

Carla Dandone leaned back against her desk for support. She felt faint and she quickly poured herself another coffee. Then, as the colour gradually crept back into her cheeks, she lifted the telephone and began to try the code again with Mickey Wayne.

CHAPTER 14

Ray Fowler, the Hertsmere coach, marched into the manager's office without knocking. He and Phil Reynolds did not have that sort of relationship. Reynolds might wear the suits and handle the business side of things, Fowler might rarely be seen in anything other than a track-suit, but they were a team for all that. They had been likened to Brian Clough and Peter Taylor, but Fowler could never foresee a day when the two would have a permanent falling out. Fowler was volatile, Reynolds calm, yet even when they disagreed over tactics, or a particular player's talents, or lack of them, each would respect the other's views.

Reynolds had achieved everything there was to achieve on the field as a player, Championship medals, Cup medals, and then, when his side, Stretford United, had just won the European Cup he had chosen that moment to announce his retirement. It had come as shock to everybody, not least his wife Paula.

'Why did you do it, Phil? It's been your life,' she asked when he came home and told her what he'd done. The media had already gathered outside their house and she had drawn the curtains to get some privacy.

'I wasn't enjoying it any more. It took me that little bit

longer to get out of bed, I was just that little bit slower in training. That's all.'

And that *was* all. He never commented on it again, and he gave no interviews other than the bare statement issued by the club.

Money did not seem to be a problem. He discussed their financial situation as little as he discussed anything else, but he made it clear that he would not be rushed into taking any job just for the sake of a regular wage packet. He had always been a man who kept things to himself. It had been one of the things that had attracted Paula to him when they had first met. He'd been playing in his native London in those days, a colossus in defence, six feet tall, curly fair hair, the Roman nose giving him a classical gladiatorial appearance. He'd been a natural leader despite his taciturn approach off the field. He neither spoke nor yelled without reason and therefore players paid attention when he did. He'd captained his country for six matches, and then when he'd been forced to miss almost a whole international season because of injury he'd found himself replaced as captain. He did not complain publicly, but merely told the manager that he no longer wished to be considered for selection. The press reaction to that decision had been mixed. Some accused him of childishness, others took his side and said he had been badly dealt with by those in power. He ignored it all and concentrated on his club duties.

It had been assumed that he would go straight into management himself, but instead he took to a boat and with a minimum of experience set off on a round-the-world trip. He returned safe, bronzed and seemingly more relaxed. One television appearance as a guest commentator at a Stretford Cup match was enough to convince the powers that be that he should be given a regular berth on the Saturday night programme. He quickly became a cult figure, speaking only when he had something to say, his silences just as telling as his comments. Then, as suddenly as he had arrived, he departed, this time to take up the Hertsmere job. Again he offered no reasons, gave no excuses, Paula getting his only explanation. 'I was bored. It was time to move on.'

Ray Fowler was in complete contrast. With his old-fashioned, national service style haircut, stocky build and bow legs, he looked more like an ex-jockey than a former professional footballer; but his football career had ended in his teens with a double fracture of the leg. His old club, Stockton Rangers, had offered him a contract on the training side working with the youth team and, despite Stockton's languishing in the old Fourth Division, he had taken his kids to the semi-finals of the Youth Cup only to be narrowly beaten by Manchester United.

He had never wanted to be a manager. He enjoyed working with the players, but he was not interested in what they cost or what they earned. Often, he'd leave the training ground hoarse and sweating, his stream of invective having found its target with even the most valuable players. He was no respecter of reputations and when Reynolds had accepted the Hertsmere post he had made it a condition that Fowler would be appointed his number two. The players had still been sulking over the dismissal of their beloved John Kelly, and the introduction of Fowler with his discipline, his army-type training sessions and his refusal to accept, or even listen to, excuses had done nothing to endear him to the players; but gradually they had been won over, and as the results came and the financial problems came with them, they had bonded the players and the managerial team together far more swiftly than had at first seemed possible.

Only Mickey Wayne was out of step. Reynolds was more tolerant because he did not have to deal with him on a day-to-day basis, but he had Fowler at his wits' end on those days he turned up, and screaming into empty air on those days when he did not bother. He knew he was undroppable. The fans would not stand for it, and even the other players were past the stage of jealousy. There was one rule for Wayne and one for the rest of them. If that created a debt, he more than compensated for it with his match-winning performances, week in, week out.

Today though, Fowler had had enough.

'Phil, we've got to do something about Wayne. He's not here again today. It undermines my authority with the rest of them.'

'We've tried fining him, Ray. He just laughs it off. Simons can earn him more in a morning than I can fine him.'

The coach was not satisfied.

'He's going to be worse now this Italian story's broken. It's like giving him a loaded gun to hold to our heads. There are times when I think we might be best rid of him.'

Reynolds patted Fowler on the shoulder. There was a good six inches difference in their heights and, despite the fact that Fowler was a good twenty years his senior, there was something paternal in the gesture.

'You know you don't mean that. Believe me it'll be a cold day in hell before I agree to the transfer. All the great ones are difficult: Best, Bowles, Gazza, Maradona, Gullit. It's the unpredictability that makes them great. You have to live with it.'

'I know you're right. If he'd just phone and say he didn't feel well, I'd know he was lying. I'd know he was in bed with some bimbo, but at least it would be a gesture. I feel sorry for his wife. Laura's a nice little thing. She deserves better than Wayne. We only see him for training and matches, she has to live with him. Have you spoken to Mr Sinclair about this Italian nonsense?'

It annoyed Reynolds that, despite his years of experience, Fowler still behaved so subserviently to the board. David Sinclair was not a man who stood on ceremony. He encouraged everybody, players, staff, right down to the programme sellers, to call him David but as far as the coach was concerned he was Mr Sinclair. If Fowler'd had a forelock, doubtless he'd have touched it. He kept his thoughts to himself. Fowler was too set in his ways to change now.

'Yes, I've spoken to David. It's not good news. There's definitely been an offer. He was trying to keep it quiet, but this Barlucci character put an end to all hopes of that. That's the least of it. He's under pressure from the bank to sell, he's under pressure from our old friend Chris Handsel to let the club go, and if he does sell then it doesn't look as if any money is going to be released to us to strengthen the squad.'

Fowler shook his head in sad acceptance of the financial realities of the game.

'So we go down into the black and then we go down the tubes.'

'Got it in one, Ray. What about a drink to toast the future?'

'Bit early in the day for me. I've got to get back to the lads who did turn up for training. I left Stu Macdonald in charge. He'll make one hell of a coach himself one day. All the kids look up to him even now. I reckon he knows more about their personal problems than I do.'

Reynolds nodded.

'That's fine, as long as he remembers which side he's on. When you become a manager or a coach it's poacher turned gamekeeper, we both know that. Sure you don't want that drink? I'm going to have one.'

He made to open the highly polished oak drinks cabinet, one of the few reminders of his predecessor in the office, when a white envelope wedged between the doors caught his eye.

'What's this?' he said aloud.

'Maybe it's one of the cleaners either thanking you for the scotch or asking you to get a fresh bottle.'

Reynolds smiled, tossed the envelope on his desk and poured himself a whisky before casually slitting it open. As he read the note his expression changed.

'What's wrong?' Fowler asked. He had known Reynolds a long time and had never seen him so shocked before. Finally the manager spoke, the words coming slowly, from a long way back in his memory.

'You know that note you were waiting for from Wayne. I think you've got it.' And, as if he were handling a time-bomb, he passed Fowler the flimsy piece of paper.

CHAPTER 15

Detective Inspector Peter Jordan did not like football and he liked those involved with it even less. When he'd worked in Yorkshire in the eighties he'd seen the effect of Hillsborough on his colleagues on the force, seen them dragged through the mire by the media and made scapegoats for a tragedy that was more the fault of the game and its greed than any individuals. Before he'd moved to CID he'd never volunteered like so many other coppers to be on Saturday afternoon duty just to see a match. For Jordan an afternoon's fishing or an evening with his model railway was the nearest he got to sporting endeavour.

'Playing with your trains again, Peter?' his mother would say. 'You're forty-two years old. You'll never find yourself a wife up in the attic.'

It didn't bother Peter Jordan. He was quite happy living with his elderly, widowed mother in the three-bedroomed North-west London house that was his late father's only legacy. The sole objection he had was to the use of the word 'playing' when it came to his model railways. They were not a game. Football was a game. Model trains were a passion matched only by his love of gardening and fishing, As far as he was concerned any other sports took up space that could be more usefully converted to allotments or lakes. The only word to describe Jordan was 'solid'. Even his superiors described him as 'a solid chap' and that had perhaps been an obstacle to his further promotion. If you were solid you lacked flair and it was flair that shot you up the ladder rather than reliability. He was six feet tall, broad-shouldered, big-boned rather than fat, with a face that always bore the marks of his daily struggle with the open cut-throat razor that he insisted on using rather than the Boots electric model his mother had bought him for Christmas three years earlier. It was stubbornness that made him stick with the old methods, just as he stuck with the old methods of detection. He was stubborn about his need for glasses as well, putting them on reluctantly when he drove, holding them to his face rather than resting them on his nose when he had to read something. He liked the wrong 'uns to see his eyes with nothing to mar their vision. Once they'd looked into that stare, with the grey-green flecks of his pupils boring back at them, he knew he had an immediate advantage.

He'd sniffed when he'd been told to get down to Hertsmere United. He had little doubt that if they had a problem they had brought it upon themselves. His detective sergeant, Rob Davies, was more excited.

'Do you reckon there are any Cup Final tickets in this for us, if Hertsmere get there?' he asked as they'd driven down to the dilapidated ground.

'If there are, Rob, then you can have them. When the metropolis is invaded by a hundred thousand plus lunatics all trying to get into a stadium that gives them fifty per cent less visibility than the average TV set I want to be as far away as possible – preferably on some nice remote stretch of river.'

And now they were here in the chairman's office and quite clearly both David Sinclair and Phil Reynolds thought they were faced with a major problem. Jordan read the note again hoping something contained in it would speak to him, would give him a clue that he'd so far missed. It was a classic kidnap note, the words made of pasted letters cut from an odd assortment of newspapers. Their identification would be one for the backroom boys, but the meaning was perfectly clear.

IF You Want TO see Mickey Wayne ALIVE Again then YOU will Have TO PAY £5 MILLION. YOUR acceptance will be SHOWn By an entry in The Personal Column of WEDNESDAY's Telegraph saying Just OK Wayne. IF the AD does not Appear we WILL send YOU one of Wayne'S toes a DAY.

Jordan put the note carefully on the table. Too many people had already touched it before he'd arrived for him to have any real hope of prints, but you never knew.

'I suppose a footballer without his toes isn't much good to anybody,' he said, trying hard, but not totally succeeding, to conceal a smile.

'It's not a laughing matter,' Reynolds said. He'd only been with the policeman for an hour or so, but he'd seen enough to know he didn't like him. That was all they needed, a man in charge of the case who had some kind of a chip on his shoulder about football.

'I'm not laughing. Kidnapping's a serious crime, whoever's the victim. Do the press know about this yet?'

'We haven't said anything,' Sinclair replied.

'But in the past they've always managed to get wind of when Mickey's missed training,' Reynolds added. 'If he's not here for a few days, and we don't put out any statement, they'll start fantasizing anyway.'

Sergeant Davies had worked on kidnapping cases before. He knew that was why he was here, not because he happened to be a football fanatic. As a Thamesmead supporter he had mixed feelings about getting Wayne back in time for the semi-final in under a fortnight's time against his own team, but he was too good a policeman to let that sway his judgement. He was in his late twenties, his reddish hair, and heavy build giving him the inevitable nick-name of 'Ginga' in the force and 'Plod' when he'd played for the Metropolitan Police soccer side. He had just been tall enough to get into the force, but his strength had never been a problem, and he had struck terror into the hearts of many more talented strikers who had tried to get past him in defence. The odd forward did get past him, but rarely for more than a step or two, which had earned Davies one of the worst disciplinary records in amateur football, a record that was in wild contrast to his exemplary reputation within the force.

'If I may speak, sir?' he asked with due deference to Jordan. Davies had his own application in for promotion and was being ultra-careful not to upset any of his superiors.

'Of course, Rob. You've been here before.'

'I think we should try and keep things quiet, at least until we've put the ad in the paper and seen where that leads us. If we let the press boys in on this too early they'll be trampling all over the scene, getting in our way by talking to the same people we want to interview, family, team-mates, advisers, the Italian connection.'

'We'll be guided by you,' Sinclair said without conviction.

'Surely once you start talking to people, the news will get out,' Reynolds commented.

'Probably. But at least we'll have a start by then.'

They took down as many personal details as they could and then headed back towards the station with a promise to return in the morning.

'I'm not sure about those two,' Sinclair said as the door closed on their visitors. 'The older one wouldn't know a football from a melon.'

'Oh, I don't know. The younger one seemed to know what he was doing, and he also seemed interested. In any case they're all we've got. It's typical of Wayne to get himself into something like this,' Reynolds replied with unconcealed bitterness.

'Come on, Phil. I don't think we can blame Mickey for this one. I don't know where he is, but I'm bloody sure he doesn't want to be there.'

'Have we got him insured?' Reynolds asked.

'Yes, but only for a million. I just got a quote on increasing the cover, but the premiums were outrageous. Rest assured, he's worth more to us alive than dead.' He paused, his brow furrowed, thinking what the bank would say when they heard the news, thinking how Handsel might be able to turn the situation to his advantage. They were not pleasant thoughts.

'There has to be something more we can do, Phil. We can't simply leave the future of this club in the hands of a couple of policemen.'

'I think you're over-reacting a bit. We've won matches without Wayne before and we'll win matches without him again. Nobody's irreplaceable.'

'But these are two particular matches. A semi and a final. We win them and I think I can patch things together to keep us going, probably to get our new stadium. We lose and we're dead and buried. Even assuming we get Wayne back without having to pay any kind of...' He sought for the right word, and then, finding no alternative to the dramatic, said it. 'Ransom, yes, ransom.'

'You mean that if we don't win at Wembley we have to sell?'

'I thought I'd already made that clear to you, before this latest disaster. You know, Phil, I can't leave it to the cops. We have to call in somebody ourselves.'

'Let's not do anything hasty. I get the feeling our friend Jordan might be easily upset. Wait until Wednesday. If they've made no progress then let's get our own man on to it.'

'Any ideas? It's not every day you have to employ a private eye. We need somebody we can trust implicitly.'

Reynolds scratched his head.

'I'm just a football manager, you're the businessman.' He paused. 'Wait a minute though, didn't you tell me you'd had a letter the other week offering you some investigative services?'

'You can't be serious. Are you talking about Mark Rossetti?'

'Exactly.'

'Oh sure, we turn him away at the gate one day and offer him a job the next.'

'You saw what the Sundays had to say about that. And Rossetti's not put in his halfpence worth as yet. What he did, he's paid for. I knew Rossetti when he was a player. He was a good kid. I don't know why he did what he did, but it's over. At least he understands football, and he won't ruffle too many feathers.'

'I'm not worried about feathers being ruffled. They can burn down the whole chicken coop as far as I'm concerned as long as we get Mickey Wayne back safe and sound.'

'We've got to have some faith in our police force. After all, we pay for them,' Reynolds said.

'We pay for the cemeteries as well, it doesn't mean we want to use them,' Sinclair answered. But Reynolds had made his point and until Wednesday, at least, the fate of Mickey Wayne and Hertsmere United football club would rest in the unsympathetic hands of Detective Inspector Peter Jordan.

CHAPTER 16

As Mark Rossetti tried to tidy his flat, he realized that, short of burning the building down and starting again, nothing was going to make it presentable. He'd borrowed a Hoover from the betting office next door, acquired an assortment of cleaning materials from the corner mini-market, and even bought a bunch of flowers from the florist who had his pitch next to the newsvendor at the station.

The newspaper seller had made his comments, of course.

'Getting married again, Mark, or are you starting your own charring business?'

There was no malice in the questions and Mark had just smiled in his direction, and waved the flowers at him. He had no idea why he was even trying. He'd had visitors before and had hardly noticed the surroundings, but somehow he did not think this girl would take kindly to a dusty settee and grime-encrusted windows. It was foolish, he'd only spoken to her for less than five minutes, yet here he was trying to impress. He'd thought he was past trying to create an impression, but he'd clearly been wrong. As to whether this was good or bad he simply did not know. In the job he'd followed for the past few years he'd certainly ceased to try and differentiate between good and bad. If they paid him then they were good, if they eluded him they were bad.

She arrived dead on time, wearing a dark blue T-shirt and chinos. She appeared to have visited the hairdresser since Saturday, and the semi-crew-cut she'd received gave her a waif-like appearance. He felt himself staring and was relieved when she spoke first.

'Bit short, isn't it? I told him that with Spring in the air, he could go the whole hog. Christ knows what he's going to do when it comes to Summer.'

'It looks good,' he said, thinking how good she smelled as well, her perfume winning the battle with the disinfectant he'd used on the carpet. She looked around the flat like a prospective purchaser.

'Please don't say that I've got a nice place here,' Mark said with a smile.

'Funny you should say that. The thought never crossed my mind.' And with that she slumped on to the sofa, which creaked impolitely despite her lack of weight.

'Would you like some tea?'

'Coffee, if you've got it. Black, no sugar. Do you mind if I smoke?'

He did, but he said nothing and just bustled about his miniscule kitchen, laying some Belgian chocolate biscuits neatly out on what passed for his best china.

'It's instant I'm afraid.'

'I wouldn't know the difference. I drink so much of the stuff and smoke so many fags that my tastebuds have been well and truly destroyed.' Despite muttering something about a diet, she still took a couple of the biscuits.

'So what do you want me to tell you?' Mark asked, feeling that one of them at least should try and get round to the purpose of their meeting. She produced a tape-recorder, saw him nod and, taking that for acceptance, started it running.

'It's your story. You tell me what you want. I'll tell you if it is indeed a story.'

Mark helped himself to a biscuit. The financial investment he'd made in the domestic improvements had made deep inroads into his budget and these were all he was likely to have to eat all day.

'After a while, I thought it didn't matter any more, that people forgot, but Saturday brought it all back to me. When I first got suspended all I wanted to do was clear my name, but then I started drinking and even I didn't know if I was innocent or guilty. Now it's suddenly become important again. I'm a bit scared of stirring over the ashes...'

'They say revenge is a dish best eaten cold,' Patti interrupted.

'This is cold, all right. It's rotten as well, but then it's been eating at me until I feel rotten inside.'

'Look, Mark, I got the old file out on you when you said I could do this interview, but it doesn't tell me a lot about what really happened. I was only a kid at the time so why not take it from the top and I'll tell you when you've finished.'

'It's a long story.'

'I've got all day. Have you got enough biscuits and coffee?'

'To be perfectly honest, no,' he replied, surprised that he felt no embarrassment.

'Well then, what if I spring for lunch? By way of an advance.'

He hesitated. She might be pretty, she might be disarming, but she was a journalist for all that and it had been a long time since any of them had done him any favours.

'Let's see how it goes, shall we?'

'Playing hard to get, eh, Mark? OK, I'm used to it. I'll settle for another coffee for the moment, and then you get on with your long story.'

He used the time the kettle took to reboil to gather his thoughts. What the hell, he had to start trusting somebody again sometime. Maybe she'd been sent to him as some kind of messenger to tell him it was all over, that he'd been given an amnesty. It was too late for a pardon, he'd served his whole sentence.

He sat down in the least battered of the armchairs and paused before he began. He knew he could have got a fee for this story. He'd been offered money before and refused, even when he was at his lowest depths. None of the journalists had offered what this girl had put on the table – the right to see the article before it was published, the right to make any alterations, the right to tell it the way it was.

'I had the whole world at my feet, as they say. I was good, not yet the best as some people suggested, but if I'd worked at it then I think I could have been. The Hertsmere band wagon was just starting to roll. We were in the League by then, of course, but stuck in the Third Division. They'd had any number of offers for me from First Division clubs, but they said they were going to keep me until my contract ran out and that was two years away. I was a "symbol of their ambition" as they told the media. We were away to Tynecastle in the Cup. It was an important match for both of us. We'd already beaten Sheffield United and Birmingham and Tynecastle were on a hiding to nothing. They needed to avoid defeat against someone like us and there were all sorts of rumours about their financial situation. Then all of a sudden I'm told I'm dropped. No explanation until after the match. As it happened we got thumped 4–0 and I'm dragged in to see the chairman. This was before David Sinclair's time. Old Reggie Mortimer was in charge, very pukka, very military, white moustache, regimental tie, the lot. He tells me that one of the Tynecastle players, a defender I'd never even spoken to in my life, had taken £20,000 quid from me and that he and I were going to make sure that Hertsmere lost. He'd agreed at the time, then got a bad case of the guilts and decided to confess before any harm was done.'

'Hold on a second, what was your motive, some betting coup or other?'

'More sophisticated than that according to Mortimer. Hertsmere won't let me go, so I make sure they go out of the Cup and then the financial pressure means they have to sell me.'

'But surely that's crazy. You were a little club, you'd probably have lost anyway, and in any event without involving anybody else you could just have had an off day.'

He smiled at her enthusiasm.

'It's a shame I didn't have you to defend me at the time. They didn't just leave it there. They brought in a local bookie who swore blind he'd taken a huge bet from me on Tynecastle. Said he hadn't realized it was me at the time, but it had just dawned on him afterwards. I got set up, Patti, and, to this day, I don't know why or by whom.'

'What about the Tynecastle player?'

'A lad called Stephen Cairnes. He got a six-month suspension. Shortly after that he went off to Australia. I've tried to trace him, but no luck. He'd obviously got enough out of it to make it worth his while, to make sure he could disappear without too much difficulty.'

'And the bookie?' Patti persisted.

'Yeah, the bookie. Fellow named Bernie Lewis. Killed in a car crash on his way to Redcar within a week of giving evidence at my disciplinary hearing.'

'Inconvenient.'

'And final. End of story.'

Patti made no move to turn off the tape. 'I said I'd tell you when you were finished. That was ten years ago. What's happened since then?'

He suddenly felt very tired and hungry as if he'd been under hypnosis and had just been brought round.

'Is that offer of lunch still on the table?'

Before she could answer, the phone rang. He excused himself and picked up the receiver.

'Yes, yes it is. I'm not too bad, Mr Sinclair, considering what your club, my old club, did to me.'

The journalist watched his face with interest as the man on the other end of the line told him what he wanted. Imperceptibly, she moved nearer to him, not appearing too interested, but able to hear the Hertsmere chairman's voice.

'I see. That wasn't quite what I had in mind when I wrote to you, but yes, of course I'll come and discuss it. Now?' He suddenly became aware that he was not alone, and belatedly moved as far as the telephone cord would permit.

'No, obviously I realize this is confidential. I won't discuss it with anybody. I'll be with you in about half an hour. Yes, yes, I'll see you then.'

He replaced the receiver.

'So our lunch will have to wait.'

'I'm afraid so.'

She gave him a mock pout.

'Hard to believe there's anything more important than lunch with me...'

She gave him time to answer, but he said nothing.

Almost casually she replaced the tape-recorder in her bag, then said sweetly, 'Still, if I've got the exclusive on Mickey Wayne's kidnapping, I suppose a girl can't complain, can she?'

'Look, I've promised to say nothing. This is very important to me.'

'And it's very important to me as well. My car or yours?'

'Mine's off the road at the moment.'

'Well, that's one problem solved anyway. Now all we have to decide is how I can keep involved in this little matter.'

He was in her car before he could object. It was one of her talents to sweep men off their feet, not romantically, but mentally. She drove with the same speed at which she thought, oblivious to pedestrians, disdainful of other cars, her little Renault Clio nipping from lane to lane, and it was only when they turned into Park Crescent that it occurred to him that he had no possible way of explaining her presence.

CHAPTER 17

The Hertsmere players knew something was up with Mickey Wayne. Even he had never missed three days training on the trot, not to mention a match, and if he was injured, as they'd been told, why wasn't he receiving treatment? They sat in the changing rooms after Wednesday's session in a subdued silence far removed from the usual banter that followed a five-a-side match. Phil Reynolds had scored for the reds, whilst Greg Sergovich had left his goal to get the winner for the blues, both events that would normally have had the rest of the squad reduced to tears of laughter. They'd not been happy to come in for training today, but after they'd lost again 0–1 the previous evening to Carswell United and been booed off the pitch, Fowler had insisted they be at the ground at 9.00 a.m. sharp.

Nobody seemed to want to be the first one to get in to the showers, most of them had not even pulled off their shirts, and it fell to the captain, Stuart Macdonald, to try and bring them out of it.

'Come on, lads. You did good today. Shame you didn't do it last night. We'll take Stockton apart on Saturday if you play like that. And as for old Sid the Slav, well I don't know if we play him in goal or up front after that little effort of his.'

Sergovich looked as puzzled as ever when he was called by his nickname, Sid. He had joined Hertsmere two years earlier and although his game had adapted to the club style his English was still very much of the basic level. His main tutor had been Mickey Wayne, which meant that he had a fairly wide vocabulary of swear words and sexual references, none of which were very much use to him when he went shopping in his local supermarket and most of which threatened to get his face smacked when he used them in the wine bar frequented by many of the team.

'Mickey back tomorrow, I think,' he said, without conviction.

'Mickey not back tomorrow, or any other fucking day,' replied Nicky Collier, the big prematurely balding striker. 'They've sold him, that's what they've done and the bastards aren't telling us.'

'If they'd done that the boss would have said so,' Macdonald said, without any great conviction. He felt helpless and he didn't like the feeling. He was a man used to being in control of his own destiny. If he wanted something then generally he just got up and took it. That was how he had got his wife, after all, from that poor bastard Rossetti, but right now he wanted Wayne back and he had no means of making that happen. He knew in his heart of hearts that they weren't the same side without Wayne. He might only be one of eleven, but he could do things with the ball that were beyond anybody else in the country, let alone the Hertsmere team. They'd tried young Tommy Wallace out wide last night, but try as the Scots kid might, he was a boy amongst men. He needed time and he'd probably make it, but he wouldn't be ready for Saturday week against Thamesmead, that was for certain.

'If they've not sold him and we haven't seen him, then where the fuck is he?' Collier persisted. Wayne was not over-popular with his team-mates, but they put up with him because of his skill. Collier was a barn door of a man, who relied upon the crosses of Wayne for his battering-ram approach to opposition defences. He was a constant moaner on the field, and off it. Last night he'd virtually reduced Wallace to tears with his complaints about the quality of the service and Ray Fowler, the coach, had led the youngster off the pitch with his arm around his shoulders. Wayne might be tolerated, but Collier was actively disliked. Nobody said as much to his face. True to his name he'd grown up in a Yorkshire mining town, and was as hard as the tools that dug out the coal, his skin scarred by a lifetime of battles. He'd been John Kelly's last signing and although Reynolds had tried to replace him on more than one occasion somehow fates seemed to conspire to ensure that he kept his place. Brian Jones had been bought from Swansea and had promptly broken his leg, whilst no work permit could be obtained for Radsicz from Albania. And so Collier was still there, still scoring the odd vital goal, but without winning any medals for style. The fans who did not know him as a person quite liked him. He never appeared to give less than a hundred per cent and the sheer physicality of his game made him something of a folk hero. As another goalkeeper collapsed to the ground under his challenge the chant would go up from the crowd, 'She fell over, she fell over.' He was an intimidating sight bearing down in the six-yard box, and no less so now as he stood belligerently in his sweat-stained shirt holding forth to the rest of the team. He turned his frustration towards the diminutive Irish midfielder Pat Devine.

'You're the nearest thing he's got to a friend here. Haven't you got any ideas?'

Devine shook his head.

'If it was a lady that would explain a day, but even for Mickey she'd have to be something special to keep him amused for this long.'

Collier took a step towards him, and Devine automatically backed off.

'There's a lot of money involved in this for all of us, you thick little paddy. And all you can do is make a fucking joke out of it. You're usually not slow to get a few quid from the papers for a story. Haven't you had any of your mates on the phone asking where he is? Or hasn't anybody even noticed that he's vanished off the fucking earth?'

Devine hesitated, and Collier, seeing he'd struck a nerve, grabbed him by the front of his shirt.

'You know something, you little cunt, don't you? If you don't come clean I'll make sure you're not fit to play on Saturday, so help me.'

Devine dangled from Collier's fist, like a fish on the end of a line.

'The press boys think the club's put him under wraps to take the pressure off him. Italy and all that.'

'The club's put him under wraps, have they? So he doesn't train like the rest of us fucking mortals. I don't know why we bother. Nobody tells us the fucking truth. We might as well be machines.' He let Devine drop to the floor, and the Irishman took the opportunity to race for the showers. Macdonald had decided not to intervene until now. It was best to let Collier burn himself out and although he didn't agree with his tactics he could sympathize with some of the sentiments.

'Come on, lads, there's no point in fighting amongst ourselves. We're all on the same side. Why give the journos anything to write about? Let's get to Wembley and we can all cash in. Mickey'll turn up, he's a bad penny, mark my words.'

One by one they drifted off into the steaming water until only Macdonald and Fowler were left.

'You didn't believe any of that crap, did you Stu?' the coach asked. 'If you really think that we're playing better without Wayne than with him, then I'll take that captain's armband off you without anaesthetic.'

'What do you think, Ray?'

'I think that unless Nicky Collier suddenly grows wings we're going to get smashed by Thamesmead.'

'You mean pigs might fly.'

Fowler ignored this attempt at a joke. 'I've been in this game a long time. I've been with teams that have won the League, the League Cup, even the European Cup, but I've never been with a team that's won at Wembley in the FA Cup. I want that bad, Stu, and I'm not going to let the absence of one player, even one like Mickey Wayne stop me. Now go and get yourself showered and changed. We're a winger down already, I don't want my captain getting pneumonia.'

Fowler watched the player disappear into the haze that was now coming from the showers. Somebody was singing, and one by one they all seemed to be joining in, all of them except Collier who had already reappeared, his hair wet and sleek, his face dark with ill-temper. Footballers, who'd want to deal with them for a living? They were like kids, trouble when you had them and trouble when you lost them. They had to find this missing one and if nobody else was going to try, then Ray Fowler, at least, was going to have a tilt.

CHAPTER 18

It did nothing to help Mark Rossetti's confidence that the first person he saw on entering Hertsmere's stadium was Stuart Macdonald. The men had neither met nor spoken since Sally had left, although there had been a time when he'd regarded him as a friend. As they confronted each other in the reception area they automatically stopped, as one might when confronted by a TV personality in the street, a face known, yet unknown.

It was Macdonald who was the first to speak.

'Hello Mark, what are you doing here?'

Rossetti was lost for words. Too much was happening to him today for him to be able to control every emotion. He wanted to hit the man, to take the smile from his good-natured face, to make enough of a mess to ensure when he got home that Sally and Emma, *his* daughter Emma, would have to ask what had happened. Macdonald would have to explain and if he told the truth then Emma might understand that her real father existed and cared. He controlled himself with difficulty. If he created a scene here and now then he was likely to be out on his ear, the one chance that had come his way in a decade totally blown.

'I've nothing to say to you, Macdonald.' As soon as the

words were out he knew it was the wrong thing to say. If he got the job he'd come here after, then he'd have plenty to say to the man who had been Mickey Wayne's captain for most of his career.

'Have it your own way, Mark. Sally says you were always a stubborn bastard.'

The receptionist, Sharon, who always took a keen interest in everything that happened in the club, looked up in the hope that Rossetti would retaliate and make things really exciting, but to her disappointment he merely said, 'Can you please tell Mr Sinclair that Mark Rossetti is here to see him.'

Sharon was too young to have been around when Mark had been a player, but she gave him the smile she normally reserved for the young, good-looking first team players, who one by one learned that she was a well-practised tease who'd been going out with the same young policeman since she'd left school some five years before. She just liked to know she had the power to attract, a soccer groupie with a moral code.

'Of course. He's just on the phone. Would you like a tea or coffee?'

'Whichever's easiest.'

She made a small face as if she did not appreciate a man who could not make the simplest of decisions, and then knocked a coffee out of the machine for him.

'You've been away a while,' she said.

'You've been reading the papers.'

'Sorry. Everybody was talking about it on Monday. If you're interested, the general opinion was that you'd been hard done by.'

'Thanks for that,' he said without any trace of sarcasm. He'd lusted after praise when he'd been a player and it had been a long time since he'd heard anything good said about him. The prospect of any more compliments was brought to an end by the buzz of the switchboard. She answered it with a distinct change of voice and then directed him through the swing doors that led through to the offices, forgetting that he needed no direction.

It was like going back to school after many years. Nothing has changed, yet everything is different. He was different, not so much in size as in perspective. He spotted a change in the photographs on the wall, championship teams in which he had played no part, players he hardly recognized. They did not seem to have redecorated since he had left, or if they had then they had used the same colour paint, a dull khaki that had always reminded him of a factory cafeteria. He came to the chairman's door, and although it was ajar he hesitated before entering. He had to get over this psychological barrier if he was going to be convincing. There were raised voices inside. He'd only met David Sinclair in passing. He'd been just another fan all those years ago, but he'd heard him often enough on the radio and television to make it feel that he knew him well. The other voice he knew as well. Phil Reynolds and he had played in the same England 'B' side, Reynolds recalled from his self-imposed exile to give experience, Rossetti as a stepping-stone to the full England team. One on the way up, the other on the way out. He'd liked the man, appreciated the encouragement he'd given him. Not everybody had time for a raw youth like him. Looking back he realized how naïve he must have appeared, not just to

Reynolds, but to everybody. Well, he would show them that he was naïve no longer.

Sinclair was on the phone again as he entered the room. He was arguing angrily, whilst Reynolds looked on with a worried expression. The manager shook his hand firmly as if really glad to see him, and signalled him into a chair. Sinclair hardly seemed to notice him as he gripped the receiver with a ferocity that turned his knuckles white. Whoever was on the other end was doing all the talking until Sinclair finally said, 'No. Just no. Forget it,' and slammed down the phone.

Mark half rose out of the chair and extended his hand to the chairman. Sinclair took it, then fell back in his own chair, his face drained of colour.

'Good of you to come, but I'm not sure we've not wasted your time. You didn't speak to anybody after I called you, did you?'

'No, of course not,' Mark replied, hoping nobody had seen him arrive in Patti Delaney's car. He'd had to sit in it for long enough when she'd said she wanted to come in and wait for him.

'If you sit around a reception area long enough you see and hear all sorts of things. Sooner or later everybody passes through.'

She cut a hard bargain, but eventually he had to agree. She would stay in the car whilst he had his meeting. If it seemed that the story was about to break, then she'd have first run at it. If he got the job then she would be allowed to accompany him.

'It's a good deal, Mark. You get a pretty companion and a chauffeuse. Some men would kill for that.'

'Maybe somebody will kill, Patti.' He was amazed at how easily he'd slipped into the relationship with her without really knowing very much about her. She was good at asking questions, but not so forthcoming when it came to giving answers. 'I'm not sure I want to put you at that sort of risk.'

She patted him on the head in mock sympathy.

'There, there, little boy. Where have you been the last ten years? In hibernation? While you were sleeping, chivalry died and women got the vote. You've got me, for better or worse. It was fate that had me at your flat when you got the call and you won't regret it, I promise you. Anyway, I've a black belt in judo.'

'Really?'

'No, I lied; but anybody else I threaten won't know that.'

He'd laughed then, but he wasn't laughing now as Sinclair told him what had happened and showed him a photocopy of the letter he'd received. Gradually he'd calmed down from the call, but there was still something cool in his attitude.

'Look, I'll be frank with you, Mark, I didn't want you involved in this. You've Phil here to thank for persuading me.' Rossetti shot a look of gratitude at Reynolds.

'Yeah, so you'd better not let me down,' the manager interrupted.

'You're absolutely sure you said nothing to anybody before you came?'

'I've already told you. My phone doesn't ring that often that I'd forget and I just wanted to get here as soon as I could.'

'OK, I'm sorry.' Sinclair's tone changed. 'That was Chris

Handsel on the phone when you came in. He wouldn't say how he knew, but he knows Wayne's been kidnapped. He suggests that he's the one person who can get things moving. He tells me to forget about the police. According to our Chris, if I wait for them, then they've more chance of delivering Shergar's skeleton than Mickey Wayne in the flesh.'

Even as he recalled the conversation he was becoming agitated, his hands waving around until inevitably he knocked a cup of coffee over on his desktop. He began to mop it up still talking.

'What else did Handsel have to tell me? Oh, yes, before I can have the help of his "team" I'd have to co-opt him on to the board. I'd rather work alongside the Yorkshire Ripper. At least you know where he's coming from, and if you were a bloke you were fairly safe.'

'Do you think Handsel's behind this?' Mark asked.

'If he is, then he's got a lot of front. You snatch a player on Monday and by Wednesday you're offering to help get him back.'

'So who else knows the truth about Wayne?' Mark persisted.

'The three of us,' Sinclair replied. 'I felt I had to tell Richard Lee, he's a director and also the club solicitor. I wanted to be sure I was doing nothing wrong before getting somebody in from outside; but there's no way he would have said anything. We had to tell Laura, Wayne's wife. And now, of course, there's Handsel. Christ knows how many people he's told. And the police. Maybe it was somebody there who tipped off Handsel. I wouldn't put it past him to have friends on both sides of the fence.'

'That's it, you're sure? No family, no secretary or player drifting in and overhearing a conversation?'

Sinclair screwed up his eyes, trying to recall every detail of the last few days. 'I don't think so. What about you, Phil?'

The manager shook his head.

'I told Ray Fowler but he's like the grave. Apart from him, nobody. Certainly the lads don't know. I had Stuart Macdonald in after training telling me the hot rumour is that we're hiding him away for his own good.'

Sinclair laughed.

'I wish.' He looked Rossetti straight in the face.

'I know about Macdonald and your wife. Obviously we know all about your history with this club. Isn't this all going to be a bit personal for you?'

Rossetti didn't allow himself to hesitate.

'It's going to be a lot personal. That's why I'm your best bet. I'm not going to spin you any hard luck story about the rights and the wrongs of what happened to me, but I need this job. If I pull this off for you, maybe you'll give me a go at what I originally asked in my letter, maybe other clubs will reconsider. If you need somebody hungry, then believe me, I'm starving.'

'I don't think we've anything to worry about from the Newman Report. With the finance director we've got here, we're so clean we're squeaking. Anyway, if we're to have a club to investigate I need Wayne back in one piece, all toes attached.'

He paused, seeming to wrestle with a difficult decision.

'All right, Mark, you've got yourself a job. What do you charge?'

'Twenty pounds an hour, plus expenses, thirty pounds between midnight and seven a.m. If I get him back before the semi-final there's a bonus of fifty thousand.'

That last had been Patti's suggestion.

Sinclair didn't hesitate, and Mark realized he'd not thought big enough.

'You're on. I want a daily report. Before you incur any expenses over fifty quid you clear them with me. Now, when can you start?'

'Haven't you noticed?' Mark said. 'I've started.'

CHAPTER 19

By the time he got back to where he had left Patti with her car it was gone two in the afternoon. He'd half expected her not to be there, but she was, shouting into her mobile phone, reading from some hieroglyphics she had scribbled in her pad. She was more animated than he'd seen her before, totally immersed in her work, paying him no attention whatsoever. He felt a little deflated, realizing that he'd actually been looking forward to telling her he was on the case. She was having difficulty making herself understood, leaning forward as she spoke trying to get some clearer reception. The line obviously went dead and she shook the phone in frustration.

'They're fucking useless these things. They ring when you don't want them to, and when you need them it's like talking to Mars from the bottom of Loch Ness. The story's broken about Wayne. The Italian radio just carried it, so any minute now it'll be like the Alamo around this stadium. Let's get the hell out of here and then you can give me my exclusive. Still fancy that lunch?'

Even as she was speaking the first cars had arrived at the far end of Park Crescent and journalists and photographers were tumbling out as if it was the first day of Harrods' sale, shooting off reels of film at the stadium itself in the hope it might reveal the answer to some of the mystery. A van rumbled past with ITN written along the side, almost colliding with its BBC replica. Even without a body, the vultures were collecting.

As with everything, she chose the restaurant for lunch carefully, driving round the M25 for nearly half an hour before turning off near Amersham. They said little to each other, he trying to establish a modus operandi in his mind, she already rewriting her story. She made a couple of turns, then took a B-road that threatened to lead nowhere, but which in fact took them to a pretty country pub.

'How did you find this place?'

'Oh, you know, a girl gets taken around. Anyway, apart from the privacy and the food, I like the name.'

He looked up at the swinging sign, which showed a young girl in Tudor dress on her knees by the side of her bed and bore the title, 'The Maiden's Prayer'.

'Hoping to get it answered?' he asked.

'Bit late for that. Come on, we've work to do.'

The staff obviously knew her, as they brought her a vodka and orange almost before they'd sat down.

'The same for you, sir?'

He hesitated, remembering how he had felt the week before when he had fallen off the wagon, then said, 'Yes, but without the vodka.'

'Well done.' Patti leaned back in her chair and clapped her hands. 'Now tell me all about it.'

He waited until he had the drink before him. He had the confidence now and she had to be told this just wasn't on.

He had a client, and he owed him a degree of confidentiality.

'Patti, I don't want you to think I'm ungrateful for all your interest in me, but I think we have to make this the parting of the ways. My job's to find Mickey Wayne, yours is to find a story.'

She waved an empty glass at the barman and he immediately brought her a refill.

'If you have one more of those, then I'm walking home.'

'Ooh, I love it when you get masterful with me. Don't worry Mark. Journalists have a second stomach to hold all the booze. Anyway, the nicotine probably filters it out.'

She lit a cigarette and, noticing his air of disapproval, held it carefully to her side, blowing the smoke away from him.

'No drink. No fags. What are your failings, Mark?'

'I tell people exactly what I think.'

'I'm not so sure that's a failing.'

'You will in a minute. I think we've gone far enough down the line together. I've got my investigation to get underway, and I can't do it with the thought that everything I say may be taken down and used in an article against me.'

This time she blew the smoke straight across the table into his face and laughed when he coughed.

'And you believe I'd really do that to you. Sure, I'm after a story, but I'm not coming to the party without a bottle. You'll have people to interview, places to go, and I can help you with all that. You go to see somebody and I'll pull off a file and tell you how much money they've got in the bank, who's their mistress, and whether or not they like her dressed in leather.'

The barman put a menu in front of them and she sent it away with a flick of the hand.

'I'm not sure we're going to be eating,' she said.

'That's fine by me,' Mark said, rising to his feet.

'Where are you going?'

'Back to the car,' he muttered, 'I've wasted enough time already.'

'Well, you can waste a bit more. You want to go separate ways. That's fine with me. We start right now. I'll see you around, doubtless. I'm sure our paths will cross. Maybe I'll get back to you about your own interview. If you've got time, that is.'

She was almost at the door before she'd finished the last sentence, and automatically he came after her, catching her arm.

'And how am I supposed to get back from here? I don't even know where I am.'

She shrugged off his hand with surprising strength.

'Great start to your investigation. You get lost in the wilds of Bucks. Shame you haven't got a movie camera. You could have filmed the fauna and flora for David Attenborough. You're the great detective. Detect your way out of here.'

She was in the car, the key turning in the ignition, when he poked his head through the open window.

'All right, I'm sorry, you win.'

'Jesus, I hate a man who apologizes.'

He couldn't tell whether or not she was being serious, but she did, at least, turn off the engine.

'I'm really hungry, Patti.'

'Yes . . . ?'

'And we haven't eaten yet.'

'No. Well spotted.'

'And we have to work out a game plan.'

'Better.'

'And I've no money on me, either for a meal or a taxi.'

'I'm convinced.' And then she was out of the car and the two of them walked back into the pub for a meal.

CHAPTER 20

It was six in the evening before they got to Laura Wayne's door in St Albans and by the time they arrived the circus had already hit town. For once though, Mark was one step ahead of them. He now understood what Patti Delaney had meant about bringing a bottle to the party. What she'd provided was definitely the right stuff. And on the way he'd learnt a lot more about her.

She was twenty-six years old, with a degree in English from Kent University. She had briefly worked for a leading firm of publishers as an assistant editor and then, deciding she could write better than most of the authors she was editing, she'd walked out one day and never gone back. She was a creature of impulse and tomorrow's need for a reference didn't bother her. She'd left to write her own book, but it had been easier to contemplate than to do and as her wastebasket filled so her bank account emptied. She'd fallen lucky when Lizette Chamberlain had moved into the flat above her. They'd become good friends, and when Lizette had begun her affair with a married Tory MP, Patti's had been a comfortable shoulder upon which to cry. When the affair was discovered Lizette refused to speak to anybody except Patti and when her story was finally sold to a Sunday paper it was on condition that Patti did the interview. The editor hadn't liked the idea, he hated amateurs, but Lizette stood her ground and Patti wrote the piece. The editor had a sudden change of heart when he saw it and offered her a permanent job over lunch. To his amazement she declined, and told him she was going freelance.

'But you've only ever written one piece,' he'd said in exasperation.

'Yes, but now I know I can do it.'

As her career developed, so her book remained unfinished and eventually there was no time even to think about it, let alone write it. At first she'd followed the money, concentrating on the celebrity interview, ruthlessly using every contact she had to get to her subjects, but then she'd moved on to the in-depth investigation, the murky world of politics and espionage, of sex and corruption, The watershed had been when she'd come across a scandal involving the Hampshire-based helicopter company which had employed her father as an engineer for the last twenty years. They'd been selling machines and spares to the Middle East for years, but she had been tipped off that they were also breaking the embargo on supplying equipment to Iran. She spent a long time thinking about what she should do, and finally decided to speak to her father before she even contemplated writing the story.

'Am I supposed to be grateful to you for telling me about it?' he'd asked.

'Dad, it's illegal, not to mention immoral. I thought you'd want to have the chance to get out before this whole thing blows.'

'It'll only blow if you light the fuse. If I go now I'll never get a job in the industry. Everybody will think I gave you the information for the story.'

Her mouth had fallen open as she suddenly saw her father in a new light, not as the gentle man who always smelled faintly of Old Spice and pipe tobacco, but as an accessory to murder.

'You mean you knew about this?'

'Patricia, everybody knows. Without sales to countries like Iran we wouldn't have an aircraft industry in this country.'

'Are you asking me not to write the article?'

He'd shrugged.

'I brought you up to do whatever you think is right. All paid for by the wages of sin,' he said with a wan smile.

She'd never written the article and she'd never forgiven herself. Somebody else did it, of course, some six months later and, although her father was never prosecuted, the company folded and he'd not had another job until he threw himself under the Southampton–Waterloo express train a year to the day from her first conversation with him on the subject. He'd left no note so she didn't know whether or not that was a pure coincidence.

After that she'd had a total change of direction. She'd had enough of investigative journalism, she didn't like the thought of what she might find. Again there was an element of pure chance in her career. She'd been at a West Ham match when old Bill Turnbull had his heart attack right next to her. He'd been reporting on London games for years for the *News*. She'd phoned the sports editor on her mobile to tell him what had happened, and in desperation he'd asked her to cover the game. There was no looking back after that.

'I thought I could just watch the football, report on what I saw, that what everybody saw was what they got. I was really innocent enough still to believe that it was a different world, but I was wrong. The fans don't want to distance themselves from their heroes like they used to, they want to know everything about them and I do mean everything. And, like with everything else in life, as soon as you get up close to it, then it doesn't bear inspection. But if anybody knows that, it's you, Mark.'

'So why didn't you just pack it all in and get back to writing your book? At least you'd be able to look yourself in the face in the mirror.'

'Because every time I look in the mirror I see my father's face behind me. If I'd done what I believed in who knows what might have happened. Perhaps I could have bullied him or persuaded him into resigning, perhaps he was wrong and he could have got another job.'

Mark listened carefully. He'd almost forgotten how to listen. The men and women who'd sporadically passed through his office and his life had all been cardboard cut-outs, all with the same thing to say. They were losers and they needed his help in proving it. Some days they'd appeared to him as goldfish, soundlessly opening and closing their mouths, but with Patti he found himself hanging on every word. As she wove the fabric of her life, he could see just how good a writer she might be if she put her mind to it. She was street-wise, too, by now. The investigative work had honed her rough edges and the world of football had cured her of her innocence.

David Sinclair had given him all the phone numbers and addresses he required, together with a letter of authority, and it had seemed logical to start with Laura Wayne. He had little doubt that the police would have already spoken to her but, as Patti suggested, perhaps they had not asked the right questions. She had also anticipated the crush around the woman's house and already had a plan for getting her out.

'It's easy. Look, it says on the microfiche her father's an ambulance driver. He just needs to borrow one in his time off. We go into the house with him. He and a mate carry me out on a stretcher and you and she leg it over the fence through the neighbour's house that backs on to her's. It works. They used to do it with Gazza all the time, so I can't claim to have thought it up. But her father may not have instant access to the ambulance.'

'No, I suppose not,' he said. 'But if she's prepared to run away with us, then she's also prepared to speak to us, so why don't we just walk in the front door and lock it behind us.'

She looked at him with a mixture of amusement and pity.

'Because you are who you are and I am who I am. They'd recognize you going into the house, then that's another story for them. They see me and they panic that the main feature's moving out of their reach. So when I go in with her dad, I'm wearing a man's suit and as for you, well, you go in round the back. I've already spoken to the neighbour and said we're working for the club. They're quite excited about it, but you'd better make sure you show the letter to prove it's official.'

It had worked like a dream. Mark had done the

background work with the neighbours and Laura's father had been only too willing to help. He'd already had the news agencies round driving his wife crazy for old photographs and he saw the plan as a way of getting some revenge. Patti never quite got around to telling him she was a journalist and he never asked. They'd brought Laura back to Patti's home, a garden flat in a large converted Victorian house in West Hampstead, which Patti fondly called 'The Burrow'.

'We can't take her to your place, Mark. She'll think she's been kidnapped as well. And it could cause a permanent trauma for the kid.'

In fact 'the kid', Darren, a rather miserable two-year-old with a runny nose, had been whisked away by his grandfather in the ambulance to be cooed over by his nan for the rest of the day and it was just the three of them who sat in the Burrow on the huge scatter cushions that covered Patti's floor.

Laura Wayne was a pencil-thin girl who could not have been much more than twenty-one. When Mark had been playing football most of his team-mates had been marrying girls like her. The way to a footballer's heart had always seemed to be through a bottle of peroxide and a plunging neck-line. Most footballers were not impressed by women who thought too much. She clearly kept her figure by way of an endless succession of cigarettes that gave her clothes a permanent smell of smoke. Her hair was probably naturally fair, but she had given nature a kick-start with a blonde dye that accentuated her baby-doll blue eyes which, despite their innocent colour, had a protective hardness about them. She had married young, too young for her own good and certainly too young to guarantee she could hold her husband's interest beyond the birth of their first baby. She wore a tight jumper that, without a bra underneath, left little to the imagination.

'You've made it really nice here, haven't you? I think these cushions are great. Maybe I'll try and talk Mickey into buying some ... when he gets back. He is going to come back, isn't he?' she said nervously.

'Sure he's going to come back,' Mark said reassuringly, as Patti served them all cheese and crackers accompanied by wine for the two women and Evian for Mark.

'I'm sorry, I'm not a great one for cooking.' Another piece of information. Maybe at the end of the day he'd be better qualified to write an article about her than she about him.

'It's fine,' Laura said, 'I'm just pleased to get away from the house. I felt like a prisoner in there. They were putting notes through my letter box offering me money for my story. Being married to Mickey, I've had the press around before, but nothing like that. It was frightening. And Darren wouldn't stop crying...'

'They're very sensitive, little mites like that aren't they?' Patti said in a tone that suggested she'd shared all the pains of childbirth.

He left them chatting about the vagaries of babies and toddlers and wandered off to the bathroom. There was the same casualness of design that pervaded the rest of the flat, a casualness so consistent that it must have taken careful planning. He looked at the soaps in the Wedgwood bowl, and noted they came only from some of the best hotels in the world, the Negresco in Nice, the Plaza in New York, the

Crillon in Paris. Only when he returned to the lounge did it occur to him that perhaps it was somebody else who travelled and brought her the soaps and he felt a pang of inexplicable jealousy. He had no proprietary rights over her. He'd met her less than a week ago, yet a part of him wanted to pursue his investigation of her as much as that of Wayne's disappearance. He shook his head in annoyance like a man emerging from a pool and tossing the water from his face. He didn't want any distractions, he just wanted to get on with the job, to concentrate on finding his way back.

Patti and Laura hardly noticed him as he resumed his position on the floor. He tried to catch Patti's eye. They had an agreement. If she saw any problem she would let him ask the questions, but right now he was going to find it difficult getting a word in edgeways.

'Laura, I'm sorry to bring you back to reality, but I need some information, things that may help me find Mickey.'

'Yeah, I'm sorry. It seemed so warm and safe here. I understand why you call it the Burrow. I've not been sleeping very well at home. It was good of the club to get you in. They've always looked after Mickey well there. Not that he appreciated it. That slimy Lennie Simons always made it seem like he was being ripped off. He gave me the creeps, that bloke. We had a terrible row over him once when Mickey wanted to bring him home for a meeting and I said I wouldn't have him in the house.'

'It's that sort of thing I want you to remember. I'm sure the police have already asked you most of what I'm going to ask, but maybe you'll give me some different answers.'

He allowed Patti to replenish Laura's glass then began.

'Obvious one first, Laura. This whole thing may be

impersonal, just for the cash, and then again it may be someone who hates Mickey's guts. Is there anybody in particular you can think of who might have it in for him?'

The girl took a sip of the wine, then emptied the glass and immediately offered it to Patti for a refill. The journalist looked at Mark, who nodded. Anything that lowered her guard had to be helpful.

'Anyone who had it in for my Mickey? What's the time?' She turned her wrist in an exaggerated gesture to look at her watch. Mark noticed that the strap alone looked as if it had cost more than his entire possessions. 'Just gone seven, well we've got a few hours till midnight so I'll tell you who had it in for Mickey...'

CHAPTER 21

They'd put the advert in the *Telegraph* just as they'd been told, but by the end of Wednesday there had been no response. Sinclair had never been under so much pressure. Once the bank had read about Wayne's disappearance they'd been on to him like a ton of bricks. Their appointee, Tom Kerr, had barged his way into the chairman's office, his pointed nose virtually quivering with rage.

'How on earth did you think you'd get away without telling the rest of the board? Forget the bank, I'm the bloody finance director. Seven million pounds worth of balance-sheet assets goes missing and I don't even know.'

'We don't include our players in the balance sheet,' Sinclair murmured, but he knew Kerr was right. Yet again he was playing into the hands of his enemies.

'And now you tell me you've committed us to more expenditure on this Rossetti. The man's been banned from the game for ten years and you cast him as our white knight on an even whiter steed. It's like putting Lizzie Borden in charge of the cutlery in a school canteen.'

'I've said I'm sorry. I did what I thought was right at the time.'

There was no holding back the young Scot, his accent

thickening with his agitation to the point of incomprehensibility.

'You treat this club like it's your own personal toy. We can only play if you invite us round for tea. It's not like that any more. You're running a business here, not massaging your ego. Now, I want a board meeting called and I want it called immediately.'

They'd had their meeting and Kerr had pushed through a motion of censure on the chairman. Alone it meant nothing, but if things went very wrong then it might be the final straw to bring him down, his shareholding notwithstanding. He'd said nothing about the bonus he'd offered Rossetti; he'd had a difficult enough job to persuade them to keep him on.

The pressure hadn't stopped with the bank and the board. Barlucci had been on the phone from Rome asking whether he had a deal, always presuming that the player got back safe and sound. Paulo Versace had also called to introduce himself.

'In Italy we are used to these things, but I did not think you had the mafioso in England. Always the victim is returned sooner or later. We are better equipped to deal with these incidents than you. I make you an offer. We pay you four million pounds for Wayne and then it is our responsibility to get him back. In all the circumstances it is generous, I think. You will put it to your board?'

Sinclair was tempted to tell him to get lost, but the thought occurred to him that Versace was not going to be easily diverted. All he needed at the moment was for him to leak the story of such a proposal to the press, and for him to have said nothing to the rest of his board. He felt he was on safer ground to use his powers of persuasion on his fellow directors and had convened yet another meeting for Thursday morning.

One by one they filed into the board room. Jonathan Black made little effort to conceal his impatience.

'Unlike some of you, I've a real business to run. I've been spending so much time here lately that my wife thinks I've found another woman.'

Richard Lee had already phoned through to say he had to be in court and that he'd get there as soon as he could. Freddie Scott had taken a turn for the worse. His wife had been on the phone to Sinclair virtually hysterical.

'They say he needs private treatment if we're to keep him out of a hospice or a terminal cancer ward. We can't afford it, David, not unless he sells his shares. Freddie doesn't want to put you under even more pressure, but if you can't buy his shares, I have to look for someone who will.'

Ben Porter was there, of course, although how much he actually understood of what was going on was subject to debate. Black and Kerr against Sinclair was how it seemed to the chairman, and only Helen Archer to bring him interval drinks.

Kerr went straight to the point.

'Have you told the police about this gangster Versace's offer? It must be obvious that he's behind this whole affair.'

Sinclair had decided that he had to keep himself under control. If he lost his temper, he simply played into their hands.

'No, I haven't told the police. I've called this meeting to decide what step we take next. You censured me for acting off my own back earlier in the week and now you're trying to censure me for waiting to hear what you all have to say. As for Versace, he may be just an opportunist. Just because he makes us what might be considered a commercial offer doesn't mean he's a crook.'

Kerr's mouth sneered at the naïvety of the other man. 'You always want to think the best of people, don't you. Like this ex-con you've got working for the club.'

'Rossetti's never been to prison.'

'From what I hear that was more luck than justice. However, let's leave Rossetti out of this.'

'It was you who introduced him into the conversation in the first place,' Sinclair said, a small smile playing about his face. He could see that Kerr was becoming annoyed with all the interruptions, and for the chairman's part he was beginning almost to enjoy himself.

'Let's put this into perspective. If somebody had come along last week and offered four million quid for Wayne, we would have considered it. It's only because we've had this crazy offer from these wops...'

'Cinquante, I think you mean,' Sinclair said, this time interrupting Jonathan Black in full flight. 'Somehow or other I don't think Signor Barlucci would take kindly to being called a wop.'

Black scowled.

'I don't give a shit what he takes kindly to. If he hadn't meddled in our affairs none of this would have happened.'

Kerr was quick to jump on Black's bandwagon.

'And if you'd told us about the offer when you first received it we could have accepted and had seven million in the bank by now. There's no way that trouble-making lout is worth that sort of money.'

'He were good that Mickey Wayne, best I ever saw. The only one of this modern lot who could have lived alongside the best of my generation.' Ben Porter seemed to wink encouragingly at David Sinclair, but then as he nodded off again it could just as easily have been a trick of the light.

Kerr straightened the pad and pen in front of him. 'Ignore that old fool. I'm formally proposing that we accept Versace's offer and wash our hands of Wayne and this whole mess.'

'I second that,' said Black with some satisfaction.

Helen Archer, who was taking the minutes, wrote slowly and reluctantly.

'I vote against. I hold Freddie's proxy and he votes against as well,' Sinclair said confidently.

'Funny you should mention proxies,' Kerr said. 'I've got one here from Richard Lee.'

'That's not possible,' Sinclair said. Lee was his lawyer. He simply couldn't believe he could vote against him and on something as vital as this as well.

'I think it is,' Kerr replied with quiet satisfaction. 'Just because you appointed him doesn't mean he's not his own man.'

Sinclair leaned back in his chair and sighed, like a drowning man looking anywhere for oxygen. It came from an unexpected quarter.

'I don't agree with the sale,' Ben said in a firm voice that belied his years.

'Three all, I think,' Helen Archer said, receiving as her arithmetical reward a glance from Kerr that suggested if and when the bank moved in she would follow Sinclair closely out of the door.

'I do believe I have a casting vote,' Sinclair began to say, and then the telephone rang and everything else was momentarily forgotten.

CHAPTER 22

Detective Inspector Peter Jordan was not happy to be called away from his garden on his day off. He'd had a good daffodil display this year. No, that was modest, it had been spectacular, easily winning the prize from the local club. His mother liked daffodils and he'd sat her down in her wheelchair, blanket neatly tucked around her, just to look at them for hours in the Spring sunshine. Everything came to an end and he'd set himself the task of cutting the heads off the dead and dying flowers this morning. He liked things to be as tidy in his garden as they usually were in his mind and nothing looked more untidy than the drying, curling yellow heads of daffodils. He was like that with his cases as well, didn't like them hanging around making a mess.

The Mickey Wayne case had been hanging around, though without any kind of a breakthrough. He had simply vanished off the planet and for a while it seemed his kidnappers had gone with him. And now they'd had a call. It had been brief and to the point, the voice muffled, concealing even the sex of its owner.

'If you go down to reception you'll find a little parcel to show we mean business. Now we need to be satisfied that you mean business. Five hundred thousand pounds in used notes. There's a phone booth outside of Tesco in Hertsmere shopping centre. One person in the booth at two o'clock tomorrow afternoon, with the money. We'll call with instructions. Remember we'll know if your man doesn't come alone and we'll know if he's being followed. If you try that, Wayne loses his first toe.'

The package in reception had been dropped off by a bike messenger. Nobody could remember from which company he had come, or if he'd even displayed the name of his company. Messengers came and went all the time, they all looked the same. He'd been male, he'd been tall and he'd not removed his helmet, merely tossed the package on the counter. The only thing that struck an odd note was that he'd not asked anybody to sign for the parcel.

Jordan looked at the contents without emotion. He'd seen a lot on the force and it took more than a human fingernail removed in its entirety to upset him. Sinclair, however, had gone white, with the feeling that he was about to be sick and embarrass himself. The note that had accompanied the package had been short and to the point: 'Wayne doesn't need his fingernails to play football, his toenails are something else.'

'Tell me again about the phone call,' Jordan said.

'It was Helen Archer who answered it first,' Sinclair said.

Jordan turned to the woman who was staring as if mesmerized at the fingernail.

'They look a lot smaller off than on,' she said finally.

'Most bits of the body do,' the policeman said, from grim experience. 'Tell me, Miss Archer, exactly what the caller said to you.'

Helen made a visible effort to look at Jordan.

'He asked to speak to Mr Sinclair.'

'Did he mention your name?'

She hesitated.

'You know, I'm not sure. He might have said, "Miss Archer can I speak to Mr Sinclair". I just can't be sure. If I answer that phone, then it's almost certain to be somebody who knows me.'

'Why's that?'

She spoke slowly, as if something was beginning to dawn upon her.

'It's a direct outside line. He must have guessed you'd have a trace on the switchboard.'

'We do, but from what you've told us, and assuming he was using a call box, we'd have had no time to get to him.'

Detective Sergeant Davies had been watching Helen Archer closely. He liked the friendly look in her eyes, liked the Rubenesque curves of her body, and most of all liked the idea of a woman who knew her football. Rob Davies had seen off at least a dozen girlfriends in his twenty-seven years, as arrangements had regularly been built around, or sacrificed to, football commitments. In his spare time if he wasn't watching, then he was playing. It was something his boss would never appreciate, but he thought this girl would understand without him having to explain it to her. He tried to switch his mind back to the job in hand. Helen Archer was not going away even if Mickey Wayne was not yet coming back. As he spoke he could not help looking at her, nor could he help noticing that she was blushing.

'Don't you think it odd that they should phone on a direct

line just when a board meeting is taking place. How many people have got this number anyway?'

It was Sinclair's turn to look towards Helen for guidance and Davies guessed that was not an uncommon experience.

'It's hard to say,' the secretary said. 'In theory anybody who has ever worked for the club would know it.' She thought for a moment and then added, 'And anybody who'd been asked to call the chairman, or even asked to call anybody who might be working in this room from time to time.'

'Like who?' Jordan asked, feeling his junior was taking too much of a lead in the discussions.

Helen shook her head impatiently.

'Any number of people. When the auditors come in we let them work in here. It's one of the few rooms with a table big enough to spread out their papers. The same applies to the legal eagles. They've had meetings in here over contracts and the like. It's virtually endless. You might as well say that the decorators would also have given it out to their wives when they were painting last year.'

Jonathan Black had been silent for far too long. Anybody knowing him even slightly would have recognized that as a danger signal. Now he exploded.

'So that's it then. All we need is an accountant with a law degree who's into do-it-yourself and we've got our man.'

'Or woman,' Sinclair said.

'I'm pleased you find it so amusing. These two here,' he gestured in the direction of Jordan and Davies without actually sparing them a glance, 'don't seem to know what day it is. We may just as well have old Ben Porter on the case for all the use they are. Look, what do we do about this down payment? Do we give it to them or do we call their bluff?'

'Hold on, Jonathan,' Kerr said. 'I'm not sure the bank will give you the money.'

'You, Tom? Don't you mean us?' Helen questioned. She felt she'd already burnt her boats as far as the finance director was concerned.

'I don't need an employee to tell me what I mean or don't mean,' he replied angrily.

Phil Reynolds had been invited to join the meeting as soon as it had been decided to call back the police. He'd arrived sweating and limping.

'I'm past getting out of three-piece suits and into track suits. I've just been kicked up in the air by kids young enough to be my sons.'

He'd then watched silently as the directors tore into each other like beasts in the jungle, but now he felt it was time to make some contribution.

'Look, I know I've no money involved, but Mickey's my player in my team. We're not doing the lad any good by arguing amongst ourselves. I'm sure you've all got the good of the club at heart in your own way, you've just got different approaches to showing it.'

He had their interest now and one by one they calmed down, Kerr seating himself, Black perching on the edge of the table, Helen moving away towards the window-ledge already occupied by Rob Davies. Sinclair, too, resumed his place at the head of the table and only the manager and Peter Jordan were left standing.

'Go on, Phil,' Sinclair said, 'we were all getting a little emotional.'

'It's hardly surprising. Some of us here may not like Mickey particularly, but he's still important to us all.' Here he paused and chose Tom Kerr for a special nod. 'For one reason or another.'

'What do *you* suggest, Mr Reynolds?' Jordan asked.

'You're the policeman, you're the man with the experience of all this. I think whatever *you* say is what we should do.'

'I'm flattered,' Jordan replied. 'My feeling is that this is not a bluff. I really believe that if we don't at least make our kidnapper think we're co-operating he may do something rash ...'

'Like cutting off one of our player's toes?' Kerr asked of nobody in particular.

'Just so, Mr Kerr. Now Mr Sinclair tells me that you have some close ties with the club's bankers. Assuming the money was not going to travel very far do you think you can persuade them to make the half a million available?'

Kerr was not satisfied.

'I don't see why we have to provide all the money these thugs are asking for. Can't we make up a package to look as if it's that amount, but just have genuine notes on the outside.'

'Yes, of course you can,' Jordan replied as if he were answering a not very bright child. 'The only thing about that is if the kidnappers get away with the package or even have time to check it and communicate with one of their pals, the odds are that they might panic and you can say goodbye to your Mr Wayne. It's up to you.'

There was a total silence in the room, broken only by the distant sound of a mower being driven over the pitch. Somehow it was that perfectly normal activity within a football ground that now sounded out of place. A man's life was in the balance and another man was cutting the grass.

'So that's the choice, is it? We either gamble with £500,000 or Mickey Wayne's life.' It was Sinclair who spoke, the words coming awkwardly as if delaying them might in some small way also delay the decision.

'It would seem so,' Jordan replied.

Sinclair tapped his pencil on the desk until the point broke. Helen Archer winced. She took a great pride in everything she prepared for board meetings right down to the writing instruments she sharpened herself.

'I suppose this is something we have to put to the vote as well. I propose we approach the bank to make all the money available and then rely on the police to safeguard it,' the chairman said, looking around to see where the support was coming from.

'Seconded,' said Ben Porter who had managed to stay awake for most of the discussion.

'I suppose so,' Jonathan Black added gracelessly.

'I feel I must abstain as I've not yet spoken to the bank,' Kerr said.

'Very well,' Sinclair said with relief, 'over to you I think, Inspector.'

'Good. Assuming you've got the money together by tomorrow one of you will go to the phone booth. If I'm not mistaken...'

'You'd bloody well better not be,' Kerr muttered loudly enough for Jordan to hear him.

'None of us is perfect, Mr Kerr. All we can do is our best. As I was saying, I'm fairly sure the call will be from another box telling the carrier to go to yet another venue. That will give the kidnappers, and we have to assume there's more than one of them, a chance to observe, to make sure the carrier's not being followed. We'll have to make certain that they're satisfied on that count. Somewhere along the line, maybe two or three calls away, there'll be a final instruction to dump the money. That's when we'll move in.'

'And what happens if you lose the money and whoever picks it up? It happens, I know. I've read it in the papers: money swinging from hooks on bridges, motorbikes in fog.' Black spoke as if he had good reason to doubt the efficiency of the British police force.

'We'll have a fail-safe in so far as there'll be a small electronic tag in the bundle. We'll be able to trace it to its final destination.' Jordan leaned against the door, arms folded, daring anybody to argue with his plan.

'Who takes the money?' Kerr asked, seemingly more concerned with the banknotes than the welfare of whoever was going to act as the carrier.

'That's for you to decide,' Jordan answered.

'I don't think it should be a woman,' Davies added almost too hurriedly, and again he saw from the corner of his eye that Helen coloured slightly.

'I agree,' his superior said. 'I'm not saying this is dangerous, but it could be.'

The men in the room looked at each other as if waiting for a volunteer to go over the top behind enemy lines. It was Kerr who spoke first.

'Well, who wants to be a hero? You were the ones who voted for this cockeyed idea.'

Phil Reynolds, again, brought the voice of reason to the table.

'We've got Mark Rossetti on the payroll, why don't we get him to earn his money?'

'That seems like a sensible suggestion,' Sinclair said, with evident relief. He had been just about to assume the responsibility when Reynolds had intervened.

'I'll call him, shall I?' Helen asked and, receiving no objection, she went to make the call. If anything was going to go wrong now it would be Mark Rossetti's fault.

CHAPTER 23

While Mark Rossetti was being appointed to carry half a million pounds into the unknown, he and Patti Delaney were sitting in the lounge of Mickey Wayne's house. The media circus outside seemed to have died down and, apart from a few waifs and strays hoping for the odd photo, the press seemed to have decided that if Wayne was going to surface anywhere it was not going to be at home.

His son Darren, now returned by his exhausted grandparents, played quite happily with large pieces of Lego on a rug in the centre of the room, seemingly unaware of the absence of his father.

'Mickey's hardly ever here anyway. Darren sees more of the window-cleaner than he does of his own father.'

Laura Wayne had a cockney accent that she had made just a small effort to improve and the effect of her efforts made her sound like a character from a class-war TV sit-com. Despite the early hour she had worked hard on her make-up and her jeans looked to have been sewn on to her, whilst the white blouse was topped off by an expensive gold necklace that would have looked more in place with an evening dress. It was she who had asked them over after the session at Patti's flat. There she had given them a list of her husband's enemies within the club, a list that just stopped short of the entire playing staff. Now she seemed willing, even anxious, to talk some more, particularly as with the departure of the main press corps she could sit without the need to have the curtains drawn.

'Do you want some more tea?' she asked. Mark hoped this wasn't just a social invitation. He had enough work to do without having to act as a shoulder for a tearful woman. He shook his head and leaned back in the armchair that looked more comfortable than it felt. He couldn't understand why every player he'd ever known had the burning desire to decorate and furnish his house in the same style, a kind of 'soccer-baroque', as once it had been unkindly described.

'Since we spoke the other day I've been thinking and perhaps I wasn't completely honest with you. I told you how Mickey rubbed all his team-mates up the wrong way, about the fight he had in training with Nicky Collier, the time he called Ray Fowler a cripple because of his gammy leg, the day he reversed into Stuart Macdonald's car just because he thought he'd taken his parking space...'

'Yes.' Mark was willing her to get on with it. The litany of her husband's appalling behaviour had gone on for hours in Patti's flat without giving him any real leads. All he'd discovered was what he'd heard rumoured already, that Wayne's personality was not his strongest point.

'Well, there were other women.'

'How many?' Patti asked gently.

'I don't know. Definitely two.'

'Do you know who they were?' Patti's voice was so quiet and gentle that Mark could hardly hear her.

'No, not exactly. One was married, I think.'

'How do you know that?'

'Just a telephone conversation I once overheard, a snatch really. Mickey would simply stop talking if I was in the room. I tried lifting an extension one night and he gave me a black eye for it; but this time I heard him say that he knew that "he" would be away and could he come over.'

'So Mickey knew this "he", did he?' Mark asked impatiently, receiving an angry look from Patti for his troubles.

'I'm not sure, knew him or of him. I didn't really want to know too much.'

'You said two other women.'

'Yes. I think I spoke to the other one. She rang here and asked to speak to Mickey. He was angry about the call, I suppose angry that she'd tried to contact him at home. I got the worst of it. He put the phone down on her and then threw his supper plate at me. Told me I was a slut who couldn't cook and couldn't be bothered to clean. Told me I wasn't a fit mother because I smoked. He hated women smoking, did Mickey. I tried to stop a couple of times for him, but he didn't even notice or care, so I thought, why should I?'

'This one you spoke to, how did she sound?' Patti asked, determined to recapture the line of questions.

'Young and posh. A bit like you really. Not Mickey's usual type at all.'

She sounded bitter but Mark thought that if Mickey Wayne walked through that door at that very instant she'd welcome him back, lead him upstairs to the bedroom and try and make him believe that she could do for him what no other woman could.

'Then last night I had Lennie Simons round here. He was effing and blinding, almost wanting to search the place. It was like he didn't believe Mickey had gone missing, that he thought he was hiding just to avoid him. He told me all about this Italian woman, said that he reckoned she'd got Mickey to sign for her in bed. I had to threaten to call the police before he'd go. I never did like him. He reckoned he owned my Mickey, that he had more right to him than I did. Are you going to find Mickey for me?' she asked in a little girl's voice. She moved towards her son, and as she held out her arms to him he toddled towards her welcoming embrace. Patti and Mark looked embarrassed. Mark ruffled Darren's hair, thinking of his own daughter who did not know her father.

'Yes, Laura, I'll find Mickey for you,' he said, whilst thinking that she might be better off if he did not.

CHAPTER 24

Rossetti arrived home on his own having left Patti to type up an article about the lives of soccer stars' wives that she'd already been commissioned to write for the *Mail on Sunday* supplement. It had been due for delivery the previous day, but she wanted to make some alterations after their visit to Laura.

'I should be getting a commission from you for all the material I'm supplying,' Mark had said to her.

She'd pecked him on the cheek as she dropped him off.

'Don't you worry, Mark, by the time we've finished with this business I'll have paid you back in spades.'

As he walked into his front room he saw Leopold Schneider had let himself in and made a pot of tea.

'Things must be looking up, Mark. The milk wasn't off and there was a fresh packet of tea-bags and some cubed sugar. Does this mean I get some rent?'

'It does,' Mark said, grinning. He pulled his wallet out of his pocket and gave his landlord two twenty-pound notes.

'Call this a down payment. I've lost count of what I actually owe you.'

Schneider did not put the money away immediately.

'You're sure you can afford this? If there are other things more pressing than me I suppose I can wait a bit.'

'Thanks, Leo, but I think you've waited long enough already. Do you want a biscuit with that tea?'

'Oy, biscuits as well. Now I don't feel so bad about taking your money. Shall I take my own bag of *kiechels* away?'

'No, you leave them. You know I like them. Probably because I've some Italian–Jewish blood way back in my line.'

Schneider took one of his own little cake-biscuits rather than one of Mark's shortbreads and munched contentedly for a moment before saying, 'By the way, there was a call for you. Somebody called David Sinclair. Wants you to call him the minute you get in.'

'But I've been in nearly ten minutes and you hadn't told me.'

Schneider's raven-like eyes creased into a smile.

'I was worried you weren't eating enough. It's the Jewish mother in me.'

Mark was dialling before Schneider had finished his sentence.

'Such devotion to duty,' the old man said, shrugging himself into his heavy coat despite the heat of the day. 'What I'm only missing out on because you won't work for me. I'll be on my way. If I got rent from you maybe it'll be a *mazeldik* day all round.'

Mark waved his thanks to Schneider's back as he made his way down the stairs and waited while Sinclair was found and brought to the phone. When the chairman told him what he wanted him to do he felt all the old familiar butterflies assemble in his stomach. He'd taken on this job because it was his only chance. So far he'd achieved little and what he'd done he'd done with Patti by his side. Although he'd said nothing to her of his fears and self-doubt he now felt terribly isolated. He knew that not everybody at Hertsmere wanted him there, that they were waiting for him to make a major mistake and now he had been given the opportunity to do just that. The rest of the day stretched out before him endlessly. He had planned to talk to the rest of the players, but all he could think of was the following afternoon. He hesitated over telling Patti what he'd been asked to do. If she knew she'd want to be there, probably with a photographer, and that was the last thing he wanted. She'd doubtless see this as a breach of their unwritten agreement, but if this was just a step away from catching the kidnappers then their uneasy alliance would be over in a day or so anyway. The worst she could do was change her mind about doing the feature on him.

At two in the morning he lost the battle against temptation and went downstairs into his office to remove the bottle of whisky he'd secreted in the filing cabinet, placing it as a private joke carefully between 'v' and 'x'. He promised himself that he'd just take enough to get himself to sleep, but by six a.m. the bottle was empty and he was still awake. He'd been told to be at the club by ten to be briefed by the police, but as he looked at his red-eyed, gaunt reflection in the mirror he didn't see how he could possibly make it without another drink. He cleaned his teeth and then tried to test his breath to see if the smell of alcohol could be detected. He thought not and opened a bottle of vodka for his breakfast, mixing it liberally with tomato juice, ice-cold from the fridge.

He began to feel better, felt he had made the right decision. Just a little bit of courage from the bottle and he could do anything. As he left the club and his police briefing he was even hoping that he would lose the police backing and become the hero of the hour on his own. Yet, as he made his way towards the Hertsmere shopping centre, the drink was beginning to leave him and he felt cold and tired. In case he'd have to drive after the first message the club had lent him a car and he just hoped that Detective Sergeant Davies, who'd given him his instructions, didn't try to breathalyse him when he got back. The man had been a fan, although he could have done without the endless questions about a career that was long dead.

'Don't try any heroics,' were the words that lingered in his mind. He certainly did not feel heroic. Lured by the morning sunshine, and comforted by the haze of drink, he had come out wearing only a T-shirt and thin cotton trousers, not even bothering with socks before he pulled on his well-worn, scuffed trainers. Now he felt cold as, with typical English Spring perversity, the sun had turned to cloud followed closely by a chilly drizzle. He had shopped at Tesco often enough himself, but today he had nothing in common with the men and women who piled out of the store with their carrier bags spilling over with food. As the rain got heavier, umbrellas began to sprout like so many mushrooms. Mark had no such protection. He carried the parcel that Rob Davies had given him under his thin shirt to keep it dry, wondering if anybody could conceivably guess at what was contained therein. With his luck he'd probably get mugged; he could not help but imagine the look of incredulity on the face of any attacker who got away with half a million pounds, a look that would soon disappear as the police descended having followed the electronic bug.

By the time he'd got to the phone box the packet felt as if it was swelling in size under his shirt. He'd found it hard to believe that £500,000 could be reduced to such a small size, ten thousand fifty-pound notes, more than he'd ever see again in his lifetime. If he'd been allowed to stay in the game then he could have earned that sort of money and more; but this was no time to dwell on his own bitterness. Whatever he could do, he couldn't bring back his lost youth, the edge of pace, the spring in his step. The best that he could hope for was that one day, with a slice of luck, he could prove his innocence.

He glanced at his watch. Five minutes before two. The phone box was already occupied by a fairly bulky woman who had left her pram outside with a large black umbrella hooked into the spokes of the wheels. He wondered what would happen if the woman stayed on the phone for any length of time. Presumably his contact would keep on trying. If the police were right then he had someone watching him even now, and if they were watching him then they were able to report that the box was occupied. Then it all happened, so quickly that when he tried to piece it together later he could not even remember the order of events. The door of the phone box opened, the woman seemed to tumble out, reached into the pram and then let the canister of gas off in his face, whilst almost in the same movement ripping the bundle from his hand. He tried desperately to grab her, but he was operating blindly, his eyes burning with pain. He got one hand on her shoulder and almost managed to swing her round, thinking all the time that if he could just hold on for a few seconds the police would be across the road and it would be over. He'd forgotten she still had the canister, and she swung it at him and he fell to the floor. She took off with the pram, pushing it rapidly between the streams of shoppers, disappearing from view in a matter of seconds before the first of the plain-clothes men in the precinct had even realized what was happening. Later, Mark seemed to recall there being something odd about her face, as if it were not a face at all but a mask, and when the police questioned him he could not be sure that his attacker had even really been a woman. It wasn't that alone that concerned the police. They had found the pram in amongst the supermarket trolleys just a few moments later; but what they also found was what had led them there, the outer packaging of the bundle of money and the tiny electronic device that had been hidden amongst the notes.

It was as if the assailant had known exactly what to look for, concluded Detective Inspector Peter Jordan, which meant that somebody who had been in the meeting with him the day before had told him ... or her. As he looked down at Mark Rossetti having treatment to his eyes in the local hospital it was either that or Mr Rossetti had himself told him. Mark groaned. He had a terrible hangover in the middle of the afternoon not assisted by the swelling on his forehead, he could see nothing out of his left eye, whilst his right one would not stop watering. In the space of a few short minutes he had lost half a million pounds that did not belong to him and had turned himself from an investigator into a suspect.

CHAPTER 25

By Saturday afternoon David Sinclair was regretting his decision ever to get involved with a football club. He'd been happy as a fan, but that had not been good enough for him. He had wanted to be at the centre of things and now he was at the epicentre of a tornado. They had heard no more from Wayne's kidnappers and whoever had been in the phone box had vanished without a trace. In his darker moments it occurred to him that perhaps half a million had been enough, that Wayne was dead, his body dumped somewhere and there would be no further contact.

Tom Kerr had blamed him entirely for the loss of the money, and none of his efforts to place at least some of the responsibility at the door of the police, whose operation had been such a miserable failure, met with any success whatsoever.

'You were the one who proposed we make the money available. I had the devil's own job to get the cash out of the bank, even to the point of saying I was in favour of it. I know my responsibility is to support a board decision and this is my reward. And as for trusting that drunk to handle the money, well I've nothing to say. One of the policemen at the scene told me he could smell the alcohol on him. Somebody's head will roll for this, I promise you.'

Sinclair did not know what to do about Rossetti. He couldn't see what anybody could have done about the assault and he'd done all he could and more. He was lucky not to have been permanently blinded. It had been the one thing they had not been expecting, and he did not think that Jordan was serious when he talked about the ex-player being a suspect. They were all suspects, all of them who had been parties to the plan, and that depressed him more than anything else. No, that was not quite true. What had depressed him more than anything was the ultimatum he had received this morning from Freddie Scott's wife, Vera.

'I've had a firm offer for Freddie's shares, six hundred thousand. If you can get near to that, David, they're yours, if not, then come next Thursday, I'm selling.'

He did not even need to ask her who the other purchaser was, he knew the answer would be Chris Handsel. He'd already heard from Helen that she'd received applications to register some thirty other transfers in favour of Handsel within the last week. He'd been working his way through the list of shareholders, picking out likely widows with no interest in football, pensioners to whom his generous offer for an otherwise worthless piece of paper would be irresistible.

Sinclair had asked Helen rather than Richard Lee if there was anything he could do about it.

'You could try refusing to register the transfers, but while he's taking you to court all he'd need to do is get the voting proxies from his potential vendors. If he puts those together with Freddie's shares then he's in a position to call an Extraordinary General Meeting and put it to the shareholders and the waiting world that you're not fit to run this club and ought to resign in favour of someone who is.'

It had not been a comforting analysis of his situation.

At home he tried to put a brave face on things whenever Holly visited. She seemed to be spending more time than ever with him in a silent gesture of support and, although he was grateful, he could see it was getting to her as well. Her social life appeared to be non-existent and he couldn't help thinking it was unnatural for an attractive girl of her age to have so few friends of either sex. Here at the club on match day he tried to joke her out of it, but she appeared even more upset as the cameramen besieged her every time she moved.

'It's only because you're prettier than me,' her father said, but she raised no more of a smile for him than she had done for the photographers.

Handsel had not bothered to speak to him. He had a seat in the directors' box again, only this time the demonstration in his favour seemed more organized, a hundred times more raucous, the placards more hurtful. 'Sinclair lost Wayne, Handsel will find him.' All this was accompanied by singing that would have not been out of place at an Eistedffod.

> Who lost Mickey Wayne?
> Who lost Mickey Wayne?
> You fat bastard, you fat bastard,
> You lost Mickey Wayne.
> Who'll get him back again?
> Who'll get him back again?

Chris Handsel, Chris Handsel,
He'll get him back again.

It wasn't poetry, but it had a hypnotic quality all of its own.

'I'm not fat,' he said to Holly, but raised only the glimmer of a smile. Today there was another visitor to the directors' box in the shape of Claudio Barlucci. He had not been shy in speaking to the press before the match. Many of the Italian reporters had travelled with him, drawn by the melodrama that was being enacted off the pitch. It had all the qualities of a story that they would normally have needed to invent in accordance with the grand tradition of Italian journalism.

Barlucci had turned to his countrymen from the steps to the main entrance of the stadium.

'Wayne could not come to Cinquante, so Cinquante has come to Wayne. If Hertsmere cannot deliver, then Cinquante will collect and I am merely the humble errand boy.'

From an open window, Helen Archer listened to the broken-English version and said to Sinclair:

'All he needs is a toga and he could play Julius Caesar.'

'As long as I get to play Brutus I'm not too bothered. He's all I need today, an excitable Roman who seems to think we've deliberately wafted Wayne away to push up the price,' Sinclair replied.

'What does he hope to gain by coming here today?' Helen asked.

'Some credibility with his fans, I would think. He's dug himself a hole by promising them Wayne and he has to show them he's doing something to dig himself out of it.'

Barlucci embraced Sinclair as if he was a long-lost brother, ensuring that several paparazzi photographed the hug for posterity.

'We must talk later, but for now we enjoy the match.'

Barlucci may well have enjoyed it, but for Sinclair it was purgatory. Under normal circumstances Stockton Athletic would not have been the most awesome of opponents. They were almost certainly safe from relegation, a million miles from any chance of qualifying for Europe and their two Cup trails had ended after their first matches. If any team was marking time until the end of the season it was Stockton and, as one journalist unkindly put it in the *Independent*, their players were just as likely to come on to the pitch in swimming trunks and sunglasses as their red and white Stockton strip.

It was not that Stockton raised their game or even played particularly well. From the third minute it was clear that Hertsmere were on a suicide mission. Stuart Macdonald, of all people, back-passed to Greg Sergovich only to see a previously unseen Stockton forward swoop on to the ball and waltz past the Slav keeper to tap the ball into the back of the net. Ten minutes later the eighteen-year-old Tommy Wallace, playing in place of Wayne, finally got past the Stockton right back and was flattened for his troubles about halfway into the Stockton half. The referee was already on his way over to book the defender when Wallace got to his feet and felled the opponent with a perfect right hook to the jaw. Within seconds there were nineteen players milling around the incident – the only exceptions being the two keepers and the Stockton man who still lay unconscious on the turf. When he finally got to his feet he was substituted to the accompaniment of a yellow card and a severe dose of concussion. By then Wallace was back in the dressing-room and Hertsmere were not only reduced to ten men, but also 2–0 down, Stockton having scored with a speculative twenty-five yard shot that caught Sergovich prowling around the penalty spot and unusually oblivious to any danger. By half-time Pat Devine had mowed down the Stockton striker in the Hertsmere penalty area and in trying unsuccessfully to save the resultant kick, Sergovich collided with the post and dislocated the little finger of his left hand. Bobby Maxwell, the reserve keeper, hadn't played a first-team match for nearly two seasons and it showed when, just after the interval, he went up for a corner, tried to punch it away and succeeded only in diverting the ball into the top right-hand corner of his own net.

The fans had seen enough. The first dozen or so who ran on to the pitch attracted the attention of the stewards, but they and the police were helpless to stop the flood-tide of bodies which followed. The referee promptly abandoned the field to the army of fans, whilst the small group of visiting Stockton supporters sat down on the terraces to enjoy the Spring sunshine and the internecine warfare which was considerably more entertaining than anything they had seen from the Hertsmere team during the game. There were about five thousand on the pitch within ten minutes, gathered beneath David Sinclair's seat, their fingers pointing at him in a united gesture of hatred, the chant of 'Sinclair Out' echoing around the stadium like a chant from a Nazi rally. Helen Archer made an appeal over the loudspeaker, thinking that perhaps they might respect a woman, but all she received for her pains was a response of, 'Sinclair's whore'.

Tom Kerr looked down at the scene beneath him in disgust.

'And this is the lot you want to build a new stadium for? We'd be better off spending the money on cages.'

Chris Handsel ambled across to the chairman, looking suitably upset in case anybody might be on hand to capture the encounter on film.

'Look, Sinclair, I know you don't like me, but we've got to get this game underway again. We're going to be in enough trouble with the League over this anyway when the referee puts in his report. We're into damage containment.'

'So what do you suggest?' Sinclair could never have anticipated himself asking that particular question of Handsel, but he knew he had no choice.

'You let me go on the public-address system and talk to them.'

'Are you crazy? That's almost an admission that I've given you control of the club,' Sinclair replied in horror.

'Suit yourself. I reckon that if this match doesn't get finished and there's a real clamp-down you could even find yourself kicked out of the Cup before the Thamesmead match next week. After Millwall they're looking to make an example of somebody. I don't think we'll be seeing any more football today, so I'm off. If I leave now I'll be home to hear a report of this mess on *Grandstand*.' He turned to leave and Sinclair caught him by the arm in a gesture of self-preservative weakness for which he despised himself.

'If I let you speak to the crowd, what will you say?'

'I'll just tell them to go back to their places and let's get on with the game. That's all. Don't worry, I'm not going to make a political speech. I don't need to, do I?'

'I'll have to ask the referee's permission. You're not a director or officer of the club.'

'So ask him. If you don't ask then you don't get, as my dad always used to say.'

'I'll bet he did,' Sinclair thought furiously to himself as he made his way down to the match officials' room. He'd been outmanoeuvred and he hated the feeling.

The referee was only too pleased to allow Handsel to try and bring some order to things.

'It's about time somebody at this club did something positive.'

Sinclair could not bring himself to tell Handsel that he'd been given the green light and sent Helen with the message and the authority to take his rival to the public-address room. However, he could not help but hear what Handsel had to say and there was no way that he could avoid seeing the effect of his words. He was beginning to realize just how a party leader felt on the night of a general election defeat.

Handsel was nothing if not a showman. He'd got the resident disc-jockey to play Queen's 'We are the Champions' and having got the attention of the crowd he simply said, 'Chris Handsel here. When I was a player we never needed to stop a match. You've got a semi-final next week and a final in May when you've won that.' There were cheers at this. 'I understand your frustration. Everybody's doing all they can to get Mickey Wayne back. The best way you can help this great club of ours is to get the hell off the pitch, let the game restart and cheer the bollocks off our boys to help them get four goals back this afternoon. As for me, I'm going to do just that. I'll see you all soon.'

The crowd lifted their arms again, this time not in a gesture of abuse, but one of adulation. With cries of, 'Handsel for Chairman,' and 'One Chrissy Handsel, there's only one Chrissy Handsel,' they left the field like an army that had achieved its victory and could afford to be magnanimous.

Within five minutes the game was under way again, and almost from the restart Nicky Collier bulldozed his way through to score from five yards. The crowd cheered as if he'd just displayed the virtuoso talents of a George Best in converting the goal of the season.

Handsel and Collier, heroes to the crowd. If only they knew, Sinclair thought, if only they knew.

CHAPTER 26

Mark Rossetti had watched the game from the stands in an agony of expectation. His eyes were still not completely back to normal and he wore a pair of dark glasses that not only kept out the light but also had so far kept him safe from recognition. He had an appointment with David Sinclair immediately after the match and he did not think it was going to be about his bonus. The club had not only lost their star player, but they had also now lost half a million pounds, which sum of money had last been entrusted to the care of one Mark Rossetti.

He had already been the target of Patti Delaney's wrath.

'You got what you deserved. We had a deal and you broke it. If I'd been there who knows what might have happened. I might have had a photographer in just the right position to get this "woman" on camera.'

He'd tried to argue his corner with her, but it had been hopeless.

'Patti, the police were involved. They took photos, but it's done them no good. She, or he, was wearing a mask. I couldn't just announce what was happening to all and sundry.'

It wasn't the most tactful thing he could have said.

'Oh, so I'm all and sundry am I? I heard you couldn't keep sober when I was away from you for five minutes. And you want me to help you clear your name? Well, if you want that, then why go dipping it back into the shit every time I turn my back on you.'

He'd invited her to come to the match with him, and then for a meal after, but she'd declined both offers.

'I've still got my press pass, remember, and as for a meal I'm not sure you could keep off the drink long enough to be able to pick up the tab. I'm not ready to act as your unpaid driver.'

He'd left it at that. His experience with women told him that she would decide when the time was right to talk to him again.

The game had finished 5–2 to Stockton. He went through to the administrative block sensing the feeling of despair amongst the homeward-bound supporters, picking up fragments of their conversations as he ducked and dived against the flow of the human traffic.

'Fucking useless. If we don't get Wayne back for next week we'll be better off not turning up against Thamesmead.'

'I reckon they ought to dope-test that cunt of a keeper. No wonder he hasn't played for all that time.'

'Best performance of the afternoon was from good old Chris. The sooner we get that wanker Sinclair out and Handsel in, the sooner we'll start winning something.'

The mood of gloom and despair travelled with Mark into the offices, even if here it was reflected in a less obscene form. The doorman nodded him through with a half-smile this time.

'Reckon on that display you could get back into the side,' he said, and Helen Archer echoed the sentiment when she asked him if the club still held his registration.

'Good luck,' she added as he knocked on the chairman's door. He could hear raised voices and thinking that they had probably not heard him he pushed the door gently open to attract some attention. He had never seen Claudio Barlucci before and from the first impression the man seemed to fill the room not merely with his body, but also his voice. His English may have been stumbling, his accent atrocious, but there was no doubting the message he was giving David Sinclair.

'The player, he is mine. When he goes you should tell me. We would know what thing to do.'

Sinclair was on the point of desperation.

'Signor Barlucci,' he spoke slowly, as if the speech he was making was familiar, which it doubtless was as this was about the fifth time he had said the same thing to the Italian, 'the player was not yours. We had not even agreed the fee...'

Not for the first time in the conversation he was not allowed to finish the sentence.

'We agree. I say seven million. It is more than the player is worth. You want eight, I give you eight. It is the same to me...'

'Signor, please listen to me. There are some players who do not have a price.'

'We speak to player's agent. She agrees the money. All is settled. He is our player, I have told my people, he is our player.'

'That doesn't make him yours,' Sinclair said, realizing

the stupidity and childishness of the argument, but forced to bring it to a conclusion despite himself. He looked up, suddenly aware of the presence of Rossetti.

'Mark, come on in. You've arrived at just the right moment. Can you please explain to Signor Barlucci in his own language that we had not agreed to sell him Mickey Wayne, that Wayne is under contract to us, that we have not given him or anybody else permission to talk to the player and, that while he is always welcome at our ground as a visitor, we would prefer it if he did not use our front steps for the purposes of a press conference.'

It had been a while since Mark had spoken Italian, but it had been the language of his childhood and as soon as he spoke the first words it all came flooding back. He was in Sinclair's office, yet at the same time he was in his father's cafe, his grandmother still alive, the two of them engaged in good-natured banter, their voices warm and loud, filled with the sunshine of Palermo where his father and generations of Rossetti's before him had been born. He had gone back only once after his father's death, to try and find himself as the doctor had advised in the midst of the depression that followed his suspension. He remembered kneeling in the beautiful old church at the *Martorana*, the Church of Santa Maria dell'Ammiraglio, praying for his own private miracle which had still not come. The priest had touched him gently at the nape of the neck,

'Are you troubled, my son?'

And he had fled, just as he always fled when anybody got too close.

He had not realized how regionalized was his accent, but Barlucci identified it immediately, listening more intently to Rossetti's Italian than he had to Sinclair's English, and whilst he did not agree he at least did not argue. Finally he spoke rapidly in Italian, then shook Sinclair's hand, kissed Rossetti on both cheeks and was gone.

'Thank goodness you got rid of him, he was all I needed today. What did he say at the end?'

'That he will not leave without Wayne, dead or alive. I think he's an honourable man and he's made some kind of pledge to the fans which he's determined to keep.'

'It doesn't sound too honourable to me to announce you've signed another team's player, when you've hardly opened negotiations.'

'Yes, well, he's Italian. They do things differently there. You wanted to see me, David, and I don't think it was just to use me as an interpreter.' He paused. 'I'm really sorry about Thursday, if anybody wanted it to go right it was me.'

'Hey, come on. Nobody could have expected a mother with a pram to pack a knock-out punch.'

'Yeah, but I'd been drinking. It didn't help. I've been on the wagon for years and now twice in a week or so I've fallen off. It won't happen again, I promise.'

'Most of my board don't want to give you a chance to let it happen again.'

'And you?' There was a pleading note in his voice that Sinclair could not fail to miss.

'I don't think you've been given a fair crack of the whip, but I'm afraid as from today you're off the club payroll.'

'I see.' Mark felt tears pricking his still-sore eyes.

'I don't think you do,' Sinclair said, 'you're off the club payroll, but you're still on mine. Just keep a low profile. As far as the rest of the board is concerned there are half a million reasons why you shouldn't come anywhere near the ground. Helen Archer knows what I'm doing, so if you can't get hold of me, speak to her.'

'Thanks,' Mark said in a tone that suggested there was much more he wanted to say.

'You're welcome. Where do we go from here?'

'I'd like to take a look around the stadium now that everybody's gone. I thought I'd take a look through Wayne's locker, just to try and find out a bit more about him.'

'I'm not sure how much you'll find down there. The police have had a look already.'

'Did they take anything away with them?'

'Not that I know of.' He went to a drawer and pulled out a bunch of keys. 'That small one's a master key for all the lockers, just don't tell anybody. We had it made when there was a spate of petty theft. One of the apprentices with sticky fingers, but we found most of the stuff in his locker. Do you know your way?'

'Yes, I know my way,' Rossetti replied sadly.

He walked alone through the virtually empty corridors of the stadium. It had so many ghosts, not just for him. Every match created its own memories, the great goal, the miss, the own goal, the ghastly errors that had lost a match which would forever linger to haunt the guilty men. The players' changing room had already been tidied up and cleaned, yet there was still the smell of sweat and deodorants, the invisible debris of the match.

Each player had his name on his locker, slid through two narrow metal bars, easily removable whenever a footballer moved on in his nomadic existence. Wayne's was at the end of the row and sometime in the week, presumably before the news of his kidnapping had broken, somebody had chalked on it, 'Gone Fishing,' which somebody more realistically had altered to 'Gone Screwing,' and then finally and definitively 'Gone to Italy'.

The key fitted easily in the lock. He didn't know what he expected to find that the police had not. Peter Jordan had not seemed the sort of man to overlook anything. There were the usual pin-ups Sellotaped to the inside of the door, perhaps a little more explicit than they'd been in his day. Overgrown schoolkids, that's all they were, Mark thought, then and now. The locker was not exactly overflowing with clues. A pair of shinguards, a dirty T-shirt, one sock, an expensive aftershave, a football magazine with a picture of Wayne on the front cover and a teddy bear wearing a Hertsmere shirt, a lucky mascot that had ceased to work as far as the player was concerned. He picked up the bear.

'If only you could talk,' he said. He felt an overwhelming sense of frustration. He had never met Wayne, yet he hated him. He'd had the opportunities that had been denied to Mark, yet he had only abused them. Nobody he had met had had a good word to say about him as a man, and nobody should have the right to exist only as a sporting hero. He threw the bear to the ground in anger, venting his temper on the innocent toy. The bear bounced off the tiled floor and with what he first took to be a howl of protest quite literally lost its head. That was all he needed, for Wayne to come back and find his mascot had been vandalized. He picked up the bear's torso and tried to screw the head back on. There were little grooves in the neck, like a bottle-top, but the head refused to turn. He tried again and then saw there was some paper in the way. He pulled at the corner and the crumpled paper came out easily, not one sheet but two. Now the head fitted on perfectly. He examined the animal and saw no apparent sign of damage. He replaced everything in the locker just as he had found it and closed the door. He looked for somewhere to throw away the papers and then he saw they were not just stuffing, they were hand-written letters. They were two letters written to Mickey Wayne and, as he read them, he could not decide if they were a testament to the player's ego or a key to his disappearance.

CHAPTER 27

As he stepped off the plane at Rome's Leonardo da Vinci airport on Sunday evening, Mark wondered just what he was doing there. It had all happened so quickly and there seemed no logic about looking for a missing English footballer in an Italian city; but logic had very little to do with his life nowadays. Patti Delaney was a couple of paces ahead of him and her presence was illogical too.

He tried to gather his thoughts, to take stock of the situation. He should have followed up on the two letters he had found, but he was a one-man band and he could not play in two places at once. As he had left the ground the day before to make his way home by public transport a limousine had drawn up beside him, chauffeur at the wheel, one smoked-glass window rolled halfway down to allow its passenger to speak to him.

'Signor Rossetti, I wonder if you can spare me a few moments.'

Mark was taken by surprise that someone should speak to him in Italian and it took him a few moments to realize that the request came from Claudio Barlucci.

'I'm sorry. I'm very tired. It's been one hell of a week,

and I just want to get home and put my feet up.' He replied in Italian, amazed that he had retained so much fluency in the language. He began to walk again, the car moving slowly alongside him as Barlucci persisted.

'I think it will be worth your while to speak to me. I see you have no transport. Give me five minutes of your time and I will give you a lift home in return.'

Even as he spoke it had begun to rain. Mark had no coat and the prospect of a soaking on his way to the station and a journey on a train filled with unhappy Hertsmere supporters, who would by now have had some time to drown their sorrows, encouraged him to climb into the back of the car.

Barlucci had spread his vast frame over the back seat and, despite the size of the vehicle, Mark still had some difficulty squeezing his buttocks into the space left for him. Barlucci pressed a button and the glass dividing him from the driver slid silently across.

'You would like a drink?' the Italian asked.

'Just some water.'

'Ah, yes, I have heard of your problems.'

'You have?' Mark could not help showing his surprise.

'Of course, you were highly spoken of in Italy ten years ago, the young man in England setting the lower divisions alight. I remember one article in *Corriere Dello Sport*, suggesting you might one day play for Italy. And then, the great tragedy and more articles. With a name like Rossetti you could expect nothing less.'

Mark recalled the interview with the Italian journalist, the young man who had spoken full of hope and promise, the future bright and clean.

He made to tap on the driver's window, but Barlucci gently pulled him back into his seat.

'It is no problem. He knows where to take you.'

'You seem to know a lot about me.'

Barlucci shrugged.

'I just ask the right questions.'

The traffic began to clear as they eased away from the vicinity of the ground, leaving behind them the greasy smell of hamburgers and defeat.

'So what do you want of me? I'm a bit old to sign for Cinquante now.'

Barlucci lit up a cigar and blew out smoke into the air-conditioned interior. Mark coughed, but Barlucci gave no apology.

'Not only old, but injured too, I think.'

'What is this? Are you looking to write my biography?'

Barlucci laughed, a huge roar that seemed to start in his shoes and rock his body all the way up to the top of his head.

'At the moment you have a cross between a tragedy and a farce. Let us say I want to give your story a happy ending. We have a mutual interest. You want to find Mickey Wayne for money and your reputation. I want to find him merely for my reputation and for that I will pay money. I believe you are off the Hertsmere payroll after the unfortunate incident with their money. I want you to come on to mine. If you find Wayne for me and he then signs for Cinquante I will pay you one hundred thousand pounds.'

Mark hesitated. He might not officially be working for the club, but he was still working for the chairman. How much had Sinclair told Barlucci about their arrangement? His question was answered immediately.

'It does not matter to me that you may still get something from Signor Sinclair; but I think you need a better incentive. Also I believe you need to refocus on the problem.'

'Refocus?' Mark asked.

'Indeed. Michael Wayne may have no enemies in Italy, but I have made some over the years. Signor Versace would be pleased to see me as the English put it, with noodles on my face.'

'It's egg. Egg on your face,' Mark said, with a smile. He was beginning to like this man.

'It may be. With the English who can tell? I would like you to come to Italy for a day or so. Make yourself active there. Be sure that Versace knows you are sniffing around. Forget you are Italian. Be the British bulldog. Perhaps you will dig up a bone.'

And so he had accepted. He had decided to tell Sinclair what he was doing. If he was to serve two masters then neither should be kept in ignorance. He refrained from telling him about the two letters as yet. He needed time to think about them, to decide whether or not he should simply hand them over to the good Detective Inspector Jordan and leave him to get on with the job that he was doubtless more qualified to do than he was himself. However, he had offered the letters to Patti as a peace offering and found himself relieved when she not only accepted but also decided to accompany him to Rome.

'You're not to be trusted on your own,' she said not

unkindly, 'last time I turned my back you were mugged for half a million quid by a mother with a pram.'

'It could have been worse. It might have been the baby.'

They'd both laughed and it was as if the argument had somehow sealed a contract that until then had merely been the subject of negotiation.

There had been another reason for her willingness to go to Rome which she did not mention until they were sitting in the restaurant of the Hotel Hassler with its panoramic views of the city at night. Even then, before she told him she looked around to ensure nobody was listening and, although the tables on either side of them were empty, she still spoke in barely a whisper.

'I know you think I'm a liability who's just blackmailed you into letting me come along for the ride, but I've been doing a little digging around the subject myself.'

'And?' He helped himself to some mozzarella cheese and a slice of Parma ham.

'And, as I told you, I have access to information that could be useful. I ran a few checks on some of the leading characters in our plot. It's quite amazing how boring people connected with football can be.'

She yawned in his face to make her point, but by now Mark was anxious to hear more and ignored the joke. She poured herself another glass of white wine without giving the waiter a chance to earn his tip.

'You're on to something, Patti. I don't know you that well, but I can see that little reporter's nose of yours twitching.'

She took a sip of her drink and, tantalizingly, paused again to light up a cigarette. He could see she was enjoying keeping him in suspense and he guessed he probably deserved it.

'It may be nothing. Probably whoever's got Wayne have nothing to do with the club. For all we know they may only be a couple of chancers who saw the way to making a quick buck.'

'But you don't think so?'

'No. Do you?'

'No.'

'So, my research. The chairman, David Sinclair, he's under a lot of pressure. He's about to lose control if Freddie Scott sells his shares elsewhere. He hasn't got the money to buy and he's very stretched financially in his own business. The property market's not what it once was and he's got too much money in the club for him to bow out gracefully.'

'You're not suggesting Sinclair arranged this kidnap himself. He doesn't just live for Hertsmere, I think he'd die for it. The man's a fan.'

'I'm not suggesting anything. I'm just putting everything I've got on the table. Just like I'm sure you're going to do from now on in.'

'Look, I've said I'm sorry about the ransom drop. What else do you want me to do?'

'Wear a hair shirt and be whipped through the streets of the Vatican, but the apology will do for now. That and another bottle of wine. I seem to have finished this one. And don't say I drink too much. I'm a journalist.'

He signalled the waiter over, who seeing his glass unused and the bottle empty looked at Patti with a certain admiration replacing the initial lust that as an Italian he had shown as a matter of course. Mark could understand his emotion. It was far warmer in Rome than in London and Patti had acknowledged that by wearing a short-sleeved pale blue cotton top that was little more than a vest, and through which her prominent nipples made a positive announcement that they were free of restraint. The dark blue cotton skirt gave a first impression of modesty as it swirled as she moved, but when it caught the light it was translucent and showed that at least she was wearing panties, even if they were tiny and white.

'What are you looking at?' Patti asked.

'Him looking at you.'

'He's Italian. I'd have to be the Elephant Woman before he wouldn't try to chat me up. It's a matter of national pride.'

'You were telling me about Sinclair.'

'I've told you all I know of interest about him. Then there's your old friend Chris Handsel.'

'I thought he was my friend once.'

'To be perfectly honest I think you're better off with him as an enemy than a friend. There's a long history of things happening to friends of that family which are not entirely pleasant. He takes after his father in that he's a very determined man and a very bad loser.'

'He was like that when he was a player.'

'It seems he gets upset if he doesn't get what he wants and what he wants right now is Hertsmere United.'

'Why should he be that keen? I can't remember him having anything good to say about the place when I knew him. He was one of life's great moaners.'

'That was puzzling me too, and then I found out something else about Handsel. I'm not sure how it fits in, or even if it has a place in the Mickey Wayne jigsaw, but at least one of Handsel's companies banks with Banca di Fratelli.'

'So what? They have to bank somewhere.'

Patti sliced herself a large chunk of cheese, speared an olive on the same knife, then hesitated with the utensil in mid-air.

'Of course they do. It just strikes me as a little more than a coincidence that Banca di Fratelli and Roma Ulisse Football Club both have the same owner. Paolo Versace.' Only when she had seen the effect of this information on Mark Rossetti did the food complete its journey into her mouth.

CHAPTER 28

By Monday morning David Sinclair felt tempted to surrender. If whoever had taken Mickey Wayne wanted him that badly then they could keep him, along with the half a million pounds. And if his shares meant that much to Chris Handsel, then he could have those too. A plague on all their houses. He had got to the stage where he simply did not bother to read the newspapers. Handsel seemed to have most of the tabloids in his pocket and whatever he might say himself was twisted and turned in the hands of journalists until it bore but the merest resemblance to the truth.

It was the visit of his solicitor Richard Lee that changed his mind. Lee's attitude had been giving him more and more cause for concern. He'd thought he'd known the man. He'd used him as his lawyer from the very start. They'd met as young men on a supporters' club coach travelling away to Yeovil in the Cup. Sinclair had been about to buy his first property and Lee had just completed his articles. He was hungry for work and Sinclair was hungry for success; and they both had an appetite for football and Hertsmere United that knew no bounds.

Throughout his business life Sinclair had used no other

lawyer and had seen Lee's clientele grow and grow until he was no longer his biggest client. Sometimes he'd complain to Lee that his work was being delegated to a junior member of staff, that in some way Lee had outgrown him, but his old friend would always shrug the complaint off with a joke.

'Whatever happens you'll always be my oldest client.'

'I will be as long as I keep on instructing you,' Sinclair had replied.

'Who else would have you? No other lawyer would spend half a meeting talking football to you.'

And no other lawyer would charge for the privilege, Sinclair thought, but he said nothing.

Richard Lee had been at the ground by ten in the morning, and had breezed past Denise into his office without any prior warning. Sinclair was at his desk, just staring into space, his mind running riot over a hundred possibilities. He felt a mild annoyance that Lee had arrived without an appointment. If he had done the same to him he would have been greeted by his secretary with his diary ready to send him away with a flea in his ear and a meeting scheduled for a few days on.

'Morning, David. Any news?'

'Nothing. It's as if Mickey and the money have been beamed up to another dimension.'

'If we don't get him back by Saturday we've got no chance against Thamesmead. I take it you've seen the papers. They're not exactly kind about our performance on Saturday.'

'I've stopped reading them. They weren't exactly kind about anything. What do you think it takes to become a journalist? I remember when Holly was young once we came back by train from some match to King's Cross. Some cub reporter from the *Sun* was with us and Holly saw a whole line of hookers outside the station. She asked me what the ladies were doing and I said they were waiting for their husbands. That wasn't good enough for our lad from the *Sun*. Oh no, you've got to be honest with your children, tell it like it is, mate. They're prostitutes, he says to Holly. I'm not sure she even knew what a prostitute was, but she looks again and asks me what happens when a prostitute has a baby. That's easy, I said, that's how you get journalists. I was only joking at the time, but now I'm not so sure.'

Lee nodded as if he understood.

'Any chance of a coffee?'

'Look, Richard, I'm a bit busy this morning. Unless it's urgent, do you think I could drop by your office later in the day? I've a few things to discuss about the Ipswich development anyway.'

'I don't think this will wait, David.'

Sinclair sighed resignedly. Why was it that nothing anybody had to say to him could ever wait? He opened the door and asked Denise to bring them a couple of coffees. Lee seemed unwilling to start until he had the drink in his hand and the door had closed behind Sinclair's secretary.

'It's Freddie. I spoke to his wife this morning.'

'Why did Vera call you and not me?' Sinclair asked, already certain he was not going to like the answer.

'It was on a legal point. Freddie's very bad, you know.'

'I know, Richard. I'm not a fool. Why do you think he gave me his proxy? He knew he wouldn't be back again.'

'I think you can forget about that. Freddie's given Vera a power of attorney. She's sold the shares, David. She's sold them to Handsel.'

'I see.' Sinclair felt the same sinking sensation in his stomach that he'd experienced the day his mother had come to his school to tell him his father had been killed in a car crash. There was no kind way of breaking bad news.

'Last week she said she'd give me a bit of time to find the money to buy them.'

'That was last week, David. A week's a long time in football. It's even longer when you've only a matter of weeks to live.'

'Like Freddie?'

'Like Freddie,' Lee responded. 'And even so could you have got the money together?'

'You know how the property business is at the moment.'

'So the answer has to be no. Call it a day, David. You've fought a good fight. Why do you need all this aggravation? Call up Handsel. If you don't want to do it yourself, I'll talk to him and try and get you the best possible deal. That way you wash your hands of it all. I'm sure we can swing a deal so that you have a permanent seat in the directors' box. You can go back to being a supporter again. It'll stop being a business and start being enjoyable.'

Sinclair drained the last dregs of his coffee.

'So that's your advice is it? As my lawyer?'

'Not just as your lawyer, it's my advice as your friend.'

Sinclair bit his lip and nodded as if he had taken it all in.

'Well, thanks, Richard, for the advice. You're not charging me for it, are you?'

'Hey, come on. I'm pleased to see you've not lost your sense of humour.'

'No, I've still got that all right. I'll let you know shall I?'

'Sure, sure. I just want the best for you and Holly. You shouldn't have to take all that crap they're throwing at you.'

Again Sinclair nodded. At least Lee was right in that respect. Holly was acting more and more strangely, withdrawing into herself just as she had done in her last year at school when the pressure of exams became too great. The headmistress had advised he take her to a psychiatrist then, but after half a dozen sessions she was treating it all as a joke. Maybe he should see if the doctor she had seen was still around. He'd like to find something that would put a smile back on her face. Resignation and the sale of his shares wouldn't do it, he was sure of that.

'And you'll pop in later to discuss Ipswich?' the lawyer asked.

'Yes, what time will be good for you?'

'Well, actually I'm not dealing with it. It's young Jane Summers who's got the file. She's very good, my latest rising star. You'll like her.'

'I'm sure I will,' Sinclair said.

As the door closed behind Richard Lee, Sinclair counted to ten. Lee would have said goodbye to Denise. To twenty; he'd be through her office and in the corridor. To thirty; into main reception and passing a cheery word with Ted the long-serving security man. To forty; into the main road. He thought he heard his car alarm switch off. Then and only then did he draw back his arm and hurl the empty coffee cup with all his might against the office door, shattering the white china into as many pieces as his broken life.

CHAPTER 29

Mark Rossetti insisted he went alone to the meeting with Paolo Versace. Patti was not happy about it, but eventually agreed to see some of her own contacts in the city. They had arranged to meet up for lunch at the large air-conditioned Ponti's Pizzeria just off the Via Veneto, but as he was led into Versace's office his own words to his travelling companion came back to haunt him.

'I don't want you involved with Versace. He's a dangerous man.'

'I deal with dangerous men every day of my life,' she'd answered.

'Yes, but they're dangerous Englishmen, this one's Italian.'

Versace's headquarters were situated next door to the Banca di Fratelli building just off the Via del Corso near to the Villa Borghese. A security door behind bullet-proof glass allowed only one person to enter at a time, and the X-ray machine that lay behind was as efficient as anything he'd seen at Heathrow. The man who operated it wore dark glasses and a bright white shirt that could have been used for a detergent advert, set off by a black tie and a suit of grey shiny mohair. The whole impression was that of a man who was not only used to going to funerals, but also of causing them.

He had phoned through to make an appointment and when speaking to a secretary whose English was considerably better than several footballers he'd played alongside, the key to the door had been the mention of the names of Mickey Wayne and Chris Handsel. It had all sounded so good in theory. Go to see Versace and rattle his cage. Only now that he was here he did not seem to be a man whose cage would be easily rattled.

Versace's office itself was in direct contrast to the rest of the building. A wall-to-wall heated aquarium in which swam fish of myriad colours gave off a restful air, reflected in the pastel colours of the decoration and the limited-edition lithographs on the walls. Even the desk had a subtlety all of its own, with its gently curving design that could only have been Italian. Versace signalled Mark into an armchair that seemed to take him prisoner as its upholstery moulded itself to the shape of his body. The Italian lit a cigarette with an Art Deco lighter and offered Mark one.

'I don't smoke, thank you.'

'Very wise, but then I believe you are a trained athlete.'

'I was, once.'

Versace nodded sympathetically and Mark wondered how much this man knew about him. He was getting tired of attending meetings where the person to whom he was talking was ready to go on *Mastermind* with a specialist subject of the Life and Times of Mark Rossetti.

'Signor Rossetti. Would you prefer it if we spoke in English or Italian?'

The question was asked in Italian and Mark got the distinct impression he was being tested. But tested for what? He couldn't believe this man was also going to offer him a job. There he'd been just a week or so ago with no future prospects of employment and now it seemed that almost everybody he met wanted to pay him. He doubted that it was his charisma charming them down from the trees.

'Italian is fine.'

Versace smiled, although his eyes did not.

'I think you are merely being polite, Signor. I will use English. If I make any mistakes I hope you will point them out to me. I rarely like to make the same mistake twice.'

Mark took a deep breath, hoping the Italian would think he was affected by the smoke that wreathed the room rather than nerves.

'Signor Versace, I don't know whether or not you can help me. I've been helping Hertsmere in their efforts to recover their player Micky Wayne.'

'Is that not a matter for the police?'

'Yes, but that doesn't mean the club can't take its own steps.'

'And these steps, are they leading anywhere?' Versace was still icily polite, taking stock of his opponent before deciding whether to go on the attack or the defence.

'They led me here.'

'Here? To this office? I do not have your missing footballer on my person.' He began to pull open drawers in an exaggerated fashion. 'Nor is he in my filing system, at least not under W for Wayne or G for giocatore. Perhaps you can give me another clue as to where I should help you locate him.'

'I didn't mean here, I meant Rome,' Mark said, not knowing whether or not he was supposed to enter into Versace's seeming frivolity. If he had known the Italian better he would have realized that he was never frivolous.

'Rome is a big city, a beautiful city. It is like a beautiful woman and as such it conceals many secrets. Perhaps also the secret of the whereabouts of Mr Wayne.'

'Can you help me unlock those secrets, Signor Versace?' Mark asked.

'Why should I do that? So Wayne can sign for Cinquante. I think in English terms you are asking the owner of Tottenham Hotspur to help the chairman of Arsenal sign a player he would like himself.'

'So you want to sign Wayne as well?' Mark said, just a little too eagerly.

'Of course, he is a fine player. His style will be more appreciated here than in his own country. Here we give our artists a huge canvas on which to paint their pictures. In England, I believe, they are restricted to miniatures. We had been following the player's career for some while. I heard of the situation and made an offer. It was a business proposition.'

'So you were gambling four million pounds on your ability to find Mickey?'

'I believe I have a better chance than you, or your English police. Money can buy you a lot of information and I have a lot of money. If Barlucci would have paid seven million for him then, although I am not a mathematician, I believe I have a little under three million to play with and still finish ahead of the game. Now if you have no more questions I must ask you to leave. I do not wish you to consider me impolite, but I have a very busy schedule and I fitted you into it at short notice.' He rose to shake Mark's hand.

The Englishman moved to the edge of his seat, but did not rise.

'Just one more question, Signor Versace. How well do you know Chris Handsel and what part are you playing in his takeover bid for Hertsmere?' He threw the question from left field, like a man shooting an arrow in the air at a fast disappearing flock of birds.

Versace furrowed his brow as if a vaguely unpleasant thought had just crossed his mind.

'Handsome. I know handsome men ... and woman, but nobody by that name.'

'Handsel, as in Gretel.'

'*Babes in the Wood*. I enjoyed that story as a child. Signor Rossetti, I must tell you that there are grave dangers in venturing into deep and dark woods. You can trust nobody to keep you from harm, not even the woodcutter.'

'I'm too old to be a babe,' Mark replied, this time making to leave.

'When you are dealing with a wicked witch who has magical powers, you are never too old. I wish you good luck in your search for Mr Wayne, but remember to stay in the sunshine. I think, perhaps, that once you go into the woods, you will never come out again.'

It was only a short walk from Versace's office to the Via Veneto and Mark needed a longer time to think. He was not due to meet Patti for nearly an hour and so, instead of heading straight for the restaurant, he turned left towards the Piazza del Popolo and left again on to the Ponte Margherita. He stood on the bridge for some time looking down into the swirling waters of the Tiber. It had not been so long ago that he had stood on Westminster Bridge, a bottle of whisky in his hand, another bottle already inside him. He had been trying to anaesthetize himself that night so that when his body hit the water he would feel nothing. Only a passing tramp had saved his life, although the man could never have known it. He'd stumbled towards him, smelling of cheap booze and stale vomit, demanding money for a cup of tea, and Mark had felt fear. He was about to throw himself into the Thames and yet he was scared enough of the vagrant to realize suddenly he wanted to live. He had thrust the second bottle of whisky into the man's hands and run for home. Now here he was on a bright and sunny Rome day with no thought of suicide but with an irrational fear that some catastrophe was about to befall him. He really wanted to live. If he could only pull this job off he would have enough money to get out of the dump he called home, enough money to fight for access to his daughter. He had to pull this job off, yet just as he felt that Mickey Wayne was coming within reach he moved out of sight again.

He looked across the river to the inscrutable churches and palaces of the Vatican. Perhaps if he had been religious it would have helped. Both his parents had been Catholic, but as soon as he was old enough to make decisions for himself he had opted first out of mass, then confession, then the church altogether. There had been the odd prayer, please let me win this match, let me score this penalty, but he did not know who he was asking for these favours. Maybe if he had time he would go to sight-see the papal buildings before he went home. He glanced at his watch. Nearly twelve thirty. He began to retrace his steps, watching the lunch-time traffic decline as the Romans began their daily two or three hour shutdown. The cars were a mere trickle, all the mopeds with their short-sleeved, helmeted drivers seemed to be heading some-where, each treating all other road users as if they were competitors in some great uncharted race. And then gradually, apart from the crowded restaurants and side-walk cafes, the city began to slumber.

He felt very tired himself by the time he got to the pizzeria. He looked around for Patti and saw she was already seated in the smoking section.

Rome, with its nicotine-dependent population, was only just falling into line with the rest of Europe in offering any kind of sanctuary to its non-smoking inhabitants and visitors. She waved to him and he went over to join her, coughing his way through the smoke like a wraith coming through the mist on a haunted heath, determined to persuade her to move to the innovative non-smoking section the restaurant provided.

'Hi, how did your day go?' she asked and he noticed she had already worked her way through half a bottle of Verdicchio.

'Puzzling. Do you think you could bear to go through a meal without a fag and we can move away from this cancer factory?'

She had no time to argue before the explosion hit the

other half of the restaurant. The window seemed to shatter in slow motion, its lethal slivers of glass finding random targets who screamed as blood began to pour from their wounds. He pulled her to the ground fearing another attack, but there was just the shocked silence that follows any outrage and then the screams of the injured as they realized they were not dead but hurting. For a moment he could not be sure she was breathing. Even in the swirling smoke that clouded the restaurant like an old London smog her face looked deathly white. He felt a total panic that he might be left alone to deal with all the chaos that would follow in the wake of the attack, then a sense of anger that despite all his precautions she had still been dragged into a fight that was not hers.

'Patti, Patti.' He called her name loudly even though he was lying on top of her, his mouth just a few inches from her ear. What did you do in circumstances like this? Did you give her the kiss of life, smack her face to try and bring her round or try and keep her still until the ambulance arrived? He put his mouth upon hers and tried to remember the very basic first-aid he had learned as an apprentice footballer. What to do when another player swallows his tongue on the field. It did not go much further than that.

'You smell of garlic and if you don't get off of me, I'm first going to hit you with my fist and then with a paternity suit.'

He rolled off her immediately.

'Pleased to hear you're back to normal,' he said.

'Not really. Mark, just get me out of here. Please.'

Much later when the police had told them it was merely a smoke bomb, meant to cause panic rather than injuries, it

222

occurred to him that if he had had his way they would have been sitting with the other non-smokers who had suffered cuts and shock. He also remembered that he had declined Versace's offer of a cigarette. He felt angry, then slightly flattered that if it was Versace who had had him followed and ordered the attack, then he was taking him seriously. Something he had said had obviously managed to rattle his cage. But what? If Versace had wanted to warn him to keep out of the woods, then he had only succeeded in making him sharpen his axe.

CHAPTER 30

They decided to cut short their stay. They had learned
nothing, yet they had learned too much.

'I never even saw the inside of the Coliseum,' Mark
complained.

'Don't worry. It looks like a stadium after the England
fans have visited and just seen their team lose,' Patti
consoled him. Despite the bravado she had been more
shaken than him by the attack. She had left the restaurant
dusty and unhurt, clutching the unfinished bottle of wine in
her hand.

'At least we got out of paying the bill,' she'd said,
then burst into tears. He produced a handkerchief, but
she was shaking uncontrollably and virtually threw herself into his arms as they stood amongst the excited crowd
who had gathered to see the result of what they believed
to be yet another terrorist attack. Apart from lying on top
of her on the floor of the restaurant it was the first time he
had actually touched her since they had met and, as she
pressed her body against his for comfort, she felt much
frailer than she'd appeared before. All the tough world-
weariness had been stripped from her and all that was left
was a frightened little girl. As soon as he felt himself

becoming aroused he gently pushed her away, partly from embarrassment, partly because he simply did not wish to get involved. Patti Delaney was expedient, she was a means to an end. One failed marriage had been enough for him. She had emptied the bottle, slugging the drink back like a thirsty wino in a cardboard box under Waterloo Bridge. The effect was as immediate and as dramatic as Popeye's spinach.

'Come on, let's get the hell out of this country. I feel naked here.'

He felt a shiver down his spine as she used the word naked, but he too felt exposed.

'You're right, I never did like playing away.'

He had intended to talk to Carla Dandone, the lawyer who appeared to have assumed the mantle of Lennie Simons, but she would have to wait. They'd got to the airport just in time to catch the 16.55 Alitalia flight to London and by seven in the evening they were safely in the back of a familiar London cab bowling along the M4 towards central London. Patti sank back in her seat, taking a deep breath.

'Whew, I didn't think I'd ever appreciate the driving of a London cabbie, but I thought the driver who took us to the airport was going to complete what the bomb had started. I reckon the attack was a coincidence and it was the taxi-driver who was really working for Versace.'

'Perhaps it was all a coincidence. These sort of things do happen in Italy. Versace would have had to move really quickly to arrange for me to be followed, to organize the attack. And for what? He must have guessed I was whistling in the dark.'

'I'm not so sure. A little Italian birdie told me that Versace is not all he seems to be.'

'In what way?'

'Well, for a start he's under investigation already. The Italians have initiated a come-to-Jesus approach to corruption and Signor Versace has so far refused to join the party.'

'What's he accused of?' Mark asked.

'He's not accused of anything … yet. He's just being asked the questions and so far he's not giving any answers.'

'And what sort of questions might those be?'

'Questions about bribes, and corruption, and money laundering, and violent crime. Do you want the whole list or does that give you the complete picture?'

'I should have taken a long spoon even to have a coffee with him.'

Patti smiled for almost the first time since the incident in Rome.

'I think you should have taken an official taster with you. But that's not all I found out about Versace. He's got financial problems himself. A couple of Ulisse players he brought in from abroad haven't been paid some money he offered to pay himself into their off-shore companies in order to smooth the deals through. There's a very unhappy little Brazilian who threatened to go to the papers and had a preliminary meeting with a friend of mine.'

'Why only preliminary?'

'Versace didn't give him the chance to have a second one. Put the fear of God into him and then promptly sold him to a Turkish side.'

'Did he want to go?'

'It would seem he had an offer he couldn't refuse.'

The taxi pulled into Mark's street and the driver sat staring straight ahead as Mark fumbled for the money to pay him off.

'I know you, don't I?' he said as he wrote out the receipt for which Mark had asked.

'I don't know. Do you?'

'Yeah,' the driver said confidently, 'you're a footballer, aren't you?'

'Used to be,' Mark replied, as Patti stood watching the scene with some amusement.

'All the good ones used to be,' the man added and without asking for any further information drove off with a U-turn that caused the squeal of several oncoming brakes.

After the hotel his flat seemed dingier than ever. He tossed his case in the corner and put the kettle on.

'I have to get out of this place,' he said looking around and seeing it as if for the first time.

'I wondered when you were going to say that. Now I think you're really on the road to recovery. Here, I'll do the coffee. You make a lousy cup.'

So did she, but he didn't think it the right time or place to tell her.

'So where do we go from here?' she asked.

'Let's take stock.'

'Suits me. Have you got anything stronger than coffee? Whoops, sorry,' she added, realizing her mistake.

'No.'

'I don't think you're telling me the truth, Mark. I hate liars.'

'And you're a journalist.'

Suddenly, the lightness had gone from her tone.

'I write the truth as I see it. Sometimes it hurts and I'm sorry for that, but unlike some of my fellow scribes, I don't make it up as I go along.'

'So the public has a right to know,' Mark said bitterly.

'It does. If someone wants to get all the benefits of being in the shop window he has to take all the problems of having a sales docket hung around his neck. I won't go snooping around the back door of some grief-stricken widow for a photo of the husband who's been killed saving a cat from a tree, but if some pop star is snorting coke then I reckon he's fair game.'

'And if some football star is trying to throw a match?' Mark asked, although he knew the question was not fair.

'Then he's fair game too; but if he can show he's innocent then he's entitled to just as much publicity for that as well. Is that the end of the moralizing? Assuming it is, then just go and get the bottle you've got hidden in some old sock and at least one of us can be a little more constructive.'

The half-bottle of scotch wasn't in an old sock. He'd put it inside a spare pillow, but he fetched it just the same, together with one glass.

'You're going to swig it straight from the bottle are you?' she said jokingly.

He was beginning to get used to her mercurial swings of mood.

'I thought I'd let you finish it on your own and put temptation beyond my reach.'

She poured herself a whole glassful of the whisky and

knocked it back almost in one gulp. She'd had a few brandies on the plane as well.

'You know, if I'd have had your capacity to hold my drink I don't think I'd have ever realized I was an alcoholic,' Mark said.

She ignored the comment and simply poured herself another glass.

'I see it as my duty to keep you off the booze. You have no such obligation towards me. Now, I feel suitably refreshed and I thought you were about to do a bit of stocktaking.'

She always seemed to demand the last word, the decision as to when it was time to change the subject, but he remembered how he had felt when he thought she was seriously hurt, perhaps even dead, and he let her have her own way without further comment.

'We have a missing footballer. We have a ransom note and, as far as we know, the kidnappers have half a million quid and the player. We have a club in financial difficulties and we have a chairman under pressure to sell his shares. We have two Italian clubs who want to buy the player and either one of them goes a long way to sorting out the club's problems. But we also have a club with an important Cup semi-final next weekend and no star player. We have the player who seems to have two agents, one in England and one in Italy, and we have a player with a wife and at least two mistresses, a player about whom we've not yet found anybody with a good word to say. We have an angry Italian in the shape of Versace and he obviously doesn't like something I said to him...'

'And don't forget Mr Handsel who banks with your angry Italian and wants to buy the club; and also don't forget the innocent player trying to clear his name.'

For once her speech was slightly slurred and she put a hand out to stroke the side of his face.

'I'm sorry if I was a bit tough on you before. It's not every day a girl has a bomb thrown at her and a man jump on top of her. I really do believe you, you know.'

She had leaned towards him on the sofa, her eyes half-closed, but he could not be sure if it was from emotion or exhaustion, nor could he be certain what she expected him to do next. It had been a long time since he had reason to read any woman's mind save that of a vengeful wife. If he was misreading the signals he could destroy the whole of their relationship and that was the last thing he wanted to do. He moved fractionally towards her and still she did not move away.

'We still haven't decided what happens next,' she said, her eyes now fully closed, her voice dreamy. In the distance he could hear the insistent beeping of his answerphone and realized that he had not even bothered to play his messages since they arrived home. She immediately sensed his mind had wandered elsewhere and whatever thin silken chain that might have been woven between them was broken. She pulled away, as if remembering something more urgent.

'The letters you found. Who do we tell first, the husband or the wife?' she asked, once more the business-like journalist.

'Or the police? Or Sinclair?' he added.

'You're trying to duck out of responsibility again, Mark.

Why should we let anybody else in on our story? We can sort this out ourselves.'

'If we're not blown up first. And it may be a story for you. For me it's a job of work.'

'Same thing as far as I'm concerned. Now why don't you get those messages that are obviously playing on your mind? And then let's decide what to do.'

There was only one message. It had been left just an hour or so before they returned, but once they had heard it then the decision was made.

'Hello? Mark? I don't know if you remember me. It's Paula, Paula Reynolds. Phil's wife. I have to talk to you. Please call as soon as you get in, or better still come straight round. It's 28, Walton Close, the private road behind the golf club . . .' The message broke off as the woman began to cry. 'Please Mark, just as soon as you can. It's Phil. He's disappeared.'

CHAPTER 31

The Reynolds' home was far bigger than he'd expected. He knew the man had done well for himself out of the game, but he had never realized he had done this well. The numbering in the road at the expensive end of Potters Bar was a mere concession to the postman, as each house was almost invisible beyond its tree-lined drive. Only an individual name revealed each property's true identity. Reynolds's was called 'Sardan', after his children, Sarah and Daniel. Mark had seen their photograph on the manager's desk, polished, well-scrubbed, slightly in awe of whoever held the camera. The house itself was the inevitable mock-Tudor with ivy and climbing roses cunningly covering the twentieth-century brickwork to give the appearance of age. The gardens were lovingly laid out, a testimony to the daily visits of an expert gardener, and looked even more impressive illuminated by subtly placed lights within the boughs of trees that were old enough to have pre-dated the house. There was an isolated feel to the property. Reynolds' children were nine and ten, yet no toys littered the lawn, abandoned by kids going reluctantly in for their pre-supper baths, and the house itself was unlit and totally silent. The house may have been inhabited, but it was certainly not lived in. A high fence divided the property from the golf course at the back where a zealous groundsman still played a sprinkler over the greens despite the lateness of the hour and the almost total darkness. As they pulled at the bell rope, a deep resonant ringing could be heard echoing around the house and for a moment they thought there was nobody at home, that their journey had been wasted.

'Not bad for a footballer,' Patti said and could not see the flicker of pain that passed across Mark's face. He could have had all this. They were about to turn back to Patti's car when they heard a sound from inside and a woman, whom Mark recognized as Paula Reynolds, opened the door the width of the security chain.

'You came,' she said, sounding surprised, and then unlocked the door to let them in, looking at Patti with some hesitation.

'It's OK, she's with me,' Mark said, offering no further explanation.

Paula led them through to a lounge that seemed never to have been used before. The white carpet bore no trace of a stain, the light blue furniture might just as well have been delivered from the store that very day. It was not a room in which to relax, but then Paula Reynolds did not look like a woman who relaxed very much at any time. She seemed like a coiled watch spring, ready to overwind if she was given one more tiny turn. She was not unattractive to someone who liked his women thin. She bore all the signs of somebody who worked out regularly and then used the sunbeds at the same, doubtless expensive health club. Her hair was pulled back off her forehead, accentuating the elfin shape of her face and from the way she walked on the toes of her feet Mark guessed that at some stage in her life she had received some dance training. She must have been in her mid-thirties, but in the gloom of the house she could have passed for somebody ten years younger.

She gestured weakly around the room and Mark perched himself on the edge of an armchair all too aware that his shabby clothes made him appear, in these surroundings, like a beggar seeking charity; but then beggars were not usually telephoned to make house visits. Patti was far more confident, and indeed far more in place with her suede trousers and white silk shirt which she had produced from her case and changed into at Mark's before they left. There was something of the chameleon about her, Mark had decided. Wherever she was and whoever she was with, she would look the part.

Paula flicked on the lights and, as she blinked, they could not help but notice the swelling under her left eye. Neither of them commented. If she wanted to tell them then, doubtless, she would do so in her own good time. She did not look like a woman who would react well to any pressure at the moment.

'Now you're here, I'm not sure I've done the right thing,' Paula said, her hoarse voice testifying to the hours she had spent crying.

Patti got to her feet.

'Point me in the direction of the kitchen and I'll make us some coffee. Or, better still, show me where you keep the hard stuff.'

'I would have thought your nose would have led you

straight to that,' Mark said, still uncomfortable with her incessant drinking.

'Oh, listen to Barney the boozy bloodhound,' she replied as if only the two of them were in the room.

'You two sound just like Phil and I used to sound,' Paula said. 'Have you been together long?'

Mark and Patti looked at each other, not knowing quite how to answer without leading to more questions that might divert them from their objectives.

'A lifetime,' Patti said, 'or at least it seems like it.'

Patti found a half-empty bottle of white wine in the fridge and poured a full glass for both herself and Laura, then found a can of Diet Coke for Mark and added some cashew nuts to the tray for good measure. If she was going to entertain herself then she might as well do it in style. She noticed a bottle of Dom Perignon in the cooler as well and decided that would be her next target.

'There you are,' Patti said, distributing the drinks. Paula drank as if to satisfy a long-existing thirst.

'Thank you. I got my mother to pick the kids up. They seem to prefer it with their grandparents nowadays anyway, so they didn't put up too much of a struggle.' She paused, hoping somebody was going to seize the initiative, but her two guests merely held their glasses, taking the occasional sip, the silence an invitation for the manager's wife to proceed with her story.

'There's no easy way of saying this,' Paula said, taking a deep breath. 'I rang Helen Archer first at home. I've always liked her. She suggested I talk to you rather than the police. I got the impression the detective sergeant on the job is pushing his luck with Helen and she doesn't know how to handle it.'

Mark leaned forward so far in his chair that he was nearly falling off.

'Good for Helen. I'm here, Paula. I've nothing else to do this evening except listen to you.' And get to bed, he thought, realizing that he'd woken up that morning in Rome, probably had a bomb thrown at him and then flown back to England. The last thing he really wanted to be doing was trying to concentrate on Paula Reynolds' problems and then, perhaps, have to do something about them. Not for the first time he considered the fact that he was not a natural gumshoe. None of Raymond Chandler's heroes ever seemed to go to bed and Humphrey Bogart's eyes were clear evidence that he had dispensed with sleep.

'Phil came home from training today in a foul mood. The last few weeks, with all the problems at the club and then Mickey disappearing, he's not been himself.' She poured herself another glass of wine. It seemed to give her the necessary courage. 'No, scrap that. He's not been himself for a long time. Maybe he never was the self I married, perhaps I fell for the image like everybody else.'

Mark knew all about that. The public hero and the private demon. The more talented the genius, the more flawed the player. Only when the genius fades does the demon threaten to leave with it, and then comes the gradual rehabilitation, the adjustment to obscurity. Only some would make it through the long dark night.

'Anyway, today he was worse than usual. He wouldn't tell me what was wrong at first and then I pushed him, which was a bit of a mistake. You'd think I would have learned over the years. When I kept asking he suddenly started asking all sorts of questions about Mickey.'

'What sort of questions?'

'About calls he'd made to me, whether we'd met up for drinks.' She paused, her eyes shifting from Mark to Patti, then back again, searching for something that she had suddenly realized was there, the reason why neither of them had expressed any surprise at her call to a virtual stranger.

'You know, don't you? You know about me and Mickey.'

'Yes, we know,' Mark replied. 'I found your letter.'

'He got mad with me about that letter. Told me never to reduce things to writing. It was more like a business lesson than a lesson in love. But he kept it, did he?' She was almost talking to herself, as if Mark and Patti had left her alone; but then with a noticeable jerk of the body she was back with them.

'Where did he keep it, the letter?'

'Inside his mascot in his locker.'

'A bear?'

Mark nodded.

'I gave him that. It was after we had spent our first afternoon together.'

'How long ago was that?' Patti asked.

'Six months, almost to the day.'

'I'm sorry, you were telling us about your husband.'

'Yes, my husband.' She spoke as if she had only just recalled somebody who had once passed through her life. 'He'd found out about Mickey. At first it was just the questions, but then he started shouting, asking how long I'd been making a fool of him, who else knew. That everybody was laughing behind his back, he was a changing-room joke. And then...' She began to cry again and when Patti handed her a handkerchief she winced as she dabbed the injured eye. 'Then he hit me. And he was gone.'

'How long ago was this?' Mark asked.

Paula looked at her watch.

'It's nearly ten now. I suppose he's been gone about seven hours.'

'Seven hours. That's not a lot of time for a husband who's just found out his wife's been screwing around to get his head together,' Patti said a little brutally.

'He had some commitments. Phil never missed anything he was getting paid for. He had a Radio 5 interview about the semi-final and I had them on the phone saying he hadn't turned up. He had a photo-session for one of the football magazines back here and after I'd made the photographer his third cup of tea he'd had enough of waiting and made tracks...'

'Maybe he'd had enough of your tea,' Patti said and received a wan smile in return, a smile that even in its reluctance gave a glimpse of what both Reynolds and Wayne had seen in the woman.

'Then the golf-club secretary called to complain that Phil hadn't arrived to make a presentation and it was then I panicked and phoned Helen. I thought maybe he'd gone back to the ground, and she seems virtually to live there, so if anybody would have seen him it would have been Helen.'

'And that's it?' Mark asked. He had seen enough of the women seeking divorces who had passed through his offices to know when something was being held back. He decided on shock treatment. He had the distinct feeling in his guts that as far as Mickey Wayne, and indeed Hertsmere, were concerned they were running out of time. Getting no reply he ploughed on.

'Paula, I have to tell you something about Mickey. Inside that bear, your letter was the only one that was signed, but there was another note there, anonymous, but high on emotion. You weren't the only one Mickey was seeing outside his marriage. Even his own wife told us there were two on the go.'

Paula gaped at him.

'No. I don't believe you. You're only telling me that to cause trouble.'

'It's not my job to cause trouble, Paula. My job's to find Mickey. Once I've done that then you and he, and Phil, have to work things out for yourselves. Now have you any idea of who could have written this?'

He produced the other note he had found during his search of the locker and Paula took it between two fingers as if it were a poisonous serpent that might strike at any moment. She read it slowly, then seemed to force herself to read it again, before handing it back to Mark, still in slow motion. She bit her lip, trying to keep her feelings under control. There had been too much pain to show any more.

'He couldn't even be bothered to think of something fresh to say, could he? You know I was never honest with myself before tonight. I knew Mickey's reputation with women, I knew his wife for heaven's sake. I liked her. We'd sit next to each other at matches and for ages I'd listen to her complaining about Mickey, how he was this and how he was that, and I actually felt sorry for her. And then we were in the players' lounge after a match one day. They'd won five-nil and Mickey had scored a hat-trick and made the other two. He was on a high, like footballers are after a special performance; but you know that don't you, Mark?'

'Yes, I know.'

'So there he was, with the match ball, heading it up and down, doing all his little party tricks, and he flicks the ball over to where I'm sitting and knocks my drink to the floor. He's over to me like a shot, and he's mopping up the table, and then he's mopping me down, and his touch was so gentle, like he was really sorry. He was like a little boy. I was lost as soon as he looked at me and he knew it, and kept on drying me off long after he needed to, and I thought to myself, Laura, you don't know what you've got here, if you've nothing good to say about him. If you don't want him, then I'll have him. Phil and I had nothing really going for us by then. After the kids came he reckoned he'd done all he needed to do in our marriage. He was a media star. I must admit I was a bit surprised when he took the Hertsmere job. He'd always said he didn't fancy management, but then he didn't discuss things like that with me. I don't want you to get totally the wrong picture.' She waved her hand around the room, like a disinterested tour guide. 'We never wanted for anything. I could run up accounts wherever I liked and he never complained, but to come out and choose something with me, well that was a different story. Mickey, though, he was different. If I'd bought a new dress he'd like to see me try it on, and then...' Again she was in her own world. 'Then he'd like to take it off me. He encouraged me to be more daring than I'd ever been before. He'd say, it's not only the clothes that show that matter, it's what you've got on underneath, that only you know about. When I'd bought some lacy underwear, he'd whisper to me when we were in company, even with Phil and Laura, "have you got them on? I'd like them off." Once we did that, went out to the back of somebody's house at a party and he took me against a wall like we were teenagers. He was much younger than me, of course, but he made me feel young, you understand, while Phil and the kids they made me feel old before my time.'

She saw the glass empty in her hand and it was she who suggested that Patti go to the fridge to get the bottle of champagne.

'We were saving that until Hertsmere won the Cup, but it doesn't look as if Phil and I are going to be toasting that together.'

Mark heard the pop of the cork from the kitchen.

'Is that it, Paula? Have you told me everything?'

She hesitated, wondering if what she was about to say was a flight of fancy.

'No. There's just one more thing. I asked Phil how he'd found out. Who else knew? He didn't say, but I got the distinct impression that he'd heard it from Mickey himself.'

'But Mickey's been missing for over a week. Why did he take so long to confront you with it?' Mark asked.

'You don't understand. I don't think he waited any time at all. I think he heard it from Mickey today.'

CHAPTER 32

By Wednesday morning there had been no news of either
Phil Reynolds or Mickey Wayne, nor had Sinclair heard
anything more from the kidnappers. They had all gone to
ground. But one person had surfaced: Carla Dandone. She
had been in touch with Mark that morning.

'Mr Sinclair suggested I telephone you,' she had said
when she called first thing, her English perfect, with only
the hint of a foreign accent.

'That was good of him. Why did he do that?' Mark said.
He was not in the best of moods. He had felt after the visit
to Paula Reynolds that they were really making progress.
Somehow there had to be a connection between the two
disappearances, but for the moment it continued to elude
him, as did the identity of the other woman in Mickey
Wayne's life. Wayne himself was becoming a spectre, no
sooner did Mark feel that he was in sight than he drifted
again beyond reach through solid walls.

'He felt that you were making better progress than the
police. That you were close to finding my client.'

'I think he's being somewhat optimistic. If I were the
man in charge of team selection for Saturday then I'd be
making my plans without Wayne.'

'That is unfortunate. And negative. I understand that you nearly had an unfortunate accident in my city. Perhaps that means you are nearer than you think.'

'Unfortunate. Yes, you could say that. The whole of my trip was unfortunate.'

'Ah, yes, your meeting with Signor Versace. Not the most pleasant of men in opposition.'

'How did you know about the meeting?' he asked, feeling he was giving more than he was getting from the conversation.

'Rome is a village. I merely listened to the gossip. I think I may come to England this week, perhaps tomorrow. I would like to see this Cup semi-final on Saturday and I would like to see my client play.'

'Would you indeed?' Mark was becoming irritated by the woman. Either she thought he knew more than he did or else she knew more than she was letting on. Either way he was being toyed with and he did not like it. He was beginning to feel that he was a pawn in a game of chess where the rules were continually changing. The only rule to remain constant was that the pawn could be taken by anything and anybody.

'So. I hope we will meet up. Perhaps I will be able to be of service to you some day. We will both be operating in the same world, I am sure of it.'

Lawyers, he thought, the same the world over, like Sally's lawyer denying him access to Emma. Using words as their weapons. They were not to be trusted, none of them. He hated them all.

If Mark had known precisely what Richard Lee was doing

at the very moment he was talking to Carla Dandone then his feelings towards the legal profession might have been even more violent. Lee was an ambitious man, and as such selected his clients rather than have them select him. He knew that given an hour alone with most people he could persuade them that the services he could render, the advice he could give and the fees he would charge would all be far more advantageous than those of whoever was advising his target at that time. And he'd had his hour with Chris Handsel. Handsel was on the way up just as David Sinclair was on his way down. Lee had decided that there could be only one winner in the contest and he wanted to be on the winning side.

It was not the first time he had sacrificed an old friendship. He had set up in practice nearly twenty years ago with Colin Sykes. Colin had been to school with him in West London, and they had then gone to Manchester University together, sharing digs, sharing exam notes, even sharing their women. It had been a David and Jonathan relationship, only when a large City firm had head-hunted Lee after working with him on a major transaction they had made it clear that they were not looking for a merger or a takeover of the practice of Sykes and Lee. Lee could come, but Sykes must stay. The two old friends had never seen the need for a partnership agreement and Lee had walked away with most of the clients and not even a goodbye kiss.

It had been his idea to use the Freddie Scott situation to strengthen Handsel's position. Vera Scott had been easy meat for a predator like Lee. He had taken her out to lunch, listened sympathetically, then pressed all the right emotional buttons to ease Vera's conscience over Sinclair.

'Look Vera,' he'd said over the second brandy which he'd ordered for medicinal purposes, 'it's not as if you've not given David his chance. I mean he's my friend for Christ's sake, nobody wants him to keep control of the club more than I do; but there comes a time when you have to look after yourself and your loved ones. David wouldn't want Freddie to die on a ward in a National Health hospital, or some hospice with nuns mopping up after dying old men. This is his one chance to meet his end with dignity. Believe me I thought long and hard before I agreed to talk to you for Handsel. I made it clear to him that I wasn't acting for him in any way. I know where my loyalties lie. I mean, David was virtually my first client. He set me up. Even if there weren't the rules of conflict, I wouldn't work against his interests, but sometimes there are things more important than your professional ethics, when a man's life is at stake. So, when Handsel asked me how to get in touch with you, I thought the least I could do was speak to you myself.'

Vera Scott was in her early sixties. Freddie had been ill for so long that she could not remember the last time she had dressed up to go out, but for this lunch she had really made the effort. The powder had been heavily applied to skin that already had a powdery texture of its own, her hair was freshly set from the morning's visit to the hairdresser, the lacquer glinting under the harsh lights of the restaurant. The dress she wore, black with a lace bodice, might have been fashionable twenty years before and it may have fitted her then, but as her husband had wasted away with his illness she had gained weight in almost inverse proportion.

She put her hand on his.

'You're very kind. Freddie always spoke . . . speaks, very highly of you.'

'You didn't tell him you were meeting me, did you?'

She completely missed the note of panic in his voice. That had been the gamble, that she would tell her husband and he would tell Sinclair.

'No, I promised you I wouldn't and I always keep my promises.'

She favoured him with a coquettish smile that made him feel physically sick. He detested unattractive people. He had once read that, after the Jews and the Communists, the Nazis were going to rid themselves of all the ugly people and he had some sympathy with that ideology.

And so the bargain had been struck and, not satisfied with that, Handsel had sent Lee to persuade Sinclair to sell his shares without a struggle. Again there had been no great struggle with his conscience. Handsel was persuasive.

'Dickie boy . . .' Richard did not like to be addressed in that way, but did not think the relationship was as yet strong enough to protest. 'Dickie,' Handsel continued, 'you've done the old man and his old lady a favour in getting them to agree to sell to me, now you can do your old mate Sinclair a good turn too. He's well out of it. He's not a football man, like me. The game belongs to us, not to him. Johnny come lately. I did all the hard graft out on the field and I've done all the hard graft in my business to make sure I've got the money to turn this club around. Sinclair's got nowhere with the local council, but then he doesn't know the right people like I do. Life's a case of always knowing the right people, isn't it Dickie? And now you know me and I know you and that's how it's going to be from now on. I know the way Sinclair treated you. If you didn't dance to his tune then he never invited you to the ball.' He laughed, a deep throaty noise that could just as easily have been the sound of an animal being strangled. 'Ball, get it. You know, foot*ball*.'

Lee smiled politely. One thing he'd learned in his years as a solicitor was that you didn't have to like your clients. Sometimes it helped, but it wasn't a prerequisite of the trade. You had to make them trust you and you had to make them pay. Anything else didn't really matter. In any event he'd not been able to persuade Sinclair to sell. He'd popped in to see him whilst the chairman was discussing his Ipswich project with the lovely Jane Summers. She herself was another subject to be tackled at a later date. She liked football and he'd already taken her to a couple of matches on the pretext that his wife hated the sport and it was good to find a woman who actually appreciated the finer things in life.

David Sinclair had not seemed so taken with his willowy blonde assistant.

'Richard, with all due respect to Jane here, she doesn't know my stuff like you do. I've been trying to explain to her just how you did that sale and lease-back at Leamington, linked with the back-to-back off-shore financing.' Then almost as an after-thought he'd added, 'Oh, by the way, I've considered carefully what you said about selling to Handsel. It's not on. It's like surrendering to terrorists.'

'He's not that bad,' Lee had said.

'No, not that bad. Worse,' Sinclair had replied.

Did he realize? Lee wondered. He turned the subject to small talk, to the team itself, to how Ray Fowler was coping, to anything rather than the sale of the shares. No, he didn't realize, he decided, and that was what he reiterated to Chris Handsel on this Wednesday morning.

Handsel didn't seem to care whether he knew or not and for the first time it occurred to Lee that in Handsel he was dealing with a man with a reckless disregard for anything but his own aims and ambitions.

'So I'm not as bad as a terrorist, I'm worse. Got a daughter, our chairman, hasn't he?' The question was addressed to himself, not the lawyer. 'Well, fucking Mr Smartass Sinclair. Let's see how much worse I really am.'

And, as he listened, even Richard Lee with all the confidence and belief in his own abilities wondered what he had started.

CHAPTER 33

It had been a poor training session. It was not as if Phil Reynolds had actually done very much directly with the players, but his presence had always been felt. He was the eminence grise the players wanted to please and though it was Ray Fowler who gave them the skills to do it, on this Thursday morning, as Mark Rossetti stood in the directors' box by the side of David Sinclair, the motivation simply wasn't there. Fowler had been working the goalkeeper Greg Sergovich particularly hard. He had a couple of players taking corners and putting in crosses, while the attackers had been given total freedom to stop Sergovich getting to them any way they could. Every time the huge Slav rose for the ball a group of players would surround him, some even leaping on his back and being carried up into the air as he leapt to make the save. Normally this particular routine was a time for jokes and laughter, a time to grab any available bit of Sergovich and in particular his private parts, which he claimed put every other player at the club to shame. Today there was just ill-temper, a desire to hurt, to let out their anger and frustration on each other. The keeper rose from beneath a pile of bodies, dropped the ball and threw a punch at Nicky Collier.

'He know I have bad finger, yet still he go in on me.' He pulled off his glove to display the dressing that still covered the little finger of his left hand which had been injured against Stockton, held it up to support his argument, then stormed off to the dressing-room.

'Oi, Greg, you daft foreigner, we've not finished yet,' Fowler shouted after him. He felt for the first time in his coaching career he was losing control. He'd never wanted to be a manager, he couldn't be bothered to dress up in suits and ties, to pay courtesy visits to boardrooms after matches, particularly when they'd lost. He was not a good loser. He'd always considered that being gracious in defeat meant it hadn't hurt, and if it didn't hurt then it proved you didn't care enough. And then there was the press. As the coach under a personality manager you could hide away and not be bothered. That was the way it had been. Reynolds had done all the talking, all the interviews, he was good at that. He always had an answer, but for Ray Fowler there were only questions. His head had never been bothered before with anything other than tactics, but now the media demanded much more from him. They seemed to have learned a lot more about him as well, as if he were a new subject appearing for the first time on a school curriculum. They'd even found out about his daughter, Josie. Eighteen she'd been when she'd had the car crash, but that had reduced her to a two-year-old and that was how old she would always be now. The bastards had even gone to the home to grab some photos. Human interest, one of the reporters had said to him before Fowler had him thrown out of the ground. He couldn't cope with all this and he knew it, but he also knew he couldn't turn and run. Not just now. It wasn't in his nature to give up when a job was not completed. If he got the sack that was one thing, it was outside of his control, it happened all the time in football. But as long as he had a contract he'd battle on, however helpless or uncomfortable he felt.

Sergovich turned around from some twenty yards away. 'You not finished. I finished. Cup finished. Whole fucking club finished.' And with that he tossed down his gloves and ran down the tunnel.

Nicky Collier stood there with a singularly nasty smile on his face. On another man it might have made him seem amused, but on Collier it gave his craggy features the look of a death mask.

'Very nice, very nice indeed. You bring them in from these fucking third-world countries, you dress them up, try and teach them the lingo, and that's the gratitude you get. I'd ban the whole lot of them. If you're an English club then you should have Englishmen playing for you, not a bunch of fucking foreigners who cry for their mummies when the going gets tough,' he said.

'Why don't you fuck off yourself, Collier,' Stuart Macdonald said. 'You knew the finger was still hurting him, so why try and kick his hand off?'

'Because he's a poofta, that's why. OK, so he dislocated his finger, and then it got put back. If he's fit to play on Saturday then he shouldn't be worrying about a little challenge. Have you seen that centre forward of Thamesmead?'

'The big blond Swede, Erstrom?' Macdonald asked.

'Yeah,' Collier continued, 'another fucking foreigner.'

'All right fellers, let's call it a day. Take a jog around the pitch, then we'll warm down,' Fowler said dejectedly. He liked the continental idea of warming down at the end of training and he'd even tried to do it at the end of matches. Every new signing thought the other players were having him on, that it was some kind of initiation rite, when showered, dressed and ready to go home, he was told to go back out on to the empty pitch for a few exercises.

Fowler did not know who he was missing more, Reynolds or Wayne. He'd never liked Wayne as a person, but that didn't mean he couldn't respect him as a player. All he hoped was that if they lost on Saturday and Reynolds did not reappear, that it wouldn't mean he'd lose his job as coach. They could keep the manager's post and welcome to it, but he knew full well that in the cold and ruthless world of football a new manager would bring in his own coaching team, notwithstanding the historical success of whoever was in the job. He just wanted to turn back the clock, to have everything exactly the way it was. He tried to convince himself that Reynolds was sure to turn up by Saturday. He'd been told there had been some domestic problems, but no more than that. Yet the fact that the police had wanted to talk to him about Reynolds, as well as Wayne, made him think that they, at least, believed there was more to his disappearance. He felt totally frustrated. He'd done what he could to find Wayne. He'd asked around the pubs where he usually drank, wandered into wine bars and clubs where he appeared quaintly out of place, like a father looking for a wayward son when it was past his bedtime. But he had turned up nothing new. Yes, Mickey was one of the lads, yes he might have one drink too many, and everywhere the story that he was never seen without a pretty girl, nor ever seen with his wife. There had been one thing though, and it troubled him. One description of one particular girl and her car; it was vaguely familiar, yet he could place neither of them out of context. He wondered if he should tell the police or, perhaps, Mark Rossetti. He hadn't liked the inspector, Jordan or whatever his name was. The man obviously knew nothing of football and Fowler had an inbred suspicion of anybody who had no interest in what was, for him, the very essence of life. The detective sergeant was different though; but he seemed more concerned with Helen Archer than the case itself, following her around the stadium as if she was going to turn a corner and stumble upon both the missing men herself. No, he'd tell Rossetti, when he had a little more to go on. A few more visits, a bit more clubbing, he smiled to himself, making up for lost time. A girl had actually tried to chat him up at one club, but any thought that her approach might have been a compliment had been dispelled when the bouncer on the door had said, 'You'd better steer well clear of her mate. She's into rough trade.'

Sinclair had seen the players begin to drift off the pitch and called Fowler over.

'Not going too well, is it, Ray?'

'We'll just have to hope it's all right on the night, Mr Sinclair.'

'What did you think, Mark?' the chairman asked.

Rossetti was taken by surprise at being brought into the football discussion. It was the first time that anybody at the club had actually acknowledged he knew anything about the game.

'I don't want to tread on anybody's toes,' Mark said awkwardly.

'It's not a problem,' Fowler replied, realizing he was being asked a question.

'Are you sure?' Mark still asked.

'I always talked to Phil after a training session. Sometimes he could see things I didn't, even if he'd only watched a few minutes.'

'It's Collier,' Mark said, 'he thinks he's better than he is. He's got his strengths and you should play to them. He's good in the air, awkward and hostile, but he's got no first-time touch. We had a player like him in the youth team when I started here. I just adjusted my game, got the ball to him early. Long-ball stuff they'd call it nowadays, but this lad scored any number of goals. I quite like the kid, Wallace. When does his ban start?'

'Not until after the Thamesmead game. I wasn't going to play him on Saturday anyway. I thought I'd leave him on the bench to teach him to keep his hands to himself.'

'I'd give him a chance, but I reckon he'd be happier with a free role. He needs his confidence built up. At the moment he's playing wide on the left, same position as Mickey Wayne so everybody expects him to be Mickey Wayne. Maybe he'll be that good one day. When you were working with the defence I saw the kid doing some tricks with the ball that were out of this world. He's got to be persuaded to try that sort of thing in a match, not in his own half, but when he's got a bit of space. If he pulls it off once, he'll have the crowd behind him and that's all he needs.'

The crowd behind you, he thought. The adrenalin pounding through you, the roar of the crowd, like the roar that had filled the ancient Coliseum that he had not seen on his Roman trip. They all wanted blood, the taunts of the winners, the frustrated rage of the losers. Yes, if young Tommy Wallace could get them going he would see that he could feed off it for the rest of his career.

'Will you have a word with Wallace then?' It was Ray Fowler talking to him, dragging him reluctantly back to the present.

'Sure,' Mark replied, pleasantly surprised. 'When do you want me to do it?'

'Now's as good a time as any. I think he's scared to death of me. Some players it works with, some it doesn't. I'll go and drag him away from a mirror. He spends more time combing his hair, that one, than he does playing.'

As he hurried off to fetch the young player, he felt a sense of relief that he had somebody with whom to share the responsibility, and in his relief he completely forgot what it was that he was going to tell Mark Rossetti.

CHAPTER 34

Mark did not know what had drawn him to the stadium that day. Perhaps it was because he needed a focus for his questions and could not get that focus sitting alone in his flat. Or maybe it was because he was becoming increasingly at home at the Park Crescent ground, a ground which should have been his home for the past ten years. He felt good today, far better than he'd felt for many years. It was the conversation with Ray Fowler followed by his chat with Tommy Wallace that had helped to exorcize so many ghosts of the troubled past. He had been made to feel useful. The investigation into the kidnapping of Mickey Wayne may have helped to swell his non-existent bank balance, but it was not the way he would have chosen to return to the world of football.

Tommy Wallace had proved to be a nice lad, quietly spoken, an attentive audience despite the dire warnings Mark had received from Fowler as to his attitude. He had a round choirboy's face, with close-cropped red hair set above a mass of freckles and a Glaswegian accent that at times was impenetrable. He said nothing about Mark's past and it occurred to him that he might know nothing of it. If indeed he was yesterday's news there was every chance of a fresh start.

He'd lost all track of time and it was only when the young player had mumbled his thanks and said his reluctant goodbyes that he realized it was nearly four in the afternoon. Patti, as she had put it, had gone off to 'do some real work,' and he was once again without transport. He had begun to become accustomed to the convenience of the car, when for so long he'd waited patiently for trains and buses. If he wasn't careful he'd catch the main rush-hour and he wanted to avoid anything that might put him back on the emotional downhill.

He asked if he could use the telephone in the front office and Sharon on reception, who was by now quite used to his presence at the ground, cheerfully waved him towards it, whilst carefully positioning herself within earshot. With so much happening within the club her days were simply flying by, and she herself was the centre of attention when she went for a drink in her local with the boyfriend. Most of the fellow drinkers were Hertsmere supporters and they clung to her every word regarding the latest drama at the ground, looking forward to her revelations more eagerly than the next episode of *Neighbours*. She didn't know who Mark was going to phone, but she was sure it was going to be interesting. Before she had met him, Mark Rossetti was just another name from the past, a face in old team photos, but now whenever he was around things seemed to happen. Mark dialled Patti's number. He felt in some small way that he had something to celebrate. He wanted to share it with her. However much time they spent together he still felt there was much more to learn about her and to his surprise he found himself wanting to attend the lessons. They'd never even really discussed in depth her passion for football. He recalled that first meeting when he had just been turned away from the stadium where he now seemed to have the freedom of the park. What had she said? 'I was just going because I like Mickey Wayne.' After all their joint efforts to find him he didn't know whether or not she had ever met him.

All he got was her answerphone and he left a message with a sense of disappointment. He had planned to ask her out to dinner and now he was left with the awful thought of the journey home on public transport and a take-away meal from the local Chinese. It was Helen Archer who changed all that. As he was putting the receiver down without having provided the receptionist with any new material for her nightly cabaret, the club secretary came into the reception area holding a file of papers.

'Mark, I was hoping to catch you. Could you spare me a few minutes?'

'Sure, I was just about to go home, but there's no rush.'

There was never any rush to go home, he thought, but then he drove the image of the flat from his mind, determined not to become self-pitying. He was on an up, he had to keep telling himself that, and if he did then eventually he would believe it. He'd kept off the drink since the disaster with the money and if he could keep that up then he was well on the way to winning the battle against himself. He did not want to rediscover the arrogance of the player of ten years ago, but he did want to maintain the self-belief of the man he now was. Helen looked around her and, seeing the receptionist listening with ill-concealed curiosity, said, 'I'll give you a lift, if you like. We can talk in the car.'

She went back to her room to get her coat.

'She's nice, Miss Archer, isn't she?' Sharon asked pointedly. She had already decided to spread the news that the club secretary had gone off for a private drink with the ex-player. It had all the makings of a new twist to the plot.

'Yes, very nice. And good at her job.' The answer was less than satisfactory, but Sharon was sure that given time and a flexible memory she would be able to make something of it.

Helen Archer's car was as tidy and utilitarian as she was herself, a no-frills version of an Astra that had all the personality of a hired car. He almost expected to find the glossy book with the details of emergency services and vehicle return on the back seat. She asked for directions to his home, nodded when he gave the address to show that Southgate was familiar territory and then drove at exactly thirty miles per hour.

'So what was it you wanted to talk about?' Mark asked.

'I'm not sure,' she replied, reddening slightly in the same way as she had done when Detective Sergeant Davies' eyes had lingered on her.

'In your own time,' Mark said, watching in the wing mirror the line of cars behind who seemed somewhat keen to overtake at the first possible opportunity. He was learning all the time as to the best way of prising information from people, and also learning that he was getting good at it.

'I told Paula Reynolds to speak to you, I hope I did the right thing.'

'Yes, you did. It was very helpful.'

'Good, good,' she said as if still trying to justify her decision not to co-operate fully with the police. ' It's unlike me not to play strictly according to the rules. I was never in trouble at school. I've never even had a parking ticket let alone a speeding ticket, but somehow I think our best chance of getting Mickey back rests with you.'

'I'm flattered,' Mark replied. 'I really believe I'm getting closer. I just need that little bit of luck to break through the wire.'

For the first time during the drive she gave him a smile, and although she did not take her eyes off the road, he saw the whiteness begin to fade from the knuckles that were gripping the steering wheel.

'Yes, I guess you've been out of luck for quite a while. My father used to say what comes around goes around.'

'Wise man, your father?'

'Not really. He was an MP. And he hated sport. Except he'd go to the university rugby match. And the soccer match as he always insisted on calling it. He liked to be seen where it was useful to be noticed. MPs and Yanks, they're all intellectual bankrupts when it comes to football. I hate amateur sport, don't you? There's something unnatural about not getting paid for what you do. All that happens is that it leads to cheating.' She paused for breath, contemplated for a moment as if surprised she had opened out so much to a relative stranger. 'Do people always tell you their deepest darkest secrets?' she asked.

'Not always, but often. More often recently. I think it's because they sense a fellow loser who's been wherever they fear they're going.'

'I reckon it's because you listen, and don't interrupt. Most of the people I meet through the game have such massive egos that they're already thinking of the next thing they can say to ambush the conversation before you've finished. We need to expand the directors' box to accommodate the egos of some of the chairmen and managers we entertain.'

'But David's not like that.'

'No, he's not,' she said softly, and it occurred to him that perhaps she wished there could be more between them than just a working relationship. The streets became more familiar and he realized that he was nearing his own neighbourhood.

'We'll be there in about ten minutes,' he said, hoping to encourage her to come to the point of their meeting. What he didn't want to do was to have to invite her up for a coffee.

'Is there somewhere we can go for a drink? Somewhere quiet.'

'There's a little deli which serves teas and coffees. And nice cakes.'

'That'll do. I do like a nice cake for tea.'

I'll bet you do, Mark thought, observing her ample hips, and generous bosom.

She sighed, and for a moment he feared he might have spoken aloud.

'That's always been my problem, a sweet tooth. I have tried very hard to diet in the past, but somehow lately there's not been a lot of people to diet for, so I've fallen into my old wicked ways.'

He directed her towards a parking space right in front of the deli, into which she reversed as neatly and precisely as she seemed to do everything else in her life. They were ushered to seats at the rear by the Italian owners, who greeted Mark as if he were a long-lost son.

'Marco, it has been too long. You don't like my pastrami any more? My pasta is not *al dente*? My cappuccino has too much froth?'

'Why do they call you Marco?'

'Gianni and Maria, who own this place, were friends of my father,' Mark explained as they sat down. 'He thought my name was Marco, but my mother defied him for the only time in her life and had Mark put on my birth certificate. It's always been my guess that she thought Rossetti was a big enough cross to bear if you were going to school in England. If you can avoid telling people your surname, you've a reasonable chance of them not calling you a wop. Now, what'll you have?'

She ordered a cappuccino which was perfect despite the fears of the proprietor and his wife who fussed around them as if they were inspectors from Egon Ronay, and then added a slice of *torta con nocciole*, a hazelnut cake with a generous proportion of his home-made *gelati*.

'Why is it that nobody makes ice-cream like the Italians?' she asked, the spoon half-way to her mouth.

'We're naturally hot-blooded. We need something to cool us down.'

He sipped his own little cup of strong black coffee, having declined the temptation of the cake on the grounds of a newly created diet, but had been forced to agree to take a couple of slices home in case he should become hungry in the night.

Gianni, who was a small, rotund man with a bald head that shone under the strip lighting, gave him a knowing wink behind Helen's back, and said in Italian so that she should not understand, 'I give you two slices in case you are both hungry.'

Mark made a little circle with the thumb and forefinger of his left hand, the gesture that was expected of him. Why was it that all Italians were such romantics? It would be a cruelty to tell his father's old friend that this was merely a business meeting.

'This is really good,' Helen said, her natural reserve disappearing with every second.

'Would you like some more?'

'No. I have to get on. My mother gets worried if I'm late and the day nurse charges overtime if I'm back a second after six.'

'Day nurse?' Mark queried.

'Yes, my mother's been in a wheelchair ever since the car crash that killed my father. He'd been drinking, of course. Christ, how I hate drunks.'

She suddenly realized what she had said and put her hand over her mouth like a small child caught involuntarily swearing.

'It's no problem. I hate drunks too,' Mark said.

'I'm sorry. I won't take too much of your time, and there may be nothing at all in it, but I just felt I had to tell somebody, somebody who would understand.'

'Go on,' Mark said encouragingly, signalling for his

coffee cup to be refilled. There was only so much of the potent brew a person could drink before he had a heart attack, but he was willing to experiment with the boundaries of tolerance.

'When Mickey disappeared it was one thing. Whoever took him wanted money, and got some of it as well.' She gave Mark a sidelong glance to ensure he did not think she was blaming him for anything, but he gave no sign of interrupting or taking offence. 'But when other things started happening, I decided to go through all the relevant files to see if I could see anything that struck me as odd.' She paused needing some encouragement, and it occurred to Mark that it had taken her some courage before she spoke to anybody about what she regarded as a matter of confidentiality within the club.

'And did you see anything?' Mark asked, supplying the lead she required.

'Yes. Or at least I think so.' She put the folder of papers she'd brought with her on the table, looking around to ensure nobody else was in the deli, and pulled out a sheet of paper covered with figures, the handwriting showing signs of a fairly basic education, the spelling supporting the theory.

'These are the proposals that were put forward for Mickey Wayne's last contract.'

'From Lennie Simons?'

'No, Mickey's uncle, Arthur Glover, dealt with it. The man had his own car cleaning service so I reckon the family thought that qualified him to negotiate the deal.'

Mark read them through.

'They seem quite reasonable to me.'

'Yes, they are.'

'Now here are the typed recommendations placed before David Sinclair, and a copy of his contract, from which you'll see most of them found their way in there.'

Mark laid the three documents out before him on the plastic tablecloth and, as he read, let out a whistle of astonishment.

'The uncle asked for a signing-on fee of a hundred thousand,' he said.

'And he got two hundred thousand.'

'He was looking for a basic salary of sixty thousand.'

'And there's a hundred thousand per annum in the contract. And you'll also see the bonuses for international caps, the loyalty bonuses, the appearance money, the provision of the car. He's been given everything but the M25.'

'That was because he probably didn't want it,' Mark said, struggling to understand the significance of what he was being shown.

'He didn't want half of these things, he didn't ask for them. Now what sort of negotiation is that?' Helen asked, and suddenly for Mark it all became crystal clear.

'Somebody was earning from Mickey out of this inflated deal, weren't they? And it wasn't Uncle Arthur either.'

She nodded, grim-faced, already worrying as to whether this was a matter she should report to the Premier League.

'Who did the initial negotiations on behalf of the club?' he asked, and when she told him it was Phil Reynolds it no longer came as a great surprise.

CHAPTER 35

He'd been looking for a change of luck, and the lady had brought it. Mark was now convinced of one thing above all, that Phil Reynolds' squeaky clean public image was just a façade. David Sinclair may have dismissed John Kelly, but he had hired another dishonest man in his place. Ever since he'd met Paula Reynolds he'd had the feeling that he was getting closer to the real Phil Reynolds and now he was sure of it.

Reynolds had been smarter than Kelly. He'd played hard to get when it came to football management. He'd been a media star after he'd won the hearts of the nation on the pitch, and still it had not been enough. He'd been greedy just like his predecessor and at the end of the day he'd made a mistake. Once Helen Archer had given Mark the papers the rest had been easy. Wayne's uncle presented himself with a modest deal probably because he simply did not know the value of his nephew and what he had sought had seemed like a lot of money to him. Reynolds had taken him or Wayne aside, Mark guessed probably the player, and he'd told him he'd give him a much better deal, but there had to be a sweetie in it for him. How much had he charged? Ten per cent? Again Mark thought it was likely to have been more, perhaps as much as fifty per cent of the uplift. The argument was attractive. Fifty per cent of something was always going to be more than 100 per cent of nothing. So, on the figures before him, Reynolds would have received some £70,000. And who was to say that the Wayne contract was an isolated incident with the sort of agents there were around. Sinclair trusted Reynolds. If he told the chairman that he had struck the best deal possible then there was no reason why he should not believe him. It still left him trying to work out the connection between the disappearance of the two men, if indeed there was any.

Patti had finally returned his call and having refused his offer of dinner had made a counter-proposal to come over and bring some food with her. She'd arrived shortly after eight, laden with packages.

'The bottle of wine's for me,' she said, 'just in case you get any ideas.'

She unpacked the various bags and containers.

'There we go; won-ton soup for three . . .'

'But there's only two of us.'

'Yes, but I like won-ton soup. Then there's this crispy duck, pancakes, fried rice, and a bit of Szchewan beef and chicken, oh, and some lychees for dessert. I hope that's enough.'

'I'm not sure I've got enough plates,' Mark said with a smile.

'Don't worry about it. We can pig out from the cardboard like they do at the start of *Roseanne*.'

'If you eat all this you'll start to look like Roseanne. Let's at least have the soup out of proper bowls.'

He moved towards the kitchenette and she called after him, 'Don't forget the wine glass for me. And an ashtray please. If I have a fag I'm sure that'll help keep the weight down.'

They began to eat and he told her what had happened at the ground and then what had come from his meeting with Helen Archer.

'So I turn my back and you're out gallivanting with other women. Very nice.'

'It was all in the course of duty, and believe me Helen Archer's not my type.'

'So who is your type, Mark?' she asked and he did not know whether she wanted him to say that she was.

She was still a paradox as far as he was concerned. He wanted to think her brittle, bantering surface hid something more tender and although she seemed to come and go as she wished without the need to offer explanations to anybody, there was no reason why there should not be a man in her life. He did not see her as the celibate type, nor did he think she was into women. He decided to turn her question into a joke, at least for the present.

'A woman who pays for her own food and doesn't drink or smoke.'

She did not look too happy with the reply.

'You'd better start hanging around the local nunnery then, that's about the only place you're likely to find her.'

They ate a little in silence and Patti knocked back three glasses of wine in quick succession, at which point her good humour seemed restored. Mark wanted to warn her of the dangers of getting happiness out of a bottle, but did not think she was likely to prove receptive. The one thing he

had learned about her was that she did not react kindly to
lectures.

'I've been busy today as well. Perhaps not as successful as
you though. I went through the picture library at the
Tribune today. You never know what might turn up.'

'And did anything?'

'I'm not sure. I borrowed these. I thought they might
mean a bit more to you than to me.'

She removed some glossy prints from her case and
spread them on the floor rather than removing the food
from the table. There was Mickey Wayne, a teenager with
his hair cut short; Wayne with John Kelly, the old manager;
Wayne with Phil Reynolds announcing his new contract;
Wayne, Reynolds and Sinclair. Mark shuffled through
them, sorting them into groups as if he were looking for the
edge pieces in a jigsaw. The faces of Reynolds and Wayne
smiled back at him, keeping whatever secrets they held.
Were they the faces of live or dead men? Finally he shook
his head.

'No, they tell me nothing.'

She looked a little crestfallen and poured herself another
drink. He couldn't stop himself saying, 'If you're going to
drive home, I'd call it a day with the wine, if I were you.'

'Well you're not me,' she said harshly, 'and if I decide
I'm not fit to drive then I can always stay here.' Her tone
changed, became more gentle. 'Can't I?'

He didn't know whether to be annoyed or relieved when
the front doorbell rang. He didn't usually have visitors at
this time of night, but if it was merely a salesman or
Jehovah's Witnesses (he couldn't remember if they only
called on Sunday mornings, it had certainly seemed that

way when he and Sally had wanted a lie-in during the early days of their marriage) then at least it gave him a little time to gather his thoughts about what may have been a proposition from Patti. He gave her a pecked kiss on the top of her head which could have meant anything and then went slowly down the stairs. The bell rang again insistently and he opened the door on the security lock. Since the attacks in the telephone booth and the restaurant he had become, not unreasonably, a little nervous. He need not have worried. It was Leopold Schneider, his face chalk-white, leaning awkwardly against the door, obviously in some distress. He undid the chain and the old man virtually fell into his arms.

'I'm so sorry to trouble you. I was nearby, collecting rents. All of a sudden I don't feel so good. I think maybe I'm going to collapse in the street. Then I remember, if you collapse in the camps you never get up, so I see I'm near to my best tenant...'

'And you decided to drop in,' Mark said, surprised at how little his landlord weighed and most of that in any event was overcoat.

'Always, you make me laugh, Markie. Maybe that's why I come, to be cheered up by you.'

'Listen, Leo. Do you think you can make it up the stairs? And then I can call for a doctor.'

'And if I can't make it up the stairs? You'll leave me here all night?'

In all the time he had known him, Mark had picked up the cadences of his speech and had assumed that all of his questions were rhetorical. At least Leo had never complained when he did not answer him.

'It's your property, Leo, you can stay where you like, but either way I'm getting you a doctor.'

Schneider, with some difficulty, pulled himself out of Mark's arms and, to Mark's astonishment, began to climb the stairs.

'I just need one of your special cups of tea in one of your beautiful chipped cups and I'll be fine.'

Mark followed him, ready to catch him if he fell, but step by step, though his breathing became increasingly more laboured, he made it to the top and crumpled into the oldest armchair, hardly noticing the presence of Patti.

'Leo, this is Patti. She'll look after you while I make the tea; but first I'm making that call.'

The old man made a feeble gesture with his hands, half apologetic and half dismissive. For the first time since Mark had known him he seemed terribly frail, like a wounded bird unable to fly after a fall from a tree. All his experiences had given him an inner strength which had diverted attention away from his physical weakness – until now.

'Ach, I'm sorry, you've got company. If I'd have known I would never have bothered you. I'll have my drink and I'll be off.'

He fumbled for his glasses and, producing them out of a well-worn, old-fashioned metal case, he put them on to take a better look at Patti.

'Nice, very nice. If I was thirty years younger and she was Jewish. Leopold Schneider, my dear,' he suddenly said, remembering his manners, and trying to rise to his feet whilst at the same time extending his hand.

'Patti, Patti Delaney,' she replied, taking his hand gently, 'and if you don't sit down and wait for the doctor,

I'll refuse to go out with you and you can forget all about my conversion.'

With ill-disguised relief he sank back in the chair and tried to make himself as comfortable as the battered chair would allow. Mark came back into the room with a steaming cup of tea in one hand and a couple of painkillers in the other.

'It's all a bit basic, I'm afraid, but it'll have to do until the ambulance gets here.'

'Phone them back, do me a favour,' Leo said. 'Once they get you into hospital, they find all sorts of other things wrong with you. Then they carry you in and they carry you out.'

'Don't worry, Leo. It'll take more than a minor heart attack to stop you. The whole of the SS couldn't do it.'

'Who said anything about my heart? I was feeling a bit faint that was all. You'll have to remind me to buy you some better furniture next time you pay me any rent. That is if you're intending to stay,' he added with a pointed look at Patti.

He took a sip of the drink, and his hands were shaking so much that Patti had to steady the cup for him and then take it away from him as if at the bedside of a sick child. Again he rooted around in the seemingly depthless pockets of his overcoat, this time producing an ornate little pill-box. He took two tiny tablets out and slipped them under his tongue.

'TNT,' he said by way of explanation.

'I think they're called GTN,' Patti said. 'My grandmother used to take them. But you said you didn't have a heart condition.'

'No,' Leo said calmly, as if they were arguing about the quality of fish, 'I asked who had said anything about my heart.'

'You're a bolshie old bastard, Leopold Schneider. They'll take one look at you at the hospital and then probably expel you.'

He drank some more tea, this time able to help himself without any disasters. His face now had a hint of colour and his voice also sounded stronger.

'Honestly, I don't need a doctor. Tell them to go and look for some sick people and leave me alone. Maybe though I'll go home by taxi, just for once.'

Mark found it hard not to smile.

'I don't believe you. You mean you drag around London collecting all these rents in cash and then travel home on the tube?'

'No, I usually take a bus. I like to see where I'm going.'

Leo peered at the photographs spread out on the floor.

'What's this, you're thinking of opening a gallery now? I recognize one of those men.'

'You should do. Mickey Wayne's face has been all over every newspaper for the last few weeks.'

'I never read the papers, who has time? I stopped reading the papers when they stopped publishing the Yiddish daily. Wayne, he's the young man you chose to look for rather than working for me, no? You see, if you'd taken the job, I'd have had less strain and I wouldn't be here now.'

'Are you trying to make Mark feel guilty, Leo? He's not your son and you're not a Jewish mother.'

'With a name like Delaney what do you know about Jewish mothers?'

'My father was Irish. My mother was Jewish.'

'That's good. So you don't need to convert to marry me. In the Jewish religion we follow the mother's faith. At last I've got something to recover for.' He hesitated as another spasm of pain coursed through his chest, then, as if the rest of the conversation hadn't happened, continued, 'Yes, I know one of the men in those photos; but not the young one.'

Mark picked up the picture of Sinclair, Reynolds and Wayne and held it close to Schneider's face.

'Which one do you know, Leo? And where from?' he asked, sensing the answers were going to be significant.

'He's like you, he rented a room from me, a couple of weeks ago. Only he paid his rent in advance.' As he spoke he pointed to the smiling face of Phil Reynolds.

CHAPTER 36

Wood Green, in north London, was not the sort of place Mark Rossetti would have chosen for a Thursday late-night date with a pretty girl. It had all moved so quickly after Leo had identified Reynolds, and the earlier part of the evening now seemed to belong to another life, another person's dream. What might have happened if Leo Schneider had not rung on the door, if Patti had finished the bottle of wine, if she'd stayed the night he would never know, nor would he now know whether he would have wanted her to share his narrow lumpy bed.

The ambulance had come to take away Leo, who was still protesting even as they fixed the oxygen mask on his face. Before then he'd handed them a huge bunch of keys that made Mark wonder just how little the old man would weigh with the coat and the keys removed. They'd had to convince him that he'd be better off in a hospital bed than accompanying them to the house where Reynolds had rented a flat. They'd finally compromised with Schneider by promising not only to visit him in hospital first thing in the morning, but also to help with his rent collections for as long as he was bed-bound.

'You see, Markie, what a devious old man I am. I wanted

you to work for me and I would have paid you, now I get you for nothing,' and then, mystified by the patient who chuckled over his heart attack, the ambulance men had put him on the stretcher and carried him away.

Once they arrived at the house they hesitated outside, not sure precisely what to do. It was a four-storeyed Edwardian end-of-terrace building, just off Green Lanes. It must have been a pleasant residence once, when owned by a single upper-middle class family who had already started the northern trek out of central London. Yet, whether it was under Leopold Schneider's steward-ship, or whether he had acquired it in that condition, it now looked that, unless it received fairly major repairs, it was not likely to survive to see its hundredth birthday. Leo had explained to them that only one flat was occupied, and when they'd pressed him for the reason for that he'd reluctantly explained that the local council had served a closing notice on the property. However when Reynolds had approached him through some local agents who, since there was cash on the table, asked few questions and for fewer references, it was the only property he had immediately available.

They sat in Patti's car looking up at the house, which from the front looked deserted and derelict. Somewhere along the street they could hear the sound of reggae music, whilst from a half-open window came the voices of a man and woman arguing in a mixture of Greek and English as to whose turn it was to walk the dog. By the sound of the barking in the background it appeared that if they did not decide soon then the animal would make the decision for them.

'If that's your friend Leo's idea of a desirable residence, I'd hate to see what he'd call a slum.'

'He didn't say it was desirable, just that it was habitable, and by the sound of things it was exactly what Reynolds was looking for. What was the name he said he took the place under?'

'Bates. That's original. Do you think he's seen *Psycho*?' she asked.

'More likely Chelsea. Anyway, I'm not going to knock Leo, he's been more than kind to me.'

'It's all right. You don't have to get defensive. I rather liked him, apart from the fact that I sense a story there.'

'I'll have to warn him about you and tell him to make sure he agrees a price before he talks to you.'

She threw him a mock punch.

'What's this, you starting to become an agent now?' she asked.

'Looking at this wreck and knowing someone agreed to let it makes me think estate agents are as bad as football agents. What are we going to do, sit here all night and soak in the local culture?'

She turned towards him, looking mysterious and beautiful in the dark as a streetlight caught her face, her perfume heavy in the enclosed car, winning its battle with the smell of smoke as she lit up the sixth cigarette since they'd left his home.

'Are you sure we shouldn't phone the police?' she said, as if it was something she ought to ask, although she knew there could be only one answer.

'I don't think Leo would thank us for that, do you?' Mark replied, placating both their consciences.

'No, he wouldn't, but then I'm not sure your landlord is the sort of man to thank anybody for anything, at least not in so many words.'

'So, let's go in then, shall we?'

'After you, Indiana, but I think I'm going to leave the car unlocked in case we have to make a quick getaway.'

'If you're going to do that in this neighbourhood then I'd take everything out that's movable and make sure the seats are insured.'

She laughed nervously and took no notice, merely stubbing out her cigarette in an already overflowing ashtray.

'I always think that once your ashtray's full then it's time to change your car.'

She closed the door softly and they moved as silently as they could up the front path, through the overgrown garden and then up the steep steps that led to the front door. The man down the street had lost his battle with his wife and was now walking the dog. Unerringly it lunged towards the gateway of Schneider's house and squatted down. The man, who wore a grimy pair of shorts and a string vest, shrugged at them as if to say that it wasn't worth making an issue of it considering the state of the property. He was a large, burly individual, with a few strands of hair brushed across the greasy top of his head and even if it had been Mark's own home he was not the sort of individual with whom he'd have picked a fight.

Mark fitted the key with the right label in the lock and it turned surprisingly easily although the door itself moved inwards with the protesting creak of a haunted house. The entrance hall was filled with rubble but, finding a light-switch which turned on a bare bulb, the two visitors were able to skirt their way around it, picking up a minimum of dust on their clothing. Leo had told them that it was the top-floor flat that he had let, but that did not stop them looking into every room as they climbed the stairs, carefully stretching their legs over the odd missing step.

They finally arrived on the top landing. It had originally been the attic of the house, converted by some previous owner who had obviously thought he and his family had a future in the property. The windows were still those from the original attic, diamond shaped, the moonlight shafting through them in tortured patterns. Now there was only one door. From behind it there was no sound but although something had been laid along the bottom of the door to ensure a black-out there was still a tiny suggestion of a light behind it. It was decision time. Did they push open the door, or turn and run back to Patti's car and the mobile phone, assuming it had not yet been stolen? Mark put his hand on the handle, pressing down only to find the door was locked. He fumbled through the keys, annoyed with himself that he had only found the front door key and not the key to the flat itself before leaving the sanctuary of the street. Leopold Schneider's writing was appalling, a spidery scrawl with a fountain pen that leaked with every loop, the labels made from cardboard cut from an old cornflakes box. He heard a cough from inside and quickly fitted the key once he had found it and threw the door open not knowing what to expect.

As the door opened wide, he saw a narrow bed, a fly-blown light, some basic plywood furniture and there, lying on the bed in a Hertsmere shirt and dark blue jeans, the thin figure of Mickey Wayne.

CHAPTER 37

'Thank God you're here,' Wayne said with a note of genuine gratitude in his voice. He moved slowly off the bed, blinking at the light from the hall like a hermit emerging from his cave. It suddenly struck Mark that Wayne might well not know who he was. He extended a hand, but before he could speak Patti said, 'Mr Wayne, I presume.'

The humour was lost on Wayne. He looked first at Mark then at Patti.

'I know you, don't I? You used to play for Hertsmere. Rossetti? And as for you, I've seen you around at press conferences.' The tone in his voice suggested that he had some regret at not pursuing her earlier.

'How long have you been here?' Mark asked.

Wayne rubbed his chin, then moved his hand up to the side of his face, tenderly touching a large bruise.

'How did you come by that?' Patti asked.

'So many questions,' Wayne said, a small unpleasant smile on his face. Mark wondered why it was that genius so often came in such a dislikeable form.

'Let me ask a question first. How did you get in here? Where have they gone?'

'They?' Mark queried.

'Yeah, that bastard Reynolds and his mate.'

'Reynolds?' This time it was Patti asking.

'Look you two. I don't want to appear ungrateful, but do you think we can get out of here before they come back, assuming they're gone. Little Miss Muffet here's going to want to file her exclusive and,' he turned directly to Mark, 'if what I've read about you is true, then you'll be needing a drink.'

Patti ignored the insults.

'We really ought to tell the police now that we've found him.' she said coolly as if Wayne were a lost purse.

'Let's just get the hell out of here and then, as far as I'm concerned, you can call Sherlock Holmes, Columbo and the whole of fucking Interpol,' the player said, moving towards the door, then peering nervously down the stairs.

It was not until he was in the back of Patti's car, cruising north, up through the leafier suburban streets of Palmers Green, middle-class Southgate and luxurious Hadley Wood towards the M25 and his home near St Albans, that he began to relax and gradually tell his story.

'Reynolds said he wanted to have a private word with me about the transfer. We went off in his car, I can't even tell you what day it was, I've lost track of time. They took my watch away.' He held up his bare left wrist for inspection. 'Fucking Rolex, I bet that's the last I see of that.' He paused, pondering the loss of the watch.

'Go on,' Mark said, as Patti drove wishing she had

brought her tape-recorder, concentrating more on remembering Wayne's words than on the road ahead.

'Well, as soon as we'd got away from the ground somebody pops up from the back seat, there's a bag over my head, and I suppose I was taken to that flat, wherever it was. I never saw the other man's face, but Reynolds was quite blatant about what he intended to do. He reckoned he wasn't so much kidnapping me, but holding the club to ransom. He knew how badly they needed the money from selling me. He tried to justify it. Said I should be glad of what he was doing. They'd freed the slaves in the States, he said, but never bothered with the footballers over here.'

'So why did he ask for a deposit, why not go for broke?'

'Sensible and reasonable fellow, our Phil. He didn't think there was any way Sinclair and the club could get all that money together. But half a mill. Well, he was sure that was on.' He leaned forward in his seat and peered at Mark. 'I've just realized, you're the poor bastard they sent to deliver the money. Reynolds said he'd been at the meeting at the club when they'd arranged it. He thought you were a prick. He said he'd even encouraged Sinclair to take you on because he was sure with you on the case he'd get away with it.'

'There were the police too,' Patti said, trying to salvage some pride for Mark.

'He had no time for them. Told me not to hold my breath for them, that the copper in charge didn't know a football from a bowling alley.'

'So that was how he knew about the bugging of the money,' Patti said.

'Yeah, it was all made easy for him.'

'But after he'd got the money, why the silence?' Mark asked. He disliked the man more and more, but he had to know the whole story.

'Bit embarrassing that. I'd been screwing his missus. She was a bit old for my taste, but then I didn't have to show her off in daylight and all cats look the same in the dark, don't they? She was hot for it, I don't reckon Phil was up to much in bed. Not exactly the best fuck I ever had, but she had a lot of enthusiasm, could never get enough of it, you know what I mean?' He got no answer, and taking that for a signal of agreement he carried on. 'Anyway, he finds out.'

'How?' Mark asked.

'I don't know. Dressing-room gossip, maybe. We'd thought we'd kept it pretty quiet, but there's no such thing as a secret in football.'

They were on the motorway by now, the lights of the cars on the opposite carriageway illuminating Wayne's face as they flashed by. Mark tried to imagine what these women had seen in him. His good looks or his cruelty, which had been more attractive?

'Whatever. Phil Reynolds is suddenly not a happy bunny. To be perfectly honest, he's a fucking crazed bunny. Now he's not going to bother with the rest of the money. He's going to kill me. Not at once. He says he wants to make it last a bit. Like your wife, I said. That was when he hits me. So I'm lying there and thinking, this is it Mickey boy, we're into extra time and the ref isn't going to add on anything and then you two turn up like I've rubbed the magic lamp.'

'So where did Reynolds go? And his accomplice?' Mark asked.

'Fuck knows. I'd tried to make a run for it once when the door was unlocked, but chummie was there, still wearing his mask. That time I got hit in the stomach. No marks, not like this.' Again his hand moved to his face. Mark saw the bandage on the finger where the nail had been removed.

'Do you think it'll scar?' Mickey asked quite seriously.

'I don't believe you, Mickey,' Mark said, 'we rescue you from a fate worse than death and all you're worried about is your looks.'

Mickey grinned, a boyish grin, and just for a moment they could both see how he could charm the birds from the trees.

'Appearances, it's all about appearances. I suppose it wasn't like that during your day.'

Mark, himself, itched to hit him, to finish off what Reynolds had started. But remembering the bonus he'd earn himself from Sinclair, and also from Barlucci if he stood by his word, he decided that he ought to return the goods in as fresh a condition as possible. Wayne, after all, had been through a traumatic experience, but it was difficult to be an apologist for this sort of man.

They arrived at Wayne's house a little after eleven. It was in total darkness.

'Do you think I'll find Laura in bed on her own? Maybe if she's got company she'll forget about my little diversions.'

'I doubt it,' Patti replied. 'We need to come in with you and phone the police anyway.'

Wayne looked troubled. 'Look, guys, I know I've been a bit of an asshole on the way back, but this whole thing's really shaken me up. If you call the police now they'll be round. It'll be questions, questions and more questions. I don't think I can face both my wife and the coppers tonight. It's not going to make any difference if you leave it to the morning. Just give me a chance to have a night's sleep and then you can call them first thing in the morning.'

'I don't know,' Mark hesitated.

'Hey come on, you've been there, Mark, you know what sort of pressure I'm going to come under when the press boys get hold of this.'

Whether or not it was the use of his first name, or whether it was because Mark also realized just how tired he was, he finally relented. Patti was made of sterner stuff.

'What if Reynolds goes back to the house? If we tell the police now they could be there waiting for him.'

'Do you honestly think he'll be back? He or his mate haven't left me alone for a minute before today. I don't know why and to be honest I don't really care, but something's spooked him. The house itself isn't going anywhere.'

Having seen the state of it neither Mark nor Patti were too sure of that, but Wayne pressed on. Finally he found Patti's Achilles heel.

'Play along with me and I promise I'll give you an exclusive interview tomorrow,' he offered. 'Now you know I can get a hundred grand for this from the *News of the World*.' She had only to hesitate for a split-second.

'OK. You've got a deal.'

'Thanks,' he said as if he almost meant it. 'By the way, what day is it?'

'Thursday, just about.'

'That's a relief,' the player said, starting to open the car door.

'Why?' Patti asked, failing to see the relevance of the day of the rescue.

'Because there's a whole day before Saturday.'

'Saturday?' Patti asked, realizing too late that she was beginning to sound like a particularly apt parrot.

Mark realized exactly what Wayne was saying.

'You're not thinking of playing in the semi-final, Mickey, are you?' he said with disbelief.

'Thinking of it?' Mickey said, smothering a cough which might have undermined his claim to fitness. 'I wouldn't miss it for all the fucking world.'

CHAPTER 38

Detective Inspector Peter Jordan was nowhere near as delighted as David Sinclair over the recovery of Mickey Wayne. He had given both Mark and Patti a hard time.

'I could charge the pair of you with obstructing the police in the course of their inquiries.'

'You could, but will you?' Patti had said, and not for the first time in their relationship Mark envied her self-confidence.

'I'm not saying I will and I'm not saying I won't. But I'm not happy, not happy at all. From what you've told me, if you'd brought us in a little earlier we'd have had a reasonable chance of getting Reynolds and his mate, not to mention the little matter of the money.'

'No clues at the flat?' Patti asked, a little more cheerfully than she felt. They'd been at the station for over three hours by then and she desperately needed a drink and a cigarette. Jordan had taken some pleasure in telling her he was a member of ASH, the anti-smoking organisation, and if she wanted to smoke then she'd have to wait either until he let her go or until he consigned her to the cells to await further questioning.

'I don't see why we should tell you anything, but as I

assume your job's at an end even if mine's just begun, the answer is no, no clues. Wherever Reynolds and his mate were going it wasn't back to the flat. They'd cleaned out the place of any trace of them. All we found was a few fingerprints and apart from that it was as if they'd never been there. From what Mr Wayne has told me he was a rather lucky fellow.'

They'd left him then, Patti to go and get her exclusive from Wayne, Mark to see Sinclair and discuss his payment. They'd both got what they wanted. Sinclair had written out the cheque there and then.

'I don't know if my board is going to sanction this or not, but even if I have to pay it myself, you've earned it.'

'Is Wayne going to play tomorrow?'

Sinclair shrugged.

'He's been to the hospital for a check-up and he seems fine considering what he's been through. Ray Fowler's having a good look at him now. He's obviously not going to be at peak fitness, but I reckon if Ray thinks he can get a half out of him, then he'll take a chance. It worked for Spurs against Arsenal in '91 with Gascoigne. I suppose you'd like a ticket for the game.'

'Can you make that two?' Mark asked.

'Of course, I was forgetting your little friend. Doesn't she have a press pass?'

'I'm hoping she'd rather sit with me.'

'Like her, do you? No problem. I'm not sure how much longer I'm going to be in a position to do anybody any favours at this club.'

'What do you mean?' Mark asked.

'Your old team-mate Chris Handsel. He's called a

shareholders meeting at the end of the month to have me removed as chairman. That is if I don't resign before.'

'And will you?'

'Would you?' He didn't wait for a reply. 'It's like a terminal illness this club. Once it gets into your bloodstream there's no getting it out. You know in my own business, when I had time to devote to my own business that is, I was always careful. I played a percentage game and I made money. Perhaps not as much as I would have done if I'd taken the risk some of my competitors did, but enough money to buy me this club anyway. Yet, somehow you put a businessman behind a desk at a football club and it's like taking a kid to the seaside. It's off with your clothes and on to the beach before there's any time to put on the suntan lotion. And then you wonder why you've got sunburnt.'

Now, sitting in the Royal Box at Wembley, Mark felt terribly sorry for David Sinclair. He could see and feel, virtually reach out to touch, the wave of emotion that greeted Sinclair's team. He'd lose all that if he lost the club. Mark had been surprised when he'd been given these prime tickets. An all-southern semi-final at Wembley was sure to attract the administrators of the game who had tried so hard to ensure that he would no longer be a part of it, no longer a player in the game. An old phrase, but one that had a particularly poignant message as far as Mark Rossetti was concerned.

Incredibly enough, Mickey Wayne was going to start the match. Ray Fowler had worked him hard on Friday and expressed himself satisfied. Even if he wasn't fully fit there was the psychological advantage of just having him on the field. Wayne's presence had brought all the interested guests to the party. Claudio Barlucci had come from Rome and was seated immediately in front of Mark, with Carla Dandone on his left. To Mark's surprise he'd not tried to renege on his deal.

'As soon as Wayne signs on the line, Signor Barlucci will sign the cheque to you,' Carla had translated for him as Barlucci beamed his huge smile in the background, looking like a bear who had discovered a new source of honey. A few rows further back, between Jonathan Black and Tom Kerr was Chris Handsel, a green and white Hertsmere scarf ostentatiously tossed around his neck despite the warmth of the Spring afternoon. Only Versace was not there in person, but Handsel himself, in his Italian silk tie and the expensive suit that he'd had specially made for the day, was a brooding reminder of his involvement.

David Sinclair sat in the front row, his daughter, Holly, by his side. Some of the fans had spotted the Italian contingent in the box and had resumed their vocal campaigns both against Sinclair and for Handsel. Holly, her young face looking drawn, was clearly taking it harder than her father.

'You'd think they'd forget about the boardroom for a day, wouldn't you?' Patti said to Mark. She had reason to feel particularly pleased with herself. She'd sold her exclusive interview to one of the Sunday tabloids and could relax knowing that whatever the outcome of the match her name would be on the by-line tomorrow. Yet, like Mark, if she had been totally honest with herself, there was an anti-climactic feeling about the day. If she and Mark had expected they would be received as heroes at Wembley by the rest of the Hertsmere board they were disappointed and indeed she'd heard Richard Lee say in his annoyingly affected accent, 'So they're letting journalists and banned players into the Royal Box now. Who knows? Maybe it'll be royalty next.' And everybody within earshot except for Sinclair and his daughter had laughed, and she could see Mark flush with anger and shame. Yet, despite that, Mark found himself drawn into the drama of the day. To his left, at the tunnel end, there were the banked Thamesmead fans, their red scarves and banners giving the appearance of a field of poppies. To his right, as far as the curve of the stadium, all was green and white, the Hertsmere supporters outnumbered, but not outsung. They had adopted the old classic 'Ten Green Bottles' as their anthem years ago and, perhaps more illogically, had backed it up with Buddy Holly's 'Everyday'. Thamesmead, with their Dockland base of fans, roared back with their version of 'My Old Man's A Dustman', the words obscene, but fortunately virtually incomprehensible, as the wall of noise rose to a crescendo.

The teams ran out on to the pitch rather than filing out in the normal circumspect Wembley fashion. Mark did a quick head count, looking for Wayne and the number eleven shirt, but he was nowhere to be seen. The thought flashed across his mind that perhaps the drama was not yet over, that somehow or other Reynolds had got him back again, but then he was there, a master craftsman at manipulating his audience, making a solo entrance to a roar from the Hertsmere end. Wayne ran over to applaud the Hertsmere supporters and they responded with the sort of reception that would have relegated the Beatles at their peak to a supporting act on the bill. It was a mutual admiration society, a private party from which the group in suits and ties in the Royal Box was excluded.

Stuart Macdonald won the toss and chose to attack the Hertsmere end. An animal-like roar from both sets of fans signalled the kick-off and they were away. Mark saw David Sinclair lean forward, his body hunched and tense, his hand clutching the rail in front of him as if it was his last point of contact with the reality. For the first quarter of an hour there was no respite for his nerves. Wave after wave of Thamesmead attacks broke against the green wall of Hertsmere's defence and it seemed that Sinclair's club had brought their uncertain League form to North London. Greg Sergovich, his injured finger forgotten, was magnificent. A huge, imposing figure in his bright new multi-coloured keeper's top, he pulled off save after save until it seemed that, once it got within his orbit, his gloves were a magnet for the ball. Wayne stayed out on the wing, apparently held there by an invisible chain. He touched the ball only once and as he controlled a long clearance by Macdonald a shiver of excitement could be sensed passing through the whole crowd, like opera-goers waiting to hear a new diva hit a high C. But, before Wayne could turn and run, a Thamesmead defender launched himself at him with all the velocity of an Exocet missile and both Wayne and the ball ended up over the touch-line.

Half an hour gone, and still the balance was with Thamesmead. Suddenly their centre forward, the Swede, Erstrom, who towered over even Nick Collier, found himself in space, ran forward past Macdonald with the grace of an awkward spider and, drawing Sergovich off his line, for once left him helpless as he toe-poked the ball into the net. Before the roar of the red end could erupt there was an audible sigh from the Hertsmere fans. The Thamesmead representatives in the royal box were on their feet as well and as Mark looked towards them he saw from the corner of his eye Handsel say something to Black and could have sworn he saw the flicker of a smile on both their faces. There could be no doubt that Handsel had a far better chance of carrying the day at any meeting if Hertsmere were out of the Cup. Then, just before half-time, it happened. The fairy-tale script had taken some time to come true, but there was Wayne getting the ball on the left-hand side of the halfway line. He gave the merest suggestion of looking up, then began his run. Collier, too, began to lumber forward, but so great was Wayne's speed, so fluent his action, that by the time he had slipped two defenders and got to the edge of the penalty area, Collier was ten yards behind him and the square pass was simply not on. The right back came to meet Wayne and the Hertsmere forward turned him in one move, leaving him lying on his backside. The Thamesmead's sweeper was still between Wayne and the goal. Collier had arrived now, screaming for the ball in the middle, but with an unerring instinct Wayne chose to chip the keeper and, finding the impossible angle, somehow slotted the ball into the only space available, a space no bigger than the circumference of the ball. Even before it had nestled in the back of the net, he was already past the goal on to the running track and receiving the wild worship of his fans. As they reluctantly pulled themselves back to their own half, after the referee had threatened to book the whole team for time-wasting, only Collier was ungracious.

'You should have pulled it back. I was in a much better position. I don't make those fucking runs for fun you know.'

'You don't run, you waddle, you stupid cunt. We scored, what more do you want?' Wayne replied.

'Why don't you go missing again? We were a sight happier without you,' Collier responded, but before Macdonald could intervene and tell them both to cut it out and concentrate on the game, the half-time whistle blew. With several hundred cameramen following every inch of Mickey Wayne's return to the dressing-room, and a bevy of cameras set to catch every word, Collier backed off, and settled for giving his own fans a two-finger victory salute. They responded to him with another cheer and a chant of his name.

Barlucci was up on his feet shouting 'Bravo', oblivious to the fact that he was aiding and abetting an increase in Wayne's value. Mark made his way over to Carla Dandone, Patti close by his side.

'Your client did well,' he said affably.

'I must thank you for bringing him back. If he scores goals like that every week he will be a saint in Rome.' She gave him a Madonna smile that suggested she had daily contact with the heavenly host. 'We hope to reach an agreement with Signor Sinclair over the next few days.' She nodded in the direction of Handsel. 'If he takes over the club before we have done a deal then I think he will sell the player to Ulisse and his friend Versace.'

'My friend, you mean. I'd no sooner met him than he tried to blow me up.'

She shook her head slowly as if Mark would never understand the ways of his father's native country. 'No, if Paolo Versace had wished to blow you up, then he would have done so. He does not try to do anything, he only succeeds.'

A thought suddenly struck Mark. He was becoming more aware of inconsistencies in life, and perhaps that was making him a better investigator, even though he no longer had anything to investigate.

'Handsel's public position is that he'll never sell Mickey Wayne if he takes over.'

'As a lawyer, may I suggest that you read, what do you call it in English?' she frowned, annoyed that her English wasn't quite perfect, 'the small print,' she added triumphantly. 'It probably says that what Mr Handsel means is that he will not sell my client to Cinquante ... But Ulisse, that will be another matter.'

While Mark turned the words over in his mind, Patti took over the conversation. She was never one to miss an opportunity, particularly when she had a cigarette in one hand, a glass of wine in the other and an interview target in front of her.

'I wonder if you and Signor Barlucci would let me talk to you while you're here. I'd like to do a feature on the mechanics of a transfer. If there were any financial details you'd want to keep out, then that would be no problem.'

Carla's guard was immediately raised.

'I will have to consult with Signor Barlucci. And, of course, Mr Wayne.'

The keenest of the spectators began to file back to their seats, anxious not to miss the opportunity to reaffirm their commitment to their heroes. Handsel and Black held back, their glasses still full, and Mark saw that Richard Lee took the opportunity of briefly telling Handsel something which had him tilting his glass against that of Black when they believed everybody had turned away to return to the box. There were still questions to be answered and Mark wondered whether he had any moral obligation to find those answers. He shook his head to rid himself of the thoughts. He was here to watch a match, he had a five-figure sum in the bank, a six-figure bonus coming when Wayne signed for Cinquante and, more than that, he had a degree of self-respect. If he respected himself who was to say that he couldn't persuade Sally to do likewise. Nobody was trying to sue him or kill him. He didn't need any problems, at least not this afternoon.

He'd even been asked by Ray Fowler to dash down to the dressing-room during the interval to talk to Tommy Wallace. Wallace had not taken his omission lightly.

'It's not like I've been playing badly. And my suspension doesn't start till next week. OK, play Mickey, but why drop me? That miserable bugger Collier could go and I could play straight down the middle.'

'You've a lot to learn, Tommy, and a lot of time in which to learn it. There are Colliers in football and there are Waynes and there are Wallaces. You need them all. You've not got Collier's strength and he's not got your skill. You'll get on today, I promise you. There's no way Mickey will last ninety minutes. And when you get on, enjoy it, savour every minute. You don't know when it's going to happen again.'

He was going to say, 'Look at me,' but he realized he no longer felt sorry for himself. He had already got his message across without gilding the lily further.

Neither side had made any substitutions and at one-all the crowd settled into the effortless concentration that preceded what was going to be an enthralling forty-five minutes, with perhaps the chance of getting even more money's worth from a half-hour's extra time.

Wallace was already warming up on the touch-line before the whistle blew to start the half and within ten minutes of the restart it was clear that Mark was going to be able to keep his promise to him. Wayne was clearly in difficulties, scarcely moving from his own half, neither making any runs nor tackling back to cover. Finally he sank to his knees and, in full view of the seventy thousand crowd, began to vomit. Fowler ran forward himself holding the eleven and twelve cards in his hands, and, in a matter of seconds, Tommy Wallace, at just eighteen years of age, was on the hallowed Wembley turf for the first time in his life.

Wallace did not hesitate. Sergovich, keen to involve him as soon as possible, threw the ball with unerring accuracy half the length of the pitch to the youngster's feet. In one movement he trapped the ball and began to run. The Thamesmead full back had already received a yellow card for his earlier tackle on Wayne and, anxious to avoid another booking and automatic dismissal, fatally backed off the winger. Wallace suddenly dropped his shoulder, threw the defender off balance and cut inside him. This time Collier had made his run early and Wallace planted a perfect cross on Collier's head from whence the ball bulleted past the Thamesmead keeper.

Mark was the first to get to his feet, feeling a more than proprietorial interest in the Scottish kid. Wallace looked up, and seeing him, clenched his fist and punched the air as if to say that now he understood why the team needed the likes of Nicky Collier. Fowler was yelling at his lads from the bench, telling them to hold their concentration, that there was still a long way to go. Wayne sat by his side, pale-faced, a bucket by his side, holding his head in his hands as if convinced that if he let go it would roll away like a spare football.

Fowler need not have worried about his team. Wallace came back to collect the ball from the left-sided Hertsmere defender, Darren Braithwaite. He played a one-two with Braithwaite just outside his own penalty area, the ball narrowly avoiding the attempted interception of Erstrom. Fowler screamed so loudly that he seemed certain to break a blood-vessel. Ignoring him, Wallace continued his run, leaving first the Thamesmead mid-field and then their defence stranded and confused by his changes of pace. He got to the arc of the opposing penalty area and without any indication that he had looked up to take aim let fly with a shot that entered the net, hit the stanchion and then bounced out with such speed that for a moment nobody but Wallace was sure he had scored.

The rest of the game was a formality. Hertsmere closed it down, their experienced defence bolstered up by the mid-field who no longer had the need to go forward. From the entertainment point of view it was dull, but effective, yet there were no complaints from those who had come to cheer Hertsmere home. Their thoughts were now concentrated on how they could get Cup Final tickets.

It finished 3–1 and David Sinclair modestly accepted the congratulations of the Thamesmead chairman.

'You can concentrate on the League now,' Sinclair said, wondering if he could have been as magnanimous in defeat as his counterpart. He looked round for Holly, but she had gone, presumably finding the occasion too much for her. Handsel, a smile upon his face which anybody who did not know him would have taken for genuine, marched up to the chairman.

'It's nice to go out in a blaze of glory,' he said softly to Sinclair, satisfied that nobody could hear them. 'I'll make sure you get a couple of tickets for the Final.'

Sinclair bunched his fist, wanting to knock the man to the ground, knowing that it was exactly what Handsel wanted him to do – another negative story to catch the headlines. Instead he merely looked into the bottomless pits of Handsel's eyes.

'And I'll make sure that the nearest you get to Wembley on Cup Final day will be by watching a television set.' But even as he spoke he knew he had no idea of how to achieve his hollow threat.

CHAPTER 39

For once in his life Lennie Simons was in control neither of his temper nor his own destiny. He'd had no problem getting in through the huge wooden gate that guarded the stadium perimeter entrance to the players' changing rooms. He represented three of the Thamesmead team and he'd got their captain Adam Barnes called to the door to facilitate his entrance. But once in the narrow corridor outside the triumphant and noisy Hertsmere changing rooms he could get no further. A Wembley security guard stood stoically at the entrance with instructions to let nobody in until the players decided they'd exhausted the singing and the champagne and decided to come out. Gordon Dancer, the team's portly kit man had come out once and had been duly dispatched with a message for Mickey Wayne to which there had been no answer.

Adam Barnes trailed off dejectedly with the rest of the Thamesmead team.

'I'll see you, Lennie.'

'Yeah, yeah. I'll be in touch. Got a lot of good things for you.'

It was his customary farewell to any players he represented, but today it carried no conviction and Barnes wondered if his man was losing his touch. He'd had no contact with him for weeks and he'd been approached by two other agents, one of whom guaranteed him a move abroad within a year, so maybe it was time for a change. Oblivious to the potential loss of another of his players Simons began to shout as the door half-opened.

'Mickey, I know you're in there. You come out and talk to me like a man. You're where you are today because of me. I've made you.'

Inside the dressing-room, Mickey Wayne was still not feeling too good. The club doctor was fussing over him and trying to persuade him that he'd had enough to drink for a man who'd been violently sick.

'Is there another way out of here, Ray?' Wayne asked the acting manager.

'Sure. You go back on to the pitch, up the stairs to the royal box and go out through there.'

'I'm going to take it. I can't face that stupid cunt out there. He made me, did he? More like I made him money. I'm off, lads. See you around.'

The rest of the players said goodbye with various degrees of enthusiasm. He'd only been back with them for a day, but he'd done nothing off the pitch to endear him to them any further.

'What about some interviews, Mickey?' the club press officer, Alastair Thompson, asked.

'Nah, I'm not in the mood. Little Tommy here can earn a few bob.' He turned towards Wallace. 'There's an agent outside who's just dying to negotiate a deal for somebody. Maybe you can make his day.' And then he was gone.

Mark Rossetti arrived just in time to see Lennie Simons

failing in his attempt to push by the security man to catch up with Wayne's retreating back.

'Mickey, Mickey, just talk to me. I can make a fortune for you. There are TV interviews, paper interviews, I've even got *Hello* interested in doing an at home. And I'll do you a better job in Italy than anybody else. What's that Italian slut got that I haven't – other than a couple of tits and a pussy?'

Wayne didn't even look back as Simons screamed his last words.

'You think I'm going to sit back and let you get away with this, you little shit. I'll make sure you don't even get to take a package tour to Italy!'

Ray Fowler came out into the corridor and quietly asked the security men to remove the angry agent. As two six-footers grabbed him by his arms and virtually carried him towards the door, Mark squeezed back against a wall to let them pass.

'You brought him back,' gasped Simons. 'You've done him no favours, I'm telling you. Do you hear me? I'm telling you.' Suddenly recovering some strength in his voice, he yelled in Wayne's direction. 'This is me, Mickey Wayne, nobody does this to Lennie Simons, not if he wants to stay a player in the game.'

That phrase again, but this time Mark found himself unmoved by it. He just wanted to talk to Tommy Wallace, to tell him how proud he'd been of his performance, to warn him about the dangers that he now faced from men like Lennie Simons. He found the lad sitting shaking in a corner, devoid of all the cockiness of which Fowler had complained.

'Hey, Tommy, you did well.'

'Yeah, thanks, Mark. I couldn't have done it without you.'

'No problem. You helped me too.'

The boy looked up surprised.

'How's that?'

'I'm not sure you'd understand. Maybe some other time. What's wrong now?'

'They tell me I've got to go out and give interviews, that half the press in the world's out there. I've never done that sort of thing before and I'm scared rotten. I thought they'd be more interested in Mickey, but he's just buggered off and left me.'

'Well that's Mickey for you. Did you enjoy the match like I told you?'

'Yes.'

'Well, now you go on out and enjoy the interviews. All you have to do is relive the match and imagine the newsboys and photographers aren't there.'

The boy got slowly to his feet, looking towards Mark for another dose of confidence. The older man nodded to him and the youngster went out the door with the slow measured pace of a man going to the scaffold. Ray Fowler and Mark were the last two left in the dressing-room.

'Drink?' asked Fowler.

'I don't,' Mark said without hesitation, almost surprised to have convinced himself he was telling the truth.

'Me neither. I had a father who liked a drop too much and when he'd had his drop liked to knock us about a bit too much. There's some orange juice over there. Some of the boys are into Bucks Fizz. I never liked their music either.'

'So what happens now?' Mark asked, not expecting an answer, but getting one all the same.

'We make our plans for Wembley. I make my plans for next season. And Mickey Wayne makes his plans for Italy.' He shrugged, both men poured themselves a glass of orange juice, and then there seemed to be nothing more to say.

On Monday morning, however, there were too many people having too much to say and Wayne's Italian adventure seemed anything but certain. They'd worked all through Sunday night and the Hertsmere boardroom smelt of stale cigarette smoke and unwashed people. It did not help communications that Claudio Barlucci's English was limited to, 'good, very good,' which he seemed to say to anything, even when it was apparent that what he meant was, 'bad, very bad'. The time it took for Carla to translate and the gulf between the parties meant that they had arrived at four in the afternoon without any sort of consensus whatsoever.

'Tea-time I think,' David Sinclair said, buzzing through to Denise and placing the order without bothering to ask if anybody actually wanted coffee. He wasn't usually that discourteous, but he'd had his fill of almost everybody at the meeting. Tom Kerr had insisted on attending despite the assertions of Sinclair that he could handle it perfectly well on his own.

'With respect, David, we're not sure you're fully committed to this deal and, even if you are, your financial track record with this club before I came on the board does not give the bank any great cause for confidence. There's also the unpleasant question of whether or not you're going to be around to see the completion of any deal we reach. There's nothing worse for new management than to have to pick up the pieces of their predecessors without anybody around to explain to them exactly what's occurred.'

Nobody could ever accuse Tom Kerr of pulling his punches, thought Sinclair.

Helen Archer was there too, not only to take detailed notes but also to advise on the technicalities that could arise from a transfer of a player abroad. She was the only one Sinclair excepted from his ill-humour. She'd been incredibly helpful, knowing just where to look, not only in the League rules, but also in the regulations for international clearances and stage payments. That had been part of the problem. The massive offer of seven million pounds which had seemed so attractive to Kerr and the bank had turned out to be a real offer of three million down and then two million a year for the following two years. Kerr had rejected it out of hand and they had therefore begun again virtually from scratch. The other complication was Carla Dandone. She seemed to have agreed Wayne's terms with Cinquante, but now as she acted as interpreter for Barlucci her position as his adviser was placed into conflict when he, Barlucci, tried to renegotiate Wayne's arrangements as Kerr sought to improve Hertsmere's position. It was a nightmare and when Mark arrived to see David Sinclair, as he'd been asked, at three thirty, he found him still locked in the meeting, and Denise a bundle of nerves as document after document was brought out for her to type, then tear up and type again.

Sinclair used the tea-break to call Mark into his office,

leaving the rest of them still arguing in the boardroom which by now was filled with smoke from Barlucci's endless cigars and Carla Dandone's Gitane cigarettes.

'Bad day?' Mark asked, wondering how comfortable he now felt about dealing with the chairman as an equal.

'A hotter than average day in hell. I don't know who's worse, Kerr or Barlucci. By the time Barlucci's finished what he's saying I can't believe the lady lawyer can remember it all to translate. If she can then I reckon she could learn any of the female leads in Shakespeare in an afternoon.'

Mark shook his head.

'I can find missing players even if I can also lose ransoms. I don't think I can pour oil on the troubled waters of his transfer as well.'

'I'm not so sure about that; but that's not why I asked you to come in and see me. I'm sorry to have kept you waiting, by the way, but once Julius Caesar and Macbeth in there are in full flight it'll take an earthquake to stop them.'

'Or a tea-break,' Mark added with a smile.

'Yes, a tea-break. Has Denise been looking after you?'

'Denise always looks after me. You've got a treasure there.'

'I know.' Sinclair glanced at his watch. 'I'm sorry, I've not got a lot of time so I'll get right down to business. I told you all about Handsel on Friday. I'm not sure whether winning on Saturday helped my position at all. The bank's still pushing me to sell Wayne. As long as they do that I can't believe I'm going to be soaring to the top of the popularity charts with the fans and in particular those fans who are also shareholders.'

'Surely they'll be pleased that you've put the club into profit.'

'Football club shareholders don't think like that. We don't pay dividends so their assessment of the value of their shares is reflected by what we do on the field.'

'But you're in the Cup Final,' Mark persisted.

'And we're about to sell our best player. Believe me, Mark, I've argued it up and down, told them what we could earn from a European run if we win, but they just don't want to know. And there's the white knight, St Chris Handsel, manipulating the press until everybody's convinced that if he takes over Wayne stays.'

'But the beautiful Signorina Dandone seemed to think that he'd sell him anyway. But to Ulisse rather than Cinquante.'

'And she's probably right, but if I say that who's going to believe me, and once he's in control who's going to stop the sale? He's got an easy way out, he just says the player insisted on going and what good was an unhappy player to the club. Also he'll be able to use the money to strengthen the club while I'm going to see it pass me by with hardly a wave on the way to the bank.'

'I thought you were in a hurry,' Mark said sympathetically.

'Yes, yes, I was forgetting. It's just a welcome break to talk to somebody who's not trying to take a slice of my flesh. What I want, Mark, is for you to see if there's anything that can stop Handsel pushing me out.'

'I would have thought that was a matter for your lawyer.'

'There are some things lawyers can't do. And anyway, my lawyer's Richard Lee. I'm beginning to lose a bit of faith in him nowadays.'

'Handsel has a rough reputation,' Mark said dubiously.

'Shouldn't be a problem to a man who's been knocked over for half a million pounds. Don't worry. Win, lose or draw, I'll make it worth your while.'

Mark had been without money too long to be altruistic, but he had grown to like the chairman, not only to like him, but also to feel an affinity with him in his love for the club.

'Don't worry about making it worth my while. I'll take it on. I've got enough to live on for a while from my bonus. You pay my expenses and, if I pull off any miracles, then we'll talk about the money.'

Sinclair gripped his shoulder.

'You're a good guy, Mark. Why is it the good guys always lose?'

'It doesn't have to be that way,' Mark replied and, as he spoke, he realized how far he'd travelled in a short space of time.

CHAPTER 40

It was nearly three on Tuesday morning before the deal between Hertsmere and Cinquante and Cinquante and Wayne was completed. Some time after midnight, Carla Dandone had decided that her client was not seeing sufficient monies from his old club as, led by Tom Kerr, they in turn had pushed Cinquante up and up. Kerr, Sinclair and Helen Archer had focused their tired eyes in disbelief when Carla had suddenly asked what Hertsmere would be paying Wayne to see him go.

'The player has a contract with you. He did not ask to leave. He must be compensated.'

'But he'll be earning fortunes in Italy,' Kerr said, the morality of his Scottish Presbyterian background rearing its head in protest.

'It is irrelevant. You are receiving many millions for him. Some of those millions could have been made available to him from Cinquante if you had not been so greedy. Now we want a little back.'

Kerr's temper, which had threatened to reach breaking point for several hours, suddenly erupted.

'It's the same fucking money going round and round, you stupid cow.'

Carla was unmoved either by the expletive or the insult. She shrugged, a mannerism calculated to irritate far more than by her meeting fire with fire.

'Either you pay or the deal is off. It would be a pity if we all go away empty-handed after so many traumas, so much time and effort by everybody.'

At this they had broken off into splinter groups, but had got close enough to a deal to wake Mickey Wayne at two a.m. From then they had somehow or other been conducted by Helen Archer to a compromise that would have qualified her for the position of Secretary-General of the United Nations rather than merely the secretary of an English football club.

When Mark arrived at the ground at ten, David Sinclair was still in his office, unshaven and rumpled-looking, a far cry from the immaculate figure he had seen on his first visit.

'It didn't seem worth going home. If my future at this club is limited then I might as well take full advantage of all the hours I can spend here.'

'The deal went through?' Mark asked.

'It did. It's just subject to a medical in Rome some time before the end of the season.'

'Why Rome?'

'I guess they don't trust our English doctors. Anyway, it's done. And I feel done too. Look, Mark, about the job offer. You don't have to feel obliged to take it if you don't want to. With the Wayne deal looking to go through and assuming Barlucci keeps his word, you're all set for the future. You're on a winning streak, why back a loser?'

'You've not got a lot of faith in me have you?' Mark asked, trying to jolly the chairman along.

'I've not got a lot of faith in myself. I don't like him, but I have to admit that if Wayne had to be sold then Kerr struck a much harder bargain than I would have done; and as for that woman ... Well give me Lennie Simons any time. At least when you've finished negotiating with him then you know when you've finished. He doesn't start up all over again when you're seeing him to the door.'

'I don't think you mean that, David.'

'I don't know what I mean. I'm shattered.'

'Why don't you just go home and get some sleep. There's no way you can get through the day looking the way you do.'

'Forget about the looking, it's the way I feel. Helen said the same thing to me, so did Denise. I suppose the three of you can't be wrong. Maybe I'll grab a couple of hours shut-eye and then come back. Is there anything you need?'

Mark shrugged. 'To be perfectly honest I don't know why I came in this morning. It just seems a good place to start. I had that feeling before and I was right. I'll have a chat with Helen and Ray and then I'll be on my way.'

'To where?'

'I thought I'd go and look up an old friend.'

'Sounds pleasant.'

'Not really. He's called Chris Handsel.'

'What do you think you'll gain by that?'

'Not sure. Maybe I'll rattle his cage a little. Last time I did that somebody tried to blow me up,' he added with a rueful grin.

Sinclair shook his head.

'All footballers are crazy even if they've stopped being footballers.'

'You never stop,' Mark said. 'It's like being a fan. However much you get punished or disappointed by your team you always come back for more.'

'You know, Mark, you're becoming a bit of a philosopher. I'm off. Close the door of my office when you've finished.'

Mark stayed for a moment looking out of the window, watching the players going through the motions on the pitch below. Ray Fowler was yelling as usual, trying to motivate them to concentrate on the bread and butter of the rest of the League programme after the caviar and champagne of the semi-final triumph. They still did not know who their opponents would be at Wembley in May. In the other semi-final, Allerton Town and Whitefield Rangers had slugged out a goalless draw that extra time had failed to bring to a conclusion and they were due to meet again the following week in the replay. Either of the north-western giants were likely to prove tough opposition. Well-supported, rich in talent, the two sides had dominated Cup competitions for the past five years. Whoever won through, Hertsmere were going to have to play a lot better than they had done on Saturday and Mickey Wayne would have to be coaxed back to full fitness and full form. A piece of paper on Sinclair's desk caught Mark's eye. It was a personal reminder to the chairman, yet it also reminded Mark of something although he could not think what. Before he could concentrate his mind on it, Fowler spotted him through the window and gave him a wave that, in his dour nature, passed for cheerful.

'Mark, could I have a word with you sometime?' he shouted. 'Maybe after training.'

'I can't hang around, Ray. I have to be the other side of London by lunch-time.'

'No problem. What about tonight? Come round and I'll make us a bite to eat.'

'Sounds fine to me. What time?'

'About eight. I'll leave my address at reception.'

Tommy Wallace also spotted Mark at the window and waved cheerfully, then juggled the ball in the air a couple of times, before executing what seemed to be an impossible chip over the head of Greg Sergovich. Wayne looked up and although he saw Mark he gave no indication that his rescuer had any further part to play in his life.

Before he left, Mark asked to see Helen Archer. He wanted to know whether she had any more thoughts about Wayne's earlier contract, the one finessed by the still-absent Reynolds, but unlike Sinclair she had gone home to what he assumed was her single bed to catch up on her sleep. He had not yet decided whether or not to confront the player with what Helen had uncovered. All he need say was that he knew nothing about it, that he'd been just a kid. Perhaps he should speak to the uncle first. He scribbled a note to himself on the little pad that he now kept in his top pocket. Another sign of professionalism. Never rely on your memory. Memory for a footballer was the greatest practical joker of all.

He left the ground to return to his hired car. If he was on expenses he felt no pangs of guilt in giving himself at least one indulgence. There was also the problem that he couldn't use Patti as his driver on this particular quest. Sinclair had been quite specific on that point.

'Your young lady's had her scoop. That's enough for anybody. This one's between me and you.'

Mark had been disappointed, but he understood, although he wasn't sure she would see it that way. His deal with Patti had related to Wayne and he had kept his part of the bargain. Yet, if he could have involved her in this investigation he would have needed no excuse to seek her company. They had parted after the semi-final like friends, promising to phone each other. And, even in the few days that had passed, he had longed for her to call and resisted the temptation to call her himself in case she said no to whatever it was he was going to ask. He might have rediscovered his self-esteem, but he still felt like an awkward teenager when it came to Patti. When he'd woken himself at two in the morning one of the muddled thoughts that had passed through his sleep-fogged mind was that he had no right to search out new relationships until he had cleared his own name. Sinclair may have treated him as if his sentence had been served, but in order to move forward he needed a full pardon. He'd fallen back to sleep denying the truth, but when he'd tried to dial Patti's number to see if she'd meet him for a meal that evening the thought had numbed his fingers and he had left the call unmade. He dreaded the idea that she might ask him to do the long-delayed interview, that all he had been for her was a good potential story, a story in which her part was merely the narrator.

The drive through London was the usual nightmare. He

could never understand how people could live south of the river. As soon as he crossed any of the bridges across the Thames he felt in dire need not only of his passport but also *The Hitchhiker's Guide to the Galaxy*. It was with some relief that he discovered Handsel's company nestled virtually on the banks of the river just across Vauxhall Bridge. At least he could keep the north bank in sight. He passed through wrought-iron gates under a huge sign that said 'Handsel & Sons' in bold letters with the words 'Scrap Metal Dealers' beneath in much smaller print, as if that were an aside. Just beyond the gate he was stopped at a security barrier manned by a man wearing a black vest which revealed bare well-muscled arms covered in tattoos. He looked well over six feet tall and not much less than that wide, and it occurred to Mark that, with a body like that to get past, the security gate itself was superfluous.

'Yeah?' the guard asked with none of the charm of the gorilla he resembled.

'I'd like to see Chris Handsel please.'

Surprised that he could read, Mark watched as the man flipped through the pages of a book in front of him.

'Mr Handsel ain't got no appointments this morning, so piss off.'

'Look, I'm an old friend. Just ring through to him and tell him Mark Rossetti's here and he'd like a few minutes of his time.'

'Mr Handsel don't see no one without an appointment.' Mark almost wanted to laugh at the traditional secretarial put-off coming from the man-mountain who loomed over his car. He tried a different tack.

'What team do you support?'

The man looked at him with a blank stare, as if he'd just asked him how to make a nuclear reactor.

'What?'

'Team, football team.'

'Hertsmere. We all support Hertsmere here.' He made it sound as if it was a condition of employment and perhaps it was. Mark tried to guess the man's age.

'I used to play for them. With Chris. Rossetti, Mark Rossetti.'

'Yeah, I remember you. Bit tasty weren't you, until you went bent.' He pondered for a few seconds, the workings of his mind as transparent as the mechanism of a carriage clock.

'Yeah, you was a bit of all right. I'll ring the boss and see what he says.' He did, and even as he was talking on the phone Mark noticed how his manner changed. He was more alert, more upright, more disciplined and Mark shuddered at the thought of crossing him in his line of duty as part of Handsel's bodyguard.

He leaned into the window of the car and Mark could smell the sweat of the man despite the coolness of the day, could feel his hot breath close to him.

'Mr Handsel says he can give you fifteen minutes now. You drive on to the bottom, then turn left and you'll see the offices in front of you. You'll need this.' He gave him a little electronic pass tag and Mark realized that this was merely the perimeter as far as security was concerned. Why should somebody who dealt only in scrap be so neurotic? When he was a kid the scrap dealers had settled for barbed wire and broken glass set in concrete on the top of the walls that surrounded their yards. Maybe there was now a premium in scrap metal.

He drove as instructed, surprised by the size of the operation. To his right was a vast landscape of broken cars, twisted metal, the debris of civilization. Amidst the carnage, forklift trucks manoeuvred their way like prehistoric animals, picking up whole cars in their huge jaws and champing them until they were no longer recognizable. Mark failed to suppress a shudder as he wondered what those same malevolent teeth could do to a man. The offices themselves surprised him too. He'd expected some ramshackle building in the mould of *Steptoe and Son*, but what he got was a state-of-the-art construction of gleaming glass and chrome built to a design that could have worked just as well in the heart of the City. Another security gate stopped him going further until he inserted the tag. He found the absence of humanity, the remote-controlled cameras rotating their eyes to take in every detail of the drive, even more threatening then the tattoos and muscles of the first man.

As the gate rose, he heard a metallic voice telling him in which bay to park and giving him the code number to open the sliding glass doors of the offices. Even in reception there was automation. He was identified, asked to sign the visitors' book, then told to take the lift to the third floor. Handsel met him there himself.

'Do you have any flesh-and-blood staff?' Mark asked as his old team-mate took his hand in an iron grip that suggested he too was an automaton.

'Cheaper this way, old love. All the investment's tax deductible and the machines never ask for time off because they've got a bad period or want to go to Granny's funeral.

Don't worry, I've enough real staff here, but they're all at the top. I've dispensed with the bottom. They're the ones who go shouting their mouths off in pubs when they've had a bit too much to drink. This is a very competitive business. Talk about industrial espionage, you've never seen the like. Come on through and I'll get you a cup of tea.'

That too came from a machine and, as they walked along the thickly carpeted corridor, Mark noted that all the office doors were closed and there was none of the usual bustle and noise that came with a successful business.

Handsel's office was a mini-version of the main building. A panoramic window gave a view over the breaker's yard that Mark had driven past, and then across the river itself. A chrome desk filled the length of one wall, an aquarium of tropical fish the other, its inmates witnessing what was going on in the silence. Hung on each wall was one large abstract, depicting twisted and tortured metal. Handsel slumped on a couch that ran at right angles to his desk and signalled Mark to sit beside him. It was a clumsy gesture, as if referring to an old friendship he'd suddenly remembered.

'Good to see you, Mark. I gather you've been around the club a lot lately. I'd have liked to have spent some more time with you at the match at Wembley but you seemed to be otherwise engaged. She looks a damn sight more attractive than Sally ever did. I'm glad you've fallen on your feet. I don't think I've ever thanked you either, for helping get young Wayne back. When I get control of the club he's a vital part of the jigsaw.'

'That's funny. I heard you were committed to sell him.'

Handsel twisted his mouth a fraction to the left as if to rid himself of an annoying piece of food stuck between his teeth.

'Rumours,' he sighed, 'you don't want to believe rumours. Who told you that? Your little newspaper girl?'

Mark decided it would be best not to answer. He was here to raise the questions, not to supply information.

'So what can I do for you, Mark?' Handsel asked, realizing that his visitor was not going to comment further.

'I'm not too sure,' Mark said, with what he hoped was disarming honesty. 'I'm just tidying up a few loose ends on the Wayne affair and, as it looks as if you're going to be in charge of the club, I thought it might be useful if we had a little chat.'

Handsel turned to face Mark and his eyes narrowed as he searched his visitor's face for an ulterior motive.

'I would have thought loose ends in a kidnapping were a matter for the police. Unless you're looking for a reward if you get back the half a mill that I gather you lost.'

'Yeah, well, you know,' Mark said, his shrug and smile hiding the sinking feeling that it might be even harder to get out of here than it had been to get in.

'No, I don't know. Tell me, Mark,' Handsel said, leaning forward, his lips parting to give a tigerish smile.

'Well, I was curious. You've obviously got a good business here. Why do you want the aggravation of a football club?'

'Are these your questions or did that little shit Sinclair write your script for you? Now you listen, Mark. You went to Rome and you upset powerful people. I'm not stupid and nor's Versace. You think he didn't tell me that you were grubbing around out there? You were always stubborn,

Mark, like your father. Now whether you like it or not I'm going to be in and Sinclair's going to be out. And when I'm in, I'm going to remember my friends and I'm not going to forget my enemies. You've done me a favour, you found seven million quids' worth of footballer, that's good. I heard you worked the oracle with Tommy Wallace, now that's good too. Asking about me in Rome, that was bad. So you're two-one up at the moment. That's a narrow lead to defend for the rest of your life. You've put the bad times behind you, that's good for you too, but it's of no consequence to me, so it doesn't get you a goal. Forget about Sinclair, he's a loser. When you're a loser in football then you get relegated, and you keep getting relegated until you're out of the game altogether. Now you've only just got back into the game, so I can't believe you'd want that, would you?'

He leaned back on the couch, and looked at his watch. Mark noted it was another Rolex and wondered why everybody who made any money at all felt the need to use an expensive watch to announce the fact.

'Well, it's been good to talk to you. Shame you didn't ring to make an appointment, we could have had lunch or something. Maybe next time. Do what I tell you and I think you've got a future.' He hesitated. 'With the club, that is.' Again the predatory smile, the handshake as firm as the metal-crushing equipment outside.

This time Mark had an escort out of the building and back to his car, a well-groomed secretary, slim, tall, who only spoke to say goodbye as she watched to make sure the gate lifted to allow him to leave.

He could understand why Handsel was in some way

linked with Versace. Everybody else he knew was descended from Adam and Eve but those two went back to the serpent. He felt sorry for Sinclair. He doubted he'd accomplished anything and he doubted if he could do anything; he was in no doubt that the chairman had formidable and determined enemies. It was only when he'd been home, made himself lunch, visited Leopold Schneider in hospital and was on his way to meet Ray Fowler that it occurred to him that as far as he was aware Chris Handsel had never met his father.

CHAPTER 41

Ray Fowler lived in Hendon, his house exactly fitting his personality. It was in the middle of an unpretentious tree-lined suburban street, semi-detached, the front garden neat and tidy, but hardly likely to qualify for a feature in *Gardening Weekly*. The front of the property had been newly decorated in a blue and white colouring that fitted in nicely with the neighbouring properties. Unlike almost every other house down the road there were no lace curtains. Instead blinds, that would have been more in place in an office, served to provide some privacy. There could be no doubting that the decoration lacked a woman's touch. Ray had told Mark over coffee one day at the ground how his wife had left after the crash that crippled their daughter.

'She blamed the football, you see. Said if I'd been home a bit more, maybe Josie would have wanted to stay in to see me. Then she wouldn't have been where she was when it happened. Illogical, really, but then there's nothing logical about women, is there?'

Mark was a little late, but at a quarter past eight there was still enough daylight for him to have had no need for any lights on the car during the drive. Fowler's house,

however, seemed to have lights on in every room, as if
they'd been switched on by a time switch. It struck an odd
chord with Mark. Fowler seemed the sort of man who
would be careful with his money, who would go from room
to room, turning off the lights as he went. He immediately
regretted not having Patti with him. At least he could have
commented on it to her, asked her what she thought,
perhaps even told her to wait outside while he checked out
the situation. He shrugged off the caution. He was
becoming neurotic. Meetings like he'd experienced that
morning with Handsel had that sort of effect. He marched
up to the front door. He'd not known what to take in as a
gift. A bottle was hardly the right thing and nor were
flowers. He'd settled rather old-fashionedly for a box of
chocolates, and he held them awkwardly as he rang the
front door bell. There was no answer, and he rang again,
this time more insistently. He didn't think Ray Fowler was
the sort of man to invite somebody round and then forget.
Still no reply. He knelt on the ground and tried to peer
through the letter box, but his view was blocked by some
obstruction. Perhaps the bell wasn't working, he thought,
and began to bang on the door with the knocker. Once,
twice, and then the door gave slightly to the pressure of his
hand. He put his shoulder to it, but although it opened
slightly it refused to yield all the way. He put his shoulder to
it again and heard a faint groan. The door moved slowly
inwards carrying with it the obstruction, the blood-stained,
unconscious figure of Ray Fowler. Instinctively Mark
glanced down at his feet and realized that the sticky
substance that was covering his shoes was a pool of rapidly
congealing blood. He dragged Ray to a sitting position

against the wall. His face was barely recognizable. Whoever had attacked him had completely lost control. The back of his head was caved in, the hair matted and mingled with pieces of bone. There was another gaping wound on his forehead, while the man's nose had been broken and crushed until the nostrils were almost invisible. His breath came shallow and irregular from the back of his throat. Mark knew he had to do something and had to do it quickly, but he also realized that too many people knew that he'd been invited to Fowler's, and here he was alone in the man's house, his clothing and person now soaked in his blood. He thought quickly. He went to the phone box a few yards away in the street and made two calls, knowing that if he'd called from the house the calls would be recorded somewhere. First he summoned an ambulance and then he called Patti, praying she would be in. He reckoned Fowler lived only ten minutes away from her flat and if she was there and put her foot down she might just beat the emergency services to the scene. He prayed that she would lift the phone, then cursed as he heard the answerphone message.

Then her voice cut in. She was there.

'Patti, don't ask any questions. I'm at Ray Fowler's house.' He gave her the address. 'Just get over here as quickly as you can, OK?'

Five agonizing minutes later she appeared, whether out of loyalty or whether led by her newswoman's instinct, he didn't care. He had about one minute with her before the ambulance arrived, one minute to explain everything and one minute to ask for help to which he had no right.

By the time Fowler was carried into the ambulance Mark

could not tell whether he was alive or dead, his breathing seemed to have stopped altogether. It was surprising he had held on at all when whoever had attacked him had certainly assumed his work was lethal. It was, however, no great surprise when a police car pulled up at the house and out of it stepped Detective Inspector Peter Jordan and Detective Sergeant Davies. Neither seemed particularly pleased to have had their Monday evening interrupted.

'I get a call. Suspicious assault on Ray Fowler, acting manager of Hertsmere. All of a sudden I'm the expert on everything that happens at Hertsmere bleeding Football Club. Am I on duty? No, I'm settling down to a pleasant evening with my latest Marklin OO Gauge controls for my railway. So I come and here you two are. Why is it that when anything happens with Hertsmere I find the pair of you? Want to tell me about it?'

Mark shot Patti a sideways glance. She hardly missed a beat.

'Ray Fowler invited Mark here to dinner. He asked me to come along. We couldn't get in. When Mark found the door ajar, he pushed it in and there was poor Fowler. Mark tried to make him comfortable, then he called the ambulance. And lo and behold you followed on apace. Weren't we lucky that it wasn't somebody who didn't know us?'

Jordan didn't smile, although Davies seemed to be having a struggle to keep a straight face.

'How is it he's got blood all over him and you haven't?'

'I can't stand the sight of blood. Mark knows that from when he cut his finger in his kitchen. As soon as he saw what there was in the house he told me to make myself scarce.'

'I see,' Jordan said, 'very thoughtful of him. When did the two of you get here?'

Mark looked down the street to his car parked a few doors away. Patti's vehicle was immediately in front of the police car. It was going to have to be her shout.

'I guess about eight or so. It took us a while to realize there was nobody there capable of answering,' she said.

Jordan fixed his gaze firmly on Mark and, although he had done nothing wrong except create an alibi for a crime he'd not committed, he felt an incredible sense of guilt. He could understand why Jordan had risen to his current rank. With that incisive stare you felt as if he could see into your soul.

'Doing anything tonight, Mr Rossetti?' Jordan asked.

'I was going to have supper with a friend, but it looks as if that's not going to be on.'

'Fine. Then you and Miss Delaney here won't mind accompanying us to the station to assist us with our inquiries.'

Mark ignored his car and clambered into Patti's passenger seat. They spoke little at first as they drove sedately behind Jordan and Davies, but Patti's face said it all. Then she finally let him have it with both barrels.

'I ought to bloody well kill you. Or myself for being so stupid. You blank me off from another part of the story – our story – and then expect me to bail you out. And like a fool I do it. And now you're in the shit and I'm in there with you. I don't believe you, Mark.'

Neither did Peter Jordan when he got him down to the station.

'You stretch the bounds of credibility, you do, Mr

Rossetti. I look you up and I see you were lucky not to be charged with corruption ten years ago. I check on your agency and I find the address from which you operate your inquiries was occupied by another sleazy inquiry agent, a sleaze-bag we'd like to interview, by the way. You turn up like a bad penny in the middle of my investigation into the disappearance of Mickey Wayne and blow me if half a million quid entrusted to you and Master Wayne's manager don't go missing as well. Then you produce Wayne like a rabbit out of a hat and it takes you until the next day to bother to get around to telling us and now you tell me you're working for Mr Sinclair and you just happen to be around when the man who's replaced Phil Reynolds gets battered not half to death, but about ninety-five per cent to death.'

'How is Ray, by the way?' Mark asked.

'By the way, he's not good. He's bloody bad. And you're either bloody bad news for everybody around you including yourself or else you're my number one suspect in the attempted murder, maybe actual murder by now, of one, Raymond Cecil Fowler, as well as the abduction of Mr Philip Reynolds.'

'No middle name?' Mark could not resist asking.

'I'm pleased you find it amusing.'

'I don't. I liked Ray.'

'But not Reynolds?'

'Did I say that?' He was feeling very tired. It had been yet another long day in what was feeling like a very long life. 'Can I go now?'

'You'll go when I say you can go. I have the feeling you're holding some things back from me. And I must tell you, Mr Rossetti, that my feelings are never wrong. Now I don't know if you're holding back to protect yourself, somebody else or because you're a bloody stubborn fool, but I aim to find out. Now maybe I won't find out tonight, or tomorrow, or the day after, but I'll find out. I'll be watching you and you are going nowhere, do you hear me? No little jaunts to Rome. If you leave North London you phone me to tell me. Do I make myself understood?'

Mark nodded wearily.

It was nearly two in the morning when he and Patti finally staggered out of the police station.

'Thanks,' was all he felt able to say. He understood now how innocent men signed confessions, how Esau sold his birthright to Jacob for a mess of pottage.

'I'm not sure you ought to be thanking me just yet. I felt I was going well with the sergeant. Then that Jordan came along and virtually called me a liar.'

'But he can't prove it.'

'I get the impression that that one could prove anything if he wanted to. In another life he was probably Pythagoras. Jesus, I'm tired. Do you mind crashing out at the Burrow? I don't think I could face a round trip and I think you should leave your car where you parked it until the police have finished at Fowler's house.'

He was surprised to see that she had a double bed, even more surprised when she told him which side he was sleeping on. But that was as far as it went. If he'd had any romantic ideas they were swept aside within seconds as she pecked him on the cheek, rolled over and immediately slipped into the deep and heavy breathing of somebody who would sleep until they were shaken awake. At first, sleep would not come for him. He lay there, frightened to move lest the body contact be misunderstood. She looked remarkably young lying there, the moonlight shining through the half-drawn curtains slanting across her face, a slight breeze wafting the odd strand of hair to and fro. It had been too long since he'd slept in the same room as a woman. He no longer knew what was expected of him, and as he thought about it he used the images of Patti to drive away the other image that was etched in his mind's eye, the image of Ray Fowler's blood-stained, battered body gasping for life. Eventually, he too fell into a deep sleep, the sleep of the exhausted, the sleep of the dead, and yet when he awoke first in the morning and found Patti's bare arm flung across his chest in a careless embrace he felt as if he had not slept at all.

CHAPTER 42

When Mark had arrived home shortly after eleven there was only one message on his answerphone and that was from David Sinclair. He wanted to see him at the club and he wanted to see him as soon as possible. The message was timed at nine and, as he was already two hours late, he decided that the twenty minutes it would take him to shower and shave would make no difference. By the time he got to the ground it was nearly one and he looked considerably better than the chairman.

Sinclair was dressed as elegantly as ever but it did nothing for the dark bags under his eyes. The pale skin drawn tight across the cheek-bones was that of a man who had forgotten what it was to have regular meals.

'I gather you found Ray,' he said to Mark, who nodded.

'You're making a habit of finding members of our staff.'

'That's what the police said,' Mark replied.

'Sit down, have a coffee,' Sinclair said nervously without joining Mark in either action. He fiddled with some papers on the desk, then walked to the window and looked out over the empty pitch as if by some miracle he could conjure up success.

'I've got to be honest with you, Mark. When I first got your letter I thought, no way. He's bad news, just another ex-footballer who can't live with the game and can't live without it; but I have to admit I was wrong. You did a job for me and you did it well. Nobody could have held on to that money and it was hard luck that you were the fall guy; but then I didn't see a queue of people offering to do the delivery. The training without Ray this morning was a disaster. I put Jimmy Townshend, the youth team coach, in charge to work alongside Stuart Macdonald but they were both out of their depth. It wasn't that they didn't know what they were doing, but there was no respect. Half the team didn't know Jimmy and the rest of them knew Stuart too well.'

'Like my wife,' thought Mark, but he said nothing. He still got the same stab of pain whenever he heard mention of the man's name. Bumping into him during recent visits to the club had hurt even more.

'It's not going to work. I know it. This is all I need, to prepare for the FA Cup Final without a proper manager.'

'How is Ray?'

Sinclair shook his head.

'He's in a deep coma. They doubt if he'll ever come out of it and if by some miracle he does, then it's unlikely he'll be much more than a cabbage. Mark, you may think I'm crazy, I'm sure everybody else will, but I'd like you to take over team affairs.'

Mark gaped. 'You *are* crazy. I've never even had any coaching experience. All it'll do is wake up all the old headlines about me. If you want to nail up your coffin from the inside then that's the way to do it.'

'Come on, Mark. It's another challenge. You told me how you'd worked with the schoolkids before they stopped you, and Ray explained to me just how you, and you alone, were able to get Tommy Wallace's head right.'

Mark hesitated, the idea tempting, the reality terrifying. He didn't know if he could cope with the pressure, the media attention, the success, or the failure. What he did know was before he could make any decision he needed to talk to Patti and Leopold. He'd grown too used to having his decisions so limited in their range of choice that they were virtually made for him.

'I'm not sure that I can cope with Stuart Macdonald on a daily basis. And I'm not too sure how he'd cope with me.'

'He'll have to cope. We all have to cope. Whatever happens to me it's vital that this club gets its name on the Cup for the first time. We owe it to the supporters.'

'I can't believe you owe the fans anything after the way they've treated you. Anyway, I don't want to appear rude or ungrateful, but are you sure you've got the authority to appoint a new manager?'

Sinclair smiled.

'You really are learning, you know. Yes, I've got the authority. It'll have to be ratified by the board in due course and who knows what they'll say. You'll just have had to win a couple of matches by then.'

'So what happens about my commission to report to you on Handsel? Do I do that in my spare time?'

'If you want to keep the job, then the answer's probably yes. Mark, this is the best time ever to get appointed. We can't go down and we can't buy new players. The team's tactics have worked so far in the Cup. Our star player's got every reason to be grateful to you, and our best youngster likes you.'

'Yeah, and the team captain stole my wife and daughter. I'll think about it and I'll come back to you. What do you do if I say no?'

Sinclair went even paler.

'I'm not sure. There's nobody really hanging around the market place and if anybody worthwhile became available they'll want the sort of long-term security contract that I'm just not able to give. That's something else in your favour when I come to tell the rest of the board.'

'You mean I'm cheap and dispensable,' Mark said, a sad smile playing around his eyes.

'You said it. Can you get back to me later today? If you're coming on board then I'd like you here for training in the morning and a press conference in the afternoon.'

'I'm not sure about the press,' Mark said and it was at that moment he realized that, whatever Patti and Leo had to say, he was going to take the job. Sinclair was right, he ought to have enough time to keep asking around about Handsel. He didn't hold out much chance of success in either role, but he had to do them. He had to do everything that came his way. He'd spent too much time running away from himself and his responsibilities. These were new responsibilities, the biggest since he'd taken on a wife and a daughter. This time round he had to succeed, he had to approach the tasks in a more positive frame of mind.

Patti was full of enthusiasm when he met her for tea in the Italian-owned deli. As a concession to the Spring sunshine the owners had put some tables out on the pavement and there was a picturesque view of the local cab rank and undertaker.

'You have to take it. I can help with Handsel, and, by the sound of it, you'll have most afternoons free. You're not going to have to traipse around the country watching Darlington Reserves to see if they've any talent. Money for old rope. They are paying you, aren't they?'

'Yes, David said he'd give me what Ray was on less ten per cent and if we won the Cup then he'd give me a fifty per cent bonus.'

'Why the discount on what Fowler was earning?'

'So he could sell it to the rest of the board more easily. Quite frankly, if Handsel gets in before the Cup Final then I can't see me lasting more than thirty seconds after he's tried out the chairman's seat in the box.'

'So you've nothing to lose, have you? And I get the exclusive interview with Hertsmere's new manager.'

'You don't miss a trick, do you, Patti? But I'm afraid you don't get your exclusive this time. He's calling a press conference for tomorrow afternoon if I say yes.'

'And are you going to say yes?'

'I am.'

'Then we'd better do that exclusive right now. If I work hard I can get the copy in to hit the later editions tomorrow.'

Mark grinned. 'Hold the front page, eh?'

'Well, the back page anyway.'

'I have to get to see Leo.'

'It's four now. Talk to me to six and then do your social work.'

She produced a tape-recorder and a notepad.

'Prepared, aren't you?'

'I was a brownie.'

'What happens if Leo talks me out of it?'

'He'd better not, he'd just better not.' And then she began firing questions at him. It was only when they were halfway through that it occurred to him that he now had a motive for taking Ray Fowler out of the game. He did not think it would take too long for that thought also to cross the mind of Detective Inspector Peter Jordan.

CHAPTER 43

Mark could not believe he'd been in the job for nearly three weeks. Not only in the job, but succeeding at it and actually enjoying his success. Three matches played, three matches won. And not just won, but victories gained in style; seven goals scored and only one conceded. He sat by Leopold Schneider's bedside absent-mindedly eating the fruit he'd brought him and signing the occasional autograph for the other visitors' children.

'You look like a million dollars,' the old man said, sitting up in the chair by the side of his bed.

'You don't look so bad yourself,' Mark replied. 'I reckon they'll be kicking you out of here in no time at all.'

'Every day I ask them and every day they tell me to be patient. I am a patient, I say, I want to stop being a patient. I think it's a good English joke, but they don't laugh.'

'I think they may have heard it before, Leo, it's nothing personal.'

'Ach, the sooner I get out and collecting my own rents the better.'

'I'm sorry that I couldn't carry on doing it for you. Isn't the agency any good?' Mark asked.

'Good? They're very good. They've given out rent-books to all my tenants. Half of them didn't know what a rent-book looked like before, but what they did know was that if they couldn't pay the rent then I wasn't going to kick them out, not unless I thought they were taking advantage. I knew the *gunafs*, but I also knew the *nebbochs*. This lot just collect the rent. Some of my tenants visit me, they tell me. And as for charging, oy, do they know how to charge. But you, Markie, I see you're paying your rent every week now, soon the place won't be good enough for you, maybe already you've grown out of it, no?'

'No, Leo. It's been lucky for me. Perhaps I'll buy a place, but I'm not moving at the moment. Where else would I get such tasty biscuits?'

Mark glanced at his watch.

'I've got to go. I want you out of here in time to come to the Cup Final. You'll be my guest.'

Schneider made a feeble gesture with his hand.

'I'm nearly eighty.' Mark realized this was the first time Leopold had ever given an admission of his age. 'I've survived so far without ever seeing a football match, I think I can live a little longer. All the shouting and screaming, the crowds, the *meshuganahs*. I'll stick to rent collecting, it's safer. Maybe you give me a ticket and I sell it?' He patted Mark on the hand to show he was only joking, and Mark could see his fingers as thin as claws, the wrist so fragile that a handshake might break it, and then just above the wrist some numbers tattooed on the flesh, numbers which seemed to have a life and vibrancy that the rest of the arm so lacked.

He drove back to Hertsmere in the new Rover with which the club had provided him. It didn't bother him that other managers might drive Porsches, Jaguars, BMWs or Mercedes. He was happy with what he'd got. Yet within days he would have to face up to reality. Today was Tuesday and the shareholders meeting called by Handsel as his first step in removing David Sinclair was due to take place on Thursday. He was tired of journalists asking how he got on with Handsel, whether he thought his old team-mate would keep him on, whether he could afford not to keep him on, bearing in mind the results he was getting. At least he had got in first with regard to the Stuart Macdonald problem. Patti had made sure that story had appeared on the day of his appointment and had also made sure that anybody reading it could not fail to feel sympathy for Mark Rossetti. But he didn't want sympathy, he wanted to keep his job, and whatever he achieved on the field the final decision in that respect would be made in the boardroom. Made by whoever owned the club at the time.

Patti had been keeping her distance for the last week or so. It was as if she had done her job in assisting in the rehabilitation of Mark Rossetti and felt it was time to move on to the next victim who needed help. Ray Fowler still lay in intensive care, his life, or what would pass for it, in the balance, whilst of Phil Reynolds there was no news whatsoever.

'He's obviously gone into partnership with Lord Lucan,' Patti had said the last time she had spoken to Mark. 'Perhaps they're running an agency for nannies and foot-ballers.'

He missed that sort of humour. He had found that he

could no longer be a part of the jokes and tricks the team played on each other. If he had any chance of keeping discipline he had to keep himself apart. He did not speak directly to Macdonald. He had been tempted to strip him of his captaincy, even to drop him from the team. Let the damn papers write what they want, conclude what they want, he'd waited a long time to have any control over the man who'd stolen his wife. Yet he did nothing, not because of the consequences, but simply because the man was a good team player as well as a good captain. He must have thought he was in with a shout of the manager's job when Fowler was attacked and, for the moment, the fact that Mark had usurped him would have to be enough.

He had nothing to do at the club that afternoon but, just as he'd homed in on it when he'd first been employed by them, so he now came there to think. But as he came through the swing doors, Sharon virtually screamed out his name from the reception area, making it quite clear there was going to be no time for quiet meditation that afternoon.

'Mark, David's been looking for you everywhere. You've had your mobile off.'

He shrugged an apology to nobody in particular. He could not get used to the idea of being available twenty-four hours a day. Even when he remembered to take the phone with him he'd invariably forgotten to charge the battery the night before. The metallic message saying that the subscriber was not available and suggesting the caller try again later was a major bone of contention, if not the only one, between him and David Sinclair. When the chairman had got hold of him finally in the past it had never actually proved to be terribly urgent, but by the expression on his face as Mark entered his office, this was different.

A woman sat crying in the chair opposite Sinclair, a black scarf wound about her hair, a white blouse, unadorned by jewellery, worn above a straight black skirt. She looked and sounded as if she were in mourning.

'Mark, I don't know if you've ever met. Vera Scott, Freddie's wife.'

'A long time ago. I was a player when your husband was a director.'

Vera pulled out a handkerchief, inspected it and, deciding it had seen too much use, dropped it into the waste-bin and produced another from her left sleeve.

'My husband was a director until yesterday, and I was his wife until yesterday, and now I'm his widow.' She broke down again. Sinclair went to his drinks cabinet and poured her a brandy whilst at the same time helping himself to a scotch. He did not offer anything to Mark.

'Take your time, Vera,' Sinclair said soothingly, and then, turning to Mark, added, 'I want you to hear what Vera's just been telling me. I want a witness.'

The woman took a sip from the brandy glass, a ladylike gesture that was reminiscent of sherry-tasting at a church social.

'He told me it was the only way to make sure that Freddie lived out his last months in comfort; but it wasn't months, it was weeks, and when I asked for the rest of the money he said that wasn't the deal. He said he'd agreed to pay so long as Freddie was alive, but as soon as he died the money stopped. And I told him that I wanted the shares back, and he said Freddie had signed everything and it was too late.'

'Hold on, Mrs Scott. Who's he?' Mark asked.

'That Richard Lee, the solicitor.'

'I'm confused,' Mark said. 'I thought he was your lawyer, David.'

'He was, and the club's. And now Handsel's too. It seems nothing's enough for our Richard.'

Mark nibbled at a fingernail on his left hand, then tapped his teeth with the same finger.

'So let me get this right, you say the offer to you was a sum of ...'

'Six hundred thousand pounds,' she said and drew a whistle from Mark.

'A sum of,' Mark continued, 'six hundred thousand pounds. That was unconditional. How you spent it was your affair and all you had to do was get your husband to sign the share transfer. Presumably you weren't to know at the time just how quickly ...' He sought the right words knowing if he chose wrongly she would again be reduced to tears. 'How near the end was.' He looked up and, satisfied she was in control, he carried on. 'Now what they're saying is that they'd pay *up to* six hundred thousand pounds and with Freddie gone their responsibility's at an end. Did you or Freddie sign anything other than the transfer?'

'I don't know, I don't think so.'

'Did he tell you to take advice on the deal?' Mark continued.

'No, in fact he said the fewer people who knew about it the better. I know you think I must be stupid. I'm not normally like this, but somehow he was so convincing. He made it sound as if it would be good for everybody.'

'So how much have you actually had?'

She hesitated.

'I'm embarrassed to say. I've been so stupid.'

'Go on,' Sinclair said grimly.

'Five thousand pounds.'

Both men were silenced for a moment, then Sinclair simply said, 'I see.'

Vera emptied the glass and refused the offer of a refill with a shake of her head.

'Is there anything we can do about it? When it was a case of making sure Freddie could go with dignity I wasn't thinking what it might do to you and the club, but now ... it's not just that they've cheated me out of the money, it's not fair that they should be able to push you out this way.'

'Are you the sole executrix of Freddie's estate?' Sinclair asked.

'Yes, I think so. He left me everything he had in the will. Without the money from the shares that's not much.'

'So, if we set aside the transfer, you've got control of the shares?'

'Yes.'

'And you'd still sell them ... To me that is. I can't afford the sort of money Handsel was paying, but at least you'll be sure of getting it.'

She nodded.

'That's what Freddie would have wanted. I don't think he ever really understood what he was signing. To be honest I wasn't sure that he'd sign it if he knew, so I didn't go into great detail when explaining it.'

'He was on painkillers?' Mark asked.

'Yes. Quite a lot. It was the only way he could get through the day.'

'David,' Mark said, 'you have to get a new lawyer on the job. I'm only an ex-pro but I've learned in the last six months. Apart from the fact that Lee railroaded Vera, Freddie, too, obviously didn't know what he was doing.'

Sinclair thought for a moment then said, 'I know exactly who to go to.'

He called directory inquiries, then dialled the number he was given and asked to be put through to Colin Sykes. As he waited, he put his hand over the receiver.

'Sykes was Richard's ex-partner,' he explained wryly. 'I think he'll enjoy this one.'

When he came on the line Sykes listened carefully, then tutted in horror and disbelief and finally gave them the advice they wanted.

'We give them no advance notice. Mrs Scott swears an affidavit and I apply for an interim injunction restraining them from voting the shares. At the same time we issue a writ to set the transaction aside. I think Mrs Scott should send the five thousand pounds back just to be on the safe side. I'll draft her a suitable letter to accompany it.'

'And what about Lee?' Sinclair asked.

'He's acted disgracefully, but then that's no great surprise as far as I'm concerned. I'm not normally a vengeful person, but I think the Law Society are going to be very interested in his explanation.'

'How quickly can all this happen?' Sinclair asked.

'If you can get Mrs Scott down here now I might get us into court first thing in the morning. We need to be able to serve the order on Handsel before the shareholders meeting,' Sykes said, clearly looking forward to the fight more than any fee that might be involved.

'She's on her way,' Sinclair said. 'I'll bring her down right now.'

Sinclair and Vera left Mark in the office. He ought to feel pleased with the turn of events. If Sinclair kept the club, then he kept the job; but now there was every possibility of security did he want to keep it? If somebody had suggested to him at the time he wrote his first letter that it would end with him being the manager of his old club, looking forward to a trip to a Wembley final, he would have dismissed the thought as fantasy. Yet now they were realities he still felt unsettled, unfulfilled. He also felt anger at himself that he could not enjoy what seemed to be the beginning of the good times after the years of famine. Was this what he wanted for the rest of his life, a career in football management, the eternal lonely walk along the tightrope? He could not decide and that, too, worried him. So long as the unattainable remained out of his reach he was content, it was only when it came too close that the problems began. He had lived for a long time without the pressure of decisions and now he had to learn how to make them.

He tried to phone Patti but the answerphone was on at home and her mobile was not switched on. He felt there was something he should be doing, that it was not enough to sit back in David Sinclair's comfortable chair waiting for results.

The sun shone in through the window, surprisingly warm for late April, the heat magnified by the glass. An early bee had found its way into the room and buzzed drowsily as Mark tried to fight off the weariness that laid itself heavily on his eyelids. He must have dozed for nearly an hour when the phone rang at his side making him leap out of the chair with guilt.

'There's someone to see you, Mark,' Sharon said, but before he could ask who it was the door to Sinclair's office opened and there was Patti Delaney.

'I thought I'd find you here,' she said and as she smiled he knew at once what was missing from his life and wondered why it had taken him so long to realize it.

Patti seated herself in the chair recently vacated by Vera Scott.

'It suits you,' she smiled. 'The chairman's seat. Player, manager, chairman, it's a natural progression.'

'I was just trying to phone you.'

'I wasn't there, but here I am. Empathy. What did you want me for?'

There was an answer to that, but Mark did not have the courage to give it. Instead he told her about Lee and Handsel and the stroke they had played on the Scotts.

'You meet a really nice type of person in football. Didn't your mother ever tell you might get hurt playing with the big boys.'

'All the time. What brings you here, apart from empathy?'

'I think I've got the answer as to why Handsel couldn't come up with the rest of the money for Scott's shares.'

'Are you saying he did actually intend to pay for them?' Mark asked.

'Let's give him the benefit of the doubt. I've been doing a bit of digging around myself. I couldn't understand why Handsel was so keen to get the shares in the first place – it doesn't strike me that love of his old club is what's closest to his heart – or why Versace should be in any way involved. At the end of the day like most things it's simple. Did Sinclair ever mention to you that he wanted to move the stadium to a site near the motorway?'

Mark shook his head.

'From his point of view it was probably ancient history. He wouldn't get the money for it from the bank anyway. He couldn't raise the money by selling this place because the local authority wouldn't give planning permission; but it seems that miraculously they *would* give Handsel planning consent for a new supermarket.'

'How did you find that out?'

'Best source of all. Where all the decent reporters cut their teeth. Local paper. They had their own mole at the council. In local politics there's always somebody who wants to turn somebody else in and can justify it by political morality. Mr Handsel wanted a high profile. You can't turn the limelight on and off when it suits you.'

'So why Versace?'

'Two reasons, I think. Handsel banks with him anyway so he cuts him in on the property deal. Then he finds a way out of Wayne's sale to Cinquante. The contract's still not been signed, I hear. He waits a bit and then sells Wayne to Ulisse at a lower price and pockets a slice of the discount, which I assume he then shares with Versace personally.'

'I'm impressed, but where's the proof? We're not dealing with choirboys here. You saw what happened when I even mentioned Handsel to Versace.'

She pursed her lips, then rummaged through her satchel bag for a mirror. 'I could do with a decent holiday,' she said, inspecting her face in the glass.

'Is that it? You come in with the whole plot uncovered and all you can say is you need a holiday.'

She smiled again, the smile of the cat who has not only got the cream but also the budgie from the cage.

'Oh, didn't I tell you? They arrested Versace in Rome this morning. One of the stringers out there woke me up to tell me. I may not have been in the newspaper business that long but I've made a lot of contacts. I'd already asked him some questions, so as soon as he heard what he thought might be answers he called me. I've been generous and left him to file the story. They've charged our charming Italian friend with being a member of the mafia and they've closed down his bank on money-laundering charges. Did you say whether or not you're free for dinner?'

CHAPTER 44

Mark could see the tension on the faces of the players and knew it was his job to remove it. There'd been all too many finals in the past when one team had frozen, had lost the match before they got out on to the pitch. Picking the team had been easy, but getting them to play on the day, to perform to the very limits of their abilities, that was another matter. The only moment of hesitation he had experienced was over the inclusion of Mickey Wayne. It was absurd, the star of the team, the most expensive sale in the history of English football, and he was thinking of leaving him out. He had good reason. On current form he'd struggle to get into any Premier League side. He'd not been the same player since he'd come back and although he could have no complaints about his efforts in training it was as if his mind and allegiance were already somewhere else.

Patti had called Handsel for an interview and as soon as he'd heard the subject matter he'd gone to ground. For anybody trying to contact him it was as if he didn't exist, had never existed. Whoever might end up owning Hertsmere it was not going to be Chris Handsel. With him out of the picture the bank had pushed through the sale of Mickey Wayne with renewed vigour.

'Don't worry about it,' Mark had said, trying to console Sinclair. 'Tommy Wallace is going to be even better, believe me. And he'll play for you with his heart and his feet, he'll perform because he enjoys it, not because of the size of his wage packet.'

'That is until some agent gets his teeth into him,' Sinclair had said cynically, and stuck to his insistence that Wayne played. It was as if he were blind to all of Mickey Wayne's faults, all of his shortcomings. He was a talisman and without him Hertsmere would not be the same for David Sinclair.

Now, in the dressing-room at Wembley, Mark focused on Wayne. He could talk to all of the other players with the exception of Stuart Macdonald, but with Wayne he could not even get close. The player had already travelled to Rome and back for his medical at the insistence of both Barlucci and the bank. If there were to be any problems then they both wanted to hear about them sooner rather than later. That had been a week or so ago and, as they had received no negative feedback, he assumed that nothing stood in the way of this being the last time Mickey Wayne would pull on a Hertsmere shirt. Somehow the money he would receive if the deal went through was irrelevant, everything was irrelevant except winning today.

The winger sat sullenly in the corner as if the afternoon's events were interfering with something far more important that he had to do.

'I don't want to see you just hugging the line, Mickey,' Mark said. 'I want you coming inside looking for the ball. Having Tommy here playing wide on the right gives you a bit of relief, and they won't know if the ball's going to be played out left or out right. If you're both mobile and both prepared to tackle back, then that'll keep them busy too. They're going to expect lots of high balls pumped on to Nicky's head so that's the way you start. Keep it up for about ten minutes, if we get a goal so much the better, but if we don't we'll have got them believing that's the way we'll play all afternoon. That's when we start playing it around to feet. We've done it all a hundred times in training. Now it's for real. Just go out and enjoy yourselves. You never know when you'll get the chance again.' He repeated the phrase almost to himself and then it was time to go.

Allerton, who had finally won through in the other semi-final replay, lined up alongside Hertsmere. Paul Nelson, their well-respected and experienced manager, leaned across to shake Mark's hand.

'Good to see you back. I tried to sign you once, you know. Good luck. Let's make it a good one for the crowd.'

As he felt the genuine warmth in the man's handshake, it occurred to Mark that were still some people around that the wonder of the game deserved. It was a shame that Allerton had to lose. Yes, they had to lose and he had to win. It was about ambition and pride and he prayed that his eleven men had ambition. You had to want to win, and for so many of his lost years he had not only been content to lose, but had contrived to lose. He clenched his fist to the banks of Hertsmere supporters who had somehow managed to take up the whole of their allocation and still kept the touts busy. When he compared the Hertsmere home gates to those of Allerton he wondered where all their fans hid on Saturday afternoons. Maybe Sinclair's ambitions for a new stadium were justified.

For once David Sinclair had actually been under pressure to find tickets for friends, family, acquaintances and people who claimed to be all three. The only place where there had been tickets to spare had been amongst the Hertsmere directors in the royal box. Lee had resigned, Scott was dead and Handsel, for once in his life, had not had the gall to ask for a ticket.

Although he had been forced to return the shares to Vera Scott, Handsel himself was still out there, running free. However hard she dug, Patti had not come up with enough hard evidence to satisfy a newspaper's libel lawyer let alone the police. As far as the Scott situation was concerned, Handsel had simply blamed Richard Lee for going too far.

'What do you expect from a lawyer who thinks he can serve two masters? All I asked him to do was negotiate for the shares. He went too far. Maybe he thought he'd get all my business, but I made him no promises.'

Sinclair had received one disconcerting phone call from him.

'You picked the wrong man to tangle with, Sinclair. Keep your crummy club. I never thought much of it when I was a player and I think even less of it now. Some of my scrap metal looks better than Hertsmere. But don't think I'm going to forget this. Stories where I don't win don't have happy endings. Watch your back, and tell that cunt Rossetti to watch his as well. Oh, and don't forget to pass the message on to that ball-breaking journalist he's too scared to screw.' And then, as an afterthought, 'And you might care to mention it to that pretty little daughter of yours. She wants to watch the company she keeps.'

Sinclair had discussed the threat with Mark and the possibility of going to the police, but he'd not recorded the call and Handsel would only deny it. He had to think they were just the rantings of a disappointed man who was not used to defeat.

Versace was saying nothing. He had made his first court appearance wearing a new suit that he had ordered from the cell in which he'd made his home after bail had been refused. He'd been represented by Rome's foremost and most expensive criminal lawyer who had then promptly found himself arrested for alleged mafia connections. The message from the newly cleansed Roman administration was that it was dangerous to the health to be in any way associated with Paolo Versace.

David Sinclair stood to applaud his team on to the pitch with mixed emotions. It was the greatest day in his life since he'd been involved with football, yet he had no one with whom to share it. Holly had phoned him to tell him to go to the stadium on his own and that she would meet him there, but she was nowhere to be seen. He couldn't believe that she was about to miss a match like this when he'd known her cancel a date to watch a Hertfordshire Senior Cup game at Hoddesdon. He'd called her at her flat, he'd called his own number and he'd tried her mobile, but there was no response. All he could think of was that she'd got herself entangled in the Wembley traffic and was as frustrated outside the stadium as he was inside.

With the kick-off he almost forgot his daughter's absence. From the very start Hertsmere launched an all-out attack as if they had been told the match was only ten minutes each way. There seemed to be no way they could maintain the pace for ninety minutes. Wallace was twisting his marker first one way, then the other, before raining an aerial bombardment on to the head of Nicky Collier, who produced save after save from the Allerton keeper, Glen Turner, justifying his position as the England keeper. The goal, when it came, was from an unexpected source. Sergovich rolled the ball out to Liam O'Donnell who played on the right of the back four. He made ground to the half-way line before playing a one-two with Wallace. Receiving the ball back, the defender found himself in almost unknown territory. He'd been with the club five seasons and it was an almost standing joke that he was the only player on the staff yet to score a goal. Even Sergovich had once come forward to score a penalty when the side were 5–0 up. He was now regularly quoted at 100–1 by the bookmakers to score the first goal in a match; when he did finally find the back of the net, Reynolds had joked that people would remember what they were doing in the same way as they had when Kennedy had been killed. Oblivious to his own reputation, O'Donnell hit the ball in the vague direction of the goal. Later he would deny he had intended it as a cross, but Turner in the goal certainly thought that was what it was as he came to cut it out, only to see it swerve in the air out of his reach and into the top corner of the net. For a few seconds O'Donnell looked in disbelief, waiting for a linesman to lift a flag to indicate he'd done something wrong, or for the referee to point to the place where the Allerton free-kick should be taken; but the one official did nothing and the other was already racing back to the half-way line to get the game restarted. The Irish defender was rooted to the spot as his team-mates launched themselves on him, wrestling him to the ground in a rolling, celebratory scrum. Euphoria swept through the Hertsmere supporters in a huge rolling wave. Only Mickey Wayne kept himself apart as if a goal in which he'd played no part was not a matter for celebration.

Mark Rossetti was off the bench, for once uncaring that a host of photographers turned their lenses on his war-dance of joy. He looked up at the Royal Box where he'd ensured Patti had a seat and saw she too was on her feet, embracing David Sinclair. He had to calm the team down. There were too many kids in the side who had no previous experience of a match like this. He needed to get the message across that one goal in the twentieth minute did not mean the game was over and won. By half-time with the lead intact he had screamed himself hoarse, but there was little more to say in the dressing room.

'Keep it going. Mickey, I want a bit more effort from you in this half. It's all been happening down the other flank, time to get them worried about you as well.'

Wayne looked at him with naked hatred.

'You know I've been meaning to tell you this for a long time. Rossetti, you're an ignorant bastard. I've been running my heart out. If the rest of this fucking team would give me the ball rather than passing it to the boy wonder there, then I could do something.'

'Leave it out, Mickey.' The warning came from Stuart Macdonald and Mark looked towards him with surprise.

'You're the right one to talk, giving it to his wife every night.' Mickey got to his feet and went for the door, although there were at least five minutes left before the end of the interval.

'Let him go,' Mark said. 'I'm only interested in winning and I'm not going to let that self-centred twat spoil it for us. Bazza.' He indicated Barry Reid, one of the substitutes. 'Go on out there and get yourself warmed up. I'm giving Wayne ten minutes. If he's not playing for the team by then I'm pulling him off.' He turned to the rest of them. 'It didn't happen, OK? Wayne wasn't here. Just keep your concentration on the football, that's all I ask.'

It was time to go.

David Sinclair had never thought that with his team 1–0 up in a Wembley final he would have wanted to leave, but that was the way it was. He could not conceive of what might have happened to Holly, but all he could hear in his mind was Handsel's voice, coarse and threatening on the phone. If he wanted to get at the Sinclair family what better time than a day when they should have been basking in glory? He spoke distractedly to various dignitaries over canapés and tea and then went down to the police room. If he was to be dismissed as an over-caring father then he could live with that. If his daughter had decided to spend the afternoon with a boyfriend she was old enough to have made her own decision in that respect. But he knew in his heart of hearts that somehow or other she would have got word to him. The officer in charge listened politely. He understood, he had a teenage daughter of his own. He took down her address and car number and promised he'd arrange to send an officer around to the flat as well as checking that the vehicle had not been involved in an accident.

'You go back and enjoy the rest of the match, sir. I had a

bet on Hertsmere after the Fourth Round at 16–1 so I'm hoping you pull it off.'

Yet, by the time he resumed his seat, there were more clouds on the Hertsmere parade. Within seconds of the restart Allerton, urged on by their fanatic followers, had caught the southern club stone-cold. It had started with a hopeful punt upfield. Pat Devine had seemed to have it covered, but had slipped and allowed the Allerton striker Tony Burton a clear run on goal. Sergovich had left his line, but the Allerton man had rounded him and left himself with a simple tap-in.

As if that were not bad enough, Sinclair was able to see Mickey Wayne standing on the touch-line refusing to leave the pitch despite the number eleven card held aloft on Mark Rossetti's instructions. There were jeers and whistles coming from both sets of supporters. The Hertsmere honeymoon with the new management seemed, in the fickle way of fans, to have ended with the equalizer and now the removal of their hero was just too much for them to swallow. The Allerton fans broke into a predictable chorus of 'What a waste of money' whilst the player and manager confronted each other face to face like two fighting dogs. The referee ran over to intervene. 'If you don't leave the field, Wayne, I'll book you and if you still don't leave I'll send you off for ungentlemanly conduct.'

For a moment it seemed as if Wayne was going to take some pleasure in seeing his team struggle on a man short, but eventually with Macdonald on one side and Sergovich on the other he was virtually carried off the pitch. Barry Reid, a stocky Geordie who had only the previous week celebrated his eighteenth birthday, ran on to the field oblivious to the distasteful events that had contrived to bring him there. With all the enthusiasm of youth he gave the Hertsmere fans a cheerful wave to indicate that their saviour had arrived and they in turn reacted with a huge cheer. Mark Rossetti breathed a huge sigh of relief. They were going to give him a chance. It had not been a move taken lightly to remove Mickey Wayne from the field of play. He realized how Graham Taylor must have felt when he'd called off Gary Lineker in his last international, but the way Wayne was reacting both to his team-mates and the opposition made him a time-bomb likely to explode at any moment.

Wayne himself refused to take his seat with the rest of the non-playing Hertsmere contingent and began to run around the circumference of the pitch towards the tunnel. As he passed the masses of Allerton banners and scarves the fans turned their hatred and derision directly towards him and he reacted with a one-finger symbol that would guarantee him an FA-imposed ban. As he disappeared into the tunnel the concentration turned back to the field of play, and immediately Reid was at the heart of the action, taking the legs of Allerton's Burton with a tackle of such ferocity that Mark wondered what colour card the referee would produce. He breathed a sigh of relief when he saw it was yellow, hoping its effect would be to calm the young man down. It did. He suddenly became aware of his surroundings and rather than being overawed by them he began to rise to the occasion. With an authority far beyond his years he took control of the mid-field and Tommy Wallace, the other teenager, now operated as a sole wide player switching wings at will. Allerton, who had obviously planned to deal with Wayne and Wallace during half-time, were totally bemused, but as the minutes ticked by the ball refused to go into their net. Turner continued to perform miracles for Allerton and when the miracles ran out there was always a post or a crossbar or a desperately flailing limb of an Allerton defender to come to his rescue. Five minutes left on the clock. Nicky Collier was brought down some twenty yards from goal. Barry Reid rushed over to take the free-kick, pushing aside his more experienced colleagues with such confidence that none of them could deny him the chance. He'd watched the seniors working on set-pieces in training for years, watched and learned, but had never yet seen what he was about to attempt put into practice. The Allerton defence formed themselves into a normal four-man wall, barely tolerating the presence of Nicky Collier and Tommy Wallace. Reid signalled the kick he was going to take, hoping the attackers would remember what it signified. Wallace, at least, did. Just as boot met ball he swivelled round so that he faced the goal, Reid chipped the ball precisely over the defenders and before they could turn or the keeper could get to the ball, Tommy Wallace had toe-poked the ball over the goal line.

Mark had to restrain himself from rushing on to the pitch. With his record he didn't think the powers that be would be likely to look kindly upon such an action. But even if he had got on to the field of play he would not have got near Tommy Wallace, who was being carried back to his own half by a throng of Hertsmere players. Allerton kicked off, but even with all the experience in the side their heads were down. Mark knew in his heart of hearts that his team ought to tough out the last few minutes in defending

their slim lead, but that was not the way he had trained
them in his short period in charge. He was an attacker by
nature and he had tried to impose his own footballing
personality on his players. Allerton were already rocked
back on their heels and, as Wallace teased and tormented
them, their frustration finally showed when he was brought
down in the penalty area. Stuart Macdonald made no
mistake with the kick and before the teams had kicked off
again Hertsmere's green and white colours were already
being tied to the cup itself. Three-one and the final whistle
came almost as a relief to Allerton. Hertsmere couldn't
believe that the ninety minutes had gone so quickly. This
time there was no holding Mark as he danced a wild
fandango, running first to Barry Reid then to Tommy
Wallace. One by one he embraced the players who had
brought the Cup home to Hertsmere for the first time in
their existence. It was only when he found himself face to
face with Stuart Macdonald that he found himself lost for
words and out of emotion. He couldn't bring himself to
have any physical contact with this man who every night
touched his wife, who every day touched his child. It was
Macdonald who spoke first.

'Well done ... boss.'

'You too. You'd better go up and get your medal. They
can't give them out without the captain.'

And then he was gone and it was only when all the
players were climbing the famous steps to the royal box that
he recognized the words that were being chanted over and
over again by the Hertsmere supporters.

'Mark Rossetti Walks On Water.'

He began to mount the stairs to collect his own medal.

He saw Patti and felt like leaping over the barrier to be with her. He saw David Sinclair talking to a policeman and hoped for his sake he'd helped make the club safe. Now there would be income from a guaranteed European season to be added to the proceeds generated from the sale of Mickey Wayne. Then he noticed Sinclair's expression change. The chairman's face was frozen in horror. Mark took his medal and shook hands with the Duchess, hardly hearing her words of congratulations, unable to take his eyes off the man who had given him another chance, who had permitted him to have this special day in the sun.

'David, what is it? What's wrong?' he called out to him, as Patti moved across towards them.

'It's Holly, Mark. Holly, my daughter.' As if Mark had never heard her name before. 'I've just been told. She's killed herself.' And amongst the still-singing crowd baying for his attention, adjacent to the visiting royalty and other dignitaries, Mark felt himself tumbling down the same well of silence into which David Sinclair, chairman of the triumphant Cup-winning side, had already fallen.

CHAPTER 45

Life went on for Hertsmere United even if for David Sinclair it had effectively ceased. Sitting in Holly's flat just outside St Albans, with Mark and Patti for company, he could not believe that there had ever been a time when he thought football to be the most important thing in the world. How many times had he jokingly said that he would give his right arm if Hertsmere could win the Cup? And now he had given his right arm. Not given it, but had it taken from him.

The ambulance had long removed his daughter's body. He had the feeling he ought to contact her mother, but he did not know how he would put into words the fact that their daughter, the child they had conceived one night in a hotel in York, a night when he truly believed he had a love that would last for ever, was gone. Nothing lasted for ever. He knew that now. Even the victory of his beloved team earlier in the day was already history, a transitory passage in a never-ending story. It was May. By the end of the summer little sides all over the country would be playing their preliminary qualifying matches for the right to shine brightly and briefly on the road to Wembley. In January his own club would have to play its first match to defend the trophy they had won today and if they lost then it was all over. They were no longer the Cup holders, all they would have left would be their name inscribed on the silver trophy, a name in dusty record books that people seldom opened, all they would have left were their memories. Which were all that was left of Holly.

The police had been more than understanding. They had offered to leave an officer with him, to arrange grief counselling, but he had preferred to be with people he knew and had come to trust. There would have to be an inquest, but they did not suspect foul play. She had been found with an empty bottle of sleeping tablets, a half-bottle of whisky, lying fully clothed on her bed. There had been no note but, as Peter Jordan had explained, that was not in itself unusual. He had been summoned to the scene as soon as the officer had discovered the body and if there had to be a policeman at the scene Sinclair was grateful it was somebody who seemed genuinely to care.

'There'll have to be an inquest I'm afraid, but it doesn't look as if anybody else was involved. I'm really sorry, Mr Sinclair. If there's anything you need, give me a ring.' He'd scribbled on a scrap of paper. 'This is my direct line at the station. If I'm not there somebody will get hold of me right away.'

'When will I be able...' He couldn't complete the question, but Jordan finished it for him.

'To bury her? I'll try and push things through as quickly as I can, but to a certain extent I'm in the hands of the medics and the coroner. I'll do my best.' And then, with a firm and comforting grip of the hand and one last sad glance, he was gone.

Sinclair moved around his daughter's room, automatically tidying articles on the dressing table, picking clothes up from the floor and carefully hanging them in the closet.

'Untidy, so untidy. When she was at home, I'd always be shouting at her about it, complaining that she needed her own personal servant to follow her around, clearing up the mess. A trail of devastation, that's what I'd call it. If I'd been more tolerant she'd have stayed home and none of this would have happened.' He sat on the edge of the bed, then in a sudden convulsive moment spread himself over the rumpled bedclothes which he still fancied were slightly warm from her body. The sounds that came from him began as gentle sob, then rose and rose until they assumed a quality beyond human grief. Mark and Patti looked away in embarrassment, not knowing whether to leave the man to his mourning or to stay to try and bring comfort where comfort was of no use. They moved into the kitchen. Patti who was not the world's best housekeeper looked at the pile of unwashed plates and dirty glasses with disgust.

'Looks like she'd been entertaining,' she said.

'Yes, but when? Some of this stuff has got the grease so well engrained its become part of the pattern,' Mark replied.

'I assume the police have taken whatever they want. Do you think it's OK to wash it up?' Patti asked.

Mark looked surprised.

'I didn't think you were into that sort of thing.'

She shrugged as if she'd been caught shoplifting with a can of beans in her hand.

'It just seems the right thing to do.' She nodded in the direction of the noises coming from the bedroom next door. 'You go back and make sure he doesn't do anything silly and I'll see what I can do in here.' He hesitated for a moment and she grabbed a washing-up brush that looked slightly greasier than the plates and shooed him away.

She opened the fridge and the smell of something that was longing to escape sent her reeling back. She decided not to be discerning and simply swept armfuls of butter, cheese, yoghurts, tuna and fruit juices into a black rubbish bag and carried them out to the dustbins at the rear. A shopping list caught her eye, a host of items that Holly would now never need to buy, and something made her rescue it from its fate in the bin. Perhaps some time later her father would want to keep everything that had some connection with his daughter and would stand the test of time. She wondered idly why the police had not done the job she was now carrying out, but she supposed there could be nothing simpler than a dead young girl, tablets and booze, no forced entry, no sexual interference. Open and shut. Like Holly's life.

She heard the phone ringing in the living-room and recalled the title of an early Le Carré, *Call for the Dead*. Could this be some revelation that was going to provide a vital clue to a death that seemed anything but mysterious? It only happened that way in fiction, she thought. She was right: it was Detective Sergeant Rob Davies for Mark, yet the expression on his face showed that what the policeman was telling him was a revelation in itself.

'Yes, yes,' Mark said, 'I'll be right down.' He replaced the receiver and contemplated the figure of David Sinclair which was now curled into a foetal shape, the sobs subsided, the tortured mind of a Lear once more reunited with his child in restless sleep.

'Patti, can you stay here until David wakes up? Then get him home, and maybe get a doctor round to give him a shot of something. That was Davies. He wants me to go down to Hertsmere General Hospital. Incredibly enough Ray Fowler's recovered consciousness, but only just. I knew he was tough, but not that tough. He's refusing to talk to anybody except me. Davies said he's working himself up into a state, that I ought to get down there as quickly as I can. I've got David's home number, I'll call you there as soon as I can get away.'

They had both their cars with them and as Mark drove away he could not help but tune into a sports station. He'd insisted the team carried on with their planned celebrations and the reporter was at the central London hotel where the players and their guests were letting their hair down. The senior players had insisted on organizing the party themselves. They weren't interested in raising any more money for the team pool that had been run with some success by Greg Sergovich's agent. This was their day and their night. It was Stuart Macdonald's voice Mark heard on the radio.

'We're all thinking of the chairman down here. He's been given a hard ride by some of the fans, but we know he's a fan himself. It's been a great day for Hertsmere and we're just sorry that David, Mr Sinclair that is, and the boss aren't here to share it with us.'

The reporter had done a bit of groundwork. 'If the papers are to be believed, there's a bit of feeling between you and Mark Rossetti.'

'The only feeling between the boss and me is for Hertsmere. He's done a great job here under difficult conditions in a very short time and all credit to him. I won't have a word said against him . . .'

Mark switched off the radio. Was Sally there celebrating with Macdonald? He couldn't believe she would not go to share in her husband's triumph, forgetting that it was also the triumph of her ex-husband. Would they have taken Emma to dance the night away or would she be with a babysitter? He contemplated the idea of going round to Macdonald's house, of seeing and talking to his daughter, perhaps even persuading her to come away with him. The death of Holly, the grief of Sinclair, had made his own daughter's existence seem even more fragile. She was lent to him, just as her own youth was lent to her, and he was not a party to either lease.

He turned into the entrance to the brightly lit architectural monstrosity that was the new Hertsmere General. Opened just five years ago when other hospitals were being closed, it had been feted as containing state-of-the-art technology. A series of technician strikes, a couple of negligence claims and the snatching of a new-born baby had rocked its reputation firmly back on its heels but there could be no doubting it had saved the life of Ray Fowler, at least for the moment. As Mark peered at him through the glass wall he wondered how the brain and heartbeat could exist where such punishment had obviously been received. His head was swathed in bandages, and where the nose should have been two tubes led through to a maze of equipment. The rest of his body also seemed to be plugged into various sockets that meant his life depended totally on the hospital's electricity system. Jordan and Davies were already outside, the detective inspector prowling the corridors with growing impatience, the sergeant watching intently as the bandaged man in the bed battled for his life.

'You took your time,' Jordan said in a tone that suggested it had been a deliberate delaying tactic on Mark's part.

'I was worried about getting a speeding ticket,' Mark said.

Jordan narrowed his eyes and gave him a stare that he normally reserved for child molesters who'd taken two cups of tea to confess.

'I suppose I should have arranged for a police escort,' Jordan said with heavy sarcasm.' Look, Rossetti, I'm telling you I'm not happy about this. Everywhere I turn in this case you pop up. I don't like tripping over a civilian's toes, it irritates me, you irritate me. Somewhere along the line, I sense you've done something wrong. And that's my job, catching wrongdoers. In the end I always catch them, because they always make a mistake, so you'd better remember that, but right now I need you. Mr Fowler in there's a very sick man. I think he's a very confused man because since he came to an hour or so ago he's refused to talk to anybody except you. I'm told that he could lapse back into the coma at any time, that he's so weak he could even die at any time, so I have to play along with him if that's the only way I can get information. But if you hold back one syllable of what he tells you then you'll spend the night in the cells, so help me.'

Mark turned his left wrist and looked ostentatiously at his watch.

'Aren't we wasting time?'

He thought Jordan was going to self-combust, but instead all he said was, 'Get yourself gowned up and remember what I told you.'

Hospitals always made Mark nervous and the glass-walled intensive care unit made him feel worse. Like a goldfish in a bowl. He didn't know if one of Peter Jordan's talents was lip-reading, but he was taking no chances and he seated himself by the side of Ray Fowler so that his body blocked any view of the patient's mouth.

'Ray, Ray. It's me, Mark Rossetti. You asked to see me. I'm here.' He held the injured man's hand and felt a slight increase in tension to indicate that he had been heard and recognized.

'Thanks,' the man on the bed said, his voice barely above a hoarse whisper.

'No problem. Good result, hey. Your team, Ray. You coached them, I only picked them.'

He saw a small tear creep out of the corner of the one eye that was visible, then vanish beneath the bandages.

'When I woke up, the match was on.'

'Yes, they said they put the radio commentary on in the hope it might get through to you.'

'So long asleep, so long.' Fowler's eyes closed again and it seemed as if Mark might have lost him, but after a few seconds the eyes, or at least the one he could see, flickered open again, this time with a livelier, more determined glint to it.

'You wanted to talk to me, I'm listening.'

The hand tightened on Mark's fingers, the grip fierce.

'Promise me first, Mark.'

'Promise what, Ray?'

'Only you, not the police, promise that it's just between you and me.' The voice had a desperate note. Mark turned to catch the eagle stare of Jordan. Yet he realized that this was no time to be arguing with Ray Fowler. He took a deep breath.

'OK, Ray, I promise, just you and me.' Whatever story he was going to tell Jordan had better be good.

Fowler paused for a moment and Mark saw the machine monitoring his heartbeat flicker, then resume its more regular beat. A nurse hurried into the room.

'Are you all right, Mr Fowler? What about a bit of oxygen?' Without waiting for his answer, she placed the mask over his face and Mark watched with a morbid fascination as his lungs filled greedily with the air and his breathing became less laboured. The nurse looked at Mark accusingly.

'I'm not happy about this. One more scare like that and police or no police I'm clearing the lot of you out of here.' She had an Irish accent and the way she pronounced 'police' made him think she had little time for authority wearing that particular uniform.

'The doctor thought it would be fine to talk with Ray,' Mark said weakly, realizing swiftly he was in the presence of a superior force.

'Doctors? What do they know?' the nurse said contemptuously. She made a dismissing sound as if they were in the pay of the police too. She stood with her arms on her broad hips, daring Mark to disagree with her and when he said nothing she finally left, muttering.

The interruption and the rest seemed to have done

Fowler some good. His breathing was even, his grip strong, but no longer desperate.

'Mark, listen to me. Who knows how long we've got before that dragon comes back.' He gave a sound that might well have been a chuckle and Mark anxiously checked the banks of equipment to be sure it had not given any adverse sign.

'I never liked Phil Reynolds, you know. I was in charge of the kids when John Kelly was around and he was a villain, but he made no secret of it as far as the lads were concerned, almost traded on it; but Reynolds liked to pretend he was respectable.'

'He convinced a lot of people he was just that,' Mark said, then paused, annoyed with himself that he had stopped Ray in midstream. He need not have worried. Ray Fowler was determined to finish his story.

'I didn't like Mickey Wayne either, but he had a talent that needed to be saved. I thought he needed to be saved from himself.' He reflected on the thought as if it had only just occurred to him and then continued. 'While you were messing about with the police I made a few inquiries of my own. I knew Mickey was one for the ladies. I found out from some of the other lads which clubs he went to. I went down to those places. Asked questions.'

Mark could not hold back a smile. The thought of Ray Fowler plodding from one trendy nightclub to another was hard to conceive. He could just imagine the attention he'd drawn to himself.

'Yes, I can see what you're thinking,' Ray said, 'but I didn't care, you see I wanted him found, wanted him back in the team. Then when he came back, he wasn't right, so I carried on with my questions. I don't know quite why or what I thought I'd find out.'

'And what did you find out?'

'Do you know, I'm still not sure. I knew Wayne was seen around one club with the same girl. I got her description, even found out they'd go there in her car rather than his. But I could never be certain who she was or whether she had anything to do with Mickey going in the first place or not being the same player when he came back. People like Mickey Wayne they come along once every ten years. They shouldn't be allowed to waste it, it's...' He sought the word. 'Immoral, that's what it is.'

'And you're a moral man, Ray Fowler, a man who sets his own standards and then lives by them,' Mark thought, but he remained silent.

'Anyway, it seems I was asking the right questions even if I didn't understand the meaning of the answers. Because I got beaten up for my troubles.'

Mark leaned forward until his face was only a few inches from the man's bandaged, disfigured features.

'So who did it, Ray?'

'I was coming to that,' Ray said after what seemed like an eternity, and when he had told Mark, he visibly slumped back and closed his eyes as if disclosing the truth had drained him of all his strength.

CHAPTER 46

'Why you? Why all the secrecy if that was all he had to say?' Jordan had asked when Mark had given him his version of the conversation with Ray Fowler.

Mark had known his story was weak, but he'd not had a lot of time to work on it.

'He's confused. He wanted to talk to somebody who spoke the same language.'

'And I suppose I don't speak English. Unless, of course, both you and Mr Fowler have taken out Chinese citizenship when my back was turned.'

Mark tried the calm and reasonable approach.

'He's a football man through and through. He wanted to talk to another football man. We'd become close while I'd been working for the club. I think he saw a bit of me in Mickey Wayne.'

'And, apart from who was likely to win the Cup next season, what did you two little athletes say to each other?'

Mark had taken a deep breath.

'He's confused, very confused, not surprising really when you consider what he's been through the last few weeks. How much was reality? How much was part of whatever dream he's been dreaming? Who can say? He thinks Mickey Wayne still isn't safe, that he needs looking after. For some reason he thought I could do a better job than the police.'

Jordan moved his mouth from side to side as if trying to disengage a small filling from a broken tooth.

'And what do you think?'

'I think some things are better left to the authorities and I told him so. And now I've told you, and it's your decision what you want to do about it.'

Jordan was still unconvinced that he was being told the whole story.

'It took a bloody long time for him to tell you just that.'

'He rambled,' Mark said, knowing how lame that sounded. 'He was asking about the Cup Final, some of the time he didn't even know we'd won it. Other times he remembered waking up to hear bits of the commentary.'

Jordan sniffed, a habit he'd developed in interrogation to let the suspect know that he didn't believe him.

'All right, that's it for now; but rather than keeping my eye on Master Wayne, it's you that I'll be watching and don't you forget it.'

He couldn't forget it any more than he could forget what Ray Fowler had told him. It was what to do about it that was the problem. He had decided to sleep on it. The one area where he agreed with Jordan was the police's decision to keep Fowler's partial recovery under wraps. If whoever had attacked him thought there was any risk of being identified there was every chance they would try to finish off what they had started. And that was the risk and responsibility Mark had taken on to his own shoulders.

One part of him knew he should have come from Fowler's bedside and given Jordan the name of his assailant; but the other part focused on his subsequent conversation with David Sinclair. Mark had gone to visit him on his return from the hospital. Patti, who had got him home in one piece and stayed with him until Mark arrived, had done one of her regular vanishing tricks explained away by the need to earn enough bread with a little butter to keep body and soul together.

Sinclair had been more coherent in his own home, away from the scene of the tragedy.

'She'd changed, Mark, even in the last year or so, she'd changed. Kids are like that, it's all subtle, so gradual that you don't notice, then suddenly one day she's a different person.'

'I'm missing all that, David,' Mark said, able for once to put his thoughts into words knowing that the other man would understand.

Sinclair had glanced up at him then had fallen back into his own grief.

'When she was little she said she wanted to marry me and when I said it couldn't happen she said she wanted to marry somebody just like me. And now she's married nobody. What made her do it?'

Mark shook his head,

'I didn't know her well enough.'

'I thought I did,' her father said, 'but it seems I didn't know her at all. What could have been so terrible that she couldn't discuss it with me?'

'Sometimes the terrors are all in the mind. I know, David, believe me I've been there.'

Sinclair grasped his hand.

'You can find out, Mark. I know you can.'

'David, you seem to think I've got some superhuman powers. I stumbled upon Mickey Wayne, it was Vera Scott who got Handsel off your back. You expect me to get into the mind of someone, of someone...'

'Who's dead. You can say it. I know she's dead. Back there at her flat I thought if I lay down on her bed, if I prayed hard enough, I could conjure her up again. But you can never turn back once you've gone down one particular path. I just need to know why. The police aren't interested, they'll close the file once the coroner and the undertaker have done their jobs. Promise me you'll try.'

Mark had protested feebly. What point was there in making a promise that could produce nothing? But Sinclair had become more and more insistent to the point of near hysteria and finally, fearing he might tip him irretrievably over the brink, Mark promised and then left him to the doctor who put him back to sleep as an act of kindness.

It was that promise that had kept him awake all night. On Sunday morning there was to be a civic reception, but celebration was far from the newly appointed manager's mind. He thought he knew now why Fowler had wanted to talk to him and him alone. It was all connected; Wayne's kidnapping, Reynolds' disappearance, the attack on Fowler. Only he had to decide whether Holly's suicide was yet another strand of the tangled web that seemed to engulf everything and everybody connected with Hertsmere Football Club.

Sleepless and hollow-eyed, he climbed aboard the team

bus that travelled from the stadium to the town hall, waving automatically, smiling a fixed and glassy smile. The players had wanted to cancel everything as a sign of respect for the chairman, but Sinclair would have none of it and, before the drugs had taken effect, had told Mark, 'Holly would have wanted to be part of it, at least the Holly I knew. She'd have been on the balcony of the town hall throwing kisses to all the players. Let it go ahead, they deserve it. If they still feel like it they can cry at the funeral.'

Mark was amazed by the inner strength of the man. If anything had happened to Emma he did not think he would have wanted to continue living. Fathers and daughters, love and pain. So it went on and who would ever want it to stop?

Mickey Wayne was the only one of the players not to turn up. His team-mates were not surprised.

'The sooner that miserable bastard goes to fill his face with pasta, the better for all of us,' Pat Devine said, summing up the sentiments of everybody.

'We won the fucking Cup without him anyway,' Nicky Collier sneered.

Mark said nothing. He did not stay for the whole of the reception. His mind was racing now, the adrenalin pumping through his whole nervous system just as it had before any football match. He had agreed to meet Patti later in the afternoon and the two of them were going to collect Leopold Schneider from hospital. He'd been ready to leave since Friday, but Mark had pleaded with them to keep him for another couple of days until he could get away to take him home in a car. It wasn't beyond the old man to attempt to get home by public transport if left to his own devices. It

387

was an arrangement he couldn't break, but he was determined to get it over with as soon as possible and concentrate on the other matters in hand. He'd give it till Monday night. If he was no nearer solving the problems he'd set himself then he would call Jordan and toss everything firmly into his lap. The detective inspector was unlikely to be very happy with him, but then he could not conceive what he would ever to do to make the policeman happy other than him providing him with a scale model of Stephenson's Rocket.

It all began to go wrong when he received no response at Patti's door. A window flew open in the first-floor flat and a female head popped out, looking as if it had got out of bed just to deliver its message.

'Are you Mark? Yes, of course you are. I've been waiting for you. Patti's had to go out. She says she'll call you later and to be sure to leave your answerphone on if you're out.'

'Do you know where she's gone?'

The girl, who looked no more than sixteen, laughed, and now Mark could see that she was really quite attractive, although the ring through her nose and the tattoo on her bare left arm did their best to conceal that fact.

'Who knows? Any way the wind blows, that's our Patti. Well done for yesterday. Can you let me have a signed photo some time? My kid brother will go bananas if I get it for him. Make it to Benjy, will you?'

Mark looked at his watch, feeling a pang of jealousy that there were parts of Patti's life of which he still knew nothing. It was nearly three. Leo would be going crazy by now.

'Look, if she comes back in the next half an hour, tell her I'll call her from the hospital so we can try and meet up.'

'No problem. Well done for yesterday.' And then she was gone, leaving behind her a sense of youthful irresponsibility that was like a breath of fresh air.

Mark drove fast to the hospital. That was all he seemed to be doing nowadays, driving to hospitals, between managing a football club. Leopold was pacing the ward with demonic intensity by the time he got there, waving away the wheelchair that the nurse told him was mandatory transport to his vehicle.

'Very nice. You leave an old man on his own while you go off chasing rainbows.'

'I caught one, at least,' Mark said.

'I know, I watched it on television.'

'I didn't think you were interested in football.'

'I'm not. But there was no chance of missing it here. It's on the box, it's on the radio, there's patients leaping up and down. It's a wonder they all didn't have heart attacks. Now can we please go? I've got a business to run, even if you've nothing better to do.'

Mark restrained himself from reacting to his landlord's apparent ingratitude. There had been too much credit given to him over the years for him to be really angry.

'No, you're right, Leo, I've got nothing to do.'

By the time they got to the car he could see that it would be some time before Leopold Schneider was up to collecting his own rents. The overcoat, which had always seemed too large for him, now hung about him loosely like canvas draped around the tent-pole of his body. His skin had the unhealthy yellowish look of a person who had spent too little time in the fresh air, accentuated by the folds of flesh where the little weight he'd had before his admission had not been replaced.

'I'd take you home, Leo, but I don't know where you live,' Mark said. It was strange, he'd been his friend and confidant over all the years yet he had no idea of the sort of roof the old refugee had put over his own head.

'You do know, you've been there.'

Mark looked puzzled. Schneider tutted impatiently.

'The house. The house in Wood Green, where I told you I'd rented a room.'

Mark still did not catch on.

'The man whose photo I recognized. I rented him a room in my own home.'

'But Leo, it's derelict.'

Schneider shrugged.

'So don't go there. Drop me at the bus stop. I'll make my own way.'

'Don't be stupid. I'm sorry, I didn't mean to be insulting. It's just that it didn't look as if anybody else lived there.'

'Camouflage. I carry cash. Nobody's going to bother to break into a place like that. I thought you were a football manager now, not an inquiry agent. If you've finished the interrogation, then take me home.'

Mark drove in a stunned silence. He knew Schneider was an eccentric, he just hadn't realized the extent of the eccentricity. Gradually though he began to talk as freely as he had spoken to Leo when he had been unable to pay his rent. Now he realized that Schneider too had seen those little chats as an escape from the drabness of his existence.

He told him about the football although he knew he did not fully comprehend, he told him about Wayne and he told him about Handsel and then he told him about Holly Sinclair as well.

'Did you like her?' Leo asked.

'I didn't really know her, but I like her father. I owe him.'

'And you always pay your debts. Maybe not always on time, but in the end, yes,' Schneider said with a teasing smile that gave a hint of the person he had been before his heart attack.

It was only when Mark pulled up outside the dilapidated house that he remembered he'd forgotten to phone Patti. He looked around for a phone box that worked and cursed that he'd once again let the battery run down on his mobile phone. He'd have to wait until he got home, and again he could not stop the slight rush of blood as he anticipated the message he hoped he would find at home. It was adolescent, he knew it, but it had been a long time since he had felt that way.

The house looked entirely different in the daylight. It was still not Buckingham Palace, but the solid pillars at the top of the flight of steps gave it at least an appearance of decaying elegance rather than the sinister feel it had engendered when he had last visited. Ivy clung doggedly to the walls, curling over gutters and paintwork in a vain effort to conceal the stains and the cracks. Wisteria in blue bloom arched over the entrance, an odd splash of colour in a black and white film.

Mark helped Schneider up the steps and handed him back the huge bunch of keys that he'd recovered temporarily from the agents. His landlord held them for a moment, fumbled with the lock then dropped the bunch with an almighty clang.

'Maybe I'm a bit tired,' he said in the nearest tone he ever got to an apology.

'Maybe,' Mark said and let him in.

It seemed a lifetime ago since he and Patti had paid their late-night visit to find Mickey Wayne, and in a way it was. He had been just another ex-professional footballer trying to make his way in life, whilst yesterday he had achieved what most men in the sport only dreamed of; he had led a team to victory at Wembley. He let Schneider lead the way and was surprised to see him take the first door on the right, climbing over discarded junk with an agility bred from familiarity. Once they were through the first room the place became more habitable. There was furniture, old and battered, but of a quality that still won through. An oak table, covered in dust, with half a dozen chairs that matched both the wood and the level of dirt. A settee, covered in black leather drawn tight over its entrails to give it a hard, forbidding look that dared anybody to relax upon it.

'Best horsehair,' Schneider said, taking up the challenge and collapsing on it. 'Have a seat or, better still, go and make us both a drink.'

Mark followed the pointing finger which led him into what could only be called a scullery, its narrow window reluctantly letting in the odd shard of light. A huge old-fashioned sink took up most of the room, with a cupboard nestling above it and what must surely have been a prototype for the refrigerator nestling beneath. Mark opened the cupboard, found some coffee and then tried unsuccessfully to clean up the chipped mugs that he saw on the draining board. In a tin he discovered some of Schneider's speciality biscuits, reasonably well preserved, and while he searched to see if there was any drinkable milk he lit a light under the whistling kettle that seemed to have lost its whistle. The fridge yielded up an unopened carton of long-life milk and he returned to the sitting room with the two steaming cups of tea. Schneider nodded his begrudging approval.

'Good, good, you found everything.'

'Leo, how can you live like this? I can't believe you can't afford something better. I can't leave you here on your own and I can't see the social services being prepared to abandon you to your fate either.'

'How can I live like this? I lived in the camps. They didn't.' He nodded in the direction of a sepia photograph of a couple awkwardly posed in front of an ornate fireplace, their artificial smiles fixed on their faces for ever. 'My parents. They went right and I went left. I never saw them again. This is luxury compared to what I went through. Forget the welfare. They'll want to stick me in a home. Do you see me living with a load of old men all complaining about their aches and pains and women on zimmer frames trying to get me to marry them so they can get their hands on my money? I'll manage.'

He got up and hobbled across to the window, looking out at the garden.

'It was a pretty garden once when I first bought this place. I still manage to grow a few things out there. French beans, strawberries, tomatoes, carrots. It's cheaper than the supermarkets. I learned that at Auschwitz. A secret patch. Life amongst death. So much death.' He shivered. Mark remained silent. He did not think Schneider was actually talking to him. The old man leaned on the window-ledge and a piece of wood came away in his hand.

'Rotten. Like me. I wonder what's happened to my little plants without anybody here to water the garden.'

'I can take you down to have a look,' Mark said, suddenly anxious to be out of the stuffy room, away from the time capsule that was Leopold Schneider's painful history.

The old man shuffled across and, taking his arm, led him back into the dark corridor and along to another door which was locked from the inside by a single bolt. Mark pulled it across for him and together they went down the three steps that led to the lawn which, in its neglected state, was almost indistinguishable from what must once have been well-tended flower beds. They reached the end of the garden, the sunniest part of which avoided the falling shadow of the house itself. Schneider gripped Mark's arm so hard that he let out a mixed cry of pain and surprise.

'Look at them, look what they've done to my vegetables. Barbarians.' He sounded as desperate as Mark had ever heard him, like a father bemoaning the death of a child. All Mark could see was some turned earth and a few dried-out plants that might at some time or other have given the vague impression they could bear fruit.

'Who are the barbarians, Leo?' Mark asked, trying to calm him down, scared that he might have another heart attack there and then.

'Your friends, the police, didn't you tell me you called them in when you found your footballer here?'

'Yes, but they didn't need to do any digging. Wayne was in one piece and Reynolds was long gone with the money. There was nothing to hide, nothing to look for...' Then he paused as another piece of the jigsaw began to fall into place in his mind. 'Jesus wept, Leo. Do you have a spade?' The old man limped slowly to a ramshackle hut, gesturing to Mark to follow him. He pointed at a cobwebbed and rusty object in the corner which seemed to have an archaeological value of its own. Without any consideration for the suit he was still wearing, Mark grabbed the ancient tool and returned to the patch and began to toss earth like a man possessed.

'What are you doing? Have you gone *meshugah*?' Leo asked. But Mark only increased the rhythm of his efforts, knowing exactly what he was doing and almost certain of what and who he was going to find.

CHAPTER 47

Mark Rossetti wanted to be, needed to be, one jump ahead of the police. He knew it was illogical, even dangerous, but he could not stop until he had finished. He did not know if the dead and battered body of Phil Reynolds that he had finally uncovered in Schneider's garden was in any way connected with the death of Holly Sinclair, but he owed it to her father to find out if it was. He knew as soon as the police were informed that it was Reynolds' body that Jordan would be called in; and he had every reason to believe that if the detective inspector saw him in the vicinity of yet another violent incident his own wafer-thin credibility would finally be blown away. He had to find Mickey Wayne, that was the first thing. From what Fowler had told him, Wayne held the answers to a lot of questions.

'I assume you don't have a phone in this five-star establishment,' he'd asked the old man, who had seemed unmoved by the grisly disinterment.

'What do you think I am, a philistine? There's a phone box at the end of the road. I've never seen anybody else use it except me. Do you need a ten p?'

Mark hadn't needed ten pence to phone the police. He'd given them details of the house and the body, told them to be gentle with Leo, and had then hung up without giving his own name. If Jordan and Davies were such great detectives then they could work it out for themselves.

He raced home, wondering if the police would actually try and stop him in his car. They'd certainly try his flat and he wanted to be in and out before they called. He needed to talk to Patti, wanted to hear from her, and the only possibility was any message she had left on his answering machine. What he did hear panicked him more than the discovery of Reynolds' body.

Somehow, disfigured and unsightly as it had been, he had been able to cope with its inanimate state; but Patti's voice was warm and alive and he wanted to keep it that way.

'I'm sorry I missed you at the flat. Tell Leo it was nothing personal, just work. You know what we newshounds are like. Offering us an exclusive does more for the libido than blowing in our ears. I had your little friend, Mickey Wayne, call me. Prince Charming himself. I think he fancies me. Offered me the last interview he's going to give before he goes to Italy. Said he'd liked the other piece I did on him after we found him. I'm not sure how long I'll be, so just hang around for my call. I know a successful man like you has got nothing else to do!'

'The time announcement is off,' the metallic tones of his answerphone told him and he remembered disconnecting it when he'd passed the Hoover over the carpet just for the sake of something to do before he went out that morning. He didn't know when she'd called and, worse still, he didn't know where she was. The second message was also disconcerting.

'Mark, *ciao*. Carla Dandone from Rome. I'm sorry to trouble you on a Sunday. My congratulations on your victory yesterday. You see sometimes the good guys do win. But I have some bad news for your Signor Sinclair. I have only your number at home and not his. Today Signor Barlucci has a call from the club doctor. Michael Wayne will not be coming to Cinquante, nor I think anywhere in Italy. He has failed his medical. If you call me I will give you the details. I am sorry, for me as well as your club and the player. I have lost a client and a fee.'

He called her back at once and when she told him the reason for Wayne's failure he knew more than ever that he had to find Patti and find her quickly. He called Laura Wayne, but she had not seen her husband since Saturday night.

Mark sat tapping a pen against his teeth. He had to get out of there before the police caught up with him, that much was clear. By the time he tried to explain to them the whole complex story it could be too late for everybody. There was every reason for Jordan to disbelieve him and he cursed himself inwardly for acting like a rogue cop in a Clint Eastwood movie. All he'd done was place another life in danger. He had to put it right whatever the cost to him.

He got into the car and began to drive although he had no idea where he was driving to, only what he was driving from. Somewhere out there in the warren to the north of London was Patti Delaney and he knew that she needed him.

Patti should have known better and, despite the desperate nature of her situation, it was that fact which upset her the most. She was supposed to have a nose for news and yet it was that nose that had let her down, had brought her sniffing like a bloodhound with sinus problems after the wrong scent.

She had not been surprised when Mickey Wayne had phoned her. It never surprised her that anybody she had interviewed before wanted to talk to her again, whether it was on or off the record. Anyway, as far as Wayne was concerned, after his tantrum at Wembley the whole of Fleet Street would have given their well-worn right arms to speak to him on their own. But the venue should have given her a warning and she had ignored it.

'Patti, don't come near my home, the tabloids have got their lads and lasses camped at the front and the back. It's not just about me I need to talk. I've got some info about Holly Sinclair as well. You know where Holly lived. I'll meet you outside there and we'll go somewhere quiet for a drink. Patti, I think this could be really big for you, so just you and me, all right?'

She'd arrived at Holly's flat by two. The police had decided there was nothing further to secure and the press had tired of taking photographs of such an undistinguished property. There was no sign of Wayne either and she'd sat in her car for a while wondering if there was such a thing as a reliable footballer. After half an hour she got out to stretch her legs. It was a typical Sunday afternoon. The streets were virtually empty as people ate their late lunches or even later breakfasts after a morning in bed with the papers, the same papers of which she was a part.

She saw the front door of the house was open and curiosity mixed with impatience drew her towards it.

Holly's flat was on the ground floor and she thought she heard a noise from inside. A forgotten cat, an ultra-cautious policeman, or an intruder taking advantage of its temporary abandonment?

The door to the flat was also open and she pushed it, wishing she'd waited for Mark, but unable to resist the temptation. She had time to take two steps inside when she felt an arm around her neck, a rough hand over her mouth. She had no chance to practise the self-defence techniques she'd learned with such enthusiasm in the draughty church hall a year or so ago. The man was too strong for her and, as the hood went over her head and ropes tightened on her arms, she heard the mocking voice of Mickey Wayne saying, 'One interfering bitch down, and one bastard to go.'

CHAPTER 48

She lost all track of time as she sat bound and hooded on Holly Sinclair's upright kitchen chair. Her hips and buttocks ached, the rope chafed into her skin and she was dying to go to the toilet. Wayne had made no further effort to communicate with her and she had no idea whether or not he was even in the flat. She felt completely isolated. Nobody knew where she was and, apart from Mark, she realized with a touch of self-pathos that nobody really cared. All that effort to keep ahead of everybody else, including herself, and this is where it ended, a prisoner in the hands of some footballing psychopath with an IQ of minus ten. But she was cleverer than him and she had to cling to that. If she used her brains he would have to make a mistake. Just one mistake was all she needed.

Then suddenly there was light and smell and pain as the hood was roughly removed. Mickey Wayne had pulled up a chair and was sitting opposite her. She had not heard him enter and she was afraid as to just how far she might have already drifted from reality.

'Dreamy time was it? How are you feeling? Comfy?' He grinned and she wondered how it was possible for such a handsome face to look so grotesque.

'I don't understand,' she said, wishing she did not feel quite so sick.

'Don't you? Oh, I think you do. Since you came on the scene you've caused me nothing but trouble.'

'We saved your life.'

He laughed, a dry brittle sound.

'You really think that? Perhaps I gave you more credit for your intelligence than you deserved. You're supposed to have a university degree. Isn't that what you told me when you interviewed me? And I'm just another thicko footballer, aren't I? At least that's the feeling I've had whenever we've talked. Well, let me see.' He lifted his right arm, then his left, shook both his legs. 'Can you do that?' She struggled feebly. 'No, I thought not. Well, who's the thicko now, little girl?'

He rose and poured himself some Perrier, thought for a moment then poured a second glass and held it to Patti's lips to allow her to take a sip.

'I need to go to the toilet,' she said, her bursting bladder recoiling at the thought of more liquid.

'Then you'd better hope your boyfriend gets here quickly because I'm not letting you loose. You're the bait, I'm afraid. If it had been you on your own I might have let it be, but Rossetti, he's blown just about everything I tried to do.'

Patti wracked her brain for all the articles she'd ever read about kidnapping and hostages. Bond with them, keep them talking, make them aware you're a human being. But he knew she was human, that was part of the trouble. He knew her and he hated her, although even now she could not quite see what she or Mark had done. She was not going to have to wait long for an explanation.

404

'I still don't understand.' Flatter him, make him feel important. He was important. He had the gift of life and death.

Wayne grinned. 'We seem to have got a bit of time. So why don't I give you a little lesson in life?'

She breathed a sigh of relief. Whatever he had in store for her and Mark, her staying alive seemed to be a part of it, at least for the moment.

'The kidnap wasn't a kidnap at all, of course. Reynolds and I set that up. He rented the flat from the old Jew. What a crap heap, and he knew how to charge for it. They always do. Greedy bastard. And he lived there himself. You should have seen it. I can't believe he ever cleaned it. I can't stand living in a mess myself. You live in shit, you think like shit. I told Reynolds we should go for one hit with the money, but no, he had to be clever, told me the club couldn't afford it, that we'd get away with half a million and once they'd paid that then they'd feel obliged to pay some more. Salami technique he called it.' He sniffed a laugh. 'Salami. The only salami I've got is between my legs.' He handled himself thoughtfully, and she tried to shrink back, trying to make herself seem smaller, less of a target for whatever he had in mind.

He yawned, removed his hand from his groin, and leaned back in the ecstasy of the moment, his erection clear for her to see in his tight trousers.

'The fingernail was a nice touch. We bought it, would you believe, for fifty pounds from a tramp sleeping rough down by the river. He didn't even seem to feel anything when Reynolds removed it. So much booze in him that he was virtually out of it. We had to clean it up a bit then dirty the bandage I stuck over my finger.' Her eyes were drawn to his hands, his perfect undamaged hands, and she shivered at his cunning. He was still talking and she could do nothing but listen. 'We had a good laugh about that, when Reynolds was still smiling. Then his stupid cow of a wife Paula had to tell him about us. Fuck knows how it came out, but it did, and then he comes roaring back all ready to kill me. She'll get hers, the bitch, oh yes, she'll get hers. Well, what could I do? I didn't mean to kill the bastard, but he wouldn't stop acting like a cunt. He hit me and then I hit him with a chair and he went down, but he wouldn't stop trying to get up.' His voice fell to little more than a whisper and it was as if he was not even aware of Patti's presence. 'He kept getting up, and saying, no, no, over and over again, and then he was lying there and still saying no, and then, then he was lying there and he was saying nothing. I cleared up the mess. I really worked hard at that, but then I had bugger all else to do. I buried him in the garden. I thought nobody would notice the difference in that mess. And then you and Rossetti screwed everything up by finding me. I couldn't believe that. You know what the biggest joke of all was? Reynolds pushed to get Rossetti involved when Sinclair talked about getting someone in from the outside. He didn't want anybody coming on the scene who might suss him out and he didn't think Rossetti could find his car in his garage. When we rolled him over for the money I reckoned he was right as well. We were just hoping he wouldn't get taken off the case. But then all of a sudden here he is, knocked down like one of those kids' wobbly toys and still coming back for more. I had to think quickly on my feet. I heard someone come in and I just had time to get back to the room. Rossetti was smarter than Reynolds thought he was, but he still wasn't Einstein. Then he goes snooping around that tight-assed dyke Helen Archer woman at the club, and she's asking me questions as well about why I got paid more than my dozy uncle asked for when I signed my last contract. My uncle wouldn't have known a bonus from a bollock. Good old Phil says to me, don't worry, we'll be generous, I'll see you all right, but you have to give me a sweetie. Some sweetie, fifty per cent of what he improved my contract by, clear in his hand and I have to pay the tax on it. That was one of the reasons why I didn't feel so bad about taking him out of the game. Who was to say that he wouldn't have tried something clever with me after he'd got the rest of the money?'

'What happened to the five hundred thousand?' Patti asked, drawn into the drama by her curiosity, despite herself.

'Oh, I've got that safe, but thanks for asking,' Wayne replied, leering at her, clearly enjoying himself. 'Anyway, I told Miss Archer that I was as shocked by what had happened as anybody else and she'd better ask Reynolds when they found him. I didn't say that he wasn't going to be in any condition to answer. She swallowed that, but Ray Fowler wasn't swallowing anything. I reckon he had something going for me.'

'He just admired you. He thought you were the greatest and you were wasting it.'

'Well, I am the greatest, aren't I?' She could see him visibly swell, then deflate as he said, 'I was the greatest,' and she did not feel it safe to ask why he referred to himself in the past tense.

'Fowler didn't care. He was jealous like all the rest. I was better than he'd ever been, better than he could ever be,' he said, his voice becoming high, his speech rapid with excitement. He began to cough, almost to choke, and Patti wondered what would happen if he choked himself to death there and then. She could starve to death here if she couldn't free herself and instinctively she tugged at the ropes, which only caused them to burn more deeply into her flesh.

As if reading her mind, Wayne said, 'Don't bother. I was a boy scout. My old woman made sure of that. Got me out of the house on Mondays and Thursdays so she could entertain her fancy men. She particularly liked the camping side of it because then she'd be on her own for weeks. That was where I started playing football, cubs and scouts, until they stopped me because I was too good. Always jealousy you see, even then. Fowler wouldn't let it alone, he was like a dog worrying at a bone. Questions, questions, of guys who knew me, and he was getting close, too close to me and the girl. I had to stop him. It was his own fault, nobody asked him to get involved.'

Patti made to say something and then bit her lip to stop herself. This man was teetering on the brink of sanity, she could see that with what little she'd picked up of amateur psychology over the years. Nothing was his fault, everything he'd done he'd been driven to, everything could be justified. He seemed to have talked himself out and he sat, seemingly deep in thought, relaxed compared to the tension he had shown whilst he'd been speaking.

The silence began to prey on Patti's nerves. She could hear the clock ticking, the man breathing, water gurgling through the old piping, the sound making her even more desperate to relieve herself. In another few minutes she knew she could hold on no longer and she could feel tears at the corner of her eyes in anticipation of the shame and embarrassment of what she was about to do. She had to say something, had to find something to concentrate upon other than this dreadful bursting feeling deep inside her.

'What are we waiting for?'

'Rossetti,' he said, spitting the word out, like an unpleasant piece of gristle trapped between his teeth.

'How long do we wait?'

'As long as it takes. He'll find you. He'll work it out and then he'll come and he'll come alone. I know him better than you. Not for him the cavalry. Oh no, he's the Lone Ranger and Indiana Jones rolled into one. He loves the glory, you could see it when he brought the money to the phone box, hear it when he found me, when he won the Cup with that load of second-raters he calls a team.'

He looked at the clock as if weighing her fate in the balance.

'We've had a nice little chat whilst we've been waiting, and I think it's time for a bit of fun. I'd be failing in my duty if I didn't keep my guests entertained.' He moved towards her and touched her T-shirt, pulling it away from her neck with one finger. She was sweating slightly and it stuck more tightly to her body with the pressure. He traced a line down with the same finger from her collar-bone to her breast, then gently circled first one nipple, then the other, watching them react and rise with a life and being of their own. She felt nausea rise within her. Then suddenly, as if a restraining rope had snapped in him, he pulled hard and the cotton ripped with his strength.

'No bra, I like that. Nice tits too. Wasted on that wop. Has he fucked you?' He looked at her quizzically, his head to one side, his eyes shining bright and beady like a dangerous bird which has spied its lunch. He was moving more quickly now, the odd jerking motions of a clockwork toy which had veered out of control. He tugged at the waist of her jeans with such impatience that the brass popper flew across the room, clanging on the polished floorboards. He unzipped the front of the blue denim and then realized he could not pull down her jeans without loosening the ropes that bound her legs. He stepped back panting like a dog on heat. He slipped his own shirt over his head and, as Patti saw the rippling muscles of the professional athlete, any thought she might have had of overpowering him vanished in that instant. She felt a wave of despair sweep over her at the sight and smell of him. How many other women had he done this to? How many others had he forced himself upon with his charade of charm?

Keep him talking, somehow keep him talking, she told herself, despite the fact you're about to be raped, although a small part of her kept saying this wasn't possible. Finally she managed to get the words.

'Mickey, satisfy my curiosity. If you'd gone to Italy, you'd have made yourself a fortune. If you'd wanted to do some deal with Reynolds over the transfer you could still have cut him in and still been seriously rich. So why the kidnap, why all the trouble and risk?' She tried to keep her voice steady, tried desperately hard to normalize the situation, but she need not have bothered. He ignored the question and, giving her another crooked smile, he began to unzip his flies and, as if in slow motion, pull down his trousers.

CHAPTER 49

It had been one of the longest afternoons of Mark Rossetti's life. He had driven round aimlessly on what should have been a day of celebration, a day upon which he should have relaxed and revelled in the glory. He did not know what he expected to find – Mickey Wayne standing on a street corner with a sign around his neck saying, 'Find Me', perhaps?

Eventually he ended up at David Sinclair's house, a huge Victorian dwelling, set at the end of a long and leafy lane in Barnet, which had formerly served as a vicarage when vicars clearly meant more than they did in the 1990s. Sinclair seemed neither surprised nor displeased to see him. He was vague, looking far older than his years, like a man who has recently retired and cannot get accustomed to his carpet slippers rather than his highly polished shoes.

'Mark, come in, come in. You'll have to excuse the mess. I've just woken up. The doctor thought it would be better if I slept.' His voice trailed off as if he had remembered somewhere he ought to be or something he should be doing. 'He gave me an injection. Asked if I had anybody who could stay with me. Only Holly, I said, only Holly.

Have I woken up, Mark? Are you part of the same dream? Tell me, Mark, I know you'll tell me the truth.'

Mark took him by the elbow and led him gently into his own house. He saw an open door to the left and guessing it was the lounge guided Sinclair into it. The curtains were drawn and there was already a smell of decay and mourning about the place. Mark drew them slightly and Sinclair recoiled from the light, blinking and shielding his eyes like a man rescued from a mine-shaft.

'Sit yourself down, David, I'll make you a cup of tea.'

The chairman protested feebly, then slumped back into an armchair which wrapped itself around his body with a long-accustomed familiarity. Mark found the kitchen by trial and error, then reeled back at the chaos that hit his nose and eyes. Dirty plates were left congealing in the sink, food had been taken out of the refrigerator and then left at random. He'd had his own times when he'd allowed himself to slip into a morass, but this had been accomplished in less than twenty-four hours. Mark located the dishwasher, piled plates into it regardless of their state and switched on the machine. He found a rubbish bag and swept the food into it, washed down whatever surfaces had now been revealed, then switched on the kettle and set off on an unsuccessful search for tea-bags. By the side of an empty caddy he found the shopping list Patti had rescued from Holly's flat.

'Tea-bags, sweeteners, fresh orange juice, Greek yog-hurts, cat food.' She obviously shopped both for herself and her father, as the intended recipient of this last item rubbed itself against his legs in a successful attempt to draw his attention to its empty bowl. He knelt down and emptied the remains of what appeared to be the last tin of rabbit and game and the cat virtually pushed him aside in its eagerness to get some food. He looked for some milk and found a half-pint that looked reasonably drinkable and poured a generous portion into the cat's bowl. The animal seemed indecisive as to whether it was more thirsty than hungry and dipped into both meat and milk with equal enthusiasm, purring its appreciation of Mark's efforts.

'You've no loyalty, moggy,' he said, wondering what secrets Holly Sinclair had confided to it at feeding time. The kettle boiled and, finding some instant coffee, he decided David Sinclair was unlikely to complain as long as it was hot and strong and he had company with which to drink it.

Sinclair held the cup in both hands, feeling its warmth with a certain amount of disbelief that he could still feel anything.

'Thanks, Mark. What happens now?'

'I don't know. I wish I did.'

'I can't understand why she would do a thing like this,' he said as if he were talking about some minor misdemeanour at school that had led to a parental confrontation with the headmistress. 'If she had a reason, she would have wanted me to know why, even if she'd not felt able to tell me to my face. She must have left a note, she must have.'

'The police looked, David, they looked everywhere. Sui—' he swallowed back the word. 'People who do desperate things don't leave notes and then hide them.'

And then it came to him with all the sudden shock of Newton discovering gravity.

'Wait right here, David,' he said superfluously, as if the man was going anywhere. Mark dashed out to his car and raced back with the file he'd pulled from his filing cabinet on Mickey Wayne. He rustled through it and produced triumphantly the two notes he'd found in the player's locker, the one from Paula Reynolds, the other, with its now distinctive handwriting, undeniably from Holly Sinclair. No question of suicide, only of infatuation, an obsession she had mistaken for love. It had been there all the time. He'd seen the scrawled note she'd left on her father's desk and it had registered then, but he'd not worked hard enough at it, and perhaps that mental laziness had cost Holly her life; but it wasn't going to cost him Patti Delaney. Mickey Wayne was out there and dangerous and he had to be stopped.

'David, have you got keys to Holly's flat?'

The question, simple as it was, still seemed to cause Sinclair an enormous effort to answer.

'David, come on, quickly.' The note of urgency in Mark's voice somehow got through to the other man.

'Yes, I think the police gave them back to me.' He looked around the room helplessly and Mark longed to smack him across the face, to bring him back into the real world, however painful that might be. Sinclair saved himself just in time.

'In the hall, on the bookcase.'

Mark picked them up and was almost out of the front door, when he realized he could not leave Sinclair on his own. In a deep, drug-induced sleep he was no danger to himself, but in this half-somnambulant state who could say?

'David, you've got to come with me, now. I'll explain in the car, but meanwhile look at this.' He handed him Holly's note to Wayne. He saw Sinclair make an enormous effort to focus, then, as he read, give out a cry of the real pain of emotional mutilation.

'Mark,' Sinclair said, gripping his manager's arm with grim determination, 'take me to that bastard, and then leave him to me.'

Mark did not argue; he had no time, but he could hardly conceive that Sinclair in his present state would have been able to deal with the cat, let alone a rampant and aggressive Mickey Wayne. He drove, grim-faced and with a single-mindedness that dared any police car to stop him. The police. He ought to phone Jordan, he knew that, but he convinced himself that he could lose valuable seconds making the call, and still drove northwards towards the flat where Holly had lived and died. Sinclair was tensed forward, straining at the seat-belt that Mark had virtually had to force him to wear. At crossroads and traffic-lights he took both their lives in his hands, his right foot playing perfunctory notes on the brake. This was no time to stop, or even think of stopping.

'I had your little friend, Mickey Wayne, call me. Prince Charming himself.' The words, rolling round and round inside his head like washing in a tumble dryer. Knowing, whatever he did, he had to get to her before her exclusive interview came to an end.

Wayne had a knife in his hand, plucked from the cutlery drawer, short and sharp, its handle a dull black. One woman had already died in this house, seemingly by her own hand, but she was sure that somehow Wayne had been involved. Exactly how was another question.

As he moved towards her, she lost her nerve, abandoned all her efforts to keep him talking, and she screamed, praying somebody would hear, but he had turned up the volume on the radio and even to her own ears the noise that came from her dry mouth seemed to merge and be lost in the cacophony of heavy metal that blasted from some local station. He touched her throat with the knife, drawing a bead of blood, then made to slash downwards as she struggled back the millimetres that an intake of breath would permit.

'Only joking,' he said in a matter-of-fact tone. She tried to stop herself shaking, to make her mind work again under her own control. He put the knife carefully on the waist of her open jeans, then slit them down, avoiding the rope but scratching her painfully. He took a step back to admire his handiwork then pulled the cloth away on two sides like theatre curtains. Naked himself save for his blue briefs which did little to hide his erection, he tugged roughly at what remained of her jeans. She was left just in her panties. The irrational thought crossed her mind that they had cost her a fortune at Janet Reger's and she hoped he wouldn't take the knife to them as well. He seemed calmer now, more in control as he stood there, watching the strip-show he'd stage-managed himself.

'Mickey, what happened to Holly?' she asked.

'She died, dozy scrubber. Couldn't take the heat, so she burned down the fucking kitchen. A sandwich short of a picnic, that one. I should never have got involved. She should never have got involved, that was for sure.' Again the humourless laugh, interrupted by a cough.

'Enough farting about. Rossetti's slow, slower than I thought he'd be. I think you need a lesson meantime.' He touched her between her legs, his fingers probing through the white satin. 'That's what you want, that's what you all want.'

Suddenly he was pressing against her and there was nothing between them except the appalling wall of noise that still rose from the radio. She longed to put her hands over her ears to block out the sound, to close her eyes and retreat into the darkness, but instead she asked one more time, 'Mickey, why didn't you just go to Italy?'

'Because he's HIV positive,' Mark said, appearing at the door, and then he dived forward to get a grip on the slippery, bare flesh of the footballer.

CHAPTER 50

He hadn't reckoned on him being so strong, but now that he was close to him, now that he could see his muscles, touch the biceps, feel the pectorals, Mark realized that he, himself, was hopelessly out of condition. Ten years ago, perhaps, he would have been a match for Wayne, but today he had to use brain rather than brawn.

Sinclair had been in a terrible state by the time they got to the flat. It was as if he had been burned out by the adrenalin, his speech slurred, his eyes closing again, the hour or so he had been with Mark now all part of the dream tunnel which drew him ever further into its dusky depths. Mark had left him slumped in the passenger's seat, all thoughts of revenge driven out by the calming effect of the drugs. And so he was on his own, on his own and losing, without a corner to throw in the towel for him.

Wayne fought like a wild animal, his teeth drawn back in a mockery of a smile, then spitting, clawing and punching without any thought other than survival. HIV positive. Even as he fought, Mark could see all the headlines, all the media programmes about people who had contracted the disease from saliva and bites, prisoners acting like untamed creatures scratching their captors determined to see others suffer the torments they suffered themselves. That was what Wayne was doing, Mark thought, he's trying to kill me, not here and now, but slowly. The player tried to sink his teeth into Mark's left arm, and automatically he jabbed his right fist into his face, momentarily causing the naked figure to reel back. A gush of blood flowed from Wayne's nose and stained Mark's white shirt like a bottle of ketchup spilled by a child at the table.

'You bastard,' Wayne hissed, clutching his nose and reeling back. Patti watched, helpless, rocking her chair back and forth in a vain effort to free herself and lend Mark some help. Wayne stood up and began to circle Mark, his arms hanging loosely at his side like an ape's, the blood still pouring.

Mark tried to balance himself, to be ready for the moment Wayne chose to pounce and as he did his eye caught the glint of the knife that Wayne had held in his hand when he had first entered the room. Wayne saw it too and was just that little bit quicker. Mark drew back. If Wayne cut him and then his blood entered the wound he was as good as dead. He had no wish to play the percentage game, waiting for years to see whether or not he had been infected. He had only just been restored to life and to die again, perhaps this time even more slowly, was unthinkable. Wayne leapt at Mark and Patti's warning cry came just in time to allow him to throw himself to his left as Wayne hurtled by.

The footballer slammed into the wall and as he was off balance Mark, aware of the wrench he had just inflicted on his damaged knee, grabbed him round the throat from behind, his arm pressing down on his gullet. Wayne's breath began to labour, words became bubbling sounds, and he felt him going limp in his arms. He couldn't kill him, he knew that, it was not in him. The man had committed some horrific acts, but he deserved his day in court. He released his grip slightly and began to drag the player's body back towards the coil of rope that lay in the opposite corner of the room, abandoned once he had completed the binding of Patti. It was a mistake. Wayne's body suddenly seemed to fill with air and expand and in a second he was free.

'You're such a soft touch, Rossetti. You must have been a mug for the dummy on the field,' Wayne said, his hands clutching at Mark's throat, the blood around the nose now starting to cake and congeal. Mark tried to knee him in the groin, but the oxygen supply seemed cut off from his body, his limbs refusing to obey his commands and all he could feel was his knee-bone wrenching in its socket. The room began to whirl around, both his legs now caving in beneath him, Patti's cries were ever fainter, even the music from the radio was nothing but a distant buzz. So this is where it ends was his final thought and then he was on the floor suffocated beneath the clinging hands of Mickey Wayne and the dead weight of his body.

It took several moments to realize that he was still alive and that it was Wayne who was unconscious and then he heard and felt the shuddering thuds as David Sinclair brought the tyre lever down again and again on what had once been his hero's head. Mark rose unsteadily to his feet and as he caught Sinclair's arm on the uplift, the chairman let himself go, surrendering to the lethargy from which he had momentarily been aroused.

'It's all right, David. It's enough, it's finished.' Sinclair let the blood-stained tool drop to the floor with a dull clang.

'Is he dead?' he asked.

Wayne stirred slightly and groaned in reply.

'He will be if we don't get him an ambulance.' Mark looked around for the phone and made the call. Sinclair toe-poked Wayne gently with his foot as if he were a wounded animal he'd found by the side of a dual carriageway.

'Holly's dead, you know,' her father said.

'Yes, yes, I know,' Mark replied gently, and then he heard the sounds of sirens in the distance and Patti's voice near at hand asking if he was going to set her free and allow her to get some clothes on before the police arrived.

CHAPTER 51

In mid-July, Mark Rossetti sat in the manager's office at Hertsmere United for what he knew would be the final time. It was the first day back for pre-season training, a season that any normal manager would be looking forward to with eager anticipation. But Mark was no normal manager, he knew that now. He had gained that knowledge, not through the corridors of power, but through the side-streets of violence and corruption through which he had walked for what seemed so long. It was also David Sinclair's first day back at the club since his enforced rest after the Wayne incident. He had yet to see how much he'd benefited from his cruise around the Greek islands. Although Mickey Wayne himself was dead, he still cast a long shadow over the club and the chairman. With his passing, Sinclair had lost his star player, his manager and his daughter. He would not be forgotten.

He had taken a long time to die, but they had finally switched off the life support system two weeks ago, although the decision not to prosecute Sinclair had already been made. Mark had got the distinct impression that Detective Inspector Jordan would have very much liked to have charged him with Wayne's murder, or anybody's murder if it came to that. He'd seen his sergeant, Rob Davies, around the ground, collecting Helen Archer, who now wore his gleaming diamond engagement ring with a certain diffident embarrassment. She had been proved to be both human and female with all the failings of both.

'You've really upset my guvnor, you know,' Davies had said one day. 'Not many people do that and live to tell the tale. He prefers to wind up his cases on his own without the help of any amateurs – or did you get paid for it?' he asked with a cheery smile.

'No, I didn't get paid for it,' Mark had replied, for even Barlucci had apologetically, doubtless on advice, declined to pay him his £100,000. Perhaps, perversely, that was all for the best. Mark rather liked Rob Davies and was pleased for Helen. She deserved a nice man in her life and at least Davies' knowledge of football was every bit as encyclopedic as her own. The thought of the level of conversation during the washing-up and later in bed defied the imagination.

He could smile now, but it had not been so easy when Jordan and Davies had arrived at Holly's flat to find the remains of the mayhem caused by Patti's capture and the subsequent fight. Despite the bruises on his neck, despite the fact that Patti was still shaking, Jordan had been brutal in his cross-examination, listening to the explanation at first with cynicism and then with annoyance when he began to realize it was the truth. The kidnap, Reynolds' death, the attack on Fowler, they were all down to Mickey Wayne, and now Wayne had been delivered to him, not in any pristine condition it had to be admitted, but delivered and defused. What Mark had not told him then, and what only

Patti knew, was that Wayne had gained consciousness for a few moments before the ambulance and the police arrived. Sinclair had already left the room and was reeling outside, gasping in great gulps of air as if he had just been rescued from drowning.

Wayne had looked up at Mark with glazed eyes, making a feeble attempt to rise before collapsing like a folding tent.

'You tell that bastard,' his voice was barely more than a whisper, but Mark still did not trust him sufficiently to come any nearer, 'tell him his lovely little girl was a great cock-sucker. Tell him that.' He'd fumbled in the pocket of his trousers which still lay by his side on the floor, while Mark watched every slow movement with wary caution. 'Here, show him this, it'll make interesting reading. I got it when I came back here that afternoon of the Final when you were all too busy celebrating. She was still alive, just. I left her there and by the time the police came it was too late. Tell the bastard that maybe I could have saved her and I chose not to.'

There was no hint of guilt or contrition in his voice, rather a note of triumph. Mark had been relieved when the voice had stopped, when the malevolent eyes had closed. He had pocketed the note which now he had on the desk in front of him. Sinclair had been right when he had said his daughter would have left him a note before taking her own life. But would this note ease his pain at all? Yes, she told him she loved him, but he knew that already, and she also told him that she, too, was HIV positive, and could not face the thought of the pain ahead. It had been bad enough telling Paula Reynolds and Laura Wayne. They'd both tested negative, but that was so far and there was still a long way to go. What purpose was there in handing this hastily scribbled note, produced by an unbalanced mind, to a father who was only just beginning to heal? He tore it once, then twice, then into strips and finally put the whole in the ashtray he kept for visitors and used his table lighter to reduce it to ashes, like Holly's body at the crematorium. It was gone, the last physical earthly reminder of the girl's fate and with it Mark felt the lifting of a burden that had been weighing heavily on his mind.

He went in to see the chairman, wondering how he was going to put his decision into words, but as ever Sinclair made it easy for him.

'Have a cup of tea, Mark,' he said in greeting, and even as he opened the door to ask Denise to make it she was already bringing the tray through.

'Telepathic now, are you?' Sinclair asked his secretary.

'No, it's just that I've had rather a long time to get it ready. It's good to see you back, to see you both back together.' She blushed like a girl of half her age and bowed her way backwards from the room as if departing from the presence of royalty.

'She's in love with you, you know,' Mark said.

Sinclair nodded.

'That's a dangerous condition. I don't seem to bring those around me very much luck.'

'You haven't done too badly by me,' Mark said

'Perhaps, but not well enough to make you stay.'

Mark put down his tea-cup halfway.

'How did you know that?'

'I can see it in your eyes. You forget that before you met

428

me I used to be successful businessman. I can tell that sort of thing a mile off. It's only the rest of my life that's a failure.'

'It doesn't have to be. Ray Fowler's back. He could be a good manager.'

Against all the odds, Fowler had gone from strength to strength after Mark's visit to him and when he'd been told of the capture of Mickey Wayne it was as if he'd been given a reason to live, to shape the fortunes of another Mickey Wayne who was out there just waiting to be discovered.

'He doesn't want to be a manager,' Sinclair said.

'Nor did I, and he's got better qualifications. The team's in Europe, you can get your new stadium, forget the bank,' Mark said, with the air of an uncle bringing a package of goods to a favourite nephew.

'What, do you mean your friendly neighbourhood police officer has given you a magic wand?'

'No, I don't think so. I think he'd like to get me up a dark alley with a good old-fashioned police baton, but magic wands aren't his style. I've been busy whilst you've been getting that great tan on your holiday.'

'Tell me,' Sinclair said, more out of politeness than any great interest.

'I had Barlucci on the phone. He was calling from the bottom of a deep, deep pit he'd dug himself. The Cinquante fans were not impressed when he failed to deliver Wayne.' He saw Sinclair wince at the mention of the player's name and rapidly continued. 'I wasn't too impressed either when I missed out on my bonus. Anyway, he had to do something to save face. What he wants is to buy on to the board here, make Hertsmere a sort of glorified nursery for his club. He reckons that any small team that can produce a player like Mickey Wayne can produce another, and by the way he'd also like an option on Tommy Wallace, although I don't suggest you agree his price. I didn't think it was any of my business to get too involved in the financial side of things, but one thing's for sure; that there's a deal there somewhere and Barlucci made it clear he's not the sort of man to want to be indebted to banks.'

'I don't know what to say. I was going to tell you that I was going to pack it in. I rather liked Greece, the peace, the quiet...'

'Yeah, but the football's crap. You saw what they were like in the World Cup. Anyway, you have to stick with it, David. The club's gone through three managers in a season, I don't think it could take two chairmen. I think Holly would want it. Clinch your deal with Barlucci, get his money, build your stadium and name a stand after her.'

'I didn't know you were a romantic, Mark.'

'I'm not. That was Patti's idea.'

'Still around, is she?' Sinclair asked, his voice softening.

'Sort of. I saw her last a week ago. She said she needed some time on her own. That I was invading her space. I told her she was reading too many agony aunt columns but she was serious. She's gone away for a while to think. I'm still waiting for the postcard.' He sounded more flippant than he really was, but he didn't think David Sinclair deserved to be told of the pain he'd felt when Patti had told him of her sudden decision to go away, or the dull ache he'd felt since she'd been gone. That was all private.

'I need to think about things myself,' Sinclair said.

'You've not got a lot of time. Barlucci is coming to see you tomorrow at ten, with the beautiful Signorina Dandone in tow. Now if you'll excuse me, I need to clear out my desk and say goodbye to the lads.'

Sinclair extended his hand. Despite the suntan he still looked tired and drawn and Mark guessed that getting involved in the day-to-day running of a football club would do him the world of good. His grip was firm and Mark thought that at least was a good sign. He passed through Denise's office on the way back to his own.

'I think you'd better get in to David,' he smiled. 'He's got a pile of work to clear.' The one person he didn't expect to see waiting for him in his office was Stuart Macdonald, but there he was looking out of his window at the view of the players in training that had so often fascinated Mark.

'Sorry to barge in, but I wasn't sure you'd see me if I made an appointment.'

'You're one of my players, or were. I always have to find time to see you.'

'What do you mean were? Don't tell me they've sacked you?'

'No. I've resigned. It was never meant to be permanent. Ray Fowler's got a louder voice than I have.'

As if he'd heard him, Fowler's tones echoed around the field at some poor unfortunate apprentice who'd not cleaned Pat Devine's boots properly.

'I'm sorry to see you go. We'll all be. I mean it.' He sought the right words, and then found them tumbling out in a rush. 'Look Mark, Sally and I, we were talking on holiday. We've not been fair to you. If you want to see

Emma at any time, well you just need to ring. Days out at first until she's got used to you, then maybe she can stay over as long as – I'm sorry, but Sally said to say – as long as you've got a decent place...' He broke off in embarrassment.

'Hey, no problem. Sally used to scare the pants off me as well.'

The two men laughed, linked by a common cause that had for so long kept them apart. Macdonald seemed reluctant to leave, as if he had said the easy bit, but the hard part was yet to come.

'I don't know how to tell you this. When you took over as manager I said to the rest of the lads this is it for me. Goodnight sweetheart. But you kept me in the team and you kept me as captain and I know that took some doing.'

'You were playing well, and, as for the captaincy ... Who else was there?'

Macdonald shifted awkwardly.

'Yeah, well, thanks, that makes me feel much better.'

Again they both laughed nervously.

'I'm not finished yet. Please, Mark, whatever you feel, just listen to me, hear me out and then do whatever you want. All those years ago, that match you were supposed to have tried to swing, I knew it wasn't you. It was Chris Handsel. He told me, enjoyed telling me, thought I'd enjoy hearing it because of Sally, and maybe he was right at the time. In any event I kept quiet about it, all this time, I never told a soul. Until now.'

Mark felt the colour drain from his face. He felt once more that somebody had their hands around his throat, squeezing the life juices from his body.

'But why? What had I ever done to Handsel to deserve that?'

'You were better than him. That was what started it off. Chris never liked anybody to be that much better than him. You were taking his headlines, taking his popularity with the crowd and he didn't like that either.'

'And just because of that he ruined my career?' Mark asked in disbelief.

'No, it wasn't just because of that, although sometimes with Chris Handsel it didn't have to be a lot more. There was the business between his father and your old man.'

Mark looked even more astonished.

'What are you talking about, Stuart? They didn't even know each other. My dad ran a little cafe in the East End, whilst Handsel senior was some big wheel.'

'If by big wheel you mean big crook, then you're right. Ronnie Handsel ran a protection racket in the East End. Still does for all I know. It was his pitch. Your dad stood up to him and, worse than that, encouraged others to do the same. It wasn't good for business. Your dad had some loyal friends, too, in the Italian community. Handsel couldn't get near enough to touch him for a while, a long while. Chris didn't say so in so many words, but I don't think that fire at the cafe was an accident. I'm so sorry, Mark. I shouldn't have kept all this back, but I wanted Sally, I wanted her really bad.'

'Yeah, she's that kind of woman.'

'As I said, whatever you want me to do now, I'll do.'

Mark thought for a moment. It would have been easier to do nothing. That was what the old Mark Rossetti would have done, but Chris Handsel was still out there and his own father was dead and buried alongside his mother in the Catholic cemetery in Hackney. His dad wouldn't have wanted him to do nothing. He lifted the phone and dialled.

'Detective Inspector Jordan please. It's Mark Rossetti. I think he'll want to talk to me.'

EPILOGUE

It was four days later that he returned to Hertsmere to say goodbye to the team who had won the Cup for him. Jordan had taken nearly all his time until then taking statements from Stuart Macdonald, asking Mark to fill in as much as he could remember of his joint playing career with Handsel, of his father's business, anything he could recall that could present a watertight case. He knew all about Ronnie Handsel and he knew that he was never going to be an easy fish to land; but Chris was different.

'He's the bait you see, Rossetti. We get him on the hook with the help of your friend Macdonald and, who knows, the old man may come sniffing around the same worm.'

'I'm not sure fish sniff,' Mark said.

Jordan had given him a look of such intensity that Mark had not tried to be facetious again.

For two whole days Jordan had worked at getting it right, and then he had invited Chris Handsel to join him for a little chat at the station. The conversation still had some way to go before it reached its conclusion. There was no doubting that Jordan was now a happier man.

'There's no substitute for careful, methodical police work,' he'd said, before making it clear that when he needed

Rossetti again to help with his investigations he'd let him know. 'We knew you were lying about Fowler. You left your car parked in the street for three days and even we simple policemen have the brains to check out the registration numbers of vehicles around the scene of a violent assault. But we decided if we gave you enough rope you'd either hang yourself or lead us to what we were looking for. The only mistake we made was not believing you'd play with the rope the day after bloody Hertsmere had won the Cup you all seem to think so highly of. You're a lucky man, Rossetti, but don't push it.'

Barlucci was still in England parading around Hertsmere as if he were some kind of messiah, shocking even his own legal adviser by the grandeur of his schemes.

'He's mad, totally mad, of course,' Sinclair said when Mark had strolled into his office, 'but I'm growing rather fond of him.'

'And Carla too?' Mark had asked, but the chairman had merely smiled and said nothing.

Barlucci had tried to persuade Mark to change his mind, even offering him the £100,000 to sign a contract, but Mark had been adamant.

'I wouldn't know what to do with all that money at this stage in my life. I think I work better when I'm likely to be hungry if I don't work.'

He'd said his farewells to everybody except Tommy Wallace who'd been giving an interview to the *Sun*. Tommy caught him on the stairs, his face looking less babyish, his whole attitude more mature, as if he had spent the summer growing out of adolescence.

'Sorry, boss,' he said.

'I'm not your boss any more.'

'To me you'll always be the boss. You can forget about Bruce Springsteen.'

'How did the interview go?'

'Yeah, good. I got paid a couple of grand for it. Lennie Simons arranged it for me. He wants to be my agent. What do you think?'

'Don't touch him with a bargepole. Be your own man.' It was the last piece of advice he had to give to Hertsmere and he knew it was a good one.

He got into the car that Sinclair had let him keep as a farewell bonus and drove back to his little flat and even smaller office. Maybe Sally was right, maybe he should move. His daughter deserved better than this even if he did not. He threw off his jacket and pulled loose the tie with some relief. Some men were meant to work in suits and some were not. He put on the ancient kettle. He needed a cup of tea; once he would have needed a drink. He also needed to think. He had resigned from the manager's post at Hertsmere because he knew that was something he didn't want to do and now he had to find something that did appeal to him. He felt a little like Mr Micawber, a character he'd discovered long after leaving school; something was sure to turn up. He went to his answerphone to play his messages. Leo Schneider was complaining that he'd not been in touch.

'You find a dead body in my garden and then you don't want to know me.'

He was right. He'd rectify that tomorrow. He still had a twenty-pound loan to repay, in any event.

And then came Patti's voice.

'Hi. It's me. I thought you'd prefer the real thing to a postcard and anyway I was bored. Nobody dies in Cornwall or if they do they keep pretty quiet about it. Give me a ring. It's about time I did another exclusive interview with you, this time without any interruptions.'

He heard the kettle boil and poured himself his drink. Then he made his way back to the phone and began to dial her number, half expecting to get her recorded message, but on the third ring she picked up the receiver.

'Hi, I was waiting for your call.'

'Good. About that interview. I think I can bring my story right up to date.'

'Can you? I wouldn't be too sure of that. Perhaps there are things that even you don't know yet.'

And then he was racing down the stairs as fast as his injured knee would take him to find out exactly what she had to tell him, although in his own heart he felt he knew already.

JOHN FRANCOME

BREAK NECK

'Francome writes an odds-on racing cert'
Daily Express

When apprentice jockey Rory Gillespie abandons his fiancée Laura Brickhill, in favour of trainer's daughter Pam Fanshaw, it's a decision made from ambition not love. And Rory has to wait ten years before Laura will forgive him.

Now one of England's leading trainers, and married to property tycoon Luke Mundy, Laura asks Rory to ride her best horse, Midnight Express, in Cheltenham's Two Mile Champion Chase. Shortly afterwards, Luke is killed on one of Laura's horses and she is arrested for manslaughter. Rory won't desert her this time and, setting out to prove Laura's innocence, he discovers that there is more than one person who will benefit from Luke's death.

Packed with intrigue and excitement, the plot unravels at breakneck speed, revealing bribery, blackmail and corruption as ingredients in this highly accomplished racing thriller.

FICTION / CRIME 0 7472 4704 8

Ophelia O. and The Mortgage Bandits

A RIOTOUS NOVEL OF LEGAL FRAUD AND LABRADORS, LOVE AND BODY-SNATCHING

TANYA JONES

Ophelia O., a newly qualified solicitor, bread-winning wife and mother of five, expects her struggles to be over on her first day at the old-fashioned law firm in the Yorkshire market town of Rambleton. But the senior partner is suspiciously still as he lies across his *Law Society Gazette* and Polly, his stilettoed secretary, conceals depths of cunning beneath her purple leather jacket. Before she can say 'Disciplinary Tribunal', Ophelia, Polly and the deep-frozen Mr Parrish are entwined in an outrageous plan to keep the practice going.

Meanwhile Ophelia's absent-minded husband has included their labrador puppy in a delivery of computers to Leafskirk. Unfortunately, the recipients are members of the East Lancashire Liberation Army who seize upon the unwitting puppy and demand a ransom.

Ophelia is pushed towards the crooked solicitor's standby: mortgage fraud. But when the senior partner is frosting over nicely behind the photocopier, a little fraud is a mere bagatelle . . .

FICTION / GENERAL 0 7472 4867 2

A selection of bestsellers from Headline

OXFORD EXIT	Veronica Stallwood	£4.99	☐
BOOTLEGGER'S DAUGHTER	Margaret Maron	£4.99	☐
DEATH AT THE TABLE	Janet Laurence	£4.99	☐
KINDRED GAMES	Janet Dawson	£4.99	☐
MURDER OF A DEAD MAN	Katherine John	£4.99	☐
A SUPERIOR DEATH	Nevada Barr	£4.99	☐
A TAPESTRY OF MURDERS	P C Doherty	£4.99	☐
BRAVO FOR THE BRIDE	Elizabeth Eyre	£4.99	☐
NO FIXED ABODE	Frances Ferguson	£4.99	☐
MURDER IN THE SMOKEHOUSE	Amy Myers	£4.99	☐
THE HOLY INNOCENTS	Kate Sedley	£4.99	☐
GOODBYE, NANNY GRAY	Staynes & Storey	£4.99	☐
SINS OF THE WOLF	Anne Perry	£5.99	☐
WRITTEN IN BLOOD	Caroline Graham	£5.99	☐

All Headline books are available at your local bookshop or newsagent, or can be ordered direct from the publisher. Just tick the titles you want and fill in the form below. Prices and availability subject to change without notice.

Headline Book Publishing, Cash Sales Department, Bookpoint, 39 Milton Park, Abingdon, OXON, OX14 4TD, UK. If you have a credit card you may order by telephone – 01235 400400.

Please enclose a cheque or postal order made payable to Bookpoint Ltd to the value of the cover price and allow the following for postage and packing:

UK & BFPO: £1.00 for the first book, 50p for the second book and 30p for each additional book ordered up to a maximum charge of £3.00.
OVERSEAS & EIRE: £2.00 for the first book, £1.00 for the second book and 50p for each additional book.

Name ....

Address ....

....

....

If you would prefer to pay by credit card, please complete:
Please debit my Visa/Access/Diner's Card/American Express (delete as applicable) card no:

Signature .... Expiry Date ....